BOOK THREE

TWELVE DAYS OF LA CLAIRIÈRE

A NOVEL

LAURA GAISIE

Purple Pearls
PUBLISHING

Praise for

Twelve Days of La Clairière

"I thoroughly enjoyed the ups & down of the characters' lives."

—Cynthia C.

"Totally engrossing. I felt as if I were neglecting the characters during those times I was away from this book. I catch myself wondering what they're doing and who will wield La Clairière next."

—Keith C.

"I thought Twelve Days of La Clairière by Laura Gaisie was an excellent story and very well written. I went in thinking that the main character was going to be Linn and the plot being how she'd keep her husband from straying, but I was glad that the story was actually about Zuellie whom I personally thought was a more interesting character. I have always been a history buff...this book called to me for this reason and this novel did not disappoint."

—Tiffany F.

"What caught my attention the most is the way in which Gaisie uses real historical themes of class and race to tell the story of a family, heaving through the adversity of segregation, laws, and differing cultures. Through four generations, the family faces differing adversity, and each character truly becomes their own. The intersection between the history of Haiti, Cuba, and America intertwines for the reader in a way that makes sense, pulls at your heart strings, and elicits the powerful magic of storytelling. This novel is truly magical. I highly recommend it."

— Laur F.

Twelve Days of *La Clairière*

Also by the Author

Book One

Book Two

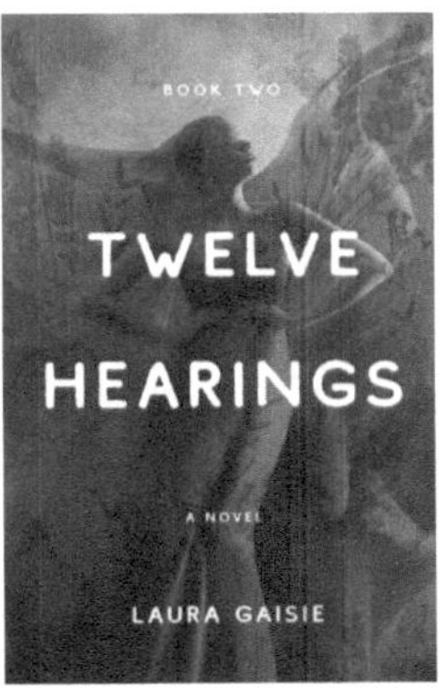

Twelve Days of *La Clairière*

BOOK THREE

Laura Gaisie

For my Mom,
Juanita Caldwell Bridges

GENEALOGY

Kolelas
Manman Linn
(pronounced mama Linn)
Kouri   Karlina   Lelo   Zuellie aka Baby Li
Rebecca
Consuelo Lynnette aka Terra-Lynn
Josephine Lynn
Reba-Lynn
(of Twelve Mondays)

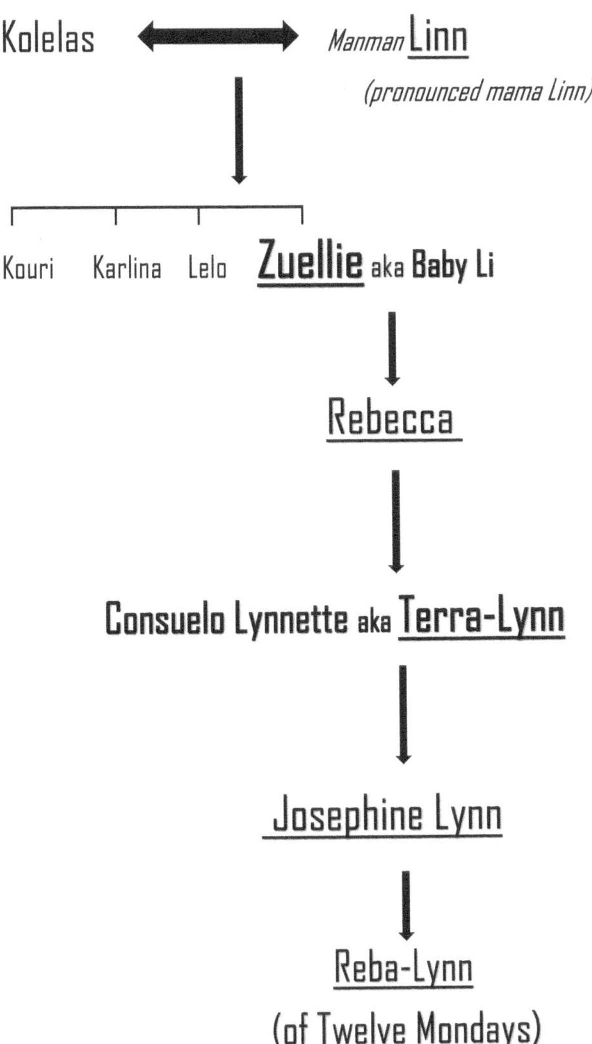

Part I:
HAITI

1

Haiti, 1901

THE DAY THEIR youngest child chose to never speak again was just as unbearable as any other day. Standing before her open bedroom window, four-year-old Zuellie waited for *Papa Legba*, the guardian of crossroads, to grant the supernatural request. If not permitted to converse with the ancestors, she had a backup plan in mind. Paralysis…maybe that would evoke the attention of her deceased grandpapa's soul. Investigating the midnight sky, she marveled at how the fireflies below seemed to mimic the twinkling stars above.

"Shoo, hurry and carry my message," she whispered to the closest firefly. Its light dimmed, blending it into the shadowy night. If she did not receive an answer soon, next she would pray to *Erzulie Mansur*, protector of children. Perhaps she would gain more sympathy from him. With one ear she listened to the sea roaring in the far distance, and with the other, she listened for her sister's voice.

"Zuellie!" She heard a voice whisper from the dancing flicker of darkness.

Straining to hear, she pressed her tiny body against the bare windowsill, leaning far enough to see the front of her home one way and *Tante* Dorinda's backyard in the opposite direction. Her papa's elder brother, Uncle Leonide, sat with a tin can at his feet. Occasionally, he and the others would take a sip of the rum in their cups and spray the contents into the air. The drum player wore a straw hat and smoked on his pipe. Sitting cross-legged, he began to beat the skin of the drum. This was how her papa said the spirits, or *loas*, responded to their prayers. If the drummer kept playing his djembe drum, and her uncles continued to sip rum from their tin cans, *papa legba* would surely answer this night.

"*Zuellie,*" the voice came closer.

She turned just as a firefly illuminated from out of the darkness and nearly touched the tip of her nose. Losing her grip on the windowsill, Zuellie fell against the wooden frame. She let out a small moan when her tummy hit the track that should have held a screen in place. After pulling herself back upright, she fell to the floor and kicked at the wall.

"Wait a minute," she said, before standing on her feet. "That must have been my sign."

She wiggled all of her stubby toes, then bent at the knees to see if they were still flexible. Zuellie pouted when her limbs continued to bend and move as normal. That is why she needed the *loas* help. If she had not learned to walk, losing her speech would be easier to explain away. But for a healthy four-year-old to suddenly stop talking for no reason would bring more outside attention than necessary. If her hand was not played carefully she could end up in the hospital, or worse, on the other side of the trail where her papa secretly ventured for remedies from the *mambo*. Zuellie needed time to revert or freeze so her family could stay together, just as they had before the walls in the front room grew wings and carried them off in different directions. Mostly what she needed was for her papa to look at her *manman* as he had done before.

"Baby Li, don't you hear me calling you?" Said Karlina. She stood before her sister with hands on her hips.

"*Sè mwen!*" said Zuellie, in their native language. She turned back to the window, hoping for one last sign.

Karlina knelt beside the bed where she placed her hands together and bowed her head. Zuellie had gotten used to the nighttime prayers and knew she was expected to join. She listened as Karlina began to pray, thanking the Father for his son Jesus. Her eyes flew open when she noticed Zuellie still standing.

"*Se, ede mwen*," said Zuellie. *(Sister help me)*. She whimpered, then gasped for air.

Zuellie knew her sister wanted them to speak French when they were alone, but tonight she would have to settle for their native tongue. She listened again for the sound of the beating drums, knowing soon her papa would be drawn into a dance before he passed out. She would have to act quickly to draw his attention. Now was the time for the second part of her plan, but not before she took it all in. She wanted to remember every inch of her short life just in case things went wrong. Zuellie's eyes enlarged as she scanned the cramped space of their room. She stared at a stain on the wall that had been scrubbed down with lye soap and a steel pad, what remained resembled the clenched fist used to clean it. In a corner, her eyes lingered on a molded spot, the result of the damp salty droplets mixed with the sticky heat on the hillside.

The home was mostly spotless and bug-free. Each of the Guerrier children had been taught by *Manman* Linn the most important daily chore of search and destroy. Of course, she knew nature would always find a way inside, and that way was usually through the uncovered windows. Even still, the children had been put to task, using their small swatting hands they searched out whatever creeping things they could find. Now they would be down a set of hands, the only pair that could reach into tiny cracks along the front room wall. Baby Li's small chubby fingers could even reach behind the two barrels of salt used for preserving their meat.

In what was probably no more than a few seconds, she not only marked every crack in the bedroom floor and wall but took note of the smells of the night that would forever change her existence. The sweet earth that produced their sugar cane in a small plot of land trailed along the treetops and entered through the window. And she could almost taste the over-ripened mango that drooped low on a nearby tree. Zuellie listened just a short while longer. The only sound coming from the cicadas as they serenaded the night.

"*Mwen!*" she cried out to her sister and then clawed at her throat for added effect.

"Sit down!" said Karlina. She was quick on her bare toes which had just slipped inside than out of the blanket. Before she knew what was happening, Zuellie was snatched from the window onto the bed. After realizing she was losing control of the situation, she yanked her arm free.

"*Mwe!*" She made another tiny belch-like sound before throwing herself to the floor.

Karlina began to scratch her head as she watched the fit play out before her eyes. Zuellie rolled back and forth as she wriggled on the floor, with one finger she pointed at her mouth. Karlina grew concerned, but then something fell from her sister's pocket that drew her attention. Zuellie watched as her sister held the evidence, a piece of bread she had tucked in her nightgown for a midnight snack.

"And what is this? You know how *Manman* feels about food outside of the kitchen." Karlina grabbed the younger girl by the arm and sat her carefully on their bed.

"Mwe!" said Zuellie, her tiny face twisted in pain.

"I get it already, you have a tummy ache, serves you right for sneaking food in here."

As the room grew darker, Karlina's pupils dilated as she strained to make out her sister's expression. Inching closer for a better look, she squeezed the sides of Zuellie's cheeks until her lips parted. Nothing that she could see had lodged in her throat. Rubbing her sister's arm for comfort, Karlina observed Zuellie's smooth dark skin that seemed to blend into the shadows of the room. When their eyes met she waited for the laughter that would signify the end of a prank. Zuellie remained stone-faced, studying her sister's almost colorless skin. Neither said a word.

"What are you doing Baby Li, and why won't you answer me?" She poked at the younger girl's stomach. Karlina huffed before she rose to her feet.

"Ungh!" Said Zuellie, she pointed again to her mouth.

Their papa had always said his oldest girl was intelligent, so Zuellie knew what it would take to fool a girl who devoured books and spoke four fluent languages: Haitian-creole, French, English, and Spanish. Zuellie noted the way her sister watched with a photographic memory, recording her every move and sound. Karlina was not only smart but considered a beauty. In Zuellie's opinion, it was due to her mulatto features inherited by their father. For the longest time, she thought it had been the sun that bleached her skin and left her bright hair brittle like hay. As a result, *Manman* Linn had to use a honey and beeswax concoction on Karlina's hair to soften and stretch her braids. Aside from her looks, most people adored the older girl because of her refined mannerisms.

Zuellie watched as even now sitting in the dark, Karlina sat with her head high and straight back. It was at that moment that she realized her sister's attractiveness had nothing to do with her skin tone but more with who she was on the inside. Karlina was lovely and intelligent but was it not their papa who had also said his youngest daughter was even smarter. His exact words were, "Baby Li is a quick learner, strong-willed and independent." This she knew to be an advantage over her big sister, and the source of her *manman's* sorrow. The last baby she would ever carry had grown too fast, and their papa had seemed to lose interest in his wife. So, it was up to Zuellie to fix what she created. She had to hold her grit, against her intelligent sister, the brothers, and anyone else who tried to stop her.

"Stay here and don't move, I'll get *manman*," said Karlina.

Before leaving the room, she stopped to look back at her sister. When Zuellie said nothing, she disappeared down the hallway. "*Manman*, come quick, something's wrong with Baby Li."

Zuellie listened to their murmurs as Karlina's cynical voice tried to explain her sister's behavior. She scanned the place between the chest and upholstered chair where she liked to hide during games of hide-and-seek. The chair faced the window which was the perfect spot to receive the rare breeze from the Caribbean Sea during the rainy season. It was also her favorite place to sit with the ragdoll her papa's boss had given her on the day she had been born. He liked to tell the story of how the doll had been brought from a far-off country beyond their sea, and *Manman* Linn said it was the only way they would ever know anything of the world beyond the Caribbean. Though she claimed not to be superstitious, *Manman* Linn often spoke of the omen pronounced at her birth, giving this as the reason she kept her children close.

Zuellie had inherited her mother's "guppy-eyes," as her siblings called them, and she had the same gangly legs as her papa and her brothers. And like her papa's legs, hers had an insatiable need to run. This was the reason the next phase of her plan to ask *Papa Legba* for paralysis had not been thoroughly considered. Losing her speech would have to do and should be enough time to keep her papa home, at least long enough to persuade *Manman* Linn to seek a remedy from the *mambo*.

In her imagination, her papa would then look at his wife the way he used to, and her *manman* would be happy again. She was old enough to remember the days when he came home with a smile, carrying meat for dinner. Her *manman* would run to her husband's arms simply because he had returned home - with or without meat. Once her papa stayed home, even if it were just for a day, Zuellie was sure their old sparks would fly. Then her uncle's wives would stop whispering as she and her *manman* passed by on their way to market.

The longer it took Karlina to return with her parents the more she wrestled with how severe her symptoms needed to be. Zuellie positioned her legs in a way that defied its natural ability. When her joints popped, she nearly yelped from the pain as it shot from her hip down to her twisted ankles. Being mute would have to do. As she lay across the bed, she couldn't help to wonder what led to her decision.

2

Haiti, 1872

~ Linn ~

ALONG THE WOODSY trail leading up the hillside, a thicket of heavy brush and wildflowers concealed a path known only to those who sought the healer. During the stormy season, torrential rainfall formed a trench, making it almost impossible to reach the *mambo's* cabin.

"Don't mind the gully," said Effia, as she scanned the clothing of her twitchy-eyed guests, "the *loas* have decided to protect me in this way." If her visitor had worn fancy threads or was blessed enough to have on shoes she knew their journey had been long, and their pockets full with her reward.

The powerful winds swept through the hills, bending palm trees and uprooting delicate crops. There was always a reason for nature's wrath, whether to punish the people's greed or to correct some form of dishonor. Before his passing, the *houngan* (male priest), warned of change to come. Now his daughter, Effia, the *mambo,* (female priestess), did the same. In the evening she walked through the forest barefooted to listen as the earth groaned and bemoaned each transgression.

"Enjoy the crops now, one day there will be nothing but dust and mud," she said. As she spoke nearby leaves shook, and when she tugged on the long braids dangling from her white headscarf the wind seemed to settle. The sharecroppers placed several Haitian Gourdes on the table before leaving.

Families like the Dupont's and the Guerrier's were farmers of citrus, and sugar cane. There were other crops, but the cane fields required hard labor of which every abled body was needed. A small grove of almond trees grew outside one particular compound, where a bright-eyed brown girl was often found stuffing her pockets full of nuts that had fallen from the leaves that hung over the wall. She would not venture outside the gate, nor would she participate in fieldwork, though she was old enough for both.

Among the four families dwelling within the compound were a herd of cattle, a coop full of hens, several hogs, and two mules used for transportation. Some of them believed in making a sacrifice to the spirit world, others turned their worship to Mother Mary, and despite these differences, they were able to coexist in peace. Mostly the town of Miragoàne had been a thriving, self-sufficient community. Their women were easily noticed at the market selling produce or purchasing goods they could not cultivate for themselves like salted fish, fine garments, and hand-carved furniture.

No matter who was selling or buying, the conditions were always hot and unbearably humid, with long days under the sweltering sun. Regardless of the heat, rains, or hurricane, the women were fashionably dressed in vibrant quadrille dresses and their heads adorned with colorful headscarves or large hats. On market days they strutted onto the vendor row and took their places. The men dressed for comfort wearing linen or cotton pants, and a sun hat. Whether in the fields or in town, children played alongside their hard-working parents; their hands and faces sticky from ripe fruit juice mixed with sweat which drew flies and mosquitos—a nuisance to the overworked adults.

That summer, an aged English woman working in the clinic helped the bright-eyed Dupont girl prepare for delivery. As they carried her squirming body into the birthing room, her pocket full of nuts fell to the floor creating a trail from the entryway, just as her water broke.

"*Linn*!" said the midwife, as she side-stepped slippery spots on the floor. "It means a stream of water, like a waterfall." She braced herself on the wall for balance.

Upon hearing the words, the hairs on the expecting girls' arms stood up. She grunted when her body was placed on the cot and in her confusion reached out for the young errand boy who had been called to clean the floor.

"Settle down child," said her grandpapa.

The errand boy frowned at them both when she released the grip on his arm.

"*Agwe* has claimed this one's offspring. Its destiny is beyond the Caribbean Sea," he said.

"No, no, take it back…please, don't curse my baby!" With a trembling hand, she crossed her heart and forehead and prayed through her tears, which at the time felt pointless, especially when the elder repeated the curse before leaving, just in case the words had been missed through the wails of her birthing pangs.

That evening after giving birth and the other mothers in the ward were sound asleep, the new mother left her recovery bed and crept onto the darkened street until she found the Catholic church. When she told the priest about the prophecy, he calmed her fears by instructing her to light a candle and pray the rosary. The young mother bowed her head in a moment of silent prayer. After feeling comforted, she returned to the recovery ward and held her baby named Linn close at her breast where she intended to keep the child for a lifetime - if it were in her power to do so.

On the same hill that same year, a light-haired mulatto boy was born to the Guerrier's. His *manman* (pronounced mama) had already selected the name for her unborn child, no matter what the gender turned out to be.

"*Kolelas*," the runner. "Because it feels as if this baby is running round and round inside my belly," she panted.

The parents of young Kolelas sought the *houngan*, and later the *mambo*, for medicine and spiritual guidance on all matters. Their way was to seek the healer, and they would never convert to the new religion introduced by the missionaries. The hillside village overlooking Miragoàne had a unique subculture. For starters, one had to get there by horse, or mule, unless you were fit for the long walk. The trail populated with loose rocks and dirt led through a thick wall of looming trees. Beyond the dangling vines, chirping birds alerted skittish animals to human interference.

Blacks like the Dupont's and lower-class mulattos, such as the Guerrier's, lived and farmed together, which at that time was rare as the country smoldered, and simmered from the revolutions of 1804. However, on the hillside, sometimes referred to as a mountain, they found comfort and even wed one another. That year, Haitians found civil peace at the expense of international unrest. Then-President, Jean-Nicolas Saget, stalled Libertarian's hunger for reform as he dealt with several military problems. Haiti's ports took the stage of a battle or two. The first was between Spanish men-of-war and the United States over a steamer thought to be a pirate carrying contraband to Cuba.

The Germans struck later that year. A gentleman named Captain Batsch took it upon himself to attack two Haitian men-of-war ships anchored in the harbor of Port-au Prince. And amid these troubles, President Saget managed to redeem the paper currency. The country formerly known as Saint-Domingue had once been the wealthiest colony in the French

Empire and all the world. The government had high hopes and expectations to recapture a fraction of Haiti's glory days.

In the capital, artists became famous for the colorful depictions of their people and culture. Haitians were spirited. Their food savory, and the music expressive—like the people. Moving beyond the narrative of poverty and violence, Haiti's beaches and hillsides were of the most beautiful in the West Indies. The coastline nurtured lush tropical vegetation of palms above and coral reefs beneath the sea. The hillsides matured into mountainous land and plains—Emerald jungles with a nutritious center where deep gorges of rock gave way to undisturbed natural baths. Vines and towering trees sagged from their ripened fruit; Moringa, Soursop, Mango, and Cacao. There were some sugar cane fields, though not as populous as they once had been, but still valuable enough to farm in one form or another.

●　●　●

1878

Each male owned a trusty machete used for whacking thicket and cutting cane. From an early age, 6-year-old Kolelas, who became known simply as Kole, learned to sling a blade with accuracy. His gangly legs moved through the bush clearing more ground than any of the other workers. His relatives speculated on his supernatural ability, many years before becoming known for the urban legend of having run from one end of Haiti to the other in a day,

The machete he used had earned the title and name of, *la clairière* (the clearing), and was never intended for use due to an obvious curvature slightly to the right. The defective blade had been given to him as a joke, just as it had been given to his father before him. However, in the right hands *la clairière* became more useful than any other cane cutter's blade, moving its wielder through the reeds with a speed of a cyclone. There was not a reed left standing after they passed.

Linn had also spent her life on the hillside. Her family converted to Christianity against the wishes of their small community and shunned the *houngan's* rituals marked by the drums. Kole had known her since they were old enough to play outdoors. She was the shy girl who watched other children from her door stoop, always silent. He would catch her on occasion giggling at the boy's horseplay. Sometimes she would disappear from the doorway for days, and he worried until her return. Linn was not an attractive girl, at least that is what the other boys said. But Kole was fascinated by her face, thinking a girl who never smiled had to have known things beyond her years. She had the saddest eyes that seemed to bulge as they observed the whole world at once. Sometimes she waved in his direction, always after looking over her shoulder first. He mimicked her behavior, checking his surroundings before he returned her wave.

"Don't even trouble yourself with her," said one of the boys, as he shook his head. "She doesn't speak and she never comes out to play with us."

Kole laughed with the others while inwardly determining he would be the one to rescue her from the porch someday. Through him, Linn would become the stream of water she had been named after. One day he would show her the place on the other side of the hill where the waterfall spilled over into the sea. And each day her curiosity pulled her back to the doorway to stare at the well-mannered boy with bright skin and smooth hair. It was more than looks that made him stand out from the rest. Kole noticed her, and soon he would learn the reasoning behind her strange behavior.

3

Miragoane, 1882

WHEN LINN WAS four years old her papa contracted a disease that left him bedbound. As a way to provide for their household, her mother left the house early each day to peddle cassava roots and plantains at the bottom of the hill, leaving the young girl as a caregiver to her father. Around the age of 10-years old, a *tante* moved into the home, relieving Linn of her duties and releasing her into the world beyond their porch. She entered the small schoolhouse, wide-eyed yet reserved, for the first time.

Kole watched from a distance as her large eyes absorbed books, admired the girls her age, and clung to their conversations. He saw the meltdown before it happened. Linn began looking over her shoulder as if still stuck on her front stoop. During one of those episodes, she collided with a well-known bad boy, and they toppled face forward into a mud hole. Never mind the fact her school uniform had been ruined, the angry boy shoved a finger in her face and threatened to correct her eyesight. Kole approached the boy and dared him to lay a finger on his friend. Later in the day, when the tough crowd teased him for his gallantry, he accepted their fate.

It started with friendship, as they walked home together each day and recounted the school day. After several weeks, Kole confirmed their relationship to his berating friends. Holding hands on a rainy day to keep from sliding on the muddy path, she was his sweetheart and he became her heartthrob. They continued this way up until the year 1888 when Kole left school to work full-time in the fields.

"We must get married." He stopped her at the gate before she left for school. It was his nature to find hidden treasure in the impractical, so his decision to marry Linn should have been of no surprise. Her nervous disposition made him love her more. "It's the only way I can protect you now that I'm no longer around."

She agreed to be his wife at 16 years old, happy to leave her overworked mother, and the impassive *tante* living in their home. After the private ceremony, Kole and four of his older brothers built their houses together in a nearby lot. The five-room floor plans were identical; two small rooms for sleeping, a slightly larger front room, a small kitchen, and an enclosed space for the chamber pot. Each home had a hand-made screen for the front and back door, and open window frames. The only difference in their homes was the vibrant colored exterior paint. They chose sky blue because it represented everything good around them. From the clear blue skies to the ocean, including the matching blue suit and dress they wore on their wedding day. Kole placed *la clairière* near the front door with pride. Linn vowed to keep her children close, as her *manman* had done with her. What she would soon learn, as each baby nursed, they eventually left her lap. They would spend less time carried on her hip, and the last baby even sooner than the others.

Running was in their blood. After all, her children were the offspring of the man who had been rumored to have run from the north end of Haiti to the south department on the day his first child was born. Of course, the story had been retold with fluid exaggeration, some details added or replaced depending on the storyteller. However, no one could deny the events encircling his oldest child's birth.

● ● ●

August 19, 1889

There was a category 1 hurricane threatening seacrafts along the Caribbean Sea. As a result, the fishing boat Kole worked on as a deckhand was docked in the northern region of Cap Haitien. It would have taken any traveler eight hours by motor car, even longer by horse and buggy; two days or more if the unlucky chap had walked. When the telegram arrived saying his wife had gone into labor, Kole left the post office dazed by the news. His first child was about to be born. He announced his good news to whoever passed by along the sidewalk, grinning and sweating as he ran wildly along the street. To everyone's surprise, he arrived in Miragoàne by nightfall in time to hear the first shrill from his baby's lungs.

They said he came running, but Kole would later tell his wife how the ship's captain received an urgent telegram at the same time and was headed back to Miragoàne to secure his cattle and crops. He rode in a brilliant red gasoline runabout, his first and only time to ride in a motorized automobile. The captain dropped him off along Route 2. From there, Kole took off running from the edge of town to the clinic where his wife was in labor. From what everyone saw, he came running.

Kole was always in motion, if not running, then walking fast. The only time his legs were at rest was during sleep. Nothing moved quicker than his feet, except for the *houngan's* hands beating on the djembe drum. Whenever the familiar sound echoed along the mountainside, Kole raced through the forest until he found rest at the drum; the velocity of the *houngan's* hands drew him closer as it drained his desire to run and he collapsed. When it was over, he rose from the ground and walked home on the swollen soles of his feet.

Linn flat out refused to attend the Calinda dances from the start. She wanted her husband and children to attend Mass as good Catholics should. Kole said they could do both. The more he participated in the wild celebrations, the more nervous she became. His brother's wives, who had not known Linn as a child, believed her isolation came from fear of the *houngan*. Whatever her reasons, Linn ignored her sister-in-law's knocks on the door frame and avoided eye contact as they waved in passing. Outside of her husband, she had little interest in anyone. Then their babies started coming, so she clung to them like flour on seasoned chicken. In the presence of tiny faces and wailing tonsils, Linn's condition was scarcely noticeable.

Their first child came out coffee-bean brown like Linn but favored his papa in every other way. They named him Kouri, son of the runner. It seemed as though he jumped from his mother's womb and bounced against every wall of their home. Linn would later trace the source of the creaky floorboards to this moment. By the time the young mother realized Kouri no longer wanted to nurse, she began to have tell-tale signs of motherhood.

"You know what they say about a baby moving quickly, soon to be another on the way," said her mother-in-law.

Linn concealed a grin, as she massaged the unnoticeable bump on her stomach. Their second child was a girl they named Karlina. She had her papa's bright skin and reddish-brown hair. Linn exhaled, smiling into her lazy girl's face who seemed to have little interest in anything past feeding and sleeping. The children grew plump and giggled as they learned to exist within the perimeters their *manman* Linn erected and reinforced by their papa. He left before dawn each morning. On some days he ran to work, other times he rode on the back of his donkey. When he returned later in the day smelling of sea life, his wife took the small bucket of fish from his hand and replaced it with a cup of rum.

"Sit with me first." His hand tapped the cushion.

"I should put this on the kettle before the flies get in it."

"No, it can wait. Come sit with me."

Linn checked on the napping children before setting the bucket down. He took his wife into his arms, staring passionately into her large eyes.

"I go out on that boat every day and still haven't seen nowhere near the things you have."

"You're silly, I told you I'm not a seer, my eyes are just large." She nestled into his arms, inhaling fish guts and musk.

Long before he offered the sacrifice to the *mambo* Effia to seal their union, they were like one soul halved between two bodies. Knit together by an invisible string, Kole and his wife lived inside their home as if they were the only two people on the island. He knew other women found him attractive by the way their dreamy eyes lingered as he walked by. But there was not a smiling face or curvy waist that could compare to his mystical wife. Even if she pretended not to have gifts, he felt her powers with every kiss and embrace. She could see into the span of life and had still chosen him.

"I was dancing before the *mambo's* drum when the spirit of *Erzulie* came to me," said Kole.

"Hush, you know I don't like it when you talk like that." Linn pulled away from his arms.

"But it's because of her that we have this life; she told me the girl with the seeing eyes was meant to be my wife."

Linn held her stomach, silently praying for the strength to endure his superstitions. Afterward, she raised his legs on her lap and began massaging the stiffened muscles to keep him from seeking out Effia's drums for relief that evening.

$$4$$

Spring, 1894

BY THE TIME the oldest turned four and Karlina was going on three years old, Linn grew worried over her flattened stomach. Eavesdropping on the other wives' conversation as they sat on stools underneath a tree served only to increase her anxiety.

"They think we don't have sense, but we know they live here together to cover each other's trail," said Ines.

"Mm-hmm!" Monique, Dorinda, and Athalie agreed. With a snap of their wrists, hand-held fans stirred the air between them.

"This one over here who doesn't like to speak thinks she's better than us, she'll soon find out her husband is just like his brother's," said one wife. "Maybe she'll have time to speak to us then."

When their eyes cut in her direction, Linn held her breath as she stepped away from the door. The warn floorboard creaked under her bare feet as she made her way to the kitchen. She paused to see if the noise had woken the sleeping children. When there was no sound of movement, she opened the squeaky door and tossed several pieces of wood inside. Who knew if it had been the creaking, squeaking, or her sighs that finally woke the children. Kouri sprang from his bed and began running laps around his sister until their breakfast was placed on the table. A groggy Karlina sat silently at the table, and after her belly was full, she hummed songs to her brother which stopped him from running for the time being.

This was how their day began every morning. Linn kissed her husband goodbye at the door, the women gossiped under the tree, floorboards creaked then the children awoke. After being fed, they left her side. Linn would be alone to do her chores as the children played together. Kole returned with a bucket of fish for dinner. They shared an intimate moment before the children woke from napping, then he took them to play in the yard while she prepared supper. Then it was bedtime, and the next day repeated itself. There were no variations of circumstances from one day to the next until finally, she noticed the swell of her belly once more. Linn stood in her doorway when her condition became apparent and turned her nose up at the aggrieved women under the tree.

● ● ●

Their third baby was a boy they named Lelo, who wailed from the midwife's hands and continued crying for weeks at his *manman*'s nipple.

"Why the baby shaking like that?" asked Kouri.

"How come he won't stop screaming?" said Karlina, as she placed tiny hands over her ears.

Linn listened for the change in breathing which would indicate a more serious internal problem. But the baby was no different from the other two she had born, granted his cries were louder and longer in duration; otherwise, the same.

"It's just his way of letting us know he's here." Linn smiled at her two inquisitive toddlers. This was her purpose in life, not as a seer like her husband supposed, but as a fruitful mother with a running long-legged boy, a chubby lazy girl, and the sweetest crying baby in her arms.

After giving thanks to God for her fortuitous blessings; besides the children, her husband came home every night with a smile on his face, and food for the table. After praying, she placed an apron around her waist and lit the wooden stove. With the growing mouths to feed, her husband dressed quickly for the workday and barely had time to finish the toast on his plate. She waited near the door as he shoved calloused toes inside his work boots. Before he left, they shared a brief but warm kiss. From her porch, she watched as he trotted toward the gate to meet up with his brothers for the journey down the hill. The other wives waved goodbye to their respective husbands, and no sooner had the men gone, the women produced stools and sipped on hot cocoa as their mouths gaped wide from hillside gossip. Linn would never join them, even when they tempted her with a remedy that would keep their husbands' interest past child-bearing years.

"I can't, not with the crying baby and the older ones." She blushed at the thought of joining them.

"We all got crying babies," said Dorinda, the wife who lived to the left of her home.

With her arms full of soiled laundry that needed washing, she turned her back on the women. Linn made her way to the backyard, careful to step around creaking floorboards, and began her chores. After wringing the damp clothes, she hung them on the clothesline to dry. Then she checked the hen coop for fresh eggs, placed a large cauldron on the fire, and boiled water to start beans for supper. All of it completed before the wailing baby woke his siblings.

Lelo continued to expand his lungs and stretch his vocal cords as she helped the older children wash the sleep from their faces. When they were clean, she wrapped the baby around her back with a traditional cloth and moved the younger ones to the kitchen. At the table, Lelo quieted long enough for everyone to enjoy their breakfast. Linn was grateful for the few bites she was able to snatch as he nursed from her milk. The rest of the morning would be easier so long as she minded his feeding schedule. For the better part of the day, the children entertained themselves by pulling out every toy and any other object their chubby hands could find. Sometimes she made a game out of cleaning the mess, but with the crying baby, that was not as fun as before, so she waited until their naptime to tidy up.

By the time the afternoon sun cast shadows across the front room, she knew to expect her husband soon. Before the children were born, she used to meet him near the gate and walk with him across the yard, past the two small homes on their right and the other two homes on the left. Now it was Kouri who would meet his papa at the gate. Linn stood on the porch with a cranky Karlina who had been whimpering because her *manman* refused to give her another snack. When she leaned in to kiss her husband, his eyes lingered on the crying child.

"Has this been going on all day?" He frowned.

"No, it's just his way of communicating." Linn stuck a finger in the baby's mouth in an attempt to quiet him.

"It's not good, the boy shouldn't be crying like that."

Kole stepped past his wife, shaking his head as he clicked his tongue. Realizing this moment as the first time he had shown disapproval or not greeted her with a kiss at the door, she fought off an urge to defend her parenting abilities. Each day papa Kole returned from work to the wailing baby, he gave the same reaction.

"Maybe you should wait for me inside from now on," he said, after enduring a month of the noisy greeting.

Her sister-in-law who lived on the left, Dorinda, swept around her front yard and pretended not to see or hear the couple's growing frustration over the crying baby. She tried to look away after Kole left his wife standing on the porch, but she grew concerned when she noticed Linn staring at the dirt with the crying baby in her arms.

"I can come in the morning and help you some?"

Linn's eyes fixated on a dry patch of ground at the base of their steps. A peculiar oblong shape void of grass or roots with a pulsating center, like a heartbeat. The dry patch yielded to dry twigs and crumbling stones all around it and yet there was life there. Someday soon whatever was growing beneath the surface would reveal itself. The pulsating dry patch stopped beating and Linn sucked her teeth. She waited a few more seconds but there was no movement. When she finally looked up, Dorinda placed one hand over her heart as a sign of peace. Linn nodded in her direction, recognizing the need for help. She wanted to believe her marriage was different from the others, but deep down she knew this was the reason the wives gravitated toward one another after the men left for work.

Lelo was still crying in her arms when she entered the house. She bypassed her frowning husband and went to the kitchen. After Lelo was strapped on her back, she began setting the table for dinner. Kole stood in the kitchen doorway, observing his wife with the crying baby on her back. He approached slowly as she busied herself with the plates and forks. When Linn stood still, he lifted the unhappy but otherwise healthy Lelo from his mother's burden. Linn held her breath as he placed her baby close to his chest and left out the backdoor. She remembered to exhale only after she saw how her husband rocked the baby as he walked along the yard. Lelo's cries were silenced when the hens clucked as Kole entered their roosting space. When she called for her husband to come in for supper, Lelo began to cry as the baby was placed back in her arms.

That next morning, she kissed her husband goodbye and lingered in the doorway. After the men disappeared through the gate, the wives pulled out their stools. Looking back at her children's bedroom, she calculated the time before they would stir for breakfast. Her stool was in the backyard. If she walked down the hallway the wobbly boards would wake at least one of the children, and before long Lelo would be up crying.

"Can I come in?" Dorinda held out two cups.

Linn jumped from the woman's sudden appearance.

"Remember yesterday, I mentioned stopping by this morning to help out?" said Dorinda.

Linn looked from her sister-in-law to the dry patch on the ground and tried to will it to move again. If it did, she would show Dorinda what she had discovered.

"Chokola…you like hot chocolate?" Dorinda stepped closer, blocking her view of the dry patch.

"No thank you, I make my own." Linn turned up her nose after peering into the cups.

"You don't have to drink it, it's just something us wives enjoy doing together in the mornings."

"But I can't come out there, the kids—"

She stopped talking to listen as Lelo began to cry. When she left to comfort her baby, Dorinda used the opportunity to let herself in the house.

"You can wait outside, I'll come out later if I can." She clutched the screaming baby to her chest, as the two younger children placed tiny hands over their ears.

"I have a remedy that can help with that." Dorinda monitored the growing lines across her nervous sister-in-law's forehead, which seemed to deepen when Kouri and Karlina appeared and asked for their breakfast.

"I can take the baby," Dorinda opened her arms.

Linn backed away as if she had asked to suck the blood from his tiny body. She held the baby close, shaking her head as she silently prayed for Dorinda to leave her house.

"At least let me help you get the little ones fed?" Dorinda gathered Kouri and Karlina to the table. "I can even show you my secret recipe for crying babies."

Linn made peace with having the help, even if it had been Dorinda's distraction that had thrown her morning routine off in the first place. She sat down to nurse Lelo as she watched her sister-in-law, who began looking through the cupboard to search for ingredients. Dorinda was saying something, but Linn could hardly keep her eyes open. With the baby suckling and the children warming to their *tante* Dorinda's presence, Linn closed her eyes, just for a moment.

"Well, your two darlings are fed and cleaned, so I best be getting back across the yard." Dorinda removed the apron and started for the door. "If you ever need a break, I'd be happy to have your little ones over to play with my young'uns, after all, they are kin."

"That would be nice, but I'd have to ask their papa first."

"Of course…now, don't forget to give him the broth." Dorinda nodded to the baby and smiled as she left.

Linn noticed that the table had been wiped clean and the dishes put in their proper place. There was a thick-yellowy substance cooling in a kettle. She sniffed the contents before lifting the pot and pouring it on the ground outside the back door. The remainder of the day was no different than another. The children sang and played at her side as she completed chores with the crying baby strapped on her back. And before long, Kole was home.

"Why is he still crying?" He scowled at his wife.

Linn looked over his shoulders at the dark clouds forming in the sky. A storm meant no fishing boats out to sea.

"It's time Linn, we need help…I'm going to see Effia." Kole had to hold his wife by the arm to keep her from running off. Linn shook her head.

"I'm worried about you, and the baby, do you hear me?"

"Dorinda was here earlier; she gave me something to help him." She followed her husband to the kitchen, watching as he lifted the lids from pots on the stove.

"How do you expect me to believe that when all I hear is how much you turn your nose up at them." When the children came near he lowered his voice.

"But it's true, we spent the morning together, you can ask Kouri and Karlina. She made breakfast and left something for the baby to drink."

"Where is it, I don't see anything."

"He drank it already."

Linn turned away from his suspicious glare.

"Well, it's not working, she should have gone to Effia."

"The healer never helped my papa when he took ill, what makes you so sure this would be any different?" Linn shrugged, as defeat sank into her gut.

$$5$$

A TROPICAL STORM kept Kole at home for the next two days. During that time, he attempted to console the unhappy baby as best he could. When all his deliberate attempts failed, Kole diverted his attention to odd repairs around the house. Wobbly chair legs needed a nail or two, along with a shelf in the cupboard. After fixing what he could with a hammer and nails, he thought about the squeaky floorboard in the front room. Linn and the baby were seated in a chair next to the front door, which was opened for the cool but rare breeze created by the storm. Lelo was still crying in his wife's trembling arms.

"This has gone on far too long, you and I both know the healer can help us."

"You're speaking of the *mambo*?" Linn cut her eyes in his direction. "You know that's not our way, we could go to the priest for prayer."

"Tsk! The church is too far and the weather's getting worse out," said Kole, turning his back on the conversation.

The very next morning, he left the house without a word and started the journey through the thick side of the hillside. Although he had said nothing to his wife, Linn knew where he was headed. She waited at the door, watching the clouds change from white to charcoal. The wind kicked up, blowing tumbleweeds and fallen leaves across the lawn and covering the dry patch at the base of the porch. After the children went down for their nap, she thought of going out to uncover the spot. By the time she made it to the porch, Kole appeared through the gate, clutching a small bottle in one hand. He took his wife by the hand and led her to the kitchen.

"This one needs to be given to him to drink." He placed the bottle on the table. "And this goes in the cradle when he sleeps." He dangled a root-filled satchel before his wife.

Linn nodded, thinking she would do the same thing with the bottle as she had to Dorinda's broth. But when he pulled a rubber nipple from his pocket and placed it on the bottle, her stomach dropped. She watched in horror as he went to the baby and placed the nipple in his mouth. Lelo began sucking and didn't stop until he had swallowed the last drop.

"There you go, he should be all better by morning," said Kole. When he tried to place the baby back in her arms, Linn ran from the room and out the backdoor. She flung herself to the ground, holding her mouth to block her screams and her stomach to keep from retching. She stopped crying when the sky opened up and drenched her with rain. Inside the house, Kole rocked the sleeping baby as she changed into dry clothes. In her mind, the smell of the *mambo's* potion lingered on her baby's breath. She sniffed a piece of Basil plucked from her garden on her way back inside. When Kole left the room she placed the leaf in Lelo's mouth.

Not long after papa Kole gave his son the broth, the child's temperament improved. Forgotten tears were now replaced with laughter, revealing the chubbiest dimpled cheeks when he smiled.

"I wonder what he's thinking when he laughs like that?"

Linn and papa Kole stood over the sleeping eight-month-old as he clutched his blanket, the most pleasant smile resting on his sleeping face.

"Isn't this how babies act when they arent' sickly, or have you forgotten?" said Kole.

"Maybe we didn't need that healer woman's roots at all." Linn rolled her eyes.

"But it worked, can't you see?" He pointed to their smiling baby.

She would never tell him it was not the roots that healed their son. The smell on his breath kept Linn from nursing him, and without nursing, he stopped getting the herbs she fed him through her milk. Linn would never tell him the truth. What mattered was the children were happy, her husband was pleased, and there was always hope for another baby. They smiled at each other. Kole wrapped his wide arms around her fleshy waist, the extra pounds reminded her of the babies she bore for him. When he touched the mound of her belly, an invisible cord ran up the length of her stomach and tugged at her heart.

"I sure like having my wife back." Kole squeezed tighter.

When his breathing changed, she pushed against his body and gave him her mouth. As they kissed, she prayed to her God for forgiveness; for the potion, and for her own secrets. If her prayers were answered, she believed her womb would conceive again.

●　●　●

January 1895

To Linn's astonishment, her belly did not grow that year. Or the next year. Two years quickly came and went, and still no missed cycles or a hint at morning sickness. Just when she thought the youngest had no interest in running with his brother and his father, he released her hand. Lelo was not a runner like his older brother. He seemed the most contented at his sister's side, grinning as she sang songs or read to him from a tattered children's book.

"God has cursed me for what you did," said Linn.

It was a Saturday, the day Kole and his brothers gathered to work their land. He leaned into the water bowl to rinse flecks of earth and a little blood from the goat they slaughtered to be split amongst the four households. He withheld a sigh, knowing where the conversation would end.

"Maybe God figures your hands are full enough with the three we already got." Kole covered his face with a drying towel.

Linn blocked his path so as not to be easily dismissed. When she refused to budge, Kole shook his head, knowing the conversation was unavoidable, even though she promised to stop nagging if he attended Sunday service at the new church at the bottom of the hill.

"You promised to let it go," he said.

"But the kids are growing so fast, what will happen when they don't need me?"

"Kids gonna always need their *manman*, and you can sell crop at the market like the other wives to help us out."

Linn frowned at the thought of toting a large basket on her head. Nor did she like the idea of having to endure gossiping wives on market row. In her opinion, the brief encounter with Dorinda every morning as she picked up Kouri and Karlina was enough small talk to last her a lifetime. The only time she went down the hill herself, was for church, or to purchase cloth to make the children's garments. Most people ignored Linn, as they had when she was a young girl. She thought it was because they found her to be unattractive, but Dorinda said it was the way she turned up her nose at their greeting. She held back admitting her disgust was due to their reliance on traditional outdated ways. What was the point when her own husband was the first to run to the dances at the sound of the *mambo's* drums?

"I've stopped having babies and there's no other reason except—"

"Never mind what that preacher man says, we ain't cursed, you hear me?" Kole turned his back to empty the washbowl. Afterward, he snatched his wife by the wrist and stepped quickly across the floor to their bedroom. When he released her, Linn massaged the skin on her wrists.

"I didn't mean to hurt you?" He said.

"You've known me since I was a young girl, you know it's hard for me out there."

Kole nodded. Eight years of marriage and three children later, she was still the same nervous girl on the inside. Even though he had seen the way she carried on at the church service, lifting her hands when the preacher man prompted. Sometimes she even sang out loud with the others. He also caught the way she looked at his brother's wives and stuck her tongue out at them behind their backs. Granted they mocked her first, but she matched their smirks with her nose in the air. It seemed to him, she picked when to be shy and when it served her best.

"How would we feed another mouth anyhow?" He said.

Linn expected his usual argument. Next, he would say this was God's way of helping them to survive the harder times. His brother's wives had five, seven, and eight children because they could afford them. Those wives helped in the fields and even sold their goods at the market. When he asked again if she could pitch in the way the other wives did, she turned and left the room.

6

GONE WERE THE days when the wives waited until their husbands left for work before gathering beneath the tree. If the men could sit up late drinking rum together, the women decided it was only fair they should be allowed to enjoy their chokola in the cool morning breeze. *Tante* Ines, being the older brother's wife, acted as overseer. She was the one who had advocated for their right to meet in the mornings, child and husband free, before the day began. Of course, wanting that time alone outside of delicate ears had nothing to do with her gossiping nature. When the air thickened from the rising sun, *Tante* Ines ordered the women to tie on their headscarves before piling baskets on top of their heads. As they marched downhill, their little ones skipped not too far behind with lunch sacks swinging in the air

Linn was the only wife who kissed her husband goodbye in the mornings and greeted him in the evening when he returned from work. If the women happened to catch her standing in the doorway waiting, they glared in her direction. Most of the time she pretended not to notice, but she always felt the prickle on her skin from their burning stares, except for Dorinda who remained neutral despite Linn's rejection.

"I must know, how are you able to keep your husband home at nights?" said Dorinda, who stood on their porch waiting for Kouri and Karlina after the other wives had gone.

"My job is to keep the house clean, the little ones washed and fed, and make sure my husband is happy…not outside with busybodies." Linn cupped her mouth, realizing she had said more than necessary.

"It wasn't always like this." Dorinda looked to the shaded tree. "The years fly by, and the children grow wings right when the husbands begin to lose interest."

After their conversation, Linn shivered from her sister-in-law's words. There was some truth hidden in her statement that could not be ignored. The men do leave, whether off to work or some other private undertaking. The children grow up, much too quickly, abandoning the comfort of their *manman's* yielding lap. And worse of all, the dry patch at the base of the steps still showed no signs of life. Linn knew it was silly of her to correlate her fertility to the land, after all, God was the giver of life, and yet as the days and years passed her native senses began to manifest in ways she could not deny. Although she would never admit it to Kole, the earth had been speaking to her, and she had been paying attention.

● ● ●

June 1896

The stormy season seemed to always bring about change in one form or another in the wake of its violent nature. That summer the Caribbean Sea experienced waves recorded at over 10 feet high, making it much too dangerous for fishing boats to be in the water. Thankfully, Kole was able to satiate his restless legs by working in the fields with his brothers. With all hands to the plow from each of their households, the Guerrier men were able to harvest most of the crop before it washed over the hillside. By the time the storm passed, there had been very little damage from a few inches of rain. Two more months of wind and rain kept Kole home longer than he hoped. And when the rains let up, their crop was still producing, the dry patch near the front porch sprouted little seedlings, and Linn embraced the first signs of a new pregnancy.

Lelo had recently turned three years old and refused to sit on his *manman's* lap. His behavior was no surprise to Linn, as it had been her milk he rejected from the start, and her secret attempts to nurse him when no one was around. The measures she used to seal their mother-child bond were almost forgotten. Almost. Just when she had given up hope to hold a baby and nursing again, it seemed her prayers were finally answered.

"How are we gonna feed another mouth? It's a good thing the storms are letting up." Kole ran a hand over his thinning hairline.

As Linn beamed from the thought of her growing belly, she could not ignore the strain the last baby had placed on their marriage. Without saying a word, she tied her hair in a headscarf and stepped quickly in her husband's footsteps as he left to work the fields. Dorinda toppled her basket at the sight of Kole marching down the trail with Linn at his heels, clutching her ankle-length skirt to keep the pace.

"You don't have to do this," said Kole, when he noticed the stares from the other wives.

Linn bent her head to the ground and began tugging at stubborn Malangá roots, ignoring the crook in her neck and the ache in her back. Nothing short of a hurricane would drive her from the field that day, not until she proved to her husband the next baby would not be a burden.

• • •

Winter, 1896

The hillside community experienced a cold winter that year. As the four families bundled in warm coats and continued working together in the fields, Linn's pregnancy was easily concealed. Fearing her condition would reignite smoldering embers from his brothers' wives, he asked that she keep her condition a secret for as long as possible. There was no need for an official announcement, her grin told it all. Nevertheless, when she became advanced enough to where her baby bump could no longer be hidden, Kole suggested she forego the laborious work and remain at home. On the first day of her absence from the fields, Dorinda appeared on her doorstep.

"Well, well, well, I see congratulations are in order. When is the new baby due?" Dorinda forged a smile.

"We wanted to wait, just in case something went wrong before saying." Linn cut her eyes in her children's direction.

"Oops, where are my manners? I assumed, being as though you are so far along that your little ones would have known by now." Dorinda placed a jeweled hand over her heart, showcasing the Edwardian gold and sapphire wedding ring.

"A baby? I sure hope it's another sister," said Kouri, as he sprang through the door to greet his favorite *tante*.

Linn may have suffered for a time when Lelo refused to nurse in her lap, but it was Kouri who felt the sting of rejection daily as his younger brother clung to their sister, sleeping in her cot and at her side during every waking hour. Kouri often complained of how Karlina robbed him of being a big brother. But even Linn had to admit that Karlina had a way of charming the younger child with her made-up fairy tales. If allowed, Lelo could lie on his belly all day and listen with wide eyes to her animated stories and songs. To Karlina and Lelo's displeasure, Papa Kole was the one who forced the brothers to spend more time together. Lelo was not a rough-natured child like his older brother. He whined when Kouri was too aggressive, and he cried when shoved to the ground or pounced on from behind. Kouri would sulk until his brother forgave him, then the rough play started over again until Lelo learned to throw a punch, and play pranks on their sister. Linn had to admit having a sister would bring a much-needed balance into their home.

7

1897

THE NEWBORN WAS given the nickname Baby Li because her siblings could not properly pronounce her full name. Zuellie (pronounced Zoo-lee) Linn Guerrier had her mother's large seeing-eyes and the most delightful shade of coffee-brown skin. Kole fell in love with the youngest born who reminded him the most of his wife. Kouri was pleased with the new arrival, who represented a built-in spectator for his precocious sister, and guaranteed his uninterrupted freedom with Lelo. Karlina made plans straightaway to teach her younger sister the many ways to charm their papa and pacify their manman. Lelo was relieved to see his mother's attention shift from him to the baby, and that he would no longer have to feel guilty after dodging her embrace that always ended with him on her lap. Linn wore a smile that stretched from jawbone to jawbone.

"*Manman*, look at the way she stares at me?" said Lelo.

The newborn's eyes followed as he hopped around the room. Linn giggled as the baby turned at a 180-degree angle to follow her brother as she continued nursing.

"Come sit here with us, I have enough for both of you to drink." Linn created space for him on the chair.

"Yuck!" He frowned. "Papa says I'm not a baby anymore, so I don't have to."

She had told him numerous times that the baby would not change his need to nurse, but Lelo behaved as if her milk tasted like a mouthful of bitter roots or sour fruit. As she reached for his arm, he slipped past and ran from the room. Her shoulders slumped from the weight of his rejection until the newborn's eyes locked on hers. Time seemed to stand still, and at that moment Linn was transported to the day of her own birth, of water, fear, and an omen.

"It's just you and me now, so tell me, what is it dem eyes see, eh?" Linn held her baby close enough for their noses to touch.

"*Ou*!" Baby Li's lips curled around the familiar word of her *manman's* native language.

What she just heard had to be a coincidence, she was sure of it. Peering intently into her newborn's soul, Linn became aware of Kole's fascination with her large eyes. It was like staring into a looking glass and waiting for a glimpse of anything from the past, present, or future. A hint that the pangs of yesterday would lead to brighter days. But what Linn saw was nowhere close to hopeful as her gaze was met with the darkness of awful secrets.

"Things aren't easy for people like us, do you understand me, little one?"

Baby Li stopped suckling long enough to watch her mother's mouth as it formed shapes to sounds not yet understood.

"If you really are like me, that means we here for one purpose, best you know that now," said Linn.

The baby stiffened in her arms as frown lines formed on her tiny forehead. After Linn repositioned, she placed the baby over her shoulder and begin to pat her on the back. A tiny belch and the baby relaxed. When she settled, Linn placed her in the same hand-made cradle her husband had made twelve years ago for Kouri. As the baby slept, Linn wrestled with visions of her newborn growing into a young girl about Karlina's age. When her sadness became unbearable, she lifted her baby from the cradle and placed her on the opposite nipple.

● ● ●

Not long after her neck and leg muscles strengthened, Baby Li was ready to crawl. In the evenings, Kole liked to sit in the backyard with his brother's drinking rum and bragging about how the baby began scooting across the floor within three months. They knew he exaggerated, but no one could argue the fact that Baby Li would soon be walking. And at nine months old, as Karlina held her chubby hands, and her brothers cheered from the sidelines, Baby Li took her first steps.

The elders would say Baby Li was preparing to make room for the next child, but Linn knew she had given birth for the last time. She convinced herself of being okay with knowing there would be no more babies. Then her husband began to change, so she decided it was better to withhold certain truths. Kole talked less and drank more often in the yard with his brothers. He was tired when he came home from work and often fell asleep as he waited for Linn to finish cooking their meal. Sometimes she questioned whether to wake him to eat with them at the table.

"The baby isn't nursing as she should." Linn waved a fan across her face to create a small breeze as she attempted to start a conversation.

It was a hot evening, which made sleeping a sticky uncomfortable experience. Kole had his back to her as they lied in bed, a half-crescent moon illuminated the lines of his body.

"You know I need my sleep," he said, as he pinched his eyes shut.

Linn fanned in his direction, and when he gave no resistance, she rested her head on his shoulder.

"I'm serious, it's hot and I'm tired. I'll be lucky to get at least two hours to sleep at this rate."

"Can't we talk for just a little while? Seem like you always busy lately, and there's never time for just us."

She noticed when his mood shifted. When Kole turned over, his brewing anger was quelched by the delicateness of her face.

"Tomorrow I will make time for us, okay? Now can we get some sleep, please?" And with the blink of an eye, his kindness passed over as quickly as ocean waves.

Linn turned her back with a solemn, "Good night."

Kole was not the only one who had changed, but it was somewhat of a surprise that no one, not the children, her husband, or even Dorinda, noticed her lack of interest and frequent drifting thoughts. Except for Baby Li. She knew that *Manman* Linn's soul was dying, as she took in less and less of the outside world and fewer delights with caring for their home. The baby, although growing fast, watched as her *manman* receded into a shadow of herself. Whenever Linn tried to shield her tears from the children, it was Baby Li who stopped what she was doing to come to her *manman's* aid.

"Don't cry, don't cry." She would hug whichever limb or body part was closest.

At twelve months old, Baby Li's vocabulary was growing just as quickly as her legs and torso. She would stand out of sight to listen as the small girl formed words almost as perfectly as Lelo. Linn was devastated, so she reacted in ways that shocked the children as well as herself.

"Hush up now, stop all that noise." She snapped and swatted at the playing children.

As Lelo questioned their mother's scorn, baby Li connected with her *manman's* eyes. The two of them lay motionless with their backs to the floor, and feet propped against the wall. Linn moved around the room picking toys from the floor and refolding a pile of clean clothes.

"Repeat after me, Mir-a-goane," said Lelo.

"Mir-uh-gone," Baby Li repeated, with a toothy grin.

"I said be quiet!" Linn shushed again.

"But we are talking low!" said Lelo.

Baby Li looked from her brother back to their mother. Lelo may not have noticed, but their *manman* continued to shush them whenever the youngest attempted to speak. There was not enough time in the mornings for Kole to have noticed what had taken place right underneath his nose. Everything was changing, except Linn intended to do everything within her power to have the smallest being in their home remain the same.

"You can't leave me." Linn would whisper to her last born when nursing. "There will be nothing left for me to live for after you're gone."

8

1899

BABY LI MARVELED at how long it took for her siblings to notice. If at least one of them, preferably Karlina, had paid closer attention the problem would have been detected sooner. The boys were distracted with their yelping laughter as they played pranks on each other. Karlina was more concerned with her looks, though soft and attractive, she despised the bright skin and encouraged her younger sister to be proud that no one would ever question who her parents were. She had also been the first to suggest that Baby Li was ugly; not because of the color of her skin, the decided unattractiveness had more to do with how the younger sister's eyes protruded like a carp fish.

Yesterday while she was taking a nap, the older siblings were allowed to play in the yard. When their *manman* called them in for lunch, Baby Li overheard the tell-end of a confusing yet curious conversation.

"Watch how she look at us, tell me if you think she is scared or frightened," said Kouri as he corralled the siblings around their sleeping younger sister.

"It's her eyes, they remind me of the stories we hear of zombies in the night without a soul." Karlina shivered from the image conjured in her mind.

Kouri shushed her when they saw Baby Li awake on her mat. As the older two siblings continued to whisper, Lelo moved closer. She reached for him. After kissing her on the cheek, he used the opportunity to slide in beside her and wrapped what had been his nursing blanket not too long ago around their back. Lelo was upset, she could tell by the way he clung to her as if trying to shield her from harm. Baby Li may have favored their *manman* the most in features, but she was also kind and warm like their *manman* had been to him. Lelo clung tighter until the older siblings left the room.

"I'll always protect you," he said, as he squeezed her once more. "Do you understand what that means? You can always count on me."

Baby Li nodded, but the decision had already been made. No one could help her now, at least none of the children. She was going to do what needed to be done for all of their sake, and nothing short of divine intervention would change her mind. Maybe her Papa could help, but it would require finding the words to explain what was happening to her, and *manman*. Karlina would know how to approach their papa, but Baby Li knew she'd prefer such favors to be saved on a yummy sweet treat, or better yet, a reading book. This was a matter the youngest had to take on alone.

Linn held her last child in her arms even when she could walk and shushed her when she tried to speak; her pleading eye's begging for the girl to remain a baby, just a little while longer. Baby Li clung to her mother's hip as she distanced herself further from her siblings. As she withdrew in silence, she conformed to what her *manman* needed her to be and less of herself. Baby Li continued to be breastfed, not seeming to mind the extended time in her mother's lap – not until the day came for Lelo to start school.

It was a sad, cold morning for both Baby Li and Lelo. Their manman wiped tears from her eyes as she explained the process of walking down the hill and meeting up with other children, Lelo tried not to cry as he held on to his baby sister. When Kouri entered the room, Baby Li watched as Lelo released her hand and squared his shoulders.

"Alright already, we're going to be late if we don't hurry," said Kouri, as he pulled his brother away from their younger sister.

"After you eat then you can leave," said manman.

The three older siblings ate their hot oats quickly with steam trailing from their bowls to wide-opened mouths. Karlina was first out the door with her book sack in hand, but it was Kouri and Lelo who made it to the compound gate before anyone else. When they were gone, Linn slumped into her seat and avoided looking at her remaining child who watched her like a little eaglet waiting to be fed. Baby Li waited for her mother's approval before climbing onto her lap. As she nursed, *manman* Linn turned to the front room wall and whispered inaudible words that slipped through the cracks of the stone. Baby Li imagined the small chirping bird outside their window carried her mother's message over the treetops to a hiding place deep in the forest.

As Linn relaxed, she was able to search within her mother's eyes hoping to find a trace of her secrets. When her eyelids became too weighty to hold open, Baby Li imagined a large pair of wings lifting and carrying her tiny body over the hillside. She marveled at the sloping trail her papa and siblings had journeyed on that morning. As her eyelids opened and shut, her manman's protruding eye sockets enlarged, allowing space to peer through the shared vision. Then they were together, holding hands as they soared above the town below their hillside. From the dockside, they saw a rugged fishing boat. Papa Kole yanked fish overboard, some he tossed in a small bucket to be brought home for dinner.

At first glance, her papa looked fine, but there was something slightly off. Maybe it was because she was looking so intently but he seemed slower, which could explain the worry on his face. Baby Li could sense there were other things, hidden within troubling him. When she tried to press forward a gust of wind pushed her back to the docks and nearly knocked the breath from her lungs. After regaining her composure, they turned to the trail and before long she was back in the comfort of her *manman's* lap.

Baby Li yawned from her nap then opened her eyes to the sound of her brother's laughter. With hardly a glance in her direction, they ran to the kitchen to sneak a piece of whatever they could find to snack on. Karlina moped a few minutes behind them. As she complained to their *manman* of having to run all the way to keep up with the boys, Kouri and Lelo shared stories from their day. After eating the curried meat and rice their mother prepared for lunch, Baby Li followed them to the bedroom.

"I saw the way she smiled at you," said Kouri as he poked a finger in his brother's back.

"Will you quit it?" Lelo spun around and swatted his hand away.

"But you do like her, admit it." The older brother continued to tease.

"Can I have a moment with him now?" Karlina stepped forward with a pencil in hand. "Come on, let me show you how to write your name so the other kids don't use it to pick on you."

Before she could push Kouri aside, he grabbed Lelo by the hand and yanked him away. As they ran out the back door Kouri did a hand flip off the back porch. Baby Li laughed when she saw her brother's bottom hit the ground.

"That's okay, I'll teach Baby Li because she's smarter than both of you anyway." Karlina grabbed her sister's hand and led her back into the room.

"Me? You gonna teach me to write?" Baby Li pointed at her chest.

Karlina nodded as she prepared space on their bed for the lesson. No sooner had Baby Li placed the pencil properly in position than a dark shadow filled the doorway.

"What are you doing that for? You know she's not like the rest of you," said *Manman* Linn as she folded her arms.

"Just like we can learn, she can learn too and I'm going to be the one who teaches her." Karlina stood with two hands on her boney hips. When she returned to the bed she intentionally ignored her *manman's* glare. Baby Li followed her sister's pattern as she traced the letters of her name. When Karlina clapped her hands, she could hear *Manman* Linn's breathing increase.

"See here, that's the letter Z." Karlina held the paper up. "It's the first letter of your name, your real name is Zuellie Guerrier—not baby Li."

"That is enough, you hear what I say?" *Manman* Linn frowned at the two girls.

Karlina and Baby Li watched as she snatched the pencil away and tossed it onto the floor.

"I have to potty," said Baby Li. She ran from the room and shut herself inside the washroom. While washing her hands she could not help but wonder what life would be like for her at the schoolhouse down the trail. After washing her hands, she followed her papa's voice to the front room.

"Papa, can I go to school?" She tugged at his pant leg.

"Of course, are you ready to learn to read and write?" Papa Kole lifted her into his arms.

She grinned, shaking her head up and down as her braids bounced in the air.

"My sissy taught me to write a letter."

"Is that right? Well, sounds like you are ready for school then."

When his wife entered the room, she smiled at the sight of her husband. Baby Li noticed the smile leave her papa's face as he placed her on the floor and grunted.

"Zuellie is ready for school," he said politely.

Baby Li's eye's widened as she awaited her *manman's* response.

"She needs to stay home a little longer. You know how shy she gets and can hardly talk," said *manman* Linn.

Papa Kole noticed Baby Li staring so he closed his mouth that was gaped open. She could see his mind spinning as he struggled with the appropriate words. Baby Li looked from one parent to the other. When her eye's connected with her *manman's*, Baby Li could hear her silent plea.

"I will die if you leave me." Whispered the unspoken words.

Kole patted his daughter on the head as he turned to leave. *Manman* Linn followed in his footsteps until he reached the backdoor and stepped outside. Linn watched as he took a seat next to his brother's and was handed a tin can to drink from. Baby Li came to her manman's side and stayed there as she cleaned the kitchen and prepared the family's dinner.

9

1901

MANMAN LINN ENTERED first; her earthen brown skin glowing from the cocoa butter used during her night-time ritual. Papa Kole followed, still clothed in his high-waisted work pants held up by a thick leather belt wrapped twice around his pole-thin waist.

"What the trouble, eh? Come sit." *Manman* Linn tapped her legs. When Zuellie climbed into her lap, the smell of cocoa filled her nostrils. Manman Linn placed a warm hand across her forehead, next she kneaded the young girl's belly to check for pain. In the shadows, Papa Kole seemed to tower over them like a swaying palm tree.

"Any fever?" His protruding lips clicked as they usually did when agitated or worried. Papa Kole moved around the darkness with ease. He slid a hand underneath the mattress, next he crawled around the floorboards to check for small critters.

"I found this in her pocket." Karlina produced the smashed bread slice.

"Take it to the kitchen," said *manman* Linn.

Zuellie avoided their scorn as she continued to groan. When she noticed her papa diligently continuing his search, her legs itched with a desire to join him.

"Keep still, or you will make things worse." Manman Linn massaged her daughter's legs until she settled.

Zuellie continued to groan as she nestled into the crook of her mother's armpit. Papa Kole stood on his feet and smacked his teeth. With her eyes closed, Zuellie overheard him mumble something about bad spirits that lurked where they had not been invited.

"I'll get a broom and a matchstick, the flame will drive out any bad spirits," he said.

Manman Linn rolled her eyes at his shadow as he left the room. When he was gone, she tucked the youngest girl into a nursing position as she had done before. It had been many days, and months upon months since Zuellie had abandoned her *manman's* milk. For a moment, she questioned her mother's intention. She fought the habit to lean into her *manman's* breast.

It had been Kouri who had given her the best news when she was about two-and-a-half years old. After inspecting her opened mouth, he declared the time had come for her to eat and drink with the rest of them. Karlina and Lelo stood close behind and nodded their approval. Maybe they were not aware that *Manman* Linn had been the one to seek her out to nurse, even when Zuellie refused—always with those saddened eyes. Now here she was again in her *manman's* lap. The other children had not known she still nursed when they were not around. Sometimes it seemed she was held on their *manman's* lap for hours. Zuellie would stare around the room daydreaming of running down the hillside with her brothers.

As she searched her *manman's* expression, the surrounding rooms grew quiet. By this hour it was so dark, Papa Kole had taken one of the oil lamps with him, the other remained unlit in the front room. In the darkness, it was hard to make out the head nod that signaled her to nurse. *Manman* Linn refused to take her eyes off the room door. One hand tightened around her daughter's back as the other pushed her gown aside. Just as Zuellie was about to position herself, Karlina reentered the room. *Manman* Linn sat forward and closed her gown.

"Papa said put this at the head of the bed." Karlina placed a bundle of pungent-smelling roots on the bed. She folded her arms across her chest.

Manman Linn twisted her lip in disgust. In one movement, she pushed her daughter aside and rose from the bed. Zuellie eyeballed the dangling pouch as her mother left the room.

"I told you, this isn't our way," said Linn.

"Ssshh, let's not wake the boys too, there's enough upset in here for one night." Papa Kole pulled his wife from the doorway.

As their parents whispered away from earshot, Karlina used the time to cross-examine her sister.

"Okay, tell me now if you are pretending. I promise it'll be our secret," she said.

Zuellie ignored her sister's request, especially since her parents were speaking to one another. Now all she needed was for papa Kole's frown to disappear, and the sparkle to return to her mother's eyes.

"My wife," he used to tease the children when they pestered and nagged for their *manman's* attention.

"My wife," he said proudly to his parents, and relatives whenever the conversation allowed.

"I can't leave my wife overnight." He had once boasted of how he told the captain his reasons for not excepting long fishing trips, excursions that would have provided enough fish for their entire compound. Papa Kole stood his ground and was always home in time for supper with his wife.

If she stuck to her plan long enough, maybe by morning or even tomorrow evening, her papa would call for his wife again and *manman* Linn would be happy. Zuellie would no longer have to carry around the guilt for rejecting her mother's lap. Then she would be free to run and dance like her papa and Kouri.

Zuellie groaned when she saw her sister waiting for a response. Karlina frowned, and when her sister refused to answer she struck her hard on the thigh. Zuellie screeched from the throbbing sensation. Water formed in her guppy-shaped eyes as she rubbed the sting.

"I'm so sorry, Baby Li…I just don't know what to do. You won't talk, and you're acting strange. What's wrong? I promise you can tell me." Karlina held her fingers up in a pinky promise.

"Papa Legba, can we trust her?" Zuellie whispered to the open window.

The night had gone silent; not a beating drum, nor a flicker from the lightning flies, or a twinkling star in the sky. Karlina had been like a spare mother to Baby Li, carrying her when she could not keep up with their brothers, wiping her face when mango nectar trailed down her chin. She had even taught Zuellie things their *manman* had not, like eating properly with a spoon and teaching her letters in her name.

"If only you knew how to spell then we could write to each other." Karlina put her arm around her sister's shoulder.

Zuellie reached for her sister's hand and placed it over her heart. If Karlina could turn off her brain for a moment, then maybe she could understand. Zuellie held onto her sister's hand until she believed the unspoken words had penetrated her soul.

"My sister, listen," said Zuellie without moving her lips. *"I can't speak now, not until manman becomes papa's wife again. And after she stops looking at me with those sad eyes then I'll talk."*

Karlina closed her eyes as her hand rested on her sister's chest. With each heartbeat, she silenced her breathing to still her pulse. When she had listened for as long as she could tolerate, she opened her eyes and stepped back.

"I won't let you do this," she said.

As Zuellie looked out the window, small hints of light had begun to break through the darkness. Morning would come within a few short hours and their parents were still talking in the front room. Zuellie could tell the conversation was unpleasant, but at least they were communicating. Occasionally she heard her *manman's* weary plea before her papa's gruff response. He wanted to seek counsel from the *mambo* in the forest. *Manman* Linn refused him, saying it was better to take the girl down the hillside to a medical physician. Papa Kole was willing to do both.

Karlina had fallen asleep some time ago after she pulled her younger sister underneath the blanket. By morning they were still lying close, hands placed at each other's heart, silently protesting the other's will. When their brothers awoke, Zuellie had won her first battle.

"What's going on in here? She should be up by now." Kouri pointed to his sleeping sister.

Lelo stood behind his brother, grinning more than usual. Today was his 7th birthday, and he was officially a "big boy," as his brother and papa Kole explained yesterday at the dinner table.

"Yeah, did somebody die or something?" said Lelo.

Karlina stirred when he held her eyelids open. After she rolled over, Lelo hopped onto the bed and curled up beside his sister as he had done dozens of times before. Zuellie looked away from Lelo, knowing his intuition was just as keen - if not more - than their sister.

"Baby Li is not feeling well," said Karlina.

She pushed against Kouri's leg with her foot until he moved away from the bed. Then she shoved Lelo out as well.

"Come on big boy, let's get ready for school." Kouri shrugged before he escorted the younger boy from the room.

Neither of them looked back as they made their exit. After they were gone, Karlina pulled Zuellie into her arms and placed her hand back against her chest. When *manman* Linn entered to check on the girls, Karlina asked if she could stay home to help watch her sister. Zuellie was relieved when both parents refused her request. She stared at her sister when *manman* Linn announced she and papa Kole would stay home together to take care of baby Li. When Karlina had finished dressing for school and was about to leave, she gave her sister another glance. Zuellie beamed like the morning sun sitting between her manman and papa.

There was not much progress on that first day. Yes her parents were talking more than they had in months, but their disagreement continued until the afternoon. In the end, *Manman* Linn surrendered to her husband's desire; they would utilize every means possible to help make their baby well. Papa Kole and his wife walked down the hillside with their youngest child between them. Zuellie walked for the first two miles but when her legs grew tired, Papa Kole tossed her on his back for the remainder of the journey.

After the examination at the clinic, Zuellie listened as the physician scratched his head while reading the charts. There were no medical findings to explain her symptoms. Time and maybe additional testing could reveal the answers. Zuellie could not conceal a smile when the physician suggested "patience and a boatload of love" should cure what he labeled as, "selective mutism."

"Now do you see why I didn't want to come down here?" said Papa Kole.

Their faces weighted down with concern as they embarked on the long walk home. Proud of herself for having the will to outlast both her parents and the probing physician, Zuellie rejoiced as she sucked on a small piece of sugar cane.

"It is not only our duty but our way," said papa Kole.

Manman Linn nodded, knowing the argument would not end unless he had his way. Halfway up the hillside, Kole took Zuellie from around his neck and placed her on the ground. When he placed his lips on his wife's mouth, *Manman* Linn closed her eyes and lingered after the kiss. When she opened them again, he had crossed the street and turned onto a heavily wooded pathway until he vanished out of sight.

Later in the day when Karlina and her brothers returned from school, they approached their sister with extra care. Zuellie sat silently at the wooden table as *Manman* Linn explained that Baby Li had a case of selective mutism. Karlina eyeballed her sister before placing a kiss on her cheek.

"Is it okay for us to play together?" said Karlina.

Zuellie reached for her hand as *Manman* Linn intervened.

"The doctor says I need to keep a close eye on her."

She moved between the two girls and lifted Zuellie onto her lap. Karlina looked to her sister before she left the room.

"Not yet sissy," Zuellie's heart spoke to her sister. *"Maybe by this time tomorrow night manman's sadness will have gone…and I will be free."*

10

1906

SHADOWS ARE CAST when a larger object, or body, blocks a path of light. The body projecting the shadow appears larger and the silhouette may shape-shift depending on the light source. One thing is for certain, a shadow ceases to exist if the blockage is removed. Zuellie learned it was not difficult to become her mother's shadow. When *Manman* Linn rose early to warm the stove for cooking, Baby Li was close at her side. The first stop was at the chamber pot. Next, they would fill the washbowl with water to brush their teeth with a boars-hair toothbrush. Afterward, *Manman* Linn made haste to change from her night garments to a flour-stained peasant dress. By this age, Nine-year-old Baby Li had learned to imitate her every move. Her mother was barefoot, so she did the same.

In the kitchen, she watched as *Manman* Linn tied an apron around her waist - no matter how quickly the young girl moved, her mother had to go first. Afterward, Baby Li did the same. She tied a smaller apron around her waist, then watched the kettle and frying pan leave the shelf in her mother's hands as they were placed on the stove. Zuellie helped fill the kettle with water from a hand pump in the yard to boil, then went to the cupboard for lard. She followed as *Manman* Linn selected peppers and herbs from her garden. With arms bowed from the veggies, they tiptoed to the hencoop, where her mother reached for enough eggs to feed the family.

Papa Kole would be the first to sit at the table in his suspenders and rubber boots. The very eloquent (with a small dash of conceit), 16-year-old Karlina sauntered in next with her favorite book in hand, *De l'égalité des races humaines*: On the Equality of Human Races, by Haitian anthropologist, Joseph Firmin. 17-year-old Kouri and 12-year-old Lelo, entered last, cross at their *manman* because they still needed to be shaken from their bedsheets. After they were fed, Papa Kole put on his straw hat, grabbed his lunch pail, and waited by the door. Baby Li moved alongside her mother As Papa Kole kissed his wife, she waved goodbye to her siblings from the porch.

Kouri and Lelo hunched their backs as they fell in line to start the long journey. Halfway down the hillside, Karlina and Lelo would veer eastward toward the schoolhouse. Kouri and their Papa continued down the hill, marching with extended necks through town until they reached the docks.

After the rest of the family left through the compound gate, *Manman* Linn stepped off the porch to sweep around the yard. The other wives would watch as their withdrawn sister-in-law moved with her small shadow. *Tante* Dorinda was the only wife to wave at *Manman* Linn, who would return a curt head gesture in her direction. Baby Li waved at her *tantes*.

"*Gade li, timoun nan frize.*" (Look at her, the frozen child). The oldest *tante* sucked her teeth.

"Doctor says she might—" said Linn before she was interrupted.

"Tsk, if she can go about like this then why doesn't she speak, eh?" The *tante* placed a hand on her squared hips.

"She has a disorder, selective mu-mute—mutation," Linn stuttered, shrugging her shoulders.

Baby Li smirked at her mother's obvious discomfort, as another *tante* eyeballed them. *Manman* Linn put her head down and continued sweeping. Baby Li smiled when her *Tante* Dorinda approached.

"Don't pay them no mind," said Dorinda. "She just jealous because her husband ain't come home last night, and yours come home every night." Dorinda sighed.

Baby Li leaned against the porch railing when *Manman* Linn stopped to listen. She watched the two women as they spoke, her mother's stone-set expression matching Dorinda's melancholic voice. One woman's pain the same as the other, but *Manman* Linn would see nothing past her own sorrow.

"I'm really busy today, getting ready for Lelo's party." Manman Linn averted her eyes.

"I know, same as the rest of us. You let me know if you need any help," said Dorinda, she turned to leave without waiting for a response from Linn.

At that moment, for the first time since the night she waited for *Papa Legba*, Baby Li felt a tiny glimmer of hope. Dorinda was the answer to her prayers and had been there all along. Another woman - a friend - who could relate to the woes of having children grow up and husbands lose interest. As they parted ways, Baby Li observed her *tante's* hesitant steps as she returned to her place under the tree.

In the kitchen, *Manman* Linn cleared the dishes and threw out uneaten scraps of food. Zuellie usually followed no more than three steps behind, as she went through rooms picking up soiled laundry and removing rubbish from the wooden floor. Normally as they worked her mother sang an old hymn, but this time she was silent. Baby Li poked her *manman* against the arm, then spread her arms wide, a hand gesture she created which meant, "Look at me," or "What do you want?" Whichever happened to fit the situation.

Her first year of silence had been fun, like a game almost. Baby Li became the teacher and her family was her students. As she focused attention on living in silence, she developed a unique system using her hands and facial gestures to communicate. *Manman* Linn saw no further need to nurse the child after realizing her youngest born was handicapped and determined instead to teach the girl everything she knew.

"Today I will teach you how to sew." *Manman* Linn placed the sewing needle and spool of thread before them. "That boy's so rough on his clothes, we'll need to patch these up before the party." She spread Lelo's torn britches on the table.

Baby Li rolled her eyes as she handled the one pair of nice trousers Lelo had left, still damp from having been removed before they had time to dry on the clothesline.

"We can't have the birthday boy show up like this, what will our guests think of us?" *Manman* Linn's face contorted into a stiff grin. "After stitching, we'll have to set the chairs in the yard for the party."

Baby Li grunted. When *Manman* Linn refused to look up, she hurried from the table to retrieve the pen and paper Karlina kept in her chest. The floorboard creaked as she returned with the pencil and paper. Baby Li's shoulders hunched forward as she scribbled hard against the paper. When she finished *Manman* Linn took the paper from her hand.

"What is my name?" She read the words aloud.

Baby Li grunted louder when her *manman* left the table to place wood inside the stove. The chair she had been sitting in rocked on its legs as she pushed away from the table and approached her mother. She jabbed at the paper until it was impossible to be ignored.

"What kind of silly question is this?" said *Manman* Linn.

Her long braids fell forward when she bent to place another log into the belly of the stove. After the stove was hot, Baby Li blocked her from returning to the table. When she refused to move, *Manman* Linn went to the cupboard and came back with flour and other ingredients to knead into dough. Baby Li was not at her side, nor would she watch the precise movements of her *manman's* recipe, even if she would be the only one to know the secret technique.

It had been seven long years, as Baby Li studied at her *manman's* hip; watching every move, mimicking every gesture, learning skills she was told would help her later in life. When Lelo awoke this morning, he announced to the whole world that he was 12 years old today. Kouri congratulated his younger brother by proclaiming he was, "almost a man and would someday find a girl to marry, as he had."

Kouri would soon be married, which meant before long Karlina would do the same. Then Lelo. There someday had been marked by growing older and leaving their *manman's* side. The realization of "someday" never coming for Baby Li made her stomach turn. She returned to her seat and continued writing where she left off.

> *My name is Zuellie, not Baby Li. I am nine years old. I can do more things now, like read and write. I should be in school so I can learn things like Karlina. Papa thinks it's time too.*

After reading her note, *manman* Linn continued kneading as if nothing had changed. While waiting for a response, Baby Li thought of the many lectures her *manman* had given over the years. There was nothing for people like them in the world; no fulfillment in marriage, or children. Like herself, the youngest child had gifts that were meant to be hidden. She told her on the eve of each of her birthdays. Baby Li had been born to help her *manman,* and that was it. The other children had accepted this truth, so she should as well.

Karlina believed her sister could at least learn to write, not just cook and clean at their mother's side. She was the one who gave Baby Li the spelling and writing lessons late in the night beside an oil lamp. Papa Kole had his doubts about her supposed disability, questioning his daughter with a weary look after each grunt. He shared his worries with his wife, but she rolled her eyes and shrugged off his concerns. Kouri and

Lelo gave her space, mostly because they were ever around much. Five years she heeded *Manman* Linn's orders, ignoring her developing body and enduring scrutinization from her *tante's* chattering lips. But today was different, Lelo's "someday" was difficult to overlook.

Manman Linn seemed clueless as she continued mixing and kneading. Without saying a word, Baby Li stepped onto the back porch. In the far distance, she could make out a large body of water with waves as they rippled across the Caribbean Sea; miles and miles of an ocean filled with adventure, excitement, and life. Papa Kole and Kouri were out there somewhere on a fishing boat, she imagined them laughing together as they enjoyed their time at sea. Someday Lelo would be on that same boat if he chose. Someday Karlina might even get to ride on one of the fancier passenger ships. As she thought more about life beyond her *manman's* shadow, Zuellie found herself at the edge of the yard, past the chicken coop and bob-wired fence. Far beyond the tree stumps where her papa and his brothers sat sipping homemade rum from tin cups, down to the place where the trees began to slope against the hillside.

"*Zuellie!*"

A voice called to her from the forest, drawing her further into the thick of the trees.

"I thought you had forgotten about me," she said, kneeling to listen with her ear to the ground.

"*Zuellie!*"

11

WITH HER EAR and body pressed to the ground, Zuellie closed her eyes and held her breath. Determined to meet the guardian spirit face to face, she waited for the second time in her life for a sign. A low murmur began and rose until it caused a tingle inside her eardrum. Zuellie flinched from the vibration but kept her face planted. As she continued to listen, the familiar sound of the sea grew louder.

"Zuellie!"

Her eyes flew open and enlarged the way *manman* Linn's had done when they had shared her vision. Hovering above her image on the ground, Zuellie watched in amazement as the sea rose until it covered the hillside and washed over her body. A gigantic wave carried her far away, planting her in a foreign land with people who spoke a different language, and laughed at her ignorance. Despite her shame, she embraced their ways until she became like one of them. When the wave returned to carry her back home she fought against the current. The wave rang in her ear until the sound of drums matched the thumping in her chest. Then it all stopped.

By the time she awoke, a light tapping from a woodpecker drew her back to reality. Zuellie stood up and half expected to be drenched in water instead of leaves and dirt. When she could not see the top of their home, her steps quickened as she followed the smell of her *manman's* bread and roasted meat.

"ZUELLIE!" A voice called out.

Rocks and twigs dug into the souls of her bare feet as she ran toward the sound of familiarity. Just as the sight of her backyard came into view a thorn pricked her heel and caused her to stumble to her knees.

"There you are…she's over here," said *tante* Dorinda. She waved to *Manman* Linn who emerged from the woods several yards down.

Zuellie put her head down when her mother approached.

"I have been worried sick out my mind." *Manman* Linn placed a hand over her chest.

After thanking her sister-in-law, she snatched her daughter by the arm. As they marched across the yard and up the back steps, Zuellie glanced back at her *Tante* Dorinda, who remained in the yard setting a long table with chairs all around. Dorinda's mouth gaped open when she noticed her niece smiling in her direction

"Okay, you're not a baby anymore and you want to be called by your name." *Manman* Linn stuck her head over a bubbling pot of beans and stirred. After she had tasted the contents she faced her daughter.

"You win, now please go change out of those clothes?" She pointed at a mud stain on her daughter's skirt. "But first, mop up this mess from the floor." Her eyes traced the dirt trail from the backdoor.

Zuellie was so excited she ran to her mother and kissed her face. After wiping away the mud trail, she skipped down the hall and thought of the different ways to reintroduce herself to her family members. By the time she had washed and changed into clean clothes, the sound of laughter filled the front room. Zuellie left her room feeling a little nervous and approached her *tante's* who each carried their pots filled with vegetables, meat, and rice. Her *Grann manman* stepped over the threshold hunched over with a cane in her hand. Zuellie ran to escort the elderly woman to a seat.

"You remember my youngest? Baby—I mean Zuellie." *Manman* Linn pushed her daughter aside to hand her mother-in-law a glass of brewed tea.

"Mm-hmm. This is the one who refuses to speak." *Grann* waved Linn away and motioned for the young girl.

Zuellie moved closer to take her grandmother's hand.

"*Oui, Madame,* this is the one who pretends," said *Tante* Ines, pushing Linn further out of Zuellie's view.

"*JELE!*" said Ines, with a snarl that caused Zuellie to shrink on her knees. "They call this frozen child Baby Li."

The front room filled as papa Kole's brothers with their children and wives arrived. When her *grann* asked why Effia's medicine failed to heal the girl, Zuellie peered around the guests in search of anyone to divert the attention away from her condition. Her Grandpapa Baptiste walked by and patted the top of her head. Her uncles shook their heads, as her *tante's* hovered together in a circle.

"Her name isn't Baby Li anymore, she wants to be called by her rightful name, Zuellie, ain't that right Dorinda?" A pathway parted as *Manman* Linn reentered the room wearing her fancy yellow and red Quadrille dress. She looked goddess-like with her loosened hair falling around her face in crinkles. Zuellie used the opportunity to scamper away from the crowd as her *manman* snagged the spotlight.

"If the child can use her throat to grunt, that same sound can be used to speak with," said her *Grann Manman*.

Manman Linn took a deep breath. Before she could respond the front door opened, and Papa Kole entered with the grinning birthday boy at his side. Kouri and Karlina were not too far behind them. Kole looked to his wife, who put her head down.

"Linn's been doing a good job working with the girl's disability," said Kole, as he stood next to his wife.

Lelo stood beside Zuellie to show his support. He slid his arm around her shoulders as she leaned on his chest. One of the elders zeroed in on him, which caused Lelo to straighten up. When he continued to stare, Lelo marched across the room and stormed out the front door. As he passed by, Zuellie overheard their uncle mumble a harsh word to their papa, something about, "making him a man and less of a girl."

The family moved from the front room to the backyard where the chairs had been placed. Pans filled with food were brought out and covered the table before them. Dressed in their best, the wives sat beside their partners who wore hats to shield them from the blazing sun. As Zuellie picked up a calabash bowl and began to pile it with rice and beans, she noticed the twinkle in her *manman's* eyes as papa Kole placed a hand on her knee. The day had turned out perfect, and there was only one thing left to do. As Zuellie contemplated her next move, the back door swung open as Karlina and Kouri joined the party. Her brother filled his bowl and took his seat. Karlina stood next to Zuellie as she piled food into her bowl.

"I saw your note on the table, it's about time you stood up for yourself." Karlina grinned at her sister.

Zuellie opened her mouth to speak but was distracted as Lelo emerged from the side of the house with a friend. *Manman* Linn asked for him to stand in the middle of the circle. When the family began clapping and cheering, he covered his face with both hands and blushed. After his initial shock had ended, Lelo began skipping as he sang, "Happy Birthday to me," in a high-pitched voice.

"Okay, son, that's enough," said Papa Kole.

Zuellie noticed the way his nostrils flared as his brothers began whispering amongst themselves. Lelo returned to his friend, whom he introduced as Pieter, and they finished the shrill of a song together. Papa Kole looked to their mother when Lelo placed an arm around his friend's shoulders.

"Hey baby sis, I want you to meet my friend." Lelo passed the eyeballing elders to introduce her. "She doesn't speak for some reason but she's really smart."

Zuellie put her food down to shake Pieter's hand. A warming sensation shot up her arm and caused her stomach to quiver when he held onto her hand longer than was necessary. Pieter's slanted dark eyes held her gaze until it seemed they were the only two people standing in the yard. When Lelo pulled them apart, his arm slid back around his friend's shoulders. As he bypassed their parents, Papa Kole pounced from his seat. Lelo bent to shield his father's fist. Zuellie waited for the elders to stop her papa, but most of her family turned their backs and the others watched as if it were a drama or motion picture. With each blow, *Manman* Linn lowered her head. Kouri and Karlina acted as they had when Zuellie had been held hostage in her perpetual state of infancy.

"It's time you start acting like a man now!" Papa Kole's chest heaved as he spat on the ground. Then he turned and frowned at Pieter, who bowed his head and stepped away.

Zuellie had seen enough. For the second time in one day, she took off running. Leaving behind the blur of shadows in her backyard, she ran past *tante* Dorinda's house and through the compound. She continued through the gate, running until she felt liberated of her *manman's* pleading eyes and Papa Kole's disappointment. When her foot turned on a pebble, Zuellie bent to remove her shoes and kept going. When the trail sloped downward, she paused briefly to look back. That's when she noticed the remote pathway near the edge of the trees. The dry branches snagged the hem of her dress as she left the trail that soon led her to an open field with tall shoots. Running through a muddy creek, she followed it until the fields turned to woods. Stopping to survey her surroundings, she headed back North, hoping to return home, but the forest grew thicker.

Zuellie continued walking until a mysterious chiming sound caused her to look up. Shells strung through tree limbs clanked against empty bottles that were strung by twine. When the sun gleamed on the reflection of the glass, she shielded her eyes. There was no need for a mailbox or door number, anyone who ventured this far knew it to be the sacred dwelling of the *mambo*. A gust of wind blew, causing the swinging bottles to sway back and forth. The further she walked the louder the chiming became until Zuellie stood still. A bone-shaped object on the ground caught her attention, reminding her of Karlina's crazy tales about the *mambo*.

"What them see, can't be unseen."

Zuellie spun around to face an older woman. She had large seeing eyes like *Manman* Linn's and was dressed in all white from her headscarf to her ankle-length dress.

"This be the one they call the frozen baby, come way down to see me, eh?" Effia raised her eyebrows. Her thin limbs cracked as she approached. Zuellie was about to say something when the woman held up a hand to shush her.

"No need," said Effia, as she waved for the girl to follow.

Once inside, Zuellie was struck by the darkened interior. The windows were covered over with wood slats, and the only light seeped through tiny gaps in her thatched roof. There were mysterious hand drawings on the wall and shelves of jars filled with murky fluid; some with bark and twigs, but mostly unidentified specimens. When Zuellie noticed a floating eyeball in one of the jars, she checked to see if both the *mambo's* eyesockets were intact. Effia cackled when Zuellie searched her face.

"Come here, this way child," she moved deeper into the room until they reached a spot where the sunlight landed.

"Give him this to drink," said Effia, she reached for a jar before sitting in a rickety rocking chair. "It's what your papa wants for the boy, it should work."

Effia waved her away and began plucking leaves from a nearby plant and placed them into a bottle. When Zuellie frowned at the stench, Effia's laugh cut through the silence.

"Never mind the smell, if you can get him to drink it then his little problem will go away. Then your papa gets what he wants, but he will lose something he needs… he's been warned about the cost."

Zuellie turned the bottle in her hand to admire the contents. There was enough trouble at home for one day, and if *Manman* Linn knew about the *mambo's* medicine the evening would be worse. Zuellie slid the bottle in her side pocket and turned to leave. When Effia's cackle filled the room, she ran from the hut and fled through the field and woods until she was out of breath. Zuellie exhaled when the front gate of her compound was in view.

By the time she reached home, Papa Kole and his brothers were sipping rum on their tree stumps. The others sat around the table gossiping as they finished the remainder of the food. When she entered the house, *Manman* Linn and Lelo sat alone in the front room. Zuellie clutched her pocket as she went into her room to hide the bottle for safekeeping. Sometime after midnight, the house cleared and the house went dark. Zuellie tiptoed from her bed and went to her brother's room.

"What you doing still up sissy?" said Lelo.

Zuellie held a finger to her lips. She pulled a pencil and torn piece of paper from her pocket and began to write.

"You-must-drink-this? Did you get this from the medicine lady?" said Lelo.

Zuellie pointed at his mouth and nodded.

"They're worried about the way I act." His shoulders slumped as his head lowered.

Zuellie reached into her pocket and handed him the bottle. When Lelo opened the top, both of them pinched their nose from the stench.

"How am I supposed to drink this?" said Lelo.

Zuellie made a hand gesture as if milking a cow.

"But you know how much I hate milk," he said.

Zuellie placed a hand on her hip and grunted. Without further complaint, he turned the bottle to his lips and drank it down fast. When he was finished, he squeezed his nostrils to keep from gagging. Zuellie ran to pour him a glass of tea, which he drank quickly. Moving on autopilot, she plucked a leaf from *Manman* Linn's mint plant and waved it underneath her brother's nose. After Lelo's stomach settled, they sat on the floor and leaned against each other for support.

12

A ROOSTER CROWED in their backyard at the same time Lelo and Zuellie pushed from the hard kitchen floor where they had fallen asleep. Lelo's bones cracked as he twisted and stretched. After Zuellie had finished yawning and wiping sleep from her eyes, Lelo raised a hand and saluted his sister. Whether it was to honor her vow of silence or to share in her pain, she was unsure.

"Papa is worried about me because he thinks I'm soft like a girl, but I'm more concerned about you sissy." His smile faltered. "We're getting older now and—"

Zuellie grunted, then dropped her head to avert his sorrowful eyes. She could end this charade now, but her words were snuffed out somewhere between her mind and mouth, and there was no explanation as to why.

"Maybe the medicine was for you," he said.

Zuellie shook her head back-and-forth, causing her neck to crack as her four long braids whipped the air.

"Don't worry about it, I'll never leave you here alone. We will get through this together."

When Zuellie smiled, he gave her another tight squeeze. Still dressed in yesterday's clothing, the two of them hunched their shoulders as they moved down the hallway. She heard someone whistling outside their kitchen window and knew Papa Kole was preparing for work in the cane fields. It was a Saturday morning, but everyone besides the Guerrier brothers would take advantage of the time to rest.

Zuellie stepped lightly into her room and slid into bed beside her sister. Laying with her eyes closed, she thought about her brother's words. Her papa and older brother mistook him as weak, but his vow to watch over her proved otherwise. Together they could maneuver through the next phase of life, watching each other's backs, and caring for their aging parents. Maybe her life was just as her *manman* had always said, she had been born to care for them. Having peace with her brother's alliance, Zuellie's thoughts rocked her to sleep.

"WE'LL BE RIGHT THERE!," said Karlina.

Zuellie opened her eyes to find her sister dressed in her long field skirt and head wrap.

"Papa says he needs our help in the field today." Karlina placed a bonnet over her headscarf to shield her delicate skin.

"He hasn't been feeling well, and the cane must be harvested today or we lose the crop," she said.

Zuellie pulled herself out of bed and quickly changed into suitable clothing for the fields. Papa Kole and the boys waited near the back door. She noticed the crooked blade they called *la clairière* in his hand and knew hard labor awaited.

"Pick up your steps or else find your way down without us," said Papa Kole. "There's rioting in the capital over food shortages, we'll need all hands on deck to get what we can to market. These are direct orders from President Simon himself."

Papa Kole led the way through a cleared trail behind the hen house. Zuellie hurried to catch up as the family trooped through the bush with heads down and lips pressed together. Kouri and Lelo jogged alongside their papa, each brandishing a machete at their side. Karlina waved for her sister to hurry and then slowed down as she caught up.

"Something's wrong with papa, he says his stomach's been hurting him for some time now." Karlina turned her head and whispered.

"I think it's the stress from the rioting…if the President focused more attention on getting the railway built, the goods could get to Port-au-Prince quicker and the riots might stop."

Zuellie looked to her papa, his long strides quick and steady as he led his children down the path. Wearing a straw hat to shield the sun, he moved as gracefully as she always remembered. What was of more concern were the growing lines of uncertainty etched in his brow beneath his hat.

"I overheard him talking to *manman*." Karlina continued to whisper. "He says if his stomach doesn't get better it could interfere with his work. That's why we're here, to help out in case—"

Karlina stopped talking when Papa Kole stood still. He pointed in one direction and instructed his girls to get in line with the other women who bundled stalks. As Papa Kole barreled through the fields a clear path was left behind for his sons. Kouri and Lelo followed him into the tall reeds, each pulled the blade from their hip and began to slash through the remaining canes. Kouri held his machete tight until his knuckles jutted outward, not his father's technique but it worked for him. Lelo slung his handle almost too hard. One of the men jumped as his blade came near. Zuellie could see the relief on the man's face as Papa Kole came over and demonstrated the correct swing.

"Twist at the wrist as you press your weight into it." Papa Kole patted his son on the back when he mastered the technique.

Zuellie beamed as she watched his machete knock over the thick vegetation.

"Don't just stand there gawking, there's plenty of work for everyone out here," said *Tante* Ines. She sucked her teeth when Zuellie appeared startled. "This one is just like her *manman*," she complained to the other wives.

"Come this way Zuellie, we'll gather what papa knocks down," said Karlina, as she pulled her sister close.

Tante Ines frowned and mumbled indistinguishable words as the girls passed. When Zuellie noticed the beating of the djembe drums, she turned in the direction of the sound.

"That's papa's elder brother, Honorè, he does that sometimes to encourage the workers." Karlina rolled her eyes.

"Nevermind that, why did *manman* allow you to come this time, what happened yesterday?"

Zuellie took a moment to remember yesterday. She had defied their *manman* for the first time in her life and took her name back. She had also run off and found that beautiful place in the forest, which was nowhere as spooky as Karlina had made it out to be. When she smiled, her sister wrinkled her nose.

"Let's write notes about it later," said Karlina.

She seemed pleased when Zuellie nodded.

They worked until the sun had crossed over the sky and began its descent on the other side of the hill. When Papa Kole's legs ran out of steam, he removed his hat, wiped the sweat from his forehead, and called it quits. On the way home, Zuellie tapped her papa on the arm then gestured toward his hip. She hesitated as he held out *la clairière*. When he urged her, she grasped the handle, turning it over to admire the crooked blade in the sunlight.

Whoosh!

Her arm swung upward then down on a nearby branch.

Thwack!

The branch split and fell to the ground.

"BE CAREFUL, it's sharper than it looks," yelled Karlina, as she jumped out of the way.

Zuellie smiled at *la clairière* when it passed from her hand to Papa Kole. He nodded at his youngest, causing her cheeks to flush. As they marched up the trail and reentered their back yard, each of their faces lit up at the smell of *Manman* Linn's homemade bread. Zuellie washed her hands and hurried to the kitchen table. The savory Pork with onions saturated her taste buds and before swallowing she shuffled in a spoonful of beans. The table went silent as spoons and forks clanked inside their bowl. *Manman* Linn grinned at her family, proud of the feast she had prepared by hands that mixed ingredients with love. For Zuellie, it was the first time she had experienced the joy of coming home to a warm meal after a hard day's labor. When her bowl was empty, she watched as Papa Kole piled on his second helping, her siblings followed his lead.

The family ate everything in sight until there was nothing left besides tomato stains and gnawed over bone and gristle. Zuellie watched as *Manman* Linn removed their empty bowls and placed the orange cake in the center of the table. Next, her *manman* would set a cup out for each of them and fill it with her refreshing mint-leaf tea. When *manman* Linn approached to place a saucer and cup in front of her youngest child, Zuellie wrapped her arms around her mother's waist and buried her face in her apron.

"You should have seen her out there today," said Papa Kole. "She worked hard, just like a true Guerrier."

Zuellie tried not to blush as her oldest brother agreed with their papa. When Lelo demonstrated the way she swung *la clairière* she giggled. Karlina remained silent.

"Well, if you would like, somedays you can work in the field when you want and on other days help me out here…how does that sound?" said *Manman* Linn.

Zuellie nodded, recognizing the ache in her back and feet as her head spun from the sun exposure and dehydration. Karlina frowned in their *manman's* direction, who ignored her daughter's hostility as she cleared the table. They all knew how much Karlina craved a world beyond the hillside as she preached - countless times - about the importance of having an education. As her family members left the table, *Manman* Linn continued to remove dishes and rinsed them out. Zuellie noticed that not one of them offered to help, not with cleaning the dishes or sweeping the floor. After Karlina placed her chair under the table, she stuck her nose in the air and floated down the hallway as if she were a direct descent of Toussaint L'Ouverture, leader of the Haitian revolution. Zuellie stood up to follow her sister, but when she reached the hallway she looked back to her *manman*. She knew the floors needed to be waxed before morning. Someone would have to wring a chicken's neck, pluck the feathers and clean out its bowels for tomorrow's supper. The vegetables in the garden had to be picked before the Hare ate them up.

Zuellie returned to the kitchen and placed her apron around her waist. *Manman* Linn reached for her daughter's hand and squeezed it with a sudsy grip. When Zuellie gestured, *Manman* Linn took a seat at the table and reached for her sewing needle. After the dishes were put away, Zuellie went to the yard to pick ripe vegetables. When she returned with a basket full of tomatoes, yellow onions, and snap peas, *manman* Linn pretended not to watch as her daughter moved around the kitchen with ease. Zuellie emptied her arms before returning to the yard. She marched over to the coop where she pounced on the first plump unsuspecting chicken. The bird squawked and jumped in her arms. On the way back to the house she noticed Lelo's haggard machete tossed aside in the grass. Zuellie walked over to the blade and carried it with the chicken to a tree stump.

"NO, WAIT! Let me do that." *Manman* Linn stood at the backdoor with her mouth gaped open.

Whack!

Zuellie held the headless bird in the air with its blood oozing down her arm.

"You shouldn't be fooling around with that blade." *Manman* Linn removed the machete from Zuellie's hand. "You should go clean up, I'll finish the rest," she sighed.

In the bedroom, Karlina had her head buried in a book. Zuellie leaned over her sister to see what she had been reading, purposely touching her with bloody hands.

"YUCK! Go clean up," said Karlina.

Zuellie chuckled as her sister sprang and ran from her bloody outstretched hands.

"Quit it, what's gotten into you lately!"

When Zuellie grew tired of chasing her sister around the room, she left to clean herself. In the washroom, she smiled at the memory of Karlina's contorted face and realized why her brothers teased her so often. When she returned to the room, Karlina turned her back and gave her the silent treatment. Zuellie fell onto the bed like a rock and was asleep within seconds.

13

1910

IT WAS A muggy Sunday morning, but no different from any other day on the hillside. The family was expected to attend church together, however, to their parent's despair, the older siblings found the change much easier to adapt to than the youngest children. Karlina, who was now 20-years-old, and still unhitched, was the only sibling who truly shared their mother's faith, yet they opposed each other on every other matter. Nevertheless, each Sunday morning *Manman* Linn insisted on waiting for her chippy-natured daughter so they could walk down the hillside "proper as a family ought to."

"Come on here now girl, church will be over by the time we get there," said *manman* Linn, cooling herself with a hand-held fan as she and papa Kole waited at the front door.

"JUST A MINUTE!" said Karlina, humming as she carefully selected her outfit.

After pinning down one of her sandy-brown braids with a bobby pin, she glanced in her sister's direction.

"We are leaving now, so you can quit pretending you still sleep." Karlina paused for a response then leaned over her sister and kissed her forehead.

Zuellie pinched her eyes shut. After checking herself again in the Victorian mirror that had been given to her as a birthday gift from their *tante* Ines, Karlina left the room. Zuellie pulled the quilt over her head and exhaled as she listened to *Manman* Linn and Karlina's tense exchange. She imagined Kouri waiting at the Church house with his wife, whom he married a year ago - a devout Christian who attended Sunday services with the same fervor as one attending a celebration or festival. Zuellie suspected the new daughter-in-law was the only reason her mother had so willingly converted from catholicism to the new faith and the fact the young couple was now expecting their first child.

Papa Kole went along because it was the only way *manman* Linn left him alone when it came time for the Vodou festivals he frequented with his brothers. Lelo who was now sixteen years old had left school to work in the fields and on some days peddled large crops at the market. Labor was beneath Karlina, whose self-appointed job was to finish college and become a schoolteacher. Their parents expected nothing less, although the household could use the money since Papa Kole worked less due to his continued stomach pain and nausea. Even Zuellie had to be hired out to her aunt's home, where she exchanged services for pay.

When she was certain the others had gone, Zuellie rolled out of bed and entered the kitchen to prepare breakfast.

"Umm, that sure smells good, sis, do you mind sharing with your favorite brother?" said Lelo.

Zuellie sized up his grass-stained trousers and rubber boots as he stood at the entryway drying his face and hands with a washrag. He knew *manman* Linn insisted no work should be done on a sabbath day, but he also knew the time it took for the church service to end and their parents to return home. Zuellie nodded as she dropped another egg and slice of ham into her skillet. After placing two settings on the table, she reached for the wooden serving spoon. Lelo rubbed his hands together as he pulled out a chair. A knock at the front door caused him to abandon his seat. Zuellie watched the frown appear across his face as he left to answer the unwanted visitor. While he was gone, she filled their cups with Chokola and began spooning eggs onto each plate. When he returned, she noticed the heavier creak in the floorboards and the extra body that followed.

"I guess it's about that time—you want something to eat before we head out?" Lelo nodded to his guest.

The friend, who had been introduced as Pieter, smiled graciously but shook his head back and forth. Lelo took no offense, he shrugged off the rejected offer then proceeded to devour the cooling plate before him. When Zuellie noticed his shameless indulgence she attempted to mimic her brother but just as the fork was within an inch of her mouth, Pieter's staring eyes came into view. Zuellie's fork clanked as it fell on the plate. She pushed her bowl toward him and pointed.

"No, I couldn't," he said with the same warm smile.

Zuellie grunted, insisting with stern eyes as she pointed.

"Well, if you insist, but only if we share?"

As Zuellie retrieved a clean bowl from the hutch, he began to section off a portion of the egg and ham with her abandoned fork. At first, Lelo appeared unphased as he enjoyed his vanishing meal, almost didn't notice when his sister scooted her chair closer to Pieter; but when his friend raised the fork to Zuellie's lips, Lelo had seen enough.

"QUIT IT!" He fumed at them as he frowned.

Zuellie giggled. As she touched the patchy skin on Lelo's hand, he proceeded to feed her the first bite. With her eyes closed, she savored the remarkable mouthful. It was all of ten seconds, but within that short time, she knew this odd-looking young man was meant to enter their home and change the course of her life. When the moment passed, Zuellie opened her eyes to her brother's gritted teeth.

"What, is there a problem?" asked Pieter. "At my house, the cook always gets the first bite." He scooped a spoonful into his mouth before giving Zuellie another bite.

She giggled as she touched his hand again.

"Did you come all this way to goof off, or to work?" Lelo's chair rocked backward as he stood to leave.

After Pieter said goodbye, he ran to catch up with Lelo who had grabbed his machete and began to march down the trail at the far end of the yard. Zuellie stood at the doorway, her eyebrows knitted as she watched Pieter throw playful jabs at her brother's shoulder. When Lelo stopped to push him away, he tripped over himself and stumbled. They shared a laugh as Pieter extended a hand to help him from the ground.

A tinge of jealousy moved across Zuellie's heart as she watched them disappear into the forest. When they were gone, she searched the room for something…anything to replace the newfound emotion with the familiar. The basket of fabric wedged in a corner gave her the desired comfort. Of the many skills she'd learned from *manman* Linn, dressmaking was her favorite. Lifting the basket in her lap, she pulled out a few yards of blue fabric with white lace. After spreading the material on top of the table, she began marking the pattern for her A-line dress. If the design turned out well, she would wear it to her sister's wedding. Of course, Karlina was yet to get engaged and hadn't even begun dating, to any of their knowledge, but at her age, a worthy candidate could happen along at any moment.

As the needle pierced through the fabric, she smiled at the memory of Pieter's slanted eyes, they were confident yet mysterious. His strong jawbone and white teeth beneath his darkened mouth, somewhat misleading. He had kept his cool when papa Kole freaked out at Lelo's birthday party, and even today when her brother blew his temper. She wondered about his household, or if he had a brother with who he often bickered? When her mind grew tired of the swirling questions, her fingers throbbed from her handiwork. Zuellie admired the finished product. As she pressed the dress against her waist, a piece of thread came undone. She crumpled the material in her hands, then tossed it back into the corner with the basket.

The room grew hotter as the thoughts of Lelo's friend returned. With nothing or no one as a distraction, Zuellie's head spun as her mind raced. Hoping to cool her emotions, she sat down on the back stoop. In the far distance, she could see the faint glimmer of water from the Caribbean Sea. Somewhere over the hillside, a low murmur began, and as the sound of drums began to rise, she was shocked as her feet started to tap to the beat.

"I-should-go." Her first words came out soft and fragile as if they were a mere whisper or a thought.

Zuellie placed her hands over her mouth just as Lelo appeared at the edge of the yard. The grass stains on his trousers were now hidden beneath a layer of mud. She straightened as he approached, her lips pressed tight as if they had been sealed shut.

"I know you didn't mean any harm, but you shouldn't be kidding around with Pieter that way." Lelo flung his blade to the ground as he wiped the mud from the side of his face. Zuellie wet the end of her apron from the water spigot and wiped a stain from his cheek. When she smelled the rum on his breath she took two steps back, remembering how his temper flared when he drank.

"Come back here, I ain't gonna bite you." Lelo lost his footing as he reached for her.

Zuellie whimpered when he fell to the ground. With the sun shining on his mud-speckled face, he looked silly and less threatening. When he refused to get up, Zuellie knelt to check his pulse. Although his heartbeats came slow, he was breathing. She took a deep breath as she sat holding her knees to her chest.

"What's wrong with you little Sis?" Lelo squinted from the glare of the sun as he opened his eyes. "*Manman* screw you up the same way she did me?"

Zuellie grunted at his question. She couldn't confide in him now, not in his current condition. Besides, being the *timoun nan frize* - the frozen child – had become her identity, and it would take more than a few timid words to convince her otherwise.

"She couldn't have any more babies, so she kept us sick—you know, so she could go on caring for us…God only knows what all she did to you."

When Zuellie averted her eyes, he stood on his feet and wiped the dust from his pant legs.

"Now it's papa who's sick, just as you're getting your freedom. I guess one of us has to be the sacrificial lamb…might as well be him."

Zuellie watched as her brother stumbled onto the porch. He stopped at the door and braced himself against the frame to catch his breath before disappearing inside. His footsteps dragged along the wooden floors as he lumbered through the kitchen and into his room.

Zuellie held back the smirk at the edge of her lips. Lelo was wrong. Her silence was a gift, not an ailment, given to her by none other than *Papa Legba* who answered her prayer many years ago. Her parent's marriage had been spared from infidelity and separation because of it. When the time was right she would explain everything to Lelo, but that conversation and many more would have to wait until another day.

14

PAPA KOLE WAITED alone at the door as Karlina lingered in the bedroom mirror. Her curls had to be perfectly set, and her hair-tie had to not only match her clothes but had to feel silky soft, in case someone had the crazy urge to touch the strip of material neatly placed above her forehead. When the ensemble felt right, she puckered her lips and squinted her eyebrows; a look she believed conveyed intelligence and maturity. After all, she had more to offer than a pretty face, although, Zuellie suspected her exhaustive preparations had more to do with accentuating outward beauty than brain mass.

Manman Linn waved goodbye to Zuellie, who kissed her papa on the cheek before crossing the yard to *tante* Dorinda's house. There she would perform light housekeeping for the day, and if needed, babysit her younger cousins.

"Don't you think it's about time the girl gets some kind of education?" Papa Kole whispered when he thought she was far enough from hearing.

Zuellie slowed a bit to eavesdrop on their conversation. From her peripheral, she observed the way her two *tante's* mouths gaped open as they watched from underneath the shade tree. When she looked back in the direction of their stares, she stood in amazement as Papa Kole pulled his wife into his arms. To her knowledge, it was the first time either had shown outward affection to the other in ages. At the least it had been 10 years, she should know, as each passing year marked another vow of silence. Zuellie was sure by this age she had lost the ability to speak altogether. Now here they were on the front stoop with papa Kole's scathed lips awkwardly nibbling on the forgotten taste of *manman* Linn's mouth. His brother's wives hissed and popped their necks. None of them caught the way manman Linn tensed in his arms, but Zuellie noticed. When he refused to release her, *manman* Linn let out a defeated sigh, as she folded into his embrace.

Dorinda, who had been uncommonly late that morning, opened the door for Zuellie after several knocks. Avoiding her nieces questioning eyes, she handed Zuellie a list of to-do's and without a word, left with her stool dragging behind her across the yard. The house had been remodeled since the lot had been constructed in the 1800s. Her floors had been carpeted, and screens were installed in the windows to keep the mosquitos out. In the kitchen, oak cabinets lined the wall instead of the wooden shelves they still had at home. Despite the modern décor, Zuellie shivered from the cold, unloved surroundings.

Tante Dorinda had three small children under the age of 12, and three older ones who had married or gone off to live on their own. The younger ones left in the mornings with their papa and the others, but on this particular day, her uncle had not gone through the gate as usual. Zuellie crept toward their bedroom expecting to see his sleeping figure, but the bed was empty. After checking through every room and then the backyard, she abandoned her search to start on the chores.

Zuellie spent the morning washing and tailoring their laundry. Next, she sterilized the walls and shined the kitchen floor. The hardest part of the cleaning was in the children's bedroom where she pieced together broken toys and picked crumbs from their fancy mattresses before making their beds. Afterward, she moved to the front room where she wiped handprints from the walls and other surfaces. When everything within view had a new layer of sheen, she threw her rag into a bucket and placed them in the designated area on the back stoop. Zuellie shut the door and prepared her mind for home. Movement in the front room caused her to move cautiously down the hallway as she followed the noise. *Tante* Dorinda sat motionless watching out the front window.

"Your *manman* wants you to start dinner when you get home…they took her and your papa down the hill to the clinic, he's still not feeling well."

Zuellie stared in her aunt's face for further explanation, when none was given, she used sign language to ask for more information.

"It's nothing to worry yourself about, just a little stomach ache is all. Your papa is stubborn, and he won't let nobody but Effia treat him," she said, then sucked her teeth.

Zuellie nodded, then started for the door. On the way out, she noticed the solemn expression on her *tante's* face as she focused her attention on the front gate. Part of her wanted to stay and console her aunt, but *manman's* orders were clear. Zuellie marched across the yard and got straight to work. Imitating what her *manman* had taught her for years, she started with a vinegar rinse over the poultry for cleaning, a dash of salt, some thyme, and rosemary. By the time the hen was roasted and the rice finished cooking, her parents were home. Zuellie waited as *Manman* Linn helped her husband to the table. After he was seated, she pushed Zuellie aside to fix his plate. Within seconds, she sat a rather large serving of food before him. Papa Kole exhaled before his first bite.

"Your papa won't be going back to work. So, things will be different around here from now on, Doctor's orders."

Zuellie noticed the way *manman* Linn's face lit up as she ran around the house to ensure he had the comforts necessary for a long rest. The shortage of money seemed far removed from her thoughts, for the moment. Right now, she was a wife again—his wife, and papa Kole needed her.

That evening when Zuellie had washed her face and prepared for bed, her sister entered their room with orders from tante Dorinda to come immediately.

"Don't give me that look, she's your employer and she asked for your help," said Karlina.

Zuellie tugged on her housecoat as she slumbered to the bedroom door. In the front room, *tante* Dorinda's voice screeched as she became more agitated with papa Kole who tried with little success to console her.

"You know that no good brother of yours never came home last night? It's that same woman I caught him grinning with at the carnival—I know it's her, and I'm going to find out for sure!"

"How so? That gal lives clear 'cross in Port au Prince," said papa Kole.

He had been sitting in the armchair by the front window. *Manman* Linn was on the floor massaging his feet, oblivious as usual, to anything other than her husband and children.

"Uh-uh, she's the same one who was at that festival last week and who happens to live at the bottom of the hill," said Dorinda as her nostrils flared.

"OH! there you are." She forced a smile when Zuellie entered the room. "I need you to stay over at the house until I get back."

When Zuellie looked to her parents for approval, papa Kole rolled his eyes before he waved them away. As she left behind her aunt, a swarm of fireflies trailed before them in the shadowy darkness. Zuellie couldn't resist reaching for the closest firefly, which quickly dimmed and faded away.

"The youngins are already asleep; I just need you to be there in case they wake up and get scared," said Dorinda as she closed the door behind them.

Zuellie took the pillow and blanket from her hands as her mind lingered on the dancing firefly. She couldn't put her finger on it, but something about the night was eerily similar to the one in which she had sought *Papa Legba.*

"I shouldn't be too long, but I want you to get some rest..you should be comfortable enough here." Dorinda pointed to the sofa.

No sooner had she gone, Zuellie went to the window and watched as *tante* Dorinda crossed the lawn toward the compound gate. As she moved further away from the house, the swarm of fireflies followed until they disappeared with her into the shadowy night.

•   •   •

A door opened and shut. Zuellie yawned, somewhat surprised by her surroundings, then she remembered the previous nights' summons. She stretched to relieve the crook in her neck and stiff back. Dorinda sat in the winged chair, her focus keen as an eagle as she watched the front gate from the window. A small child cried out. Zuellie's head turned in the direction of the murmurs coming from the children's bedroom. Before she could react, the younger two entered the room and began whining as their tiny hands reached for their *manman*. When she realized *tante* Dorinda's deliberate refusal to leave the window, Zuellie intervened. By this age, the youngins' were used to their silent cousins hand gestures. When she signaled for food, they fled from their *manman* to the kitchen table. After they each had a belly full of warm cereal and milk, Zuellie ushered them back to their rooms to wash and dress. Relieved when the children took interest in a pile of mangled doll parts, she left them alone to check on *tante* Dorinda.

"Your papa thought I was crazy, but his no-good brother is down the hill with another woman—just as I suspected…and it won't be long before your papa gets bored and do the same thing." Dorinda adjusted in the chair to face Zuellie. "You, my dear niece, must be the sanest person in this entire family."

As Dorinda continued her rant, Zuellie stood near the door and waited for an opportune moment.

"Why are you standing there?" she said, noticing her niece's change in demeanor.

 Zuellie gestured toward home. When Dorinda waved her hand she wasted no time making her exit. Back in her yard, she smiled at the smell of her *manman's* homemade bread. When she reached the kitchen, *manman* Linn floated around the stove as she stirred her pots. Papa Kole sipped coffee from a tin cup, as he told tales of battling the Caribbean Sea for its fleshly rewards. He recounted the rush he felt when the fish jumped into his net and the wonder of seeing waves swell over 30 plus feet above their boat. In the hallway, she sidestepped the wobbliest floorboard to keep from disturbing their conversation. Neither of her parents noticed when Zuellie entered the kitchen nor when she slid into her room.

Alone in bed, Zuellie stretched her arms above her head as her feet touched the edge of the cot. With her eye's closed her aunt's voice echoed back…"*won't be long before your papa gets bored and do the same thing.*" He looked so proud as he spoke to his wife about working on the fishing boat. She wondered what would happen when reality set in that he would no longer be able to go out to Sea.

Not long after her nap, Dorinda was back at their door. Feeling well-rested, Zuellie placed a sunhat on her head and followed her aunt to the compound gate. She and *manman* Linn shared a quick glance as they parted. When they had reached the top of the hill, Dorinda began to speak.

"Baby Li, promise me you won't say anything, but we're not going to the market today."

Zuellie grunted to show her displeasure at the nickname.

"I'm sorry, but you still froze—I mean, you don't speak…never mind that, we're going to find that lady."

Zuellie stopped to look back at the compound gate.

"What's wrong?" she asked.

Zuellie shook her head and backed away.

"No, not that lady—we're going to see the *mambo*."

Zuellie tried to conceal her excitement as Dorinda pulled her forward. When they neared the hidden path on the side of the trail, Zuellie grunted as Dorinda continued in the wrong direction.

"Come on, hurry along. Ines said she won't keep my youngins' for any more than an hour."

Zuellie tucked into the overgrown patch, and when she was sure of the direction she waved for Dorinda to follow. Before long they had crossed a ravine and made their way around the low hanging vines.

"How is it you know the way, your papa bring you here before?" asked Dorinda.

Zuellie held a finger to her mouth, and *tante* Dorinda continued to follow. Moving silent and swift, they passed through the opened field with tall shoots and overgrown shrubs. The trail looped through a muddy creek, another field, then through the woods until the trees began to jingle from the glass bottles that hung from the branches.

"Wow, this place is amazing!" Dorinda spun around. "You should wait here, I'll go see if she's in."

As Zuellie lingered near the chiming bottles she heard a woman's voice.

"Frozen baby brought a friend this time, eh?" Effia emerged from the cabin, her long limbs and bangles on her wrist matched the chiming trees surrounding them.

When Dorinda's eyes bulged, Effia cackled.

"You came all this way, might as well come in."

When they were seated, Dorinda wasted no time. As she whined about the harlot who stole her husband from under her nose, Effia kept her eyes on Zuellie.

"I have money, and I see you like nice shiny things—I have a chest full of rare stones…name your price and I can pay it," said Dorinda.

Zuellie noticed when Effia rolled her eyes, Dorinda began sobbing.

"Your tears will do no good here, besides, for that kind of sorcery you'll need the *bokor*."

"You must tell me where I can find this *bokor*?" said Dorinda, as she dried her tears.

"The price is too high, more costly than your money and material possessions."

"But I'm willing to do anything, name the price."

"Not before you pay for my time."

Zuellie swallowed a lump in her throat when her aunt accepted the unknown terms. She watched as Effia moved to the back of the cluttered cabin and exited out a side door.

"Come this way Frozen, let me show you my favorite room."

Without giving the summons a thought, Zuellie left her aunt's side to follow Effia. In a darkened room, animal hide and feathers lined the wooden floor. Zuellie's eye's landed on a pile of chicken feet in a corner. Effia pointed to a wall stacked with jars filled with indistinguishable objects. Effia began to explain how certain combinations from the jars, like leaves and seeds, produced healing teas and remedies for many ailments.

"Next time, I'll show you how to make bush tea."

Zuellie smiled at the *mambo* as they left the room.

When they had departed, Dorinda kept silent. As they stumbled over moss and rock, their steps hastened through the woods. Finally, back on the roadside, Dorinda bent forward to catch her breath.

"Why do you think she wanted us to know about all that other stuff?" she asked, one hand over her chest to steady her breathing. "And how can I explain getting away every day to the others? You know how nosey *tante* Ines can be."

Zuellie shrugged her shoulders, as she tried to conceal a smile. The moment she had been called into her secret chambers, she knew what Effia's intentions were. Zuellie had trained many years at her mother's side for this moment. If she had her way, at the age of 14, she would become the best apprentice in all of Haiti for the *mambo*.

15

LELO AND PIETER worked in the backyard as Zuellie spied from the door. One stretched as the other tugged a rubber object onto its round metal frame. When the tire rolled from their grasp, they sat on the ground exhausted from the failed labor. Earlier that day, Lelo called the two-wheeled contraption a bicycle. He had hoped it would offer an easier means of transport for him, and eventually Papa Kole, providing more work opportunities at the bottom of the hill. Zuellie pondered over her dilemma. What would be her excuse to ask for a bicycle? Saying it was for work wasn't good enough, especially since her work was less than 8 yards away at *tante* Dorinda's doorstep. The truth wouldn't do. How could she tell him that she and their aunt had been working at Effia's cabin several times a week, for the past month? Their labor was the cost for the private ritual Dorinda needed to resolve her "problem."

As she mulled over a creative way to pose the question, she found Pieter's sweat-glistened skin to be most distracting. His face turned to watch the nearby pecking hens, but the glazed-over look of his eyes told her his focus was elsewhere. At least, that's what she told herself. Then he was staring at her. Zuellie blushed before she shifted her attention to her brother. Lelo frowned. Pieter reached for his end of the frame but when he realized Zuellie was still in the doorway, he dropped his end of the bicycle and removed his hat.

"Good morning *mademoiselle*." he smiled.

"Never mind her, if we can get to the docks today it's money in both of our pockets." Lelo furrowed his brows at his sister before returning to his work.

Zuellie sucked her teeth before she left the doorway. He was always cranky when his friend was around, and Pieter found any excuse to be there. As she retreated to her room, she tried not to think about the way his face brightened when their eyes met or the way his broad shoulders flexed as he worked. Then there was his tempting smile…Zuellie resisted an urge to return to the door. Besides, Lelo was serious about not sharing his friend with her, and a full workday lay ahead for all of them. Just before entering her bedroom, Zuellie caught the tail-end of her parent's conversation.

"It tastes funny, maybe the meats bad," said papa Kole.

"But it tastes fine to me, maybe it's the bile from your stomach," said *manman* Linn.

"No, it can't be that, the bread and the okra taste fine."

Zuellie pressed her back against the wall to keep out of sight. Papa Kole's voice was growing raspier and wafer-thin by the passing days. Without being able to work, he was wasting away into a shell of his former self before their eyes. She wondered how Kouri would feel about their papa's condition if he were home. Karlina nor Lelo seemed to care. Surely *Bondye*, the creator of all things, had not intended for her papa to end up in this condition. The last time she tried to approach the spirit world her voice had been snatched away, but this time she would ask the mambo for help.

"You know he likes you," said Karlina.

Zuellie jumped from her hidden spot as she followed her sister into their room.

"You may not be able to talk, but you can hear just fine."

Karlina moved through the room, one high-laced boot swinging from her hand. She peered beside her writing desk and behind it. Then she was on her knees scouring the floor. Her eyes darted back and forth as she scanned the room. When she spotted the familiar object beneath their cot, she pulled herself upright by using the back of the chair. After retrieving her boot, she tucked her shirt into the waist of her fluted skirt. For someone who refused to work, Karlina had acquired a rather fashionable wardrobe that seemed to coincide with her growing interest in the Presbyterian minister.

"Pieter likes you, and I suspect you know it," she said.

Zuellie shook her head as she moved away from her sister's knowing look.

"Well, don't say I didn't warn you," she shrugged. "Hey, there's a dinner at the church tonight, I could come back for you if you'd like to go?"

Zuellie shook her head again, this time adding a grunt for the emphasis. Karlina shrugged, then left the room with several quick determined steps. When she was sure her sister was gone, Zuellie stared at her reflection in the mirror. Her peasant's dress had been patched twice, and her shoes were worn with holes. She didn't mind her face and eyes, but her hips were straighter than the hairpins in her sister's bun, and her breasts little more than the size of hazelnuts. She moved to grab one of her sister's shirts to try on but stopped in her tracks when a shadow moved in the doorway.

"I wish you wouldn't tease Pieter," said Lelo, as he attempted to wipe the sweat from his forehead with a stained cloth. "It's just that we're very busy, and I need him to be focused."

He watched for a moment to ensure they had a mutual understanding. Zuellie nodded, as she withheld her grin. Then he explained how difficult it had been for him since their papa was unable to work. He worried about his ability to provide for the household, and the responsibility of Zuellie's future rested on his shoulders.

"And I want to be able to afford your school fees, being as though I had to drop out."

Zuellie's face beamed at the thought of attending school. She went to her brother and hugged him. When he squeezed back, she made a silent truce that if Lelo helped her get an education, Pieter would be off-limits to her.

"Well, there goes my plans!"

Lelo pushed her aside and went to the window. They watched as the rolling storm clouds beat away the heat as it covered the scorching sun.

"Let's pray the rain doesn't come until evening."

After he was gone, Zuellie hurried to dress, wondering if she and Dorinda would have time after the morning chores for their journey before the rain began. She recited the names of plants and roots Effia had taught them over the past month; chamomile, thyme, catnip, lemon-mint, horsemint, bitterwood, senna, ginger root, sarsaparilla root, oak bark, and Jatropha. Asosi, the cure-all plant, boil and simmer until the water turns brown—drink the tea. She remembered the day Effia demonstrated how to pick, then wash the vine, and how long to boil before the water turned brown. Effia had watched like a proud mentor as Dorinda and Zuellie each picked vines and made their tea. There was something oddly familiar as she lifted her chin, in the same manner as *manman* Linn had done when Zuellie had learned to hem her first dress. Dorinda hesitated when they were told to drink, but Zuellie swallowed without taking a breath. Knowing she wouldn't be able to return home if something happened to her niece, fear drove Dorinda to obey the command. The Asosi tea was bitter.

"Take one sip and spit," said Effia, as she passed a bottle of rum to wash the taste from their mouths.

This time, Zuellie hesitated as *tante* Dorinda guzzled the contents before she passed the bottle to Zuellie.

"That's not the first time I've seen that reaction," said Effia, as she cackled.

Afterward, she led them through the cabin and out the front door where they stood underneath the chiming branches. When the glass bottles settled, Effia pointed to a bush—the Jatropha. A plant that looked just as mysterious as its name, would require their special time and devotion.

On their way back up the hillside, Dorinda would plead with her niece, again and again, not to mention their time with the mambo. Zuellie understood her aunt not wanting anyone to know about the secret ritual, but she doubted that papa Kole or his brothers would mind the visits. Even if she could speak, Zuellie would never tell *manman* Linn or Karlina that she was learning the ways of the healer. And if Dorinda's husband left his mistress to return home, Zuellie planned to ask Effia for a secret remedy for herself.

16

BY THE TIME she left the house, storm clouds had stretched clear across the sky. Zuellie stood in the yard and listened as the wind howled through the hilltop, swishing leaves on their fruit trees, and bending the palms until they looked as if they would crack in half. With her eyes closed, she thought of the *mambo*, as the swaying trees whispered their secrets. The earth was speaking if anyone cared to pay attention. Zuellie couldn't help but wonder if it were due to her mutism that she was able to hear and see what the others could not comprehend. She envisioned the trail leading down the hill and the path that led through the wooded vines as it yielded to the moss-covered field and mushrooms. Past the field, a small patch of overgrown Plumeria and Hibiscus flowers was hard to miss. She could almost see the decorated branches swinging violently outside of Effia's cabin due to the storm winds.

When Zuellie opened her eyes, it was her hand knocking on *tante* Dorinda's door that was most startling. Her uncle stood in the doorway, wearing nothing more than his pajama bottoms and bear-chest. She tried not to stare at the way his stomach bulged like a huge ripened jackfruit. *Tante* Dorinda appeared clothed in his pajama top.

"You remember, she's been working around the house to help out until your brother can work again?"

He nodded, as he retrieved a gourd from his pocket and placed it in Zuellie's hand.

"You can take the day off," said *tante* Dorinda.

When the door shut, a smile spread across Zuellie's face. The spell had worked. It had been four weeks since the secret ritual, and Dorinda's husband had returned home. Without giving it a second thought, she walked through the gate. Once outside, she ran down the trail and crossed over where the large trees converged into thick woods before the mossy field. Zuellie didn't stop until the trinkets began to jingle in the trees, and Effia waved her inside.

"I knew you'd come."

Zuellie took the warm cup from her hands and followed Effia through the cabin to her favorite chair. The drink was sweet, unlike the bitter bush tea. Effia called it *Krema*, made with sweet milk, coconut, cinnamon, vanilla, and a small hint of rum. She relished the flavors as the frothy top slid down her throat and chased away the damp chill on her skin.

"The perfect drink for a stormy day," said Effia.

They each took a sip. Then a moment of silence.

"Dorinda-husband-home…fix-me?" said Zuellie.

Effia remained calm as if it were no miracle for the mute child to speak. A minute passed as she slurped the remaining contents from her heavy bronze chalice. Before responding, she poured them another drink.

"The one they call Frozen now has a need?"

Zuellie sunk in her seat as Effia's large eyes searched over her for the answers.

"Would you be needing the healer or the sorcerer, eh? One for you, and the other for papa Kole, yes?"

Zuellie considered the question. If she had to choose one over the other, perhaps papa Kole was more deserving. After all, their suffering began the night she made the foolish error of neglecting proper protocol and approached the spirit world. Such petitions were delicate and required help from a *houngan*, or *mambo*—which she knew now. Certain rituals called for sacred dances and offerings. She had come to this knowledge because most people mistook her silence for deafness but she heard everything.

"I can combat the effects of the poison—it won't reverse the damage but we can save the runner." Effia moved quickly from her chair and out the back of her cabin.

"What poison?"

Zuellie sprang from her seat to follow the mambo. Effia ducked through the overgrown shrubs as she barreled through low-hanging branches, moving as if she was aware of every inch of the surrounding land. Zuellie made a mental note of each intertwined vine, and which plants had what kind of root, herbs, and seeds. When Effia made her way back around from a small clearing, she sat on a wooden bench with a basket of freshly plucked leaves and roots.

"You said poison—"

"Come, sit down with me Frozen." Effia reached for her young apprentice.

"Look around..." she waved her hand in the air. "My bones may be thin but I'm not a delicate woman, never have been. I know I'm inhospitable and barren, but if you let me, I'll teach you everything I know."

Zuellie nodded.

"Good, first thing I know is, your *manman* Linn is just as much a healer as I am. I happen to know this because she is my kin, my very own niece."

"It's a lie, my *manman* hates—"

Linn bit her lip.

"Now shush girl, you been frozen all these years, you can certainly stay quiet long enough to hear what I have to say. My niece was kept away after her papa got sick, by her very own *manman*. Now because of that, and me not having any children, all this must fall to you."

Zuellie's heart fluttered at the prospect of becoming the next *mambo* but picturing her mother as a healer was silly. She laughed at Effia's words and shook her head as she processed the facts. *Manman* Linn had told Zuellie, more than a dozen times, there was nothing for people "like them" in this world. Having an education would have set Zuellie on a different path, but she chose neither for her daughter, not as healer or an educated girl as her sister was. She had become nothing more than a shadow. Effia moved closer, allowing Zuellie to further investigate what needed to be seen. The shape of her forehead was pronounced to a peak, the same as hers. There was no way to deny her protruding eyeballs, or the way her mouth set like a carp…just like hers, and *manman* Linn's.

"This seed comes from the Jatropha plant, your *manman* knows exactly how to use it—but I have a few hidden talents for situations like these."

Zuellie followed behind the *mambo,* now known as her *tante* Effia. Once they were inside, she led her niece to another area in the cabin. She called it her alter. Zuellie was instructed to repeat after her as she began the ritual with a song. Grabbing hold of her *asson,* her dancing rattled the stones and vertebrae. After the offering had been poured and the *mambo* lit a cigar, she asked *Papa Legba* to open the gate.

When Zuellie left the cabin several hours later, the sun had already dipped beyond the Sea. As she walked through the dimly-lit path, a clever plan was birthed to give her papa the healer's drink. There was also a pouch he needed to wear somewhere on his body for protection, which was more of a problem. The new price for the *mambo's* assistance was that Zuellie now had to work full-time as her apprentice until *tante* Effia decided the debt had been paid.

Vexed by the task at hand, Zuellie entered her home with a noticeable unhurried pace. Papa Kole, who had been sitting alone in his chair, waved hello. She watched as her mother moved from the kitchen to the front room, then she was gone. Zuellie listened as Papa Kole explained how Kouri's wife had gone into labor, and his brother had offered to take *manman* Linn down the hill on horseback because she was fearful of Lelo's new bicycle.

"By the way, I'm not as old as it may appear…it's just these stomach pangs, they make me so nauseous. And for some reason, I can't think straight these days," he said.

As he knocked himself against the head with a clenched fist, Zuellie sat beside him and looked into his sunken eyeballs. Effia was right. Without the medicine, Papa Kole's days were short and few. Reaching into her side pocket, Zuellie slid the vile into his hand.

"Is this what I think it is?"

Papa Kole fingered the tiny bottle with his frail hands, as he twirled the contents around for a better look.

"Drink-it-quickly," she whispered.

"What was that…you spoke?" Papa Kole jumped from his seat, his eyes wide from the shock.

"Yes, and *tante* Effia says for you to drink this, it'll stop the poison."

"What poison?" He shook his head in disbelief. "Your *Manman* won't be happy about this."

"No, papa—she can't know about this!" Zuellie leaned in and lowered her voice. "It's her cooking making you sick, the seeds she put in the food. And…*Manman* is Effia's niece, they know the same things."

"That can't be true!" Papa Kole shook his head.

Zuellie watched as his eyelashes flickered and mysteries became known in the blink of an eye. The betrayal from years of suffering, and unexplained sicknesses.

"Maybe someday soon I'll be able to attend the dances again." He smiled weakly.

"Drink it, and you must wear this for protection." She placed the charm in his hand.

After he had drank every drop of the remedy, Zuellie helped string the beads around his ankle. Then they went to the kitchen and emptied *manman* Linn's fresh pot of chicken stew. Papa Kole sat nearby as Zuellie worked fast to replicate the meal, never so grateful as now to have learned all her mother's recipes.

17

PAPA KOLE WAS up before sunrise the very next morning. Scurrying about like a field mouse as his family slept, he checked the coop for fresh eggs and picked a basket of fresh vegetables from the garden. One of the eggs fell to the ground and cracked when he bent to pluck a ripened tomato. As he tossed the broken shell aside, his foot rested on a small plant, snapping its branches as he retreated. By the time Linn opened her eyes, the fire was quenched inside the wood stove. Papa Kole smiled at the prepared food as he placed it on the table.

"It's a beautiful morning in Haiti," he said.

Linn scratched her head as she entered the kitchen.

"For some reason, I felt like making breakfast for us this morning..and I'm thinking about going down to the dock, maybe I can get my job back."

Linn's back stiffened as she took her seat.

"You sure you're well enough to walk?" She held her breath as she awaited his answer.

"Look at me, you ever see a man look any better?"

Kole opened his arms wide and stuck out his chest.

"Besides, no need to walk anymore, not after my brother bought himself that fancy buggy and horse—he'd be proud to take me down the hill."

"How about I fix us some tea before you go."

"You'll do no such thing."

Kole pointed to the teapot on the stove.

"And the bread is baked fresh, just how you like it."

Linn watched as he wiped his hands on a rag before reaching for a knife to butter his bread. Behind him was the window, and she could see her cherished garden from where she was seated. He had been out there without her knowing, doing unimaginable things to her precious herbs.

"You got those from my garden? I should go make sure nothing's trampled or needs watering."

"Nonsense, everything's taken care of."

Linn felt his stern hand grab her arm.

"Can you let me do this, just this once?" He asked.

She tried not to flinch when he kissed her forehead.

"Sure, but I forgot to wash my hands."

Linn sprang from her chair like a feral cat just as Karlina entered. Karlina jumped out of her path to keep from being trampled. When all was clear, she ran back into the room.

"Zuellie, wake up!"

She pulled the covers off her sister's face.

"Papa's in the kitchen cooking breakfast, and he looks as healthy as me and you. He's going to get his job back."

She squealed in her sister's ear. Zuellie sat up and smiled.

"We prayed for him yesterday at the church meeting, and now this…I cannot wait to tell the others."

Karlina sprang from the bed and started to get dressed. A stack of books fell over, tossing sheets of paper in several different directions. Charged from the news, Zuellie found herself bustling around the room behind her sister. If she hurried, she could slip away before Papa Kole to avoid being left alone with *manman* Linn. It wasn't until she was brushing her teeth in the washroom that *manman* Linn called for her. Zuellie washed her face, taking a moment to gather her nerve before she stepped into the hallway.

"Your uncle's giving me and papa a ride into town."

Manman Linn grabbed her handbag and the knitted blanket for Kouri's baby.

"I—" Zuellie began.

"Take care of the chores for me, will you? And start dinner, if you have time."

Manman Linn hurried to catch papa Kole, who was already seated in the carriage and grinning like a man who had sold all the sugar in Haiti and made a fortune. Karlina piled in beside him, then their mother. They were all smiling. Her uncle clapped his hands together just before he jerked on the reigns. As the two horses pulled the carriage off, Karlina turned to wave at Zuellie standing on the porch. Then *Manman* Linn turned and waved. Zuellie noticed there was something colorful dangling from her hand that resembled the charm she had given papa Kole to wear around his ankle. Zuellie swallowed her scream. The world was a blur as time stood still. When the carriage was gone, she hastened down the trail and entered the thickness of the woods. Her feet were on autopilot until the trinkets began to jingle in the tree branches. She entered Effia's hut without invitation.

"My papa went off to work today!"

Zuellie wheezed, as she tried to calm her breathing.

"That was quick…and how did Linn take the news?"

Effia sat in her darkened room. On a wooden table, she had sprawled out several tiny bones. Zuellie watched as she began crushing them into a powder with a mortar and pestle.

"She took the charm, I saw it in her hands as they left this morning."

"Hmm, she'll probably come around later to give me a good preaching, and if I'm lucky she'll bring that uppity sister of yours too."

"Karlina would never step foot in here."

Effia gave her a sideways glance.

"I mean, it's too much work to get here, she would never go through the trouble."

"They all end up here for some reason or another." Effia cackled. "Now quit squawking and help me with this."

It wasn't just that *manman* Linn knew about the medicine. She had to know it was Zuellie who had betrayed her, of all people. She thought to explain this to Effia, but what would be the point? The *mambo* had no interest in casualties, for her, every problem had a solution, and if there were tears shed, they were meant to be captured and brewed.

Zuellie left Effia's cabin by noon. She had wanted to stay for lunch, but a patron came and needed a private word with the *mambo* to discuss a delicate matter.

"Pretend as if I'm not here—besides I'm 14 now and someday I'll be the next healer," said Zuellie.

When Effia shushed her and pointed to the trail, Zuellie kicked the dirt and stormed off. By the time she made it out of the hidden path, Zuellie had mustered enough courage to face *manman* Linn. There was someone on the roadway before her. Pieter turned and waved. She found herself smiling as he approached, mindful of her uncovered hair and bare feet.

"Is your brother back there?" he pointed to the woods.

As Zuellie turned to look down the hill, her long braids whipped the air.

"No, it's just me. I felt like taking a long walk."

Pieter watched her lips as she spoke.

"Yes, I can talk, and I'm going to keep right on talking from now on," she said.

"When did this start," he asked.

"It doesn't matter, the point is that I'm not frozen and I'll never stop talking ever again."

As Pieter walked her home, neither of them cared if Lelo caught them together. He asked her questions no one had bothered to ask before, like if she felt her years had been wasted, or what she wanted to do with her life now? Zuellie realized she had rarely thought of life beyond the hillside as there had never been a need to dream before.

"Look at your brother Kouri, married with a family of his own…and Karlina, it won't be long before she's married and gone to start a family too."

"And Lelo," she added.

Pieter turned to look behind them, seeing the roadway clear, he stopped Zuellie before she entered through the gate.

"We could get married. We can make a life for ourselves outside of this compound. You could even work or go to school if you choose to."

His jawbone set like a stone as he seized their moment.

"You've given me a lot to think about."

As her thoughts caused her to blush, she looked at her hands to avoid his gaze. The life Pieter offered was promising. She wanted him, not as Lelo's best friend but in all the ways he had presented, and more.

"I should get going, my *Manman* will be back soon. She hasn't heard me speak yet." Zuellie grinned.

Pieter left her at the gate without checking to see if Lelo was home. As she watched him walk away, Zuellie suspected he already knew the answer. When she entered their home, she took a seat in her papa's chair and waited for their return. Before long she fell asleep, and when she awoke the house was dark. Zuellie lit the kerosene lamp and sat back in the chair. When the wind picked up outside, an almond tree dropped nuts onto the roof, some clunked to the ground as leaves shook with the tremble of nature. After going out to retrieve some of the nuts, Zuellie began to walk the plot of land surrounding their home. Listening with the soles of her feet, she walked from the front to the backyard. When she returned to the house, someone was in the washroom.

"*Manman*, is that you?"

Karlina opened the door.

"Now you can talk?"

Her tear-streaked face pushed past her sister. Zuellie followed her into the kitchen.

"This would've been easier if you couldn't speak," Karlina began to sob as they sat at the table.

In her years of silence, Zuellie had learned to read each of her family's moods. Slanted eyes with teeth meant joy. Low eyelids, tight lips equaled anger. Karlina had averted eyes and shivering lips which forecasted her grief.

"*Manman* or Papa haven't come back yet," said Zuellie. "I've been waiting since morning to tell her—what's wrong, did the minister man do something to you?"

"No, it's nothing like that." Karlina shook her head.

"After I talk to *manman*, I'll go with you, to that church."

"She would've given anything to hear you say that…but *manman* and papa aren't coming home," she said, with an almost inaudible voice.

"Wait here, let me fix the tea," said Zuellie.

She moved to stand but Karlina pulled her back.

"After they dropped me off, the horses got spooked and threw them from the carriage."

She held onto her sister's hand as the front door opened. Kouri and Lelo entered the kitchen.

"There was a terrible accident today," said Kouri.

He went on to explain how the horse and carriage rolled over as they approached Kouri's hut. Papa Kole had been crushed underneath the carriage, the others were thrown off to the side where they suffered their injuries. Their uncle survived with a broken leg and a fractured collar bone. Zuellie felt as if the walls of the home had collapsed and fallen over, exposing the frozen girl to the hillside, and the town below. The change had come, as promised. *Manman* Linn and papa Kole had passed over to the spirit world.

•   •   •

After the Christian funeral and vigil, the *mambo* held a nine-day ritual, which Karlina and Kouri refused to attend. Had the older siblings been there to offer a sacrifice, perhaps the *loa* of the sea would not have chosen Zuellie. Lelo was not a witness to the possession because he had already been taken over by a violent spirit who wanted more rum, and more dance until Lelo passed out on the ground. Filled with chaos and excitement, the nine-day ritual ended in a blur. How either of them made it home was unclear. The morning after, Karlina began to clear out her parents' bedroom. She reasoned that there was no need for them to continue sharing a room. Zuellie agreed. Karlina fixed a pot of coffee to combat fatigue. She had been unable to sleep since the funeral, and she now wanted to know which of them would volunteer to take their parents' bedroom.

"Why is this something we decide today?" Asked Lelo.

His hand massaging his temple to nurse the aftereffects of the rum. The only decision he wanted to take part in was how to get Zuellie enrolled in school.

"I'll move into their room," said Zuellie.

"Perfect, now I have another matter to attend to."

Karlina squeezed her sister's shoulders, as she left the kitchen. Zuellie waited until she was gone to speak.

"You know she's pregnant?" Zuellie whispered.

Lelo lifted his head from the table.

"She is, I found her love letter behind the desk. Now she's afraid I'll find out, that's why she doesn't want to sleep together anymore."

When Karlina returned to the kitchen, Lelo watched as she placed a half loaf of bread in her lunch bag before saying goodbye. When he laughed, Zuellie kicked him underneath the table.

18

1913

AMID THE GROWING frustration of laborers and rural workers, President Auguste died from an explosion in the palace. Plans for a railway line had been abandoned two years prior; so, of course, certain militia groups decided to take matters into their own hands. Down past the Cathédrale Saint Jean-Baptiste (the church *manman* Linn had attended as a young girl) farmers like the ones on the hillside began to revolt against mounting pressure. Conditions in town were crowded, tense, and sometimes violent as workers pushed harder to get food to market. Countless numbers of thatched-roof huts lined the city and farmland; the place where Zuellie now called home.

After her parent's death, Zuellie denied herself of nothing. She wanted Pieter, and their growing affection toward one another refused to smolder – despite Lelo's disapproval. None of them knew she could be so reckless, but then again, it had been her nature all along. Zuellie continued working alongside Effia, and the other half she spent with Pieter. Neither of them dared to cross the line passed handholding; not until their wedding night.

That summer, at the age of 16, Zuellie became Mrs. Pieter Bonnet. It was a small, somber ceremony. Papa Kole's brothers attended with their wives, even her uncle who walked with a cane from the horse wreck. Kouri was there, along with his wife and their two children. Even Karlina showed up with her husband (the young evangelist) and their toddler. The whole compound attended the backyard wedding—except for Lelo.

Zuellie never went to the school her brother worked hard to pay for, maybe that was why he left. After Lelo took off, Karlina moved her family into their parents' home. They had planned to relocate to the Dominican Republic, but she refused to leave Zuellie alone, even though their uncles' homes walled her in on both sides. Zuellie would have happily moved in with Effia, but the mulish woman refused her request.

"We would clash," said Effia. She was "old", and Zuellie had "already been reared a certain way," she told her.

The first year, Karlina figured Lelo went to start a life of his own. By the second year, she had to admit it was odd that he hadn't returned with good news. The third-year drew knitted brows of concern at the mention of Lelo's name. There was a failed search party just before the wedding, but still no sight of Lelo. After their wedding, Pieter moved his bride into one of the thatched huts not far from the coffee bean farm where he worked. When he left in the mornings, Zuellie journeyed up the hillside to study with Effia. On other days, she planted seeds for a garden outside their hut or collected conch shells and coconut husks from the beach.

One particular day when Zuellie was not up for the journey to Effia's cabin or beachcombing, she decided to find Lelo on her own. Not knowing where to begin, she tied on a scarf as she set out to speak with her husband in the field. Along the route, she bypassed the Cathédrale and stood to admire the large stoned building with a peak high enough to watch over the entire island. Zuellie believed, if she could make it to the top it would be easy to survey the direction Lelo may have gone. Without a second thought, she began to climb the wide steps and entered through the arched doorway. Inside, the beauty of the huge stained-glass windows behind tall pillars that stretched into the domed ceiling was striking. Mesmerized by her surroundings, she took sat on a bench to admire the statues in the vestibule.

"These might fit you, and if you come this way you'll find there is plenty of food to eat."

The priest extended his hand and offered her a pair of shoes. When Zuellie looked down, her mud-covered feet stared back at them.

"No thank you; I'm looking for my brother, Lelo?"

The priest scratched at a spot on his chin and shook his head as he explained he hadn't seen anyone named Lelo, but perhaps one of the others had.

"Would it be alright if I went up to the top?"

"You mean the sanctuary?" He raised his brow.

"Yes, the top where the peak is."

The priest made it clear that the top, or peak as she called it, was the cross, and inaccessible to enter without a ladder. When he insisted on taking her to eat, Zuellie left the building while his back was turned. On the sidewalk, she looked up once more and squinted from the sun. It was almost noon, she would have to hurry to catch Pieter before lunch. Two women passed her on the roadway, dressed in trendy clothes like Karlina's. They frowned as her bare feet slapped the pavement. Zuellie slowed long enough to stick out her tongue before running off. By the time she turned onto the dirt road, she could see the farm where Pieter worked and could smell the roasting beans.

A mile down the road, Zuellie wheezed and bent over to relax a muscle spasm. Then a sharp pain in the arch of her feet caused her to sit in the grass. The roads in town were much different than the emerald green fields on the hillside. At this rate she would never reach Pieter in time, so she gave up trying. Intending to stop long enough to rest her throbbing feet, Zuellie laid with her back on the grass as one arm shielded her face from the sun.

"No sleeping on the job!"

A man on horseback approached.

"But I'm not a laborer, *Monsieur*."

She stood and curtsied.

"Also, I was not asleep yet."

"Oh, if you're not a laborer then you must be lost."

When he raised the brim of his hat for a better view, Zuellie couldn't help but notice his sunburned skin, which was still much lighter than Karlina's.

"I'm looking for my husband, his name is Pieter."

She wiped the dust from her hands and clothes when he eyed her over.

"Come on, I'll take you down the road."

He held out a hand. Zuellie took a step back.

"I won't bite, My name is Rinaldo and your husband is one of my workers."

Zuellie was not sure if it was proper to ride on the back of a horse with a white man, but seeing no one around, she took a chance. She had been so relieved for the ride; it wasn't until the horse began to gallop that she remembered her parent's fatal accident. Tightening her grip around his waist, she buried her face into his back. Zuellie hadn't noticed the tears on her cheeks until the horse came to a halt.

"I'm sorry if I frightened you," he said.

After helping her to the ground, Rinaldo led her to the backside of one of the barns. Pieter had been sitting at a bench and stood when he saw his wife.

"Is anything wrong, what happened?"

"I found her lying in the grass outside the gate."

Rinaldo watched her as she clung to her husband's chest.

"Is she the one who used to be mute?"

"That is me, *Monsieur*, and I was only taking a moment to rest from a foot cramp," said Zuellie.

Pieter apologized to his employer, then pulled his wife close to his side.

"I knew your brother, he was a good worker. If there's anything I can ever do to help, please let me know," said Rinaldo.

"I'm going to look for him, that's what I came to tell you." Zuellie faced her husband.

"Like that, with no shoes on?" asked Rinaldo.

Pieter looked at her feet when his employer pointed. His shoulders slumped at the site of her muddy toes. He had warned Zuellie against conducting herself like a hillside girl in town. Her cheeks flushed from embarrassment.

"Tell you what, I'm headed down to the port, how about I give you a ride?" asked Rinaldo.

With a kiss on her lips, Pieter gave his blessing. Zuellie's smile faltered when she noticed Rinaldo enter into a bulky auto car. He patted the leather seat beside him, but she entered and sat in the back. Zuellie waved to her husband as the engine started and they pulled off. The drive was just as bumpy as the horse had been and caused her stomach to wobble. If she wasn't careful with her movements, her eyes would jumble, making her dizzy. Staring at the back of Rinaldo's neck helped her motion sickness. Despite the rocky drive, Zuellie was able to scan through the crowds of pedestrians as they drove. Rinaldo turned a hard right, and after the auto car rocked back on four wheels, he looked over his shoulder. Zuellie said she was alright and even encouraged him to drive faster. His hands squeezed the steering wheel as he accelerated on the gas. Zuellie braced herself against the seat, laughing as the gust of wind parted his curly hair. He yelled over the noise of the motor that they could continue the drive down route 2, as far as Les Cayes, or until the sunlight waned, whichever came first.

Zuellie and Rinaldo returned that evening without any clues of Lelo's whereabouts. And over the next two weeks, they made several more exhaustive trips to Port-au-Prince, Gonaives, and as far as Cap-Haitien. Lelo had either disguised himself, not wanting to be found, or had left the island entirely. No matter how far Zuellie wanted to search, Rinaldo agreed to keep driving. On their third week out, he asked if Pieter had any leads or information. After all, they were best buddies and had been tighter than string twisted into twine. Pieter had to know something. What were his last words? What was his mood the last time they were together? Zuellie assured Rinaldo that her husband knew nothing more than Lelo never showed for work the morning he disappeared.

Later that night, when they were in bed, she asked Pieter what were the last words her brother spoke to him?

"Not much," he mumbled. "Last time I saw him he was happy, he mentioned a girl on the other side of the island." He paused for his wife's response.

Zuellie watched him closely as she measured his words.

"There's nothing more we can do…should we stop living if he never returns?" He asked, before turning on his side and blowing out the lamp.

By morning she concluded that her husband knew more than what he would ever tell. Finding Lelo became her obsession, and no one would stop her, even if she had to go on foot by herself. Rinaldo told Pieter he could dedicate one day a week to appease Zuellie. When they were alone, he expressed concerns of his own. She was grateful for his assistance and made sure to tell him so at every opportunity that presented itself.

19

ON THE DAYS when they were not searching for Lelo, Zuellie combed the beach, questioning anyone who crossed her path. When her feet grew tired, she sat in the sand and stared out into the sea, allowing her mind to drift like the waves in the ocean. She thought of Lelo's disappointment after she turned down his offer to pay for her education, Pieter's apathy toward his missing friend, and the way Rinaldo held her as she cried for her brother. She knew it was forbidden, but alone on the beach, Zuellie imagined what it would feel like to press her mouth onto his thin pink lips. That's one of the reasons she grew to love the beach, the currents seemed to carry her craziest of thoughts out to Sea, leaving no trace of ever having crossed her mind. All that wasn't lost in the tide, she buried deep beneath the sand, close enough to reach down and retrieve them as needed. Whenever she thought of Rinaldo, she sat with her toes wiggling in the sand, allowing her fantasies to run wild.

Usually, on a Wednesday, Rinaldo would send for her. Zuellie pinned her hair the way Karlina had shown her, and put on a lace dress, with a large bow wrapped around her waist. Her eyes which were too large as a child had now grown to accommodate her long face. She had a lean torso from years of walking across the hillside and her skin was dark as burnt molasses but smoother than cocoa butter to the touch.

Yet, Zuellie had no idea how exotic and naively flirtatious she had become.

Rinaldo ran around to open the passenger door as she approached. He removed his spectacles and cleaned them with the edge of his shirt.

"You're wearing shoes!"

Holding back a wince as the leather shoe pinched her baby toe, Zuellie extended a leg to model the look.

"Do you mind if we search the back roads today? I'm thinking Lelo was headed to the Dominican Republic and maybe he's staying somewhere near the border."

"In that dress, I'll take you as far as you want to go," he said before starting the engine.

Zuellie blushed. During the drive, her imagination left its hiding place in the sand and entered her thoughts. When Rinaldo turned to check on her, she wrestled with her fantasy. Every time he spoke, she was carried away to their place together on the beach. At a halfway point, between the border where the land opened to hills and unfamiliar planes, Rinaldo pulled to the side of the road.

"I need to tell you something."

He motioned for Zuellie to sit in the front seat.

"I'm not sure how to begin, so I'll just get right to it. Maybe after today, we should stop looking and wait until your brother is ready to come home."

Zuellie knew the searches were futile, but to end it like this didn't feel right. Lelo could remain hidden just as long as she had remained mute, even longer, but she could not give up Rinaldo. She needed him like the island needed the ocean, and the beach needed the sand. The world could disappear for all she cared, but not Rinaldo, not now.

"If it were up to me, I would take you out every day, but I'm a single Spanish man driving around with a married black woman, and at some point, we'll run into a bigger problem than your missing brother."

"But my husband says it's okay, so why should it matter what anyone else thinks."

"We could get in a lot of trouble, one of us could end up jailed—maybe even executed. We have to be honest about what this is leading to."

Rinaldo pointed to her dress. Zuellie noticed how the space between them had narrowed.

"But our drives help me not to be as angry," she said.

Rinaldo rested his head on the seat. After a moment, he cranked the engine. They rode in silence. Zuellie remained in the front seat, their bodies touching when the car bumped or rocked. During the drive back, she fell asleep with her head against his shoulder. By the time he pulled outside her hut, the locusts and crickets had already begun their nightly chorus. Zuellie stood outside his car and waited for her disobedient imagination to return to its hiding place on the beach before saying goodnight.

"If Pieter is okay with us continuing the search, I'll come for you next week."

She waved goodbye as her thoughts returned to her husband waiting inside their home. She found Pieter asleep in bed, and after slipping out of the dress, she crawled in beside him. In the morning he asked nothing about the search. He mentioned taking on a second job unloading cargo at the port. It was important for him to save enough money to someday buy land and a farm of his own. After he left for work, Zuellie walked barefoot past the vendors on the street, up the hillside, and through the trail. She kept walking until the dangling charms signaled her approach at the cabin…but there was no sound. The bottles hung motionless in the tree branches. Zuellie entered the cabin expecting to see the elderly woman in her favorite seat, but the chair was empty.

She ran through the rooms in a panic as she searched for the woman who had become her only friend. Finding the rooms empty, she faced the backdoor and stepped outside. A body lay on the ground underneath a moringa tree. Zuellie approached cautiously, then knelt to check for breathing. Effia's chest rose and fell—she was alive.

"I knew you'd come; you heard me calling for you, eh?"

Zuellie held Effia's hand in hers as she checked her over. "What happened?"

"Bring me my medicine, it's on the shelf near my cot."

Effia began to cough as Zuellie tried to lift her from the ground, but the woman's body was like cement and bricks.

"Go get my medicine!"

Effia pointed to the cabin. Zuellie found a bottle near her favorite chair, but on her way back she tripped over a stump causing the liquid to spill.

"Ugh!" she cried out, "I'm so sorry, please don't die."

"It's okay, just go make me another one…use the Anise seed, Asosi, and cocoa for the flavor—now hurry!"

She waved Zuellie away.

"I don't—"

"Yes, you do, you've been studying since you were a little girl, make the medicine if you don't want me to die."

Effia began coughing until she could no longer speak. Zuellie was crying. Her hands trembled, as she muttered the ingredients. There were no excuses, someone's life was on the line. Moving quicker than she expected, she found the herbs, plucked the leaves, crushed them, and boiled them together. She added the cocoa for taste and had a fresh mixture, in less than twenty minutes. This time Zuellie stepped over the broken stump. She found Effia sitting on a bench as if the last twenty minutes never happened.

"Thank you, I feel better already."

She took the bottle from Zuellie's hand. After drinking the medicine, she hopped up, walking swiftly as a meerkat scurrying to its den.

"How long have you been sick?"

"I'm not sick, that was your exam. You passed."

She led Zuellie to the front of the cabin.

"Your debt is officially paid in full, and you're free to work on your own from here on out."

Once they were on the porch, the charms in the tree branches began to jingle. When Effia said her goodbyes, Zuellie refused to leave.

"Frozen, your desires have grown larger than this island, and the sea is calling for you."

"His name is Rinaldo, and I want him," she said.

"Mind your thoughts, it's not something I can give you—you're a married woman now."

Effia shook her head.

"Pieter knows what happened to Lelo, but he won't tell me. Because of his deceit, me and Rinaldo have found love in each other, something genuine."

"Your greed has an insatiable desire, and it will cost you everything you hold dear."

As Effia moved from her porch the charms rattled to mark her footsteps.

"If I can't have him I'll become frozen again, but this time it'll be my heart instead of my mouth."

Zuellie shivered as if the temperature had dropped or a storm had covered the hillside.

"I want to speak to the *Bokar.*"

Effia waved her off, insisting she should not make any rash decisions until after a sound night's sleep.

"You belong here with us, not with the foreigner."

Effia opened the cabin's door. She pointed at the shelves lined with jars filled with powders and leaves, stones, and seeds. Then she instructed Zuellie to look at the masks hanging from the wall. Before she could say anymore, Zuellie left the cabin and hurried down the trail.

"Don't be a silly girl, Frozen…leave things the way they're supposed to be!"

Her mind was made up, and nothing or no one could stop the runner's daughter. Her course had been set, mixed with her misguided desires, the coordinates sailed out of control. By the time Zuellie made it to her hut, her imagination fled to the Sea, but only temporarily. She would give herself to Pieter this night, afterward, if he refused to admit what happened to her brother, she planned to give him one of her *manman's* secret teas.

When her husband came home, Zuellie went to him and kissed him like she had when their love was new. She fed Pieter his meal and when he was full, they laid down together. She listened as he admitted missing her this way before her obsession grew roots and sprouted across the island. She believed him when he said Lelo left to keep from ruining her chance at happiness. As they held each other, she forgot about her search and her fantasies.

The next day, Zuellie pulled vegetables from her garden intending to sell them at the market. In the evening, she ate supper with her husband and talked about their plans to purchase land of their own. When Pieter asked if she wanted to search for her brother again, her response was quick.

"No, he'll return when he's ready."

Two weeks passed with each day a repeat of the one before. Abandoning her fantasies in the sand, it appeared as though Zuellie was finally settling into her role as Pieter's wife. She determined to be happy, no matter how bored she became. The townspeople were serious workers or regime fighters, and certainly, no one living this close to the Cathedral mentioned the Calinda dances or the Festivals.

Then one morning, after her husband left for work, someone knocked on their door. A young boy told her a man in an auto car had sent him to fetch a woman named Zuellie. Rinaldo opened the side door and asked her to hop inside.

"I thought we were done with the search," she said.

He was dressed in a formal suit and had on polished shoes. Rinaldo's white knuckles held the steering wheel as he stared at the road before them. Halfway down route 2, he pulled to the side of the road and parked.

"I'm leaving Haiti to start my own company in Cuba, do you know where that is?"

Zuellie refused to look at him as she shook her head.

"It's across the ocean. I wanted to say goodbye to you first, Pieter will find out later when I'm gone."

She moved closer, her desires filling her mind, running wild and free. *Just one kiss,* she thought, then wondered if she had said the words aloud. Rinaldo leaned closer and their lips met. Pulling her to him, he savored the mango juice still on her lips from her breakfast. It was a brief sweet kiss, but nothing like she had imagined their first kiss would be.

"If I don't leave now, I'll end up doing something stupid and dangerous," he said.

"Take me with you!"

She was not at all embarrassed by the way her words rolled carelessly from her lips, breaking the borders and restraints held neatly in place by sound judgment.

"I'll do whatever work you ask of me, just don't leave me in this dreadful place."

That day she left a note for Pieter on the kitchen table saying that Karlina needed her at home. If she didn't make it back in time, she'd stay the night and return in the morning. Zuellie did go to her parent's house that day. When she arrived, she found Karlina packing for her move to the Dominican Republic. Zuellie gave a story that she had been offered seasonal work in Cuba. They kissed each other goodbye before leaving.

When Pieter arrived to work the following day, he learned that Rinaldo had left the country. At the time, he thought nothing of it and continued to work. He found out about his wife's disappearance two days later, when she had not returned from visiting her sister. Halfway down the hillside, he entered the hidden trail and followed it through the woods. Bypassing under the dangling charms, he knocked on the *mambo's* cabin door.

"You again Pieter?"

"I come for the *bokar*, and to enslave another soul."

Part II:
Cuba

20

1913, Baracoa

ZUELLIE BOARDED THE steamship with thoughts wavering between uncertainty and expectation. Inside of her burlap sack were a few neatly folded items: a clean pair of underwear, one of Karlina's fancy sateen corsets, several seeds from her garden, and *la clairière*. She told herself the reason to take her papa Kole's old blade was that Rinaldo said laborers, or *braceros*, as he called them, were in high demand. Cuba had revolutionized a method to convert raw cane juice to crystals. Consequently, the demand for more *azucar* and workers was needed. Rinaldo was one of many foreigners to seize the moment. Purchasing land in Cuba, he settled his business on becoming a planter, prompting an influx of Haitian immigration. These were her people; cane cutters, like her family from the hillside, picked up at various ports along the Caribbean coastline.

Zuellie looked into as many of the faces as she could, noticing their need for sleep, a hot meal, and a good washing. They piled onto the gangway like a stampede of cattle. Black, brown, and yellow skin, their dreams as numerous as the coal fueling the ship. Rinaldo and his suitcases went ahead, as he kept moving through the main deck, and disappeared somewhere in the lounge. Zuellie followed the herd of blacks to the top deck, where they stood in the heat of the day and the chill of the night. Squeezing in alongside two young women, she held her sack close and gripped the railing. The two girls introduced themselves as sisters, Esther and Marie-Therese, who had made the journey back and forth over the past two years. They cautioned that although Cuba was like other islands in the Caribbean, in some ways, it was also quite different. She listened as they explained how the land was full of expressive people and savory foods. The culture was fast and rhythmic, with music influenced by Spanish guitars and African drums, like the Changui, Habanera, and Rumba. Esther said the Blacks were tolerated for their work and music but misunderstood because of their religious worship.

"They will always view us as the former slaves who used our bloody Vodou to kill our masters," said Esther. "Our freedom was much more than that, they fight for the same things as our ancestors had, freedom from colonization that oppresses the people."

"Please, sister, don't bore her with your politics," said Marie-Therese, "But you should know your place as une Noire, and learn Spanish quickly—"

"Otherwise be marginalized for your ignorance. Worse yet, stigmatized for the color of your skin and religious beliefs." Esther interrupted. "*Yo rele nou yon sosye,*" she said in Haitian-creole. They call us a witch.

"*Una bruja,*" Marie-Therese repeated in Spanish.

As the steamer sailed over 50 miles across the Windward Passage, Zuellie's mind drifted to what she knew best. She recalled the names of plants and roots, then replayed Effia's method of extracting bone marrow and living tissue, but only to be used in rare situations. Looking out to the Sea, she embraced the future, never once feeling remorse over leaving her husband, and surprisingly she had even less thought of locating Rinaldo.

"If they call me a witch, then that's what I'll be," she said.

Esther and Marie-Therese stopped bickering with one another and stared at her with open mouths. When they moved to another corner, Zuellie hardly noticed. Content with her decision, she leaned over the rail, inhaling and exhaling the damp air. She had been dreaming of this exact moment since *Agwe, loa* of the sea, took over her body at her parent's burial ceremony. The *loa* had never left, lingering like unwashed dust upon her skin. She was always mindful of him; even now, sparing her from motion sickness that caused the others to wretch and hurl their innards overboard.

After an uncomfortable day and night, the ship docked in Santiago de Cuba, under the same blue sky and shimmering turquoise sea. The harbor was outlined with tropical trees, just as brilliantly green as Hispaniola. However, there was one striking difference (which was of great concern to Zuellie)…everything was written in Spanish; roadsigns, posters, and every wagging tongue, all in Spanish. Marie-Therese and Esther switched from creole to the flowy language like a light switch being turned on. The other Haitians began to move with determination down the gangway, and onto the pier. Zuellie grit her teeth as she hurried to keep pace with the others. She found if she looked up to watch their direction her stomach turned flips, causing her head to swoon. With one hand clutched to her burlap sack and her head held low, she followed behind the others.

Thankfully, it was a short trot through the pier. Outside the gate, the crowd halted as Rinaldo stepped forward. After introducing himself to his team of laborers, they piled onto the back of a carriage truck, intended for hauling hay, cane, or small cattle. Zuellie observed the homes and storefronts as they drove the long bumpy road through town. In a city park, blanc and rouge faces with skin much lighter than Karlina's, strolled on the sidewalk dressed from formal wear to fashionable. *Le Noir,* or the blacks, wore plain slacks and straw hats, peasant skirts, and bonnets. The further they traveled away from the port, some of the blancs exchanged their fancier garments for clothing more suited to farming.

Rinaldo sat in the front beside the driver. He never once looked back to check on her, not even secretly as he turned to swat a fly buzzing at his neck; nor when the driver overcorrected, and the passengers yelped and grabbed for anything sturdy enough to keep them from falling. The wagon rocked and squeaked under the weight. Zuellie and the others swayed back and forth like waves of the ocean, their legs locked in place, and faces void of emotion. The carriage strained up a narrow country road and through miles of bush and jungle. Finally, the highway evened out and widened, as agriculture and farmhouses materialized.

Zuellie could tell they were nearer the destination when the laborers began to smile, a few men closest to the edge hopped off the back of the truck and walked off into the fields. In the distance, tall canes stood against the wind. Dark figures bobbed and moved as their machete sliced through the fields, and carts of bundled cane lay on the ground in heaps. When the house came into view, Rinaldo turned to face Zuellie for the first time since leaving Haiti.

"I hope you like the house, it was custom-built by a good friend of mine," he said.

Marie-Therese and Esther looked from Rinaldo to Zuellie who forced a lump from her throat as the sisters eyeballed each other. Oblivious to the exchange, Rinaldo lingered for a response. After she gave him a nod, he turned to focus on the approaching house, which was larger than any home Zuellie had ever seen before.

"So, our little *bruja* and *Monsieur* are on cordial terms, you must be his witch doctor?" Esther cut her eyes.

"Stop it, sister…Uhm, so how was is it that you and Señor Machado know one another again?" Marie-Therese raised her brow.

Zuellie's eyelashes flickered, as she searched for a suitable explanation. She could not tell them the truth now, not after the witch conversation. Suddenly, the wagon lurched, causing the few remaining riders to grab hold of the sides. Marie-Therese screeched as she lost her balance and Esther reached to keep her sister from falling out of the carriage. Wiping the sweat from her forehead, Zuellie quietly thanked the spirit of sorcery, for the distraction.

21

THE TRUCK TURNED down a paved driveway, lined with tall hedges and palms built like a fortress wall. They veered around a stone fountain with a carved image of Josè Marti and the Cuban flag hanging overhead. After the stretch of manicured lawns ended, a Spanish colonial home sat in the middle of the property. When the carriage came to a stop, the laborers jumped off the back of the truck. Zuellie watched as they bypassed the front entrance and disappeared down a trail leading somewhere behind the estate. Two men approached, one of them greeted Rinaldo with a forceful handshake. He spoke fast, exaggerating his words with hand gestures. Zuellie's head swooned as she tried to keep up with his movements and struggled with the language. A black man with cotton-white hair and a beard took Rinaldo's luggage and nodded at Zuellie before he left.

Then three women wearing white aprons came forward. The first was a chubby young girl, who looked to be Zuellie's age. The second woman was a middle-aged Cuban woman, who resembled the younger girl. The other woman was an older black woman. They greeted Rinaldo as, "Señor Machado," who spoke with them briefly in Spanish.

"I have told them that you are my seamstress," he said. "Settle in today and we'll work on getting you Spanish lessons tomorrow."

After he spoke, the two older women said something in Spanish, then they turned to Zuellie and scrutinized her outfit and the burlap sack jutting from her armpit. The younger girl smiled bashfully, being cautious so the women would not notice. She looked almost cherub-like with shiny curls twisted into a braided crown on her head. When she reached for the burlap sack, Zuellie stepped away.

"I'm like you," said Zuellie in creole.

The girl turned to the other women and shrugged.

"They only speak Spanish," said Rinaldo.

He motioned for the others to follow, as his footsteps tapped against the paved walkway. The women stared at Zuellie who stood gaping at the large sun-bleached yellow home. A trellis of purple vines reached from the bottom to the upper level, wrapping itself around the wrought-iron balcony and curling through the barred windows. The older woman nudged Zuellie from behind, which caused her to stumble, but got her moving. They stopped before two stone columns that held up a large archway.

"Welcome to *Casa de Baracoa*," said the excitable man, his arm swept upward in a grand motion.

Rinaldo accepted the keys as he stepped through the doorway. Zuellie entered and was struck by her reflection in the decorative window. Her two braids had come undone and were now matted from the hot and windy long journey. Although her feet ached from standing on heeled shoes, thankfully she had worn the one good pair she owned, gifted to her from Karlina on her wedding day. Hesitating before a mirror above a console table, she watched as Rinaldo removed his top hat and handed it to the cotton-haired man.

"Come with me," said Rinaldo, he spun around on his heels, eyes sparkling as he flashed his teeth.

When he noticed the others staring, he excused them from the room. The women left without saying a word, but not without sharing their glaring disapproval in Zuellie's direction. The younger girl giggled and waved goodbye before her *manman* swatted her backside. After they had gone, Rinaldo grabbed Zuellie by the arm and pulled her into a room filled with floor-to-ceiling bookshelves. She gawked at the book collection as Rinaldo sat her on his lap.

"Well, what do you think of our new home?" he grinned.

"I-I'm not sure what to think...it's amazing, I've never been in a house this big before."

"And you haven't seen it all yet," he laughed.

"My sister, Karlina, would be happy with this room alone, she loves to read."

Zuellie stared at the shelves wrapping around the room from the carved wooden door. She marveled at the stone floors, then anything and everything that kept her attention away from him. Rinaldo waited as she took it all in.

"I could fit all of my ancestors into this house at one time," she said.

"Or maybe we could fit a family of our own in here?"

She had never thought of herself as a mother. Zuellie's heartbeat quickened. She knew motherhood would eventually come, but not this soon. If she could pray the recent events away, the love and lust, her marriage, and the betrayal, then she could enjoy her newfound freedom. It had all happened so quickly, and for the first time since opening her mouth to speak, Zuellie missed her younger days of silence and solitude.

"We can be together here, sort of like husband and wife. It would be a fresh start for both of us," he said.

"You would want that, with me?"

Rinaldo nodded. Then without warning, he planted his lips on hers. Maybe if she had not been trying to recover from the uncomfortable boat ride or the motion sickness from the bumpy carriage, the kiss would have moved her at least a little as it had in Miragoàne. She felt nothing. Zuellie opened her eyes to see his reaction. Rinaldo pulled away when his kiss was not reciprocated.

"What's wrong?"

"They'll beat me, and you could get thrown in jail."

Zuellie cringed from her words, as he squeezed her hands in his. When Rinaldo leaned forward to kiss her again, she resisted him.

"Wait I said…" She stood and backed away.

"Look at me, I'm black and you're not just white, but white and rich. I'm your house help, see how I'm dressed?"

"But no one will pay us any mind out here in the bush."

Zuellie frowned, then pointed to her face and clothes.

"I'll have a whole new wardrobe brought to the house for you by tomorrow." He rose from his seat, preparing to take her in his arms.

"I need to sleep, where's my room?"

Zuellie folded her arms over her chest.

"I should probably put you in the room with the girl and her *manman*, just for now to make things look appropriate."

Zuellie followed him up a staircase with angel figures on the banister. Running her hand over the stone, she imagined the kind of woman she needed to become in a home with mosaic tiles and high ceilings. Karlina would love a home like *Casa de Baracoa*. She would know which book to read first, or what outfit to wear over the sateen corset in Zuellie's sack.

At the top of the stairs, Rinaldo pointed to his bedroom first, then led her down a long hallway and knocked on a room door. The younger of the two women answered, her smile faded as *Senior* Machado stepped forward.

"*Esta* Zuellie," he said, in Spanish.

"*Mucho gusto, me llamo* Yamilet," she said.

As Rinaldo translated, Zuellie smiled but the woman's face hardened as he explained it was her charge to give his seamstress Spanish lessons.

"And this is Pilar." He introduced the younger girl.

She greeted Zuellie with an angelic smile.

"*Pase, por favor!*" said the girl as she pulled Zuellie's arm and led her into the room.

By the time she freed herself from Pilar's grip, Rinaldo spoke a few stern words to Yamilet and left. The Mother and daughter began talking to each other, sometimes they would pause to see if their new roommate understood. There was little furniture in the bedroom; one bed, a night table, and a dresser. Zuellie stared at the bed, wondering if they would mind if she laid down for a nap, but the woman must have sensed her desire. She held out a blanket and pointed to the floor. While their backs were turned to decide who should give up their pillow, Zuellie laid down on the floor and fell asleep almost immediately.

22

March 1913

WITH ZUELLIE'S ARRIVAL, seven people were living in Rinaldo's *casa grande*. Yamilet and Pilar (who were mother and daughter), the cotton-haired man (called Obi), and his wife (the older woman named Ijemma); their room was located in the lower back half of the home. Then there was the excited man, named Bembe, who came and went at unpredictable days and times and slept in a room closer to Rinaldo's. When he was around, they spent hours in the study discussing business and politics.

Zuellie's mornings were spent with Yamilet and Pilar, at which time she received Spanish lessons as they scrubbed and cleaned the house. In the afternoons, she went into the kitchen to assist Ijemma with the pretense of learning Cuban cuisine. Then Pilar would request Zuellie's help with setting the table.

"No comemos aquí," said Pilar. We don't eat here. She placed three settings on the table.

Zuellie knit her brows and asked the girl to speak slower.

"The help doesn't eat in here," said Bembe.

When Pilar slid past him, he admired the way her curls framed her face, hen the shape of her hips as she worked.

"You and I eat here with Rinaldo…the others have a table in the kitchen."

He winked at Zuellie when she faced him.

"You speak Creole?" she asked.

"Yes, does it surprise you that a Cubano speaks your language? And yet you weren't surprised by Rinaldo."

"Because he lived among us, and he knows my people."

"And how do you know that I haven't?" His eyes settled on Zuellie when Pilar left the room.

"The house that Bembe built," he declared, lifting both hands in the air. "What do you think of it?"

He slid a hand along the wall, then down a pillar near the entryway. Zuellie watched as he admired his work, a snarly grin consuming his face. Stepping close enough to smell the lemongrass oil on her skin, he reached for one of her chunky braids and twirled it in his finger.

"What is your problem, eh?" She frowned.

A grin spread across his face. Zuellie could feel her heartbeat accelerating as she swatted his hand away. He pressed her until the sound of approaching footsteps caused him to retreat. Obi and Ijemma entered the dining room with serving bowls bulging from their arms. Bembe met the older gentleman at the door and asked for his help in the study. Ijemma ignored the men and continued to the table where she placed her bowl in the center of the table. Afterward, she faced Zuellie with pinched lips and a wagging finger.

"He's a very bad man," she said.

"I don't understand," said Zuellie, turning her back to the woman.

"Bad, bad man, muy mal." She put her hands on her hips and waited for Zuellie's response. When none came, she wagged her finger once more.

It had been two weeks since Zuellie arrived in Cuba. Between the women and Pilar, the amount of Spanish she had learned was enough to be polite. Besides, she genuinely admired the older woman who mostly kept to herself as she worked. As Ijemma turned to leave, Rinaldo and Bembe entered. She hurried to follow behind the older woman.

"Please stay," said Rinaldo.

Zuellie hesitated, being mindful of the tightly laced corset underneath her swing dress but when he insisted, she returned to the table.

"I must say, you do look lovely in that dress."

She blushed, despite her unease and reservations about Bembe, especially since he was responsible for her new wardrobe. With her chin held high, she smiled thinly, trying her best to imitate her sister's demeanor.

"Lovely as a blooming flower," said Bembe.

As Zuellie thanked him for the compliment, he reached a hand across the table and touched her arm. She thought to pull away, but knowing he fed off her fear, she kept still. Bembe may have been a bad man, as Ijemma stated, but the girl who would've shrieked from his advances was gone. She had seen with her own eyes while leaning over the steamboat railing, as the soul of Baby Li jumped overboard and drowned in the Caribbean Sea. When Bembe realized he would not receive the desired response, he shrugged and took a sip from his glass. Afraid the seam from her tight dress would come undone, Zuellie giggled. When Bembe began to laugh, she cackled, as Effia had done underneath her mysterious tree of swinging bottles and charms. Abandoning her worries over the lace and hooks of her undergarments, she cackled louder. Rinaldo held his silence with a frown.

"Excuse us for a moment, *mademoiselle*," said Rinaldo. "Find Pilar at the table in the back, I'll send for you when we're done discussing a matter."

Zuellie left the table, but not before taking a sweet roll from the basket. Then removing the tight heels from her feet, she wiggled her toes on the mosaic floor. In the hallway, she stood against the wall and watched Ijemma and Yamilet engrossed in an intense conversation. Pilar sat in a corner, shoveling rice and beans in her mouth. Instead of going to the younger girl, Zuellie went to the front porch and sat in a rocking chair as she nibbled on her roll and hummed.

A faint repetitive sound caused her to stop chewing. Zuellie could feel the excitement moving through her veins as she sat listening. Somewhere not too far in the distance she could hear drums, low at first, and increasing to a fast and persistent rhythm as the drummer called for the worshippers. Leaving her shoes behind on the porch, she followed the sound down a side walkway as it trailed behind the house.

"Zuellie," a voice whispered, as the drums beat faster.

She followed the call through the cane fields until her eyes could see the tops of the thatched roof huts. If she continued walking for about another mile or two she would find her people.

"Zuellie!" A stronger voice called out.

Rinaldo rode up beside her on horseback.

"Come on, I'll take you for a ride."

After he lifted her onto the saddle, the horse galloped down the trail. They bypassed a large barn behind a row of huts. Zuellie observed a group of faces that resembled her own, singing together in a circle. Zuellie closed her eyes, allowing the familiar songs to flood her memory. With each thump of their feet, something deep inside of her stomach yearned for them. She smiled, imagining their dance vibrating across the sea, up the hillside of Miragoàne, reaching Effia first, then further up the mountain to her parent's home.

"It's the Calinda, but I should warn you, the Cuban people don't like to see this. I figure what's the harm so long as they keep their rituals clean and out of sight," he said.

Zuellie's eyes opened just in time to see Esther and Marie-Therese twirling and jumping in the air as they sang together. She watched them for as long as she could, until the horse veered to the left, leaving the barn behind.

Rinaldo stopped once they were beyond the cane fields. After helping her down, he led them to a clearing in the grass. Zuellie watched as he removed his glasses, then he reached for her face and planted a kiss on her lips. She closed her eyes and wished for the excitement of his touch to return. There were no more sparks, not even smoldering embers. Zuellie pulled away.

"What's wrong now?"

"I'm worried about Ijemma and Yamilet. What will happen to me if they find out?" she said.

Rinaldo huffed, then reached for his glasses and placed them back on his face.

"I'm the boss, what I say goes!"

"That's why it doesn't look right." She folded her arms. "Not to mention I'm black and you're—"

"Bembe isn't black, but that didn't seem to bother you when the two of you were flirting and carrying on."

When Zuellie laughed, he pulled her into his arms and kissed her more forcefully. This time she kept her eyes closed tight, and with them shut he felt like…her husband. Pieter materialized before her, the dried tears on his dark cheeks resembling smudged ash. She kissed every streak until his skin shined and he could smile again.

"Come back to me," he said after their kiss.

"I'm not the same girl you met on the hillside, and you won't like what I've become."

Zuellie pulled away from his arms.

"I know blacks and whites are forbidden to be together, but we'll be careful and that's why I had this house built away from the city. We can live here in peace," said Rinaldo.

Zuellie blinked several times until Pieter's dark skin faded and Rinaldo's olive skin and curly hair reemerged. Confused and weakened by the vision, she leaned her head on his shoulders.

"But you must promise me you'll stay away from Bembe, as much as possible. I would hate to have an uncomfortable situation with him, he has a reputation for violence. Besides, we're business partners."

Rather than mentioning how Effia taught her to deal with problematic people (a special powder made from sea toads, and other minor ingredients), Zuellie nodded.

"It's just so hard not having anyone else to talk to, but I will try to avoid him."

When he felt as though they had an understanding, Rinaldo led her to the horse.

23

DAYS TURNED INTO weeks and several more weeks became two months. Zuellie continued to learn as much Spanish as she could from everyone in the house, including Rinaldo, who said the quickest way to become fluent was to be immersed in the culture. Despite her pleas, he refused to speak to her in French or Creole. To make matters worse, Rinaldo was hardly at home, something to do with biting off more than he could chew between the cane fields and a tobacco farm down the road. When he was around, he slept for a little while, then worked in his study for long hours, and even ate his meals behind closed doors. Before long he was on his horse and leaving again, promising he would make up for the lost time after things had settled.

Zuellie wouldn't admit it to the others, but she enjoyed his absence. Learning the new language was draining, and she found herself not only missing Effia and Karlina but her brothers as well. She thought about visiting Esther and Marie-Therese down by the barn but decided against wandering off alone until her language improved. With each passing day, the feud between Yamilet and Ijemma intensified, until they avoided one another altogether. Zuellie believed their falling out had something to do with strange activities in the night. She had watched from her mat on the floor, as Yamilet crept from their shared room after bedtime and then returned before dawn. She listened to Bembe's footsteps on the stairs, and Yamilet's laughter as he closed the door behind them. Zuellie wondered if Rinaldo knew about his business partner's affair, or if Pilar knew anything?

The two-year age difference between Pilar and Zuellie was more liken to five or eight years. In spirit, Pilar still had her youthful innocence and her giggles were like a baby chimp. Whereas Zuellie's laughter was more like a grunt of a silver-back gorilla. Pilar's cheeks had pin-dot and scars from acne outbreaks. Zuellie's face was hardened, tough like a coconut shell. No matter their disparities, Pilar sought comfort in Zuellie's company, and Zuellie found herself amused by the girls' virtue.

Because none of them knew when to expect Rinaldo, the house still functioned as if he were home. Walls and floors needed to be kept clean, and meals prepared whether he ate them or not. It was during these daily chores that she and Pilar spent most of their time together. When there was no work to be done, they would braid each other's hair. On one such occasion, Pilar separated clumps of Zuellie's thick strands and twisted them like a rope around the crown of her head. When she finished, Zuellie stood in front of a mirror to admire the hairstyle.

"*Muy bonita*," said Pilar.

Zuellie studied her features in the mirror, the face her sister had once said was ugly. The same dark skin with large puffer-fish eyes stared back at her. She still had the same thick wavy hair framing a narrow carp face and the mouth with the permanent pout that refused to smile; but Pilar was right, she was lovely. Zuellie had grown into a beautiful young woman.

"Have you ever been to the dances, the ones down by the barn?" asked Zuellie.

Pilar's eye's widened. She placed a finger over her mouth as she moved to close the bedroom door.

"Don't mention it in here…they don't think I know, but Ijemma and Obi have gone, so has my mamá."

"How about you, do you ever want to go?"

Pilar shrugged her shoulders as she began to unravel her twists so Zuellie could re-braid her hair.

"My mamá doesn't like me to go beyond the yard. She said that's how she got pregnant with me, back there by the barn. They were having one of the African dances and she went off alone with one of the boys. Sometime later, I came along."

Zuellie imagined herself at the dance as she wrapped Pilar's slick curls into a braid.

"Ouch!" Pilar reached to loosen the grip on her hair.

"Sorry about that, but I must tell you, it wasn't the Calinda that got your mamá pregnant," said Zuellie. "The same thing can happen to you here, especially with Bembe lurking around."

Pilar's head dropped as she twiddled with her fingers.

"I can take you there," she said. "Tonight when my mamá sneaks off, we can go."

● ● ●

No sooner had the sound of sleep filled the air, than Yamilet slid out of bed and crept from their room. After the bedroom door shut, Pilar flung the sheet from her body and crouched on the floor. She tapped Zuellie on the side.

"She's gone, we can go now," whispered Pilar.

Zuellie rubbed her eyes as she moved to her bag without thought. Reaching inside her sack she found her sister's corset and began to loop the hooks.

"Why are you wearing that?" asked Pilar

"You expect me to go like this?" Zuellie pointed to her nightgown.

"But it's too fancy," Pilar shook her head. "You see the way my mamá is dressed, she always goes in her nightgown."

"You think your mamá went to the Calinda?"

Zuellie rolled her eyes.

"Yes, every night when the drums start, she leaves."

Zuellie bent to pull on her shoes, using the time to decide on a tactful way to tell the girl about her *manman* and Bembe. The shoes were too tight, so she removed them.

"If she's at the dance then why are we going there?"

"Because they'll be too drunk with Rum to notice us."

She folded her arms over her chest. Pilar cracked the door to see if the hallway was clear, then the two of them tip-toed from the room. At the bottom of the stairs, she pointed to the front door. When they had made it onto the porch, the girl became so overcome with excitement that she broke out in a fit of chimp giggles. Zuellie cupped her hands over Pilar's mouth, which caused her to snort and laugh as they scurried underneath the moonlight. The closer they approached the laborer's huts, the louder the drums became. When they arrived outside of the barn, she could hear the pounding of feet on the ground as her people danced. Zuellie began to sway to the familiar lyrics.

"Dansé Calinda! Bou-doum, Bou-doum!" She sang out.

"How do you know that song?"

Pilar's mouth hung open as Zuellie took her by the hands and spun her around and around. Pilar giggled.

"Bou-doum, Bou-doum!" sang Zuellie.

Their bare feet kicked up loose pebbles and twigs as they continued dancing under the stars. Zuellie ignored the pinch when the tiny buttons on the front side of the corset dug into her waist. Before long, Pilar picked up the words and began to sing along, until something caused her to stop. Zuellie followed Pilar's finger as it pointed somewhere behind her. When she turned around, Obi stood in the doorway of the barn, a glimmer of amusement flickered in his eyes.

"Does your mamá know you're here?" He gestured in Pilar's direction.

Her smile faltered as she searched for an answer.

"Never mind, the look on your face tells me enough."

Zuellie watched the horror spread over Pilar's face, as the girl tried desperately to hold back her tears.

"It's my fault, I asked her to bring me here," said Zuellie.

Obi rubbed his chin as he decided their fate.

"Y'all come on in here. If your mamá or anybody else asks, tell them I brung you." He held the door open.

After they followed Obi into the barn, he moved to the front of the crowd, but not before giving a flimsy instruction for Zuellie and Pilar to stay put near the entrance. From where they stood, all Zuellie could make out were the backs of bobbing heads as the crowd sang and danced. When the singing stopped, the drums increased. The drummer's hands were like thunder beating a rhythm intended to awaken the spirit world. As the drumming reached its peak, some of the dancers began to sway and rock as if they were dizzy or drunk. One of the women held onto a chicken's neck with a tight grip as she whipped the bird in circles around her back. Pilar was so engrossed in the celebration that she took a few steps toward the crowd.

"We stay here out of the way," said Zuellie as she pulled her back against the wall.

Pilar nodded but her eyes never left the crowd of dancers. Within seconds, she was on the move again. Zuellie sucked her teeth, but before she could reach for Pilar, a beady-eyed man dressed in all white stepped between them. His rolled-up pant legs exposed his bare feet with crooked toes. There was a cigar in his mouth, which he puffed before blowing smoke into the air around the dancers. He stopped in front of Zuellie.

"You are the one who lives in the big house?"

His voice was scratchy, as if stripped raw from belting out a thousand Bou-doum, Bou-doums!

By chance or a miracle, Pilar snapped out of her drum-induced trance and was now standing at Zuellie's side, just in time to watch as the man drew hard on his cigar.

"Phew!" He blew out the smoke cloud.

Zuellie's eyes closed as a trail of smoke entered her nostrils and blurred her vision. When her lungs filled, she stiffened as her head snapped upward.

"NO!" Pilar cried out, as she moved to shake Zuellie.

"Don't touch her," said the man. "You see?"

He pointed at Zuellie who began to sway as the drumming continued. When her body jerked forward, Pilar covered her eyes and looked away. It was Effia's face that appeared in the smoke. She extended a hand for Zuellie to grab hold of and when their fingers touched, the air in the barn thinned. Zuellie could feel her soul lift from her chest as it floated away from her body like a feather in the wind.

"Pieter has claimed your soul," said Effia.

She sat in her favorite chair with an asson in one hand.

"What can we do to stop him?" said Zuellie, as she stepped from the vapors into Effia's darkened cabin.

"It's too late for that now, even if he had known about the baby, the wheels have already been set in motion"

Zuellie's eyes bulged as she touched her stomach.

"Oh, you didn't know either?" Effia cackled.

"It's not true, I can't be," she mumbled.

But the corset stretching tight at the seams and rolling up around her belly told her otherwise.

"It's too late, Frozen, if you were here I could help, but you're there so it's up to you now."

Zuellie looked into the eyes of the *mambo*, the auntie of her dead mother, and touched the thinning grey hair around the edges of her face. Effia's bangles clanked as she reached to pull Zuellie into her arms.

"If you come home now we can take care of your problem—both of them."

Zuellie felt a sting on the back of her scalp. When she looked, Effia held up a few strands of her hair. Zuellie stepped out of her reach until her back rested against a shelf on the wall. One of the jars knocked over, exposing a fingertip floating in a liquid substance.

"Don't ever call me Frozen again, that person died at the bottom of the Sea."

Zuellie turned to face the smoke vapors as they trailed outside the front door. Effia jumped to her feet.

"Either way you want it will require a sacrifice."

The amulets outside her cabin began to jingle with the *mambo's* movements. Zuellie ran to the door and stepped outside. As the wind stirred, the tree limbs began to shake the empty bottles dangling from the branches.

"We can fix this together, he doesn't have to know," said Effia, as she stood holding the front door open.

Zuellie turned her back on the *mambo*. She paused when her eyes landed on the trail that would lead her up the hill to her parent's home or in the opposite direction to the hut she shared with Pieter. Effia stepped aside when Zuellie returned to the cabin. Latching the lock behind them, she said there was something to be done first before they began the ritual. While the *mambo's* back was turned, Zuellie stepped through the cloud of smoke and reentered her body. When she awoke on the floor of the barn, the drums were silent. Obi had his fingers on Pilar's shoulder to console her as she wept. A passing crowd barely noticed Zuellie as their exhausted body's slumbered through the barn exit. There were no more songs to be sung that night. The mouths that had sung so jubilantly just moments ago were now closed tight.

"*Amiga, Dios Mio!*" said Pilar, her round cheeks flushed. "You blacked out, we better get out of here."

As Pilar held her by the elbow, Obi grabbed Zuellie around the waist and stood her up. She winced from what felt like bags of sand heaped on top of her head. When she stumbled, Obi tightened his grip. Black and brown faces swirled before her as she bobbed in and out of consciousness. Most of them spoke Spanish, sometimes speaking in Creole, or maybe they had not spoken at all. At one point she imagined it was a dream. Her head throbbed as the sand seeped into her brain and hardened into cement blocks that crushed her thoughts and blocked her vision.

Sometime later, when she became more alert, Obi and Pilar stopped at the back porch of the big house. They stood still and watched as the man from the barn stepped forward and blew powder before her face. Zuellie's eyes watered as the dust entered her nostrils and stung the back of her throat. As she was led into the house, she could see the mysterious man walk off into the darkness, his white outfit glowing like the moon, growing dimmer and dimmer the further away he walked. Then he was gone and for some reason, the lights turned off.

24

AFTER THE NIGHT in the barn, Zuellie spent less time with Pilar and more alone with her thoughts. Her progressing pregnancy could not stay hidden for long, and once Rinaldo found out about the baby, he would send her packing on the first ship to Haiti. Thankfully, he was gone most weeks, but then there were times when he spent days at home. It was easy to avoid him in the mornings while helping with chores and of course the exhausting Spanish lessons. Afternoons with Ijemma became the highlight of her days, as they found a common interest in the Afro-Cuban religion. As they cooked, the older woman discussed her practice of offering a sacrifice to the Orishas, the spirit guide who watched over her life.

"Which spirit is in charge of removing a curse? Where's the bruja—the one who talks to the dead?"

"Hush girl, you shouldn't say such things…not out loud at least." Her eyebrows furrowed together.

"The orisha will protect you, that's why you need to find out which is your guide, so the offering is acceptable."

She watched as Ijemma continued mixing ingredients in a bowl, measuring out spices, and dabbed a little in the palm of her hand to taste. Zuellie had been this way ever since she awoke three weekends ago from the Calinda in the barn. Whatever answer Ijemma gave incited her further.

"I want to meet him…the man with the cigar."

"Well, you'll have to wait for now." She poured her mixture into a sauce pan.

"But I don't have much time." Zuellie put her head down as she considered her next words. Ijemma looked to her stomach then averted her eyes as Zuellie folded her arms to hide her condition. Beneath her frock, the last two hooks of her corset were left undone.

"Does he know yet?"

Zuellie shook her head and exhaled.

"Keep your mouth shut—especially around that barn, and you and the child should be safe here," said Ijemma.

Zuellie remained silent as she thought of a plan. Once he found out, the only way Rinaldo would keep her around was as one of the house helpers. He had to be seduced into thinking the child was his and to pull something like that off Zuellie had to act fast. Having no one else to trust, she revealed her dilemma to Ijemma, who listened without breaking a sweat or blinking an eye. She waited until Zuellie stopped whimpering, then she explained why it was so important for Zuellie to take her position as the unofficial *Señora* of the estate, for all of their sake.

Later that afternoon, Ijemma took her to purchase a red gown embroidered with lace, and a string of pearls. She made sure to find a larger-sized corset, which pleased Zuellie. With youth on her side, the five extra pounds served as a compliment to her twiggy hips and flat torso.

"Remember, you need to wait until he has finished drinking at least two glasses of Rum," said Ijemma.

She watched Zuellie through the vanity mirror, who bent her head to the side as Ijemma bobby-pinned clumps of her hair into curls.

"After the second drink his brain will start to slow down and relax, then you make your move."

Zuellie's fingers needed something to do, otherwise, they trembled and shook. She soothed her nerves by playing with the string of pearls around her neck until Ijemma swatted her hand away. She reached for the tin of red rouge and begin massaging the color into her lips.

"This will work, this-will-work," said Zuellie.

When the room door opened, the two women were startled. Obi entered and approached his wife.

"Señor Machado is calling for her…Bembe did not come this time, so it's just the two of you for dinner."

Zuellie tried to conceal the lump in her throat as she swallowed. Ijemma stepped forward and hugged her, then she was in the hallway. With each step toward the banister, the tap of her rhinestone heels echoed on the mosaic tile. She stopped to admire herself in a beveled mirror. Her eyelids were smokey with gold tones on her cheeks, and for the first time, she noticed a striking similarity between her and Karlina around the cheekbones, nose, and mouth. This was the life her sister had dreamed of and had rightfully deserved. Ijemma must have sensed her crumbling resolve, she stepped from the room and nudged Zuellie forward. At the bottom of the stairs, she looked back and noticed Obi comforting his wife. Zuellie squared her shoulders and puckered her stained lips before she entered the dining room.

"Wow, you look amazing!"

Rinaldo placed his drinking glass on the table as he pulled out a chair for her. Zuellie blushed when he kissed her cheek but pushed away when he tried to kiss her on the lips.

"We should eat before it gets cold," she said, inhaling the smell of the roasted pork.

During the meal, Rinaldo spoke about growing concerns between the braceros and politicians. He wasn't sure which side of the argument he fell on, so he wondered if they'd be better off leaving Eastern Cuba.

"Harsh things are being said, even by my own workers, which causes me a bit of concern. Besides, in Habana, there's a better class of people and much more for us to see and do."

Against Ijemma's careful instructions, Zuellie took a sip of rum. The more Rinaldo spoke of his plans to upgrade his lifestyle, the more she drank. Not losing sight of her mission, she encouraged Rinaldo to finish his third glass, then she suggested he have another.

"I have a surprise for you," said Rinaldo.

They had just finished eating the main entrée. Taking her by the hand, he led Zuellie up the stairs. She was startled when he moved past his bedroom and stopped outside of Bembe's door. When they stepped inside, the room had been redecorated with wicker furniture and ivory-colored netting around the bed.

"Bembe is moving to a more suitable room downstairs, and besides, he's never around much. This is now your private sanctuary." Rinaldo grinned.

She returned his smile, somewhat. Zuellie noticed it was difficult to show her excitement as the rum (or her concealed situation) made her nauseous. The room spun as he leaned in for a kiss. His lips were savory from the meat and tasted sweet from the fruit that had been served with the pork. They fell back onto the bed and held onto each other. When his hands trailed to her stomach, she pulled them to her breasts, until it seemed he touched everywhere at once, and the need to hide was pointless.

●　●　●

The next morning, Zuellie did not remember removing the evening gown, or the corset. She rolled over onto her side and clutched the pillow beneath her matted curls. Rinaldo was snoring on the pillow beside her. He looked different without his spectacles. The freckles across his nose, cast a schoolboy charm across his face. As she watched him sleeping, she considered what it would be like as his wife.

'*It could work,*' she convinced herself.

The excitement from knowing the plan was a success left her feeling giddy. Zuellie's thoughts left her mind and floated to rest on her growing stomach. Fingering the lace netting around the bed, she thanked *Bondye,* the creator, for the turn of events. Rinaldo stirred from his slumber with a yawn. He reached for his glasses first, then asked if she liked her new room, the big house, and her new life?

"I'm starting to get used to it all," she said.

Rinaldo seemed pleased with her answer. He kissed her on the cheek and then left the room, saying he had pressing matters waiting. After he had gone, Zuellie sighed.

"Maybe now we can enjoy this new life." She reached under the sheets and massaged her stomach.

A tap at the door interrupted her peace. Before answering, she listened to the weight of the knock to discern the caller. Maybe if she stayed silent, they would even go away. But the knocks returned, louder this time.

"Come in, Ijemma," she said.

Yamilet entered, her eyes bloodshot from crying.

"So it is true, you and Señor—"

"Be very careful how you speak to me."

Zuellie's nostrils flared. When Yamilet froze as if she had seen an evil spirit, Zuellie slipped from under the sheets and pulled on her gown. Her narrow legs eased into the tight fabric, but she struggled with the material around the waist. Yamilet's cold eyes were piercing as she examined her undeveloped hips and thighs, and rested on the bulging tummy. Their eyes met; Yamilet opened her mouth to speak but closed it when Pilar appeared.

"Wow, you look beautiful," she said.

Zuellie had pulled herself together and began to make the bed. Pilar grabbed one side of the sheet and tucked it under the mattress.

"Señor Machado says you'll be sleeping in here now," said Pilar, she met Zuellie with a soft smile. "I know it wasn't easy sleeping on the hard floor."

"No, it was not."

Zuellie squeezed the hand Pilar offered.

"Come on girl, the house won't clean itself." Yamilet's breathing escalated as she watched her daughter.

"She's been like this since that night at the barn," Pilar whispered. "She must've found out, or maybe Ijemma told her. She's mad because the *Babalawo*, the man with the cigar, asked for you, and me too, can you imagine!"

Zuellie's eyes widened at the mention of the man. Her heart raced, as Pilar continued to explain the secret of Regla de Ocha or what she sometimes referred to as Santeria.

"Did you know that my Father is black?" said Pilar.

She shook her head up and down when Zuellie paused.

"He is, and that's why Ijemma says I should know all this stuff because it's part of my heritage."

She seemed proud of herself, standing tall as she spoke. It was almost as if knowing they had something in common had opened her eyes to a world outside of the protective walls of the big house.

"I need to tell you something," said Zuellie.

Pilar held a finger against her lips and moved to shut the room door for privacy.

25

July 1914

WITH RISING CONCERNS over what the news was calling "the great war," Rinaldo grew restless. Presuming his household would be better secured through a familial relation who worked in politics, he set his interests on a move to La Habana Bay. Before leaving for business in the North, he instructed the entire staff to attend to Zuellie's every need. After his departure, the others left the expecting mother alone, as she preferred. Except for Pilar, who had become a daily source of entertainment as she mocked her mother's resentment of Zuellie and her favored treatment.

The baby chose a good day to be born. The day after the global war began, Zuellie went into labor. From what she could gather, an Archduke named Ferdinand, and his wife was murdered, which sparked a flame that crossed the Atlantic Ocean and lit an already ticking bomb. The result was declared war between the central and allied powers. Thankfully, Señor Machado had been away for the week on business. Zuellie was grateful for the timing which allowed her to inspect the child's features. After all, she couldn't discount the slim chance of having at least one fair-skinned offspring, since her father had been half-caste.

There is something special about a baby being born. Pregnant women are met with a smile rather than disdain. Even those who are foes become considerate and kind, like Yamilet. She had been the one who found Zuellie befuddled and breathless at the foot of her bed.

"Somethings wrong," Zuellie grunted, as she clutched her large stomach.

"It's going to be okay, let me help you," said Yamilet.

She placed one of Zuellie's arms around her shoulder, then hoisted the encumbering form onto the bed.

"Your baby's coming today," she smiled.

"I don't think it's the baby, something is wrong."

Zuellie gritted her teeth as the pressure moved from her lower region to her back.

"Well, if it's not the baby then it's a watermelon, but whatever it is, it's coming out soon."

Yamilet left her wreathing on the bed and ran to the door. After yelling for help, Pilar entered.

"THE BABY'S COMING!" She squealed.

Zuellie frowned when Yamilet left the room. Pilar hopped from one foot to the other like a small child playing hopscotch. Then she was on the bed, bouncing and shaking the very mattress Zuellie dug her fingernails into. She almost cried with relief when Yamilet returned with Ijemma.

"Get off that bed, can't you find some way to be useful?"

Ijemma pulled on Pilar's arm and she came crashing to the floor.

"Go downstairs and bring the bucket, and make sure to fill it with water first."

She swatted at Pilar's backside, missing as the girl jumped out of reach. Ijemma moved as if she had delivered more than a few babies in her time.

"How long ago was the last contraction?" Was her first question.

Zuellie shrugged her shoulders.

"How much time in between the contractions?"

"They're too many, and everything hurts," she grunted.

Ijemma sucked her teeth and moved to the foot of the bed. With one motion she pulled on Zuellie's ankles and spread her legs apart.

"No, not here, not now," cried Zuellie.

"Hush your whining, Señor Machado is gone with the car, and your baby has decided today is a good day to be born."

Zuellie winced when Ijemma checked her cervix. Yamilet held her hand and began making small wispy sounds with her mouth until Zuellie repeated. The breaths helped her to relax for a moment. Another sharp pain and she assaulted the mattress again with her fists.

"Here is the water," said Pilar.

She entered with a large pail of water that sloshed around the rim and spilled onto the floor. When Ijemma shot Yamilet a cold stare, she left Zuellie's side. Pilar sloshed more water as she was led by the arm and marched from the room. While they were gone, Ijemma used the opportunity to question Zuellie further.

"You did say your papa was a mulatto?"

Zuellie gave a quick head nod as she looked away.

"Ok, then there's a good chance your baby will come out light enough to pass for Señor's child."

Zuellie bit her lip when another twinge of pain rolled across her belly.

"We give thanks to the Creator, all the saints, and baby Jesus for Señor being away. If the baby is too dark, well, we can…" Ijemma bent to recheck her cervix.

Zuellie frowned. Before she could respond the room door opened.

"I sent Pilar to check down by the barn to see if anyone's around to carry us to the hospital."

When the laboring mother groaned, Yamilet dipped a rag into the fresh bowl of water and began wiping Zuellie's forehead. A few more sharp pangs and Zuellie began to push. Yamilet and Ijemma watched each other, neither of them caring if their contorted expressions revealed their concerns.

"I can see the head already," said Ijemma.

When the next contraction came, Zuellie pushed down hard. She continued to push, even when Yamilet warned her to stop, and Ijemma cautioned her to wait. The pressure shifted from her womb to her thighs as the baby moved through the birthing canal. After the pain let up, she took a moment to catch her breath and stop the tears. Yamilet and Ijemma were silent. Thinking the baby had been born stillborn, Zuellie refused to look. When the newborn began to cry, she raised her elbows.

"Your baby is healthy," said Yamilet, her face blocking Zuellie's view. "She's a beautiful baby girl."

Ijemma peered from around Yamilet's curly hair, her expression sober as she searched for an answer.

"Please, let me see her?" said Zuellie.

Yamilet stepped back as Ijemma came closer.

"Her breathing seems a little shallow," said Ijemma.

When Zuellie reached for her baby, Ijemma wrapped a blanket to cover its tiny body. It was Yamilet who convinced the older woman to let go. She placed the baby on Zuellie's lap, who quickly removed the swaddling. A Haitian baby, dark and rich as burnt molasses, with eyes like her papa, Pieter, squirmed at her mother's touch.

"She's beautiful, just like her *mamá*," said Pilar, as she entered the room and inched forward.

"Have you named her yet?"

"No," said Zuellie, "What would you call her?"

"She's pretty as a living doll...I would name her Rebecca." Pilar grinned from cheek to cheek.

"My goodness, isn't that the name of your invisible friend," Yamilet laughed.

Pilar put her head down as she slid from the bed.

"But I like it, we'll name her Rebecca Marie Bonnet," said Zuellie.

• • •

After giving birth, Zuellie set her mind on leaving *Casa de Baracoa*. Without saying a word to the others, she planned to slip out the back door in the night with her child, and never return. Somehow Ijemma sensed her plan to escape, which was the reason she kept an around-the-clock vigil at Zuellie's bedroom door. Of course, she disguised her constant disruptions with steaming bowls and hot platters filled with her exquisite culinary delicacies. In the mornings she entered before sunrise wielding a simple platter of poached egg, toast, fresh fruit, and an herbal tea. The squeaky wheels of the iron cart were more favorable than her unnerving, screech-owl singing voice.

Later in the day, the cart sizzled with savory meals like chicken stew, pimento, and onions. Or snapper fish with green and red peppers, sometimes with red beans and yellow rice. There would always be a side dish of Zuellie's favorite…fried sweet plantains. After dinner, Ijemma returned with a warm tray of fresh-baked pastry puffs filled with vanilla cream, and a slice of a meringue pie. She watched Zuellie's countenance before checking on the baby.

"Have you thought of a name yet?" Ijemma's flittering eyes moved from mother to baby, her partly open mouth salivating to ask the unthinkable question.

"I still call her Rebecca, it seems to fit."

"Speaking of what fits, or makes sense, sometimes in life—well, there is such a thing around here as sacrificing something or someone."

Zuellie had anticipated the conversation, but now that the words had been launched in the air like a cannonball, she was torn by the weight of the decision. Yamilet lingered in the doorway, her eyes pleading for mercy. At first, she wanted nothing more than to see Zuellie tossed out with the food scraps for the hogs, but after Ijemma convinced her their security was tied to Rinaldo and Zuellie's union, she begged for forgiveness, even while Zuellie's fate dangled like a pendulum inside a tower.

"Señor Machado sent word of his return tonight," said Yamilet, as she wrung her hands together.

"Well, don't just stand there, help me pack," said Zuellie.

Ijemma held up a hand when Yamilet moved to help.

"Think about what you're doing, what will life be like for you and the baby if you go back now?"

"I'm not going back to Haiti, I'll find someplace down by the barn, hopefully, someone will take us in."

Yamilet made a mousy sound, then she ran from the doorway. When they turned to see what was wrong, Rinaldo stepped into the room with wrapped packages in his arms and a wide grin across his face. Zuellie sucked on her bottom lip as she sat forward. She looked in the direction of the cradle as Rinaldo approached carefully. Ijemma stood near the door, her eyes glued to the wall as she awaited his fury. She watched as Rinaldo removed the blanket and his shoulders slumped.

"Pieter, my old friend, please forgive me?" He exhaled.

"I was planning to leave before you returned, but—just give me a couple hours…" Zuellie shuffled from the bed.

Rinaldo turned slowly, he faced Ijemma first, who had a wet face from tears that she attempted to dry with the edge of her apron.

"I'll take supper in the dining hall," he said.

Upon hearing his command, Ijemma gave him a nod and left the room. She glanced back at Zuellie and exchanged a look of remorse as the door closed behind her.

"I'll purchase your fare first thing in the morning," he said, sitting on the corner of the bed with a heaviness that seemed to tilt the bedframe.

"I can't go back," said Zuellie. "He'll never forgive me, besides it's too late, I'm already cursed."

"Never mind that, it's just creole superstition." He waved a hand to dismiss her fears.

Zuellie shook her head, then tried to explain in as few words as necessary, but Rinaldo refused to hear any of it.

"I refuse to go back, can't I stick around and work for you, like Ijemma and the others?"

Rinaldo stood and stared out the window as he thought. After making peace with fate, he returned and faced Zuellie.

"My position hasn't changed," he said, his grip bearing into her forearm. "We can still be together."

"Why do you talk like this? What will people think of you carrying on with a black woman and a black baby?"

"I left my pride on the docks of Haiti, I no longer care what people think of me."

"But you can afford such a luxury, Señor Machado, I on the other hand must be careful never to forget my place in this world." She snatched her arm free from his grip.

She wished he would leave her alone to process her decision, but he remained standing by the door. Zuellie's chest fell, as she released her breath. Maybe it was because he felt like he owned her, like the big house and all its fancy decorations. Or perhaps, being rejected was foreign to him, whatever the reason, he refused to leave. Rinaldo wiped his forehead with a handkerchief and then placed it back in his pocket.

"This is my final offer to send you home. If you choose to stay, I'll take that as a sign of hope for us, and that you have accepted my proposal."

Zuellie watched as he moved toward the door, she had to force herself not to stop him from leaving.

"I'll send for you in a few hours, Pilar can watch the baby while we dine."

Then he left her alone.

26

THERE WAS NOTHING anyone could say to change Zuellie's mind. The Dupont's were to have a voodoo priest in every generation, and she intended to continue the tradition. True she had left her home country and severed ties with her family, but she still had their blood running through her veins. And the call of the drums would never let her forget her birthright. When she slept, invisible drums beat traditional tunes as dancers performed rituals around her bed. Sometimes she would dance with them, dressed in all white, her full gown swaying to the rhythm. For Zuellie, her nighttime visions felt more real than life itself. During the day, memories of Effia's incantations and potions filled her mind as she recorded each remedy in memory. The call of her birthright consumed most of her thoughts, except when tending to her daughter.

Rebecca was as sweet as the molasses her skin resembled and adored by everyone who met her. Even Rinaldo settled his affections onto the baby, growing less worrisome and starved for Zuellie's attention. She was thankful for the space he gave her, allowing for the time needed to bond with her newborn. On certain days, and only when he noticed she could use a break, Rinaldo would invite her to join him for dinner. He was always happy to see her, patiently waiting to be loved. She was careful with his emotions, ensuring his continued generosity.

"He's a loyal man, things couldn't have turned out better if we had planned it," said Ijemma.

Zuellie flinched as the snaps from the corset pinched her skin. When Ijemma stepped away to select a dress for her to wear, she readjusted the material, rolling her eyes at the woman's heavy-handed assistance.

"If only I could come up with a plan to keep him from wanting me," said Zuellie.

"Why do you speak such nonsense?" Ijemma turned to look over her shoulder. "Someday you may become Señora Machado, the madam of the greatest sugar and tobacco farm in Baracoa, maybe even throughout Cuba if our prayers are answered." She lifted her nose high, imitating a woman of royalty.

Zuellie laughed as she snatched the dress from her hand.

"I just know it, there are great things in store for you, and all of us. You and Senor's forbidden love will bring about change for us all."

Zuellie tried to share Ijemma's hope for the future, but she couldn't imagine a life without the *loas*, and ceremonial worship - or the drums. If only she could convince Ijemma that her path was as a healer, not to change racism or caste systems.

"When is the next ceremony?" asked Zuellie.

Ijemma lifted Rebecca from her bassinet and handed her to Pilar. When she returned, her eyes narrowed as she frowned. Zuellie sat at her vanity applying makeup to her face. With a tight grip on the applicator handle, she applied swirls of red rouge around her dreary eyes and puckered lips. Afterward, she reached for the face powder and dusted an extra thick layer on top.

"Chica, what's wrong with you?"

Ijemma removed the applicator from her hand.

"Maybe I should tell Señor Machado that you're not feeling well today?"

She reached for a napkin and scrubbed away the access makeup. After her face was cleaned, Zuellie thanked her for the help.

"Don't blow this," said Ijemma.

Zuellie squared her shoulders and prepared to leave the room. At the top of the stairs, she stopped to adjust her heel strap, lingering for a moment to rest against the wall. Ijemma moved closer, placing a hand over her forehead as she checked for fever.

"My *manman* would have liked you."

She held Ijemma's hand to her nose and inhaled the essence of garlic and oregano that lingered on her fingertips from cooking.

"She didn't like many people, but I'm sure she would've thought highly of someone like you."

"Then you should listen to me as if I were your *manman*. She would want you to have a life of luxury and class. It's what I wanted for my own daughter, may she rest in peace."

"You're forgetting one thing, I'm a black woman, pursuing a relationship with a white man is taboo."

"Yes, but maybe for you and Señor things can be different, and with the world at war, who has time to notice? Besides, he's the one doing the pursuing."

"Tell me what happened to your daughter?"

"We call them *Los Mayorales*, they whipped her at the wooden trunk. She was fine, save for the blood and open wounds but her heart never healed after they drove her white lover away…but that was then and who can stand in the way when two people are in love."

Zuellie swallowed her remorse like a lump of stale bread, remembering the days she had experienced love, first with Pieter, then Rinaldo. She wished there was a way to make amends to them both, it was not their fault she had been confused. Ijemma gave her a nod. Zuellie left the wall and hurried down the stairs. When she entered the dining room, Rinaldo met her with a glass. He swallowed his drink hard before turning to pour another.

"I don't have an easy way to say this except to speak frankly." He sat his glass down and pulled Zuellie onto his lap. "First, did I mention how lovely you look this evening?"

Zuellie smiled at the compliment and forced herself to thank him with a kiss.

"Now you kiss me, and right when I have unpleasant news. Bembe's back and making a terrible fuss about the way I'm managing the laborers—and well, I've decided to relocate to Habana, and eventually cut all ties here."

"But I can't go there, I'm not well enough to travel yet."

"Where else would you go? It's too late to return home now, I hear U.S. troops are occupying Haiti. Or do you think I would leave you here with Bembe?" he snickered.

Zuellie opened her mouth to speak but stopped when he turned his back to pour another drink. He swished the contents in his mouth and swallowed.

"You don't understand, I'm not well enough to travel, I haven't been feeling well since giving birth. Maybe I can stay in one of the huts down by the barn?"

Amusement spread across Rinaldo's face. After another gulp from his glass, he shrugged.

"You may be on to something there." He adjusted the frame of his glasses on the bridge of his nose. "I have a cabin down by the river, the bracero's use it to store equipment. It's somewhat isolated in the bush but close enough to where you could keep an eye on things for me here. After I'm settled, then I'll send for you and Rebecca."

Zuellie suppressed the smile teasing at the corners of her lips, as her head bobbed up and down in agreement. Rinaldo rubbed his beard and wrinkled his nose while brainstorming the move and snags in his plan. Overcome with emotions,

Zuellie wrapped her arms around his neck and thanked him profusely. When she finished, he rang a bell for their meal to be served.

Ijemma's head was low, as her back hunched over the serving tray. The food was served on silver so brilliant she could see Zuellie watching her in the reflection of the platter. When their eyes met, Zuellie smiled, giving her the signal that all was well. Ijemma straightened her back before returning the smile. After her cart was emptied, she hastened her steps, no doubt to relay the good news to her husband.

As they dined, Rinaldo assured Zuellie that he would make her accommodations comfortable, and most of all safe, until he came back for her. When they finished their meal, he left the room with a contemplative and determined stride, hardly noticing as Ijemma entered to clear the table.

"So, it's all settled now, right?"

Zuellie nodded, wiping the crumbs from her mouth. Ijemma placed the dinnerware on her cart, pretending to have her curiosity under control.

"Things will be much easier for us now, you'll see," said Ijemma. She patted Zuellie's hand as her cart rattled from the stacked plates.

When Zuellie left the dining room, she overheard a portion of Rinaldo's conversation in his study. His voice was quick and dismissive as he finalized arrangements. He would need two weeks to pack and move. Yamilet could stay as house caretaker but Obi and Ijemma were out of the question.

"Zuellie is none of your concern," he snapped.

After growing bored with the dispute between Rinaldo and Bembe, Zuellie went upstairs. She stopped outside of Yamilet's room and found it empty. Before leaving, she noted the plain mattress with no headboard, the scratched dresser, and the tattered rug. When the time came, she hoped Pilar would get her bedroom furniture, if not, at least the mother and daughter could finally have their own space.

When she arrived at her room, Pilar sat in a chair, resting as she gently rocked a sleeping Rebecca. They looked so peaceful together, it was almost a shame to disturb them. Zuellie thought about sneaking off for a quick walk down by the barn but before she could leave, Pilar's eyes opened.

"I can stay longer if you needed me to."

"I thought about taking a walk, but it looks like rain."

Zuellie pointed to the open window as raindrops begin to splatter against the glass.

"If it's alright with Yamilet, you can sleep in here with us tonight?"

Pilar nodded, her smile fading as she noticed Zuellie's dismal expression. "Is something troubling you?"

Zuellie could no longer hold back her emotions. Truth be told, she was fearful of the coming changes and had no more strength to pretend that she felt assured of her decision.

"Señor Machado is moving to La Habana, and—

"Moving? We can't go there…wait, are you leaving me?"

"No, no…we're staying here, well, I'm moving into a cabin down by the river, but it's close enough for us to still visit one another."

Pilar held the sleeping baby closer, her face pained with disappointment. When the baby yawned, her muscles relaxed.

"I can't leave her, Rebecca will need me to teach her things, like a big sister."

Zuellie understood more than she expressed at the moment. Pilar had lived a solitary and secluded existence before her arrival. She was oftentimes unheard and misunderstood, becoming invisible in plain sight. Zuellie knew the feeling too well, the desire to have meaning to at least one person, even if it meant fulfilling that need through the eyes of an infant.

27

1916

THE CABIN BY the river was small but cozy. There were two rooms: one large room in the front, and another in the back without a window. Zuellie and little Rebecca slept in one room and did just about everything else in the other…except for the cooking and toileting, which had to be done outside. Before moving, Rinaldo asked if she was sure about staying behind to live in what he called "sub-par conditions." Zuellie insisted that she was comfortable enough, saying it felt more like home than *La Casa Grande*, even though it was much smaller than the home she was raised in, even tinier than the hut she shared with Pieter.

The cabin had been thoroughly cleaned, thanks to the oversight of Ijemma; and with the help of Yamilet and Pilar, every bit of broken boat parts and old fishing gear had been toted away, and the oil stains scrubbed sterile. A potent combination of Borax and mothballs killed off vermin and deodorized the damp moldy wood. Initially, Zuellie refused the fancy furniture from her room in the big house, but no one listened. The wrought-iron bed, vanity, and lamps, along with the upholstered bench and chairs were moved into the cabin. She thought it looked silly, a rustic wooden cabin decorated with fancy décor. Even the lighting had been replaced with gold fixtures and trimmings, to Zuellie's disappointment. When she refused to have the floors redone in tile, Ijemma brought in a large ornamental rug to cover the rotting wood planks.

"It's for the child, to keep her hands and knees from getting splintered," she said.

There was no use protesting. Wherever the child was the reason, Zuellie's vote didn't count. She loved her daughter, but there was no denying Ijemma and Pilar's devotion toward Rebecca. When she became annoyed or frustrated at the girl's fussiness, they found her fits to be "cute," or "expressive," which Zuellie thought was foolishness. A Mother knows her own child, and she knew hers to be spoiled almost as bad as the decaying wood underneath their feet. She refrained from telling them this much, after all, they were very useful when it came to fulfilling the girl's high demands.

It had become clear, almost immediately, that Rebecca was the very opposite of Zuellie. She did not share her mother's guppy-shaped face or large eyes. She was her father's child in looks but had the mannerisms of her aunt Karlina, of all things. At two years old, she was adorable, graceful, and expressive. She hated for her feet and hands to get dirty, and she abhorred her mother's breast milk—to Zuellie's relief. One moment she could be the sweetest of angels, but if there was a stain on her clothes, or she wet herself accidentally (as any 2-year old was prone to do once in a while) she'd belt out a cry that shook the spirit world of Cuba and Haiti combined; the last thing Zuellie needed now was trouble from the guardian of children. She had to ensure that Rebecca was kept clean, a chore that required around-the-clock care. Otherwise, there was a great risk of another round of tantrums.

When the child slept, Zuellie stared at the rise and fall of her chest, watching the rhythm of her body from the tiniest pulsating veins. She waited eagerly for any indication that the girl's guardian spirit had visited. Two years had gone by and there was still not a foot stomp, or a booty jiggle at the sound of beating drums, which would be the telling sign of her birthright. If things continued this way Rebecca could end up out of sync, as *manman* Linn and Karlina had.

Every few days or so, after the laborers quit their work for the day, and long after their evening meal, the beating drums began. From her cabin, Zuellie could hear them in all directions. It never lasted long, not like during a sacrificial ceremony but more like a secret communication throughout the bush from one side of the river to the other. Just like her papa, Zuellie had an itch that started from her bare toes and spread up her legs. She wished for the freedom to neglect her duties and to run after the summons of the drummer. Instead, she resigned to dancing alone in her cabin. A few times she bounced Rebecca along to the beat, but the small child would throw a fit each time until Zuellie knew better to try again.

After breakfast, they washed and dressed for the day and then waited at the front door. The child would not have it any other way, not until her *tia* Pilar, arrived. Sometime before noon they would hear the familiar rustling of the grass, which alerted them to the much-anticipated visitor. By the time Pilar reached the cabin, her cheeks would be flushed, and her curls blown stiff. How she managed to drag the bicycle down the narrow bumpy path was ingenious at best. It had been two years of making the daily trips and she never complained, not once. Today was no different.

Pilar retrieved a few items from her bicycle rack before she greeted Zuellie and Rebecca with a wild grin. Inside one covered basket would be some type of cooked meal (like *papas rellena*, *pastelitos*, or roasted pork). The food was prepared by Yamilet, and nowhere as delectable as Ijemma's cooking; but when Rinaldo left, he took Ijemma and Obi with him. Zuellie preferred to eat the fish she caught from the river, but of course, Rebecca hated fish. The other basket was usually stuffed full of hair ribbons and bows, once a week a new dress would be crammed inside.

At 16 years old, Pilar's skin had become more radiant as her pimples cleared. Coupled with her recent growth spurt, she was developing into a fine young lady; and as the silly girl vanished with puberty, Zuellie had concerns about Bembe's tendencies toward younger women. If she could get a moment alone while Rebecca was sleeping, Zuellie planned to ask how things were going at the house. After Pilar placed the covered basket on the table, she and Rebecca sat in a chair and began to search inside the sack of bows and ribbons.

As usual, Pilar carried on about how lovely Rebecca looked in her ruffled dress, or how beautiful her braided hair was, to which Rebecca thanked her most graciously before snuggling into her surrogate aunt's open arms. Neither of them noticed Zuellie as she watched the way they stared into each other's eyes, forgetting the mother and best friend who bond them together.

"I'm taking off now," said Zuellie.

When Pilar noticed her standing at the door, she waved goodbye, but Rebecca never looked up. Zuellie had learned through Lelo's disappearance the repercussions of harboring jealous emotions. It was just as Ijemma said, no one could stand in the way of love, even if love presented itself as an innocent affection between a child and a caregiver. Zuellie hoisted her sack on her back and began her hike down an overgrown path into the bush.

During their first year living by the river, she would strap Rebecca on her back, and Pilar would follow behind them. As the child grew, she complained about the heat and the vines which seemed to reach from beyond the thicket and entangle around her tiny legs. Without Pilar's daily visits, Zuellie would be confined inside the cabin, imprisoned by her daughter's tantrums. Also, the time apart offered enough reprieve to subdue their growing vexatious nature toward each other.

Zuellie referred to her outings as scavenger hunts. She was in search of anything that could be put to good use, and everything to familiarize herself with the land. She studied the leaves of trees and vines of plants. She tasted the berries, and sometimes the dirt. Rocks, buried metal, scraps of cloth, or bone fragments were stored in her sack to be brought home. Walking barefoot along the trail, she welcomed the stones and other sharp objects that pricked at the soles of her calloused feet. In time, she learned to forecast the weather and discern movement throughout the forest from the ground.

The mosquitos that would land on her skin never bit, thanks to the oil from the eucalyptus leaf she rubbed over her arms and legs (another thing Rebecca hated, which made Zuellie smile). She recalled the tiny red blotches on the girl's arms, the likely reason she detested the bush. What would Pieter think if he knew his firstborn child had turned out to be high-nosed and smart-mouthed like her sister Karlina? She thought more of him these days, perhaps it was being so close to the water, or maybe it was the girl's eyes. He couldn't hate her forever, after all, leaving him had ensured their child would have a better future. Also, remaining here meant the removal of judgment from her family for the way she intended to live her life.

Not realizing how far she had traveled, Zuellie stopped along the path to catch her breath. Before continuing on her journey, she faced the southern sky and shook her fist in the direction of her home country. She kept walking beyond a tree with a small cutout missing from the bark, which indicated her stopping point from a previous trip. When the path narrowed, she let down the sack from her back and retrieved *la clairière*, her father's crooked blade.

"I had a feeling today would be the day."

Zuellie rubbed the rusted metal in a circular motion until the spot beneath her thumb glistened. When she finished admiring the beautiful anomaly, she raised a hand and came down with a swoosh. Zuellie swung clumsily at first, back and forth, until she made a connection with the unique rhythm of the curvature. As sweat from her brow dripped onto the ground, she inched further and further away from the inlet of the river. Forging ahead, the land yielded to her crooked blade, and Zuellie hardly noticed as the bank she had cleared of weeds became a cliff. Stopping briefly to fill her canteen, Zuellie continued to whack at every standing reed and vine that stood in her way. When the muscles cramped in one hand, she switched to the other. Finally, an ache in her spine brought her to a halt. After a good stretch to relieve the tension on her neck and back, she admired the water below as it flowed in one direction toward her cabin and the opposite way out to sea.

"CAN YOU SEE ME?" Zuellie called out, as she waved her hands high above her head.

"KOURI? KARLINA…is Lelo with you? Please, tell him I tried to make things right." Her voice choked.

Zuellie listened a moment at her echo until it faded, then she placed the machete back in its sack and retrieved the water canteen. Halfway down the cliff, she felt a pinch in her side first, then traveled around to a stabbing discomfort in her stomach. Zuellie clenched her teeth and bent at the waist. Dazed from the pain, her foot lost contact with the ground, knocking her off the trail. Zuellie knew she was in trouble when the sun beheld her face as the wind carried her back.

28

LELO HAD ALWAYS been the most thoughtful and jovial child of Papa Kole and Manman Linn's children. He was usually even-tempered and quick to forgive, but from the look on his face now, Zuellie could tell he had changed.

"See what's become of me, sister?"

He held his arms out so she could get a better look. Zuellie watched as portions of his flesh flickered in and out like an oil lamp, and other areas faded like words being erased from a sheet of paper. She wanted to touch him, but he kept fading in and out.

"What is happening to you?"

"I once told you I would never leave you, but you let Pieter take you away from me…do you remember what you told him?"

It took her only a second to remember the events she had pushed out of her mind, the reason why she had grown angry at Pieter, and left.

"You wouldn't let us get married," she said.

"That's the reason you gave him permission to do this to your own flesh and blood?"

Zuellie lowered her head when he frowned at her. As he stepped from the water, Lelo's body materialized whole.

"But it's not your fault," he softened as he approached. "We were playing with things we knew *manman* wouldn't have liked. We should have followed Karlina, and Kouri, and gone to a Christian church like *manman* would have wanted."

"I'll trade places with you, here—you can have my soul."

"You don't get it, the reason I'm able to reach you now is because they're praying for me as we speak, come look."

Lelo took hold of Zuellie's hand and led her to the water. In the water's reflection, she saw his limp body lying on a floor, as a small group stood around him praying.

"They found me wandering around deep in the jungle, crazed from the *bokor's* medicine. I can feel myself returning, soon I'll be healed from the poison and in my right mind."

When she could no longer watch, Zuellie's shaky hands clutched at his shirt. Burying her face in his chest, she whimpered.

"Forgive me, please, you must forgive me!"

She silenced her cries to listen for his response, but he never answered. The weight of him grew rigid, pressing against her face and torso. When it felt as though he would crush her bones, she shoved him away hard. Zuellie awoke face down on the ground, the river flowing over her hip and legs. When she rolled over, her back throbbed from the fall. After wiping pebbles from her mouth and alongside her face, she removed a piece of twig entangled in her hair. As she cleaned herself, Zuellie noticed a strange chalky substance on her fingertips and more of the powdery film on her toes. The pebbly bottom was filled with the mineral deposits, some of it seeped into the water and was carried out to Sea. She removed her headwrap and scooped some of the chalky white rocks inside. When she finished, she climbed back up the bank and made her way home.

There was no running water in the cabin, so Zuellie intended to show Pilar her treasure before she bathed in the river. When she arrived, Rebecca and Pilar were asleep on the bed, the girl's tiny hand clutching her auntie's blouse. Zuellie returned to the front room and began to unload her sack. At some point, she dozed off. Later on, Zuellie awoke to Pilar standing over her with a curious expression.

"What's that on your face?" she asked.

"I'm not sure, some kind of mineral, but whatever it is found me when I fell off the ridge."

Pilar reached to help her up, but Zuellie winced from the pain in her back. "Ahh, that hurts," she groaned.

"What should I do, mama's expecting me back home, she even asked if you and Rebecca could stay over in the house tonight."

"I wouldn't go there, even if I wasn't injured."

"But it's dangerous out here alone for you, and the baby, especially now that we're officially entering the war."

Zuellie rolled her eyes, wincing as she made another attempt to stand. It was always about the baby, not her well-being, at least not anymore. When she couldn't convince Pilar that the world at war could care less about a crazed black woman in the bush and even less about her over-indulged child, she insisted that Pilar take the girl.

"Are you sure," she pressed.

"Yes, take her, I'll be fine. When my back heals, I'll come to the big house, if it makes you feel better."

Pilar narrowed her eyes, as she propped her hands on her hip. Neither of them noticed when little Rebecca entered the room, until she squealed, and began jumping up and down at hearing the news that she could stay at the big house. Zuellie watched from the floor as her daughter's eyes filled with excitement. Pilar packed a bag of her clothes as the child bounced around. Zuellie tried to convince herself that her daughter really did make a bigger fuss over leaving as she listened to their parting words.

"Hold me tightly, or else you'll fall," Pilar instructed.

"Okay, I won't let go," said Rebecca.

A single tear burned down Zuellie's powder-dusted cheek, then skimmed her lip, reminding her of the tender kiss Rebecca had placed there before running behind Pilar. She allowed herself the tears now, knowing it would be the last time she would ever cry for her daughter. Zuellie knew the two of them could never co-exist here. The girl's fate had been determined by the *loa's* (or the afro-Cubano's *Orisha's*). It was better to heal from her injury and sorrow all at once, Rebecca had not been chosen by the drums, her's was the way of Karlina and Kouri.

The next day when Zuellie heard the customary rustling of the grass, she winced as she propped herself against the nearest wall. Pilar was late, she could tell by the way the sun hung to the left of her cabin and cast the shadow from a nearby tree across the room. Then she realized the footsteps were different, heavy and intense, like a messenger baring somber news. She watched his shadow cross over the wall. Rinaldo opened the door, his unsmiling face showing his concern.

"For heaven's sake, this isn't the time to be alone and injured—haven't you heard the news? We're at war, I came to carry you and the girl back with me."

Zuellie was unimpressed with the sore back that robbed her sense of humor, otherwise, she would have laughed at his statement.

"What are you doing, have you been worshipping the ancestors? I've warned you about this."

He kneeled before her and began wiping the white mineral from her cheek.

"I found this in the river when I fell, please leave it, I'll wash it away later." She placed a hand over his to stop him.

"If you pursue this way they'll label you as a witch."

"But I know what I am now, I'm meant to be a healer and voodoo priestess."

Rinaldo shook his head as he stood. Making a quick inspection of her sack filled with rocks, he disappeared into the second room.

"I've sent a telegram to Karlina letting them know how you're doing. She sent word that Lelo is back, and they're asking for you to come home."

He knelt again, this time placing a piece of paper in her hands with Karlina's return message. Zuellie laughed after she read the note.

"Please, let me send you home," he said.

She noticed when he stopped himself from touching her face, and instead, he gently stroked her arm. Part of her longed for the family reunion, but it wasn't possible to go back to the way things were; and how else could she explain to them that the girl they knew had drowned at Sea. There was no way to explain this to Rinaldo, not without sounding like a madwoman.

"I'll never go back, my place is here now."

Rinaldo exhaled, as he faced the strange woman he had fallen in love with during a manhunt for her brother. He wanted desperately to right the wrong he had done, to her, and Pieter. He remembered her as she had been in Miragoàne, barefoot and wild. No one could tame her unconventional way of existing, not him, not even her own daughter.

"Is this my punishment for wronging a friend?"

Rinaldo sat on the floor beside her.

"Let me make this right, I'll take Rebecca with me, Pilar will be there as well, she's already packing. I'll make sure she has the best education, and she'll never lack anything."

Zuellie nodded, as she realized the weight of a heavy burden had been lifted.

"Bring her to see me sometimes, and don't let her forget who her mother is, even though I fear she already has."

29

Habana, Cuba - 1925

THE YEARS FLEW by as Rebecca grew from an adorable bright-eyed toddler into an undeniable presence in the Habana home. In the flourish of eight passing years, Rinaldo and Pilar would come to realize the girl was more like her mother in ways neither cared to admit. The most telling similarity, both were as stubborn as a double-knotted stitch when it came to changing their mind. Zuellie's focus had always been on matters of spirituality, and Rebecca craved the elite lifestyle of the upper class (which was fulfilled living in Habana). To combat any wistful desires toward the traditional ways of her mother, 11-year-old Rebecca adorned herself in fanciful jewels (which Pilar gladly purchased at her request) and refused trips to the cabin as her creole language lessened.

The one-story home was brightly colored and lively. Music filled the rooms as guests streamed in and out of the dining hall to the back porch and sat around the modest pool on any given evening. Laughter and cigarette smoke filled the air (to Ijemma's dissatisfaction). It seemed Rinaldo found any excuse to entertain the business and political figures he wished to impress. For Ijemma, Obi, and the three additional servants, their days were long, too full to watch over a meddlesome and inquisitive child (hence the need for Pilar), who being childlike herself, needed something or someone to keep her occupied (insert Rebecca). Between the two girls, they seemed to be everywhere at once, and out of sight when most needed. Rebecca amused Pilar's juvenile nature, as she imitated the snobbish invitees behind their backs.

The women sat straight, their necks stiff, careful not to topple their elaborate hats. The men spoke loudly, blowing cigar smoke in ringlets, which somehow signified their importance. When allowed, or as needed, Rebecca amazed the industrialist within Rinaldo, sidling up close to him at dinner soirees and remarking on current events. The timing was important. She waited for the pause in their conversation, which always came when Rinaldo called for drinks to be served—that's when Rebecca would sometimes be allowed to entertain his guests. Her pippy voice laced with the creole accent she wished to conceal, foretold the collapse of the sugarcane industry as the decrease in global demand defied the rising cost of production. The astonished socialites leaned on their elbows to listen, while the hopeful politicians who felt the invitation gave them liberties to express their lopsided views, rolled their eyes, and cursed under their breath.

Everyone looked to Rinaldo, who by now had developed a respect for her attempts to assimilate into their new culture. When he reached for his glass, none of the guests noticed his slight nod in Rebecca's direction, a gesture for her to continue (to which she happily obliged). However, not before marking Ijemma's presence, whose back was hunched over as she encircled the room to retrieve their emptied plates. With a raised chin, Rebecca spoke proudly as she recounted facts she'd overheard on Obi's transistor radio or from Rinaldo earlier that morning at breakfast. If no one interjected, she continued to speak, eloquent yet pressured as the elder woman inched closer.

The first interruption came from a political figure. He assured the guests with the recent election of President Gerardo Machado and plans to expand Cuba's public works, the economy was sure to experience an upswing. Ijemma used the distraction to move closer. Brandishing a parental scowl, she mouthed the words, "*Silencio, por favor.*"

Rebecca imagined the pinch Ijemma wished to deliver to her arm. Motivated by Rinaldo's delighted smirk, she held her position at the table, moving only to sit in the chair Rinaldo begrudged the elder woman to place beneath the young girl's bum. Earlier in the years when she and Pilar had first moved to Habana, they trailed behind Obi and Ijemma like two abandoned baby chicks; those days were long gone. Pilar was different now, and Rebecca was desperate to secure her place, making the necessary adjustments where needed. Sometimes she pushed the limits, as in this instance, which made Ijemma nervous.

•   •   •

Later that evening after Rinaldo left with a bubbly brunette on his arm, Rebecca retreated to her room where she planned to continue reading, *The Age of Innocence*, by Edith Wharton. No sooner had she sat on the edge of her bed than the exaggerated sound of clanging plates drew her attention. With a pervasive need for survival at stake, Rebecca took her favorite blanket, along with the book, and tucked herself deep within the double wardrobe to hide from Ijemma's wrath. With any luck, Pilar would arrive soon, who had disappeared earlier that afternoon after Ijemma sent her on an errand.

Now in her twenties, Pilar had flowered into a beautiful young woman. Her oatmeal-colored skin, now free from teenage acne, was softer than the skin on her arms and legs. She told the others she had found work performing housekeeping duties for an army general's wife, but Rebecca knew better. She had seen the unnamed young man who lingered like a stray dog under a nearby street lamp every evening. Soon as the lights went out, and just before their snores erased the trace of day, Pilar tiptoed to meet her lover outside the gate. She never turned to see if anyone was watching. The magnetic force before her grew stronger as she slowly detached from the bonds within the home. Rebecca had watched them on more than a few nights and felt she could make out his height and build in a police lineup, if necessary.

The next morning Rebecca awoke in her bed, wondering when she had crawled from her hiding place. When Pilar noticed she had awakened, she moved from the chair and sat closer.

"There's something I need to tell you before you hear from anyone else."

Rebecca felt as though her heart would collapse just from the tone of her voice. Pilar had finally worked up the nerve to say goodbye, she could tell by the sorrow in her eyes. She inhaled her surrogate aunt's minty breath, and the rosewater used on her skin as a moisturizer.

"I'm getting married, so I'll be moving out."

"Can I live with you?"

Pilar refused to answer. What could she say? She had been the one who told Rebecca they would be together always. Now she was leaving and had the gut-wrenching task of telling the child she had to move back to Baracoa with her mother.

"How about I make you another promise," said Pilar after a long pause. "When our house is built, I'll send for you."

"But where will you live until then?"

Pilar and Rebecca held onto each other as they had done years ago after a frightful trek through wild fields with Zuellie for hidden treasures. When Pilar could no longer stand the heartbreak, she pressed a note into Rebecca's hands and told her to read it after she had gone. No sooner had she left, than Ijemma entered the room.

"You best get dressed now, we have a long day of travel ahead of us."

Rebecca slid the note into her wardrobe to read later. She was going to ask where they were going when Rinaldo entered the room.

"On second thought, I should be the one to take her," he said. "There are a few things I need to square up with Bembe, so you'll stay with your mother while I'm there," he said as he faced her.

Rebecca watched as he retrieved a large suitcase from the hallway and began filling it with her clothes. She had hoped he could see her as family, at the least as Ijemma and Obi, old enough to work and not as a burdensome child. But that's what she was, after all, a brat who would throw a temper tantrum if she couldn't have her way.

•   •   •

During the twelve-hour ride, Rebecca alternated between tears and sleep. When they finally arrived at *La casa grande* de Baracoa, Bembe met them at the door and quickly whisked Rinaldo away into the study. She recognized the woman standing before her as Pilar's mamá. Yamilet pulled Rebecca inside as she complained about the mosquitoes and led her to a room at the top of the stairs.

"This is the same room your mother slept in when she first moved to Cuba."

"I had no idea you knew my mother back then."

"Yes, and she looked just as scared and pathetic then as you do now…you should rest up, everyone's required to help with the housework here." She turned out the light and shut the door before Rebecca could respond.

Lying on the bare mattress, still dressed in her embroidered swing dress and stockings, Rebecca buried her face in her hands. As she had done on the long drive over, she slept some, then awoke in tears, only stopping when she fell back asleep. The next morning when a knock came at the door, she was surprised to see Rinaldo still wearing his suit from the night before, minus his glasses and tie.

"I was thinking we could drive over to surprise your *manman* now," he said.

As she stood up, the ribbon from her hair fell to the floor. When she bent to retrieve the strip of material, her shoulders slumped and seemed to remain that way as they left the house. Neither said a word as the engine started and they began the drive down the bumpy dirt road. when the car bypassed the barn, Rebecca turned to watch the laborers working in the cane fields. The car stopped where they would have to walk the rest of the way to her mother's cabin. Rinaldo held Rebecca's hand, and with her luggage in his other hand, they stumbled along the bushy trail.

"Your *manman* will be happy to see you."

When she looked up at him, his feeble smile was swallowed by the brilliant sun shining down on them. Instead of holding her decorum or using the opportunity to make a final plea, Rebecca began to sniffle. It may have been the way the sunlight shadowed his face, or because he wasn't wearing his glasses, but the eyes staring back at her appeared wet. They refused to speak until the cabin was in sight.

"Looks better than I remember it," he said.

"It's the ugliest sight I've seen in a long time."

When they reached the tiny cobble-stone walkway just before the front door, an enchanted sound caused them to look up. Hanging from the branches were pieces of glass and shells that swung back and forth when the wind stirred. Neither of them noticed when Zuellie approached, dressed in all white with dramatic tribal markings across her face.

"*Pitit fi mwen?*" (Is that my daughter?) Asked Zuellie.

"*Oui, manman*, its' me."

"And me," said Rinaldo. "You are looking quite different these days," he looked her over from head to toe.

"Why is she crying?" Zuellie touched Rinaldo's arm as she rushed to her daughter's side.

"Maybe it's because she's embarrassed by her *Manman*."

"What rubbish—come here child, this is your home."

Rebecca's legs remained planted when her mother moved to pull her inside.

"Just look at the bad manners she's picked up in Habana, and where is Pilar, hmm? Nothing would keep her from coming to see me unless something was wrong."

At the mention of Pilar's name, Rebecca pulled away and ran off in the direction of the main road.

"Now look what you've done," said Rinaldo. "There's nothing wrong, except Pilar's getting married, and I might be doing the same thing soon." He turned to trace Rebecca's path back to his car.

"Wait a minute!"

As Zuellie ran behind to stop him the glass and shells began clinking in the tree limbs. He stopped halfway down the path when his eyes caught sight of Rebecca near his car.

"Pieter's curse has found me for what we did, and now the girl hates me," said Zuellie, stopping to catch her breath.

"You silly woman, when will you start acting like a mother for heaven's sake; and what is all this garbage hanging in the trees? Have you ever considered this may be the reason she hates you?"

"My soul can't rest because of what we did." Zuellie clawed at his shirt.

"Let me send you home now," he pleaded. "She has a father and other family members she should know."

"So you want the frozen baby to return, eh? It will never happen!"

Zuellie began cackling with wild laughter when his mouth hung open.

"It's because we're here that our soul remains free."

"Bringing her down here was a mistake." Rinaldo shook his head. "I was going to leave money to help give her the life she deserves, instead you should use it to catch a train to Habana when you're ready to see your daughter—from the looks of it, the trip may do you some good."

Zuellie fell to her knees, her chest heaving as she chanted words he could not understand. Rinaldo turned and jogged toward his car. He exhaled and tried to appear calm when he saw Rebecca waiting in the passenger seat. She pointed to her mother who walked slowly behind him. Against his better judgment, he waited for Zuellie to catch up. She was still chanting when she approached the car, thankfully much quieter. Rinaldo waited for her to say goodbye to Rebecca. She kissed her daughter on the mouth, sealing the request made to the girl's guardian spirit. Zuellie imagined Pieter must be pleased knowing how tormented her life had become. He did not have her third seeing eye, but he had touched her soul, which meant he could feel what she felt.

"Now leave me alone Pieter," she whispered, as the car pulled off.

"The girl will take what I couldn't have, and that's a whole lot better than we could ever do for her."

She waved after Rebecca, who watched with concern from the rear-view window until the car disappeared.

30

1926

RINALDO'S POPULARITY GREW as news of his distant relationship with President Machado spread. At 30 years old, social acquaintances held out hopes of him claiming a seat in government, while others believed him to be a true anarchist at heart. Everyone waited to see which side of politics he would support. Rinaldo played his hand according to his audience, remaining tight-lipped about his intentions. None of them would know of his true desire to become a wealthy sugar cane planter while investing in real estate overseas.

In the meantime, Rebecca was enrolled at a small protestant school in Havana where she favored the foreign influences of the elite private school over the alternative in Baracoa (which was believed to be inadequate and overcrowded). Once she learned to overlook the minor infractions of racism and discrimination from her peers, Rebecca thrived in academics. She gave little attention to the curious stares and gentle tugs at her kinky braids from her classmates. Primary school passed by on fast-forward and by the time she entered secondary school, Rebecca was ranked as one of the top ten students in her class. The children of the upper-class society became her friends, and their parents welcomed her with looks of endearment. Their acceptance, having little to do with Rinaldo's status, was a direct result of the girl's domineering and expressive personality.

Rebecca refused to be ignored by anyone, and there was not a shy nerve to be found in her veins. She spoke before being asked a question and gave her opinion as it pleased herself. Speaking with eloquent words, she continued to entertain guests as she amazed Rinaldo with each passing year. When one of the politicians tripped her up on a topic she hadn't prepared for, Rebecca resorted to singing. Her voice was strong yet soothing, melodic, and perfectly pitched. Rinaldo would tell his guests she could calm a raging brigade, and over time Rebecca began to believe it was her presence that gained him multiple invitations throughout the community. Each new request would include a handwritten note, asking for the honor of hearing a song from his "little black bride."

Another handwritten note landed on his desk. Assuming the snobbish group had misconstrued his relationship with Rebecca and had been secretly mocking his philanthropic deeds, Rinaldo tossed the note on the floor. His colorful words alerted the house help, who quivered at the thought of his displeasure. Ijemma raced to refill his mug, as Rebecca bent to retrieve the crumpled paper. After reading the handwritten note, she squealed, which caused Rinaldo to knock over his fresh cup of coffee. Ijemma watched dumbfounded as Rebecca waved the paper around in the air.

"Ven a la fiesta, ven a la fiesta, la negra se ha casado con su principe!" (Come to the party, come to the party, the black girl has married her prince!) She sang and danced.

Ijemma laughed because the thought of them being married was absurd, but Rinaldo withheld his amusement. From that day forward, Rebecca would be at his side on every occasion, growing not only in height and fame but in looks and sophistication as well.

•   •   •

1928

By the time she turned 14 years old, Rinaldo made a business decision that would change both their fates. With each new request for his, *"Novia Negra,"* he would return an invoice to be paid by the hostess for Rebecca's entertainment fee. To his surprise, the bill was paid, and the invitations began to trickle in like granulated sugar sifting through his hands. Rinaldo deposited every peso into a separate account with Rebecca's name on it.

"By the time you turn 17, you should be able to support yourself," he said, with his head bent over the ledger as he totaled the balance.

"It would take me a hundred years to save up enough money for a house like yours."

"Maybe, but you're off to a good start—see right here, that's your balance." He pushed the rim of his glasses on his nose as he leaned to show her the total.

"But we're a team, what would I do all alone at 17 without you?" She came around the desk and sat on his lap.

"You should never do that, have a seat over there." He pushed her away and pointed to the chair opposite his desk.

Rebecca crossed her arms and pouted as she followed his command. He wasn't looking at her, which meant she had embarrassed him again with her unexpected affection.

"It's like I said before, you're getting older, and by that age, you'll meet someone and forget all about me as you start a life of your own, like Pilar."

"Must I remind you constantly, you can't get rid of me that easy," she said, leaning forward until he met her gaze.

She wouldn't admit it, but Rebecca knew she could be successful without him. If, or when, the singing engagements died off, there was always her education to fall back on, and enrolling at the University of Havana was a likelihood. The truth was, Rebecca wanted him to be a part of her future, in every way no matter the cost. She almost didn't hear when he reminded her of the upcoming trip to Baracoa. Rinaldo asked if she would be kind to her mother on their visit tomorrow as it was not only Zuelie's birthday, but her sacrifice they had to give thanks for, which allowed her to remain under his care.

"No, I'm here because she's crazy in the head, that's why you're stuck with me."

"You should respect your mother, and be sure to thank her for me. It was hard on her to let you go, but she wanted you to have a good education and a better life."

Rebecca cringed at the thought of the impending visit. This time she would be traveling alone, without Pilar, who should have been visiting Yamilet at the same time. She wanted to come up with an excuse, but Rinaldo reminded her of his promise to Zuellie, and of the importance of maintaining familial ties. In the three years since taking charge of her, he kept his word. Last month couldn't be helped, and once Zuellie was made aware of Pilar's recent troubles she would understand.

"Love your mother while you still have time," he said, nurturing his own regret at not having returned to Spain before his mother passed. "If it's okay with you, I'd like to invest some of your money into a foreign account."

Rebecca nodded, but her thoughts had already left him for the long train to Guantanamo, where she would then pay a driver to take her to Baracoa.

"Why is Pilar so upset with her mamá?" Asked Rebecca.

"You mean she hasn't told you? I figured you'd be the first person she'd confide in being as though you are close as any sisters ever could be."

Rebecca paused to consider their numerous talks over the years, which were many, especially of late as Pilar became more perplexed by her husband's violent temper. It was usually when Ijemma was around that her hysterical ramblings seized abruptly. Pilar had been this way for a long time, even before the almost forgotten attempt to return Rebecca to live with her mother 3 years ago.

"THE LETTER! It's been tucked in the bottom of my wardrobe this whole time," she gasped.

Rinaldo blinked, watching as she ran from the room, the sound of her heeled shoes tapping against the tiles as she fled. Rebecca flung open the wardrobe doors, tossing aside neatly stacked loafers and rainboots until the aged letter tumbled forward. She held her breath and carefully unfolded the paper as she began reading it aloud.

"My mamá wants to marry Bembe and she wants me to stay with Obi, who she says is my Papa. Ijemma is upset, she says my mama is a lying cat in heat, whatever that means."

Rebecca tossed the letter back into its hiding place and shut the doors. Maybe Yamilet was a liar. In all the years she had known Obi, he never acted like Pilar was his daughter. She did recall how it was Obi who shielded them from Ijemma's stern discipline. It was also true he sometimes took Pilar with him to light candles at mass, but that was because he knew not to ask Rebecca. After all, she had made it clear she wanted nothing to do with any form of religious practice.

"I have a mind to let Yamilet have it good when I see her," said Rebecca, as she paced back and forth.

Rinaldo waited for her in his study and when her emotions subsided, he advised that Rebecca should remain neutral, and focus on her own mother.

"Ijemma will bake a birthday cake, and we'll even have her send a delicious meal—you know how much she loves Ijemma's cooking," he said.

Rinaldo watched as her breathing returned to normal and she reentered his study.

"Like I said before, what would I do without you?"

Before he could object, she locked her arms behind his waist, making it harder for him to resist her embrace.

31

WHEN REBECCA EXITED the platform in Guantanamo, she found herself relieved at the sight of her mother waiting on a bench. Zuellie was wearing a plain brown dress and matching shoes (which Rebecca understood as her attempt to be less embarrassing and more presentable for the occasion). She noticed the way Zuellie touched her two customary braids hanging at the sides of her ears and positioned them neatly alongside her face and neck before she stood. Mother and daughter smiled as they held each other. After a brief mutual inspection, they hopped into a waiting car. During the long ride to Baracoa, Zuellie listened intently as Rebecca filled her in on Pilar's fateful marriage.

"I'm going to need his full name," said Zuellie. "Or some kind of personal belonging—I can take care of her problem easily."

Zuellie snapped her fingers, as her face hardened.

"No *Manman*, besides, I hardly know of him myself. Pilar has become very private, even where she lives is a mystery to us all." Rebecca shrugged.

As Zuellie settled back into her dignified act, Rebecca took note of the moment as being the first where they shared mutual respect and gratitude toward the other. After some time, nearing early evening when the bats would start to open their eyes in preparation for a night of scavenging, the car arrived at *La Casa Grande*. The intention was to share a meal with Yamilet, but she was nowhere in sight. As the two of them sat on the porch and began to eat, Rebecca filled her *Manman* in on the details of her blossoming singing career. She felt as though the proud look on Zuellie's face could be seen from across the Caribbean Sea, back to Haiti, and even beyond.

The next morning, when Zuellie mentioned needing to catch some fish for later, Rebecca accompanied her mother on the small fishing boat. For two and a half days, Rebecca lowered her high expectations, as Zuellie raised her standards, and somehow, somewhere in the middle of one's tradition and the other's modernization, a reconstructed relationship emerged. When it was time to head for the train station, Rebecca pouted for the first time in her life at leaving her *Manman*. During the drive, the space between them shrunk even more as Zuellie demonstrated how Rebecca should braid her hair at bedtime. When the driver pulled up to the station, she told her mother to expect a monthly allowance which she should spend as necessary.

"*Manman*, something is different about you this time, you seem calmer and easier to talk to."

"I was up at *La Casa Grande* when you didn't show last month…I thought at the least Pilar would," she exhaled. "Yamilet was listening to the radio and I overheard the broadcaster mention your name. He played your voice as you sang for *el Presidente* Machado—I've been waiting to show you how proud I am of your accomplishments since then."

When she leaned in to kiss her daughter on the cheek, Rebecca savored the woodsy scents of coconut fronds and sage on her *Manman's* clothing. They held on to each other until the train doors opened.

"I want to thank you for loving me enough to let me go when I was younger. It couldn't have been easy," said Rebecca.

"It was the hardest thing I ever had to do. Now I ask one favor of you…stay close to Rinaldo, no matter what it takes," said Zuellie, as the doors closed between them.

Her request was not only easy but fare. And as the train pulled further away, Rebecca made a silent promise to never skip a visit with her *Manman* again. Even as Pilar refused to see her own Mother for another 3 years, Rebecca made the journey one weekend out of every month.

•　　•　　•

1931

All of Cuba (and the rest of the world) was affected by the economic crisis known as the great depression. With demand and sales for sugar on the decline, Rinaldo placed a call to Bembe and arranged a meeting. During the drive from Havana to Baracoa, he assured Rebecca, and Pilar who accompanied them, that it would be possible to continue their comfortable lifestyle if Bembe could buy him out.

"What about the money we've invested from my singing engagements, will that help?" said Rebecca, checking to ensure Pilar was asleep before asking.

Rinaldo glanced in the rearview mirror at the sleeping figure before letting out a long sigh.

"There's no need to worry, at least not yet, your money remains put away in a safe place."

He explained that her earnings, half in pesos, and the rest in US currency, had been stored in a secret vault at an undisclosed location. He had never completed a transaction because she could not decide on a suitable investment. Rebecca remembered telling Rinaldo that she would decide when the time was right. Now she was 17 years old, the stock market had crashed, and she was grateful for the stash she too hid in a secret place, although there was no way of knowing if the money, or her gold pieces and fine jewelry would be of any value by years end.

By the time they reached *La Casa Grande*, Bembe's cheeks were as red as the coca-cola carton, now filled with empty bottles, he had drank with his rum. Back home, Rinaldo had done the same as he monitored the news of plummeting stocks and business closures. They met one another with bloodshot eyes and slumped shoulders. As they retreated behind closed doors, Zuellie and Yamilet emerged from the kitchen to greet their daughters.

"Come with me, let's take a walk," said Zuellie, she tugged Rebecca's arm. "We should give them space to talk things out."

It was getting late. The moon had barely swapped places with an orange sun, and the humidity clung to them like sticky flour dough on a rolling pin. Rebecca sat on the porch chair, fanning the wind with her hands as Zuellie looked toward the darkened outline of the fields.

"I want you to know, I have no plans to leave my cabin?"

"*Manman*, these are uncertain times. Rinaldo came all this way to sell his remaining stakes to Bembe."

"But he hasn't supported me in years. After he transferred the deed to the cabin over to me, I haven't needed him for anything."

"And what of the monthly provisions I've been sending? It's better that you come back with us, who knows what will happen with the economy next."

"No, no, I can't go. Besides, I haven't spent any of the money you've sent, it's all buried in the ground behind my cabin…don't look at me like that, what else did you expect a witch doctor to do with a heap of pesos?"

Rebecca couldn't help but laugh. She watched as her mother lifted her bare feet to squish a bug with her big toe. This time she wore her white headscarf and dress, the markings on her face neatly traced in tribal fashion. Maybe she wasn't crazy after all. The world's economy was imploding like a supernova, and her mother still rejected societal norms. Considering the current state of affairs, the cabin could end up being all they had left.

"Are you sticking close to him as I told you?" Zuellie raised an eyebrow and waited.

"Of course *Manman*, where else would I go."

"Keep your focus! Never mind Pilar and her troubles, I'm working on fixing her situation, but don't let him out of your sight, especially now that you're old enough."

"Just what is it you're suggesting? Rinaldo's like a father to me." Rebecca wrinkled her nose, as she clutched the top button of her blouse.

"But he isn't! Your papa is in Haiti, his name is Pieter."

"I know, I'm just saying—"

"GET CLOSER TO HIM!" she demanded.

Rebecca was grateful for the growing darkness that hid her embarrassment. She had loved Rinaldo for as long as she could remember (and not in a fatherly way). She had told him several years ago, but he told her never to say such things. She dropped the subject then, as she intended to do with her mother now.

32

August 12, 1933

RINALDO MANAGED TO stay afloat until the economy showed signs of recovery. He had planned for the loss of revenue after selling his sugar fields to Bembe, but what he didn't anticipate was the sudden decrease in popularity. Public opinion was that President Machado was a dictator who resorted to violence and murder to silence his critics—allegedly. The years of him remaining neutral on political matters backfired, as those in favor of a regime change marked Rinaldo as an enemy, and others assumed he was on the side of the rebellion; and with the danger of the uncertain times, he drank the days away.

Rebecca tried to console him with private serenades after dinner. If her singing didn't help, she would invite him for an evening stroll on the Malecon, where the crashing waves over the wall seemed to help them both forget their troubles. As he relaxed, Rinaldo would reach for her hand as they walked. Rebecca had become accustomed to him being one of two ways with her, amused or agitated. There were times he would get so upset that his anger made him tongue-tied, then there were moments when nothing made him smile but her singing. If he was sober, Rinaldo thanked her for putting up with his mood swings, if he had been drinking, he would yell until she left him alone.

"I've never seen him this way," said Obi, shaking his head as he walked away with a dustpan filled with broken glass, or a damp mop reeking of wine.

"Un-hunh, and he's even worse when the girl is around." Ijemma's cold glare settled on Rebecca.

She pretended not to overhear their conversation, waiting until she was behind closed doors, where she wrung her hands and paced the floor. Failing to come up with a solution, she considered seeking her mother's counsel for help. At 19 years old, and now a student at the University, Rebecca could easily manage on her own—just as Rinaldo had predicted; but she worried about what would become of him when she left. He was still single and had no family to speak of. If they could, Obi and Ijemma would abandon him for better pay, they had said so when the economy was at its most vulnerable state. Rebecca convinced herself that Rinaldo would fall apart if she left.

She needed him to sober up long enough to recognize her as a woman, capable and ready to love him. She was old enough now to say it out loud, and when the right moment presented itself, she would remind him of her confession as a young girl. Rinaldo was twenty-one years her senior, but she had never seen him as a father figure. In her dreams, she had always been his woman. Removing her sequence dress, she admired the blossoming curves underneath her slip. She was nowhere as fair as the famous singer, Rita Montaner, but Rinaldo had a thing for darker women. He had even once held up a picture of the American singer, Billie Holiday, and said she was more to his liking. In her mind, his smile said more than he could admit at the time (at least that's what she believed). Deep down, she knew he had never married because of their secret love for one another.

Wearing nothing more than the slip, and a robe she put on to appease Ijemma's ever-watching eyes, Rebecca left her room. It was just past midnight, and the hallway was empty and quiet. Their staff quarters were on the other side of the house, but still, she checked over her shoulder before approaching his door. If he wanted to know why she was up at such a late hour, she would ask to sing for him. He might ask why she was improperly dressed, and she would answer him with a song.

"Siboney, I love you, I am dying for your love," she sang outside his room door. "Honey added its sweetness," she continued in perfect pitch. Rebecca became lost in the words which reflected her desire. She never heard the phone ring at his bedside. Nor did she hear Rinaldo's expletive retort after the caller informed him that President Machado had fled Cuba earlier that afternoon. She stepped carefully over the broken shards of glass from the bottle he'd thrown against the wall. When Rinaldo reached for her, his intentions were to assure her of their safety, but also to ask if she could convince her mother to leave Cuba. Then he began to stutter, and Rebecca knew if he became more agitated he would command her to leave him. So she kissed him, and for a moment, he kissed her back.

"No, we can't do this!" He pushed her away.

Rebecca moved closer, placing another kiss on his mouth until he could resist her no more.

"I love you, I'm dying for your love," she whispered, in between breaths.

His kiss was bitter, almost hateful as he bit her lip and yanked her closer. He would hate himself in the morning, but tonight he needed her. Rebecca leaned into his weakness until they began to breathe and move in unison.

⁛

The next morning, a startled Ijemma found an unclothed Rebecca alone in Rinaldo's bed.

"What are you doing in here, where is Señor Machado?" She shook the girl awake with a frown.

"He left for an early meeting," she lied.

"Is that so, there's a note here that has your name on it." Rebecca jumped to grab the letter from her hands.

"Foolish girl, do you know what you've done?" Ijemma watched as she pulled at the sheets to cover her nakedness.

"It's an abomination, do you understand?

Believing Ijemma's disapproval was due to their age difference, Rebecca ignored the warning. If color and race were a factor, then she would pretend to be one of his house helpers. Besides, the whole countryside had already known he was her benefactor, no one would question them at this point. Ijemma held a hand over her mouth as she exited the room.

Rinaldo left Cuba that morning. Granted the letter said he would return, but he failed to say when. He wanted Rebecca to know he appreciated her devotion, and most of his happier moments in life included memories of her. He made no promise for their future but asked if she would lay low until he returned. Never mind her classes or going to check on her mother. Remain in the house until he returned, whenever that would be. Rebecca said nothing to the staff, although she saw them watching as she sipped coffee like nothing was out of the ordinary. Obi grunted when she waved for him to bring the morning newspaper.

"What did the note say?" He held the paper out of reach with his good hand, as the other hand shook from neurological damage.

Rebecca was reminded of his kindness throughout the years, even when his wife remained indifferent.

"He's away on a business trip, and left me in charge."

Obi returned to his wife who had been standing in the doorway. Rebecca listened as Ijemma sucked her teeth upon hearing the report. As they disappeared down the hallway, squabbling about who should mind whose business, she considered ways to end their tenure. The argument stopped when someone knocked at the front door.

Pilar stood on the other side of the door, she nursed a swollen lip as she clutched her overstuffed suitcase. When she saw Obi, she dropped her luggage and fell on his chest.

"I can't go back to him, he hits me for any reason he can think of," she said.

Obi looked to his wife for help, as he held the sobbing girl in his arms. Ijemma took a moment to compose herself before peeling Pilar off his shirt.

"Let me take a look at your face," she said.

Obi snatched the luggage and scurried down the hall making his escape. After Ijemma cleaned her face and applied an ointment to her wound, Pilar slept on the bed in Rebecca's room. Through the night, she flinched at every backfiring engine or noise from Obi's transistor radio. By morning her nerves were worse.

"You should get her out of the city, take her to her mother where she can rest in peace," said Ijemma.

Rebecca hesitated to give an answer, as she thought about Rinaldo's letter. He had good reason to worry, but then again he had also left her alone. If there was any danger, the threat would be in Havana. She nodded, moving quickly before she had time to second-guess her decision.

They made it to the station a little past noon. Once they were safely seated on the train, Pilar began to open up. She told Rebecca about her husband's involvement with the revolt that stripped Machado from power.

"It's no longer safe for us in Havana, and you should know they plan to interrogate Rinaldo," she said.

"If I tell you something you have to promise not to tell anyone," said Rebecca.

Pilar moved closer, almost forgetting to breathe as she listened while Rebecca whispered.

"But how can that be?"

"All of the students are involved in the revolt, and I had to pick a side—it made sense."

"What about how close you are to Rinaldo? You've clearly benefited from his status all these years."

Rebecca shrugged.

Pilar looked away, biting her bottom lip as she digested the unbelievable secret.

"He's only provided a roof over my head. I've made more money from singing than anything he's given me—I hope you told your wonderful husband that fact when you were busy running your mouth?"

Pilar swallowed a lump in her throat and remained silent for the rest of the journey. When they arrived at *la casa grande*, the air wreaked of hard times and no hope. The open-bed trucks that used to haul the freshly cut cane were stripped bare on the roadside. The mill gears had long stopped turning, and the only sound left to be heard were the drooping lush green heads of overgrown sugar cane.

"Why do you think they took it down?"

Rebecca marveled at the missing statue of Josè Marti as the driver circled around the fountain.

"Probably had to sell it for money, it's a wonder the house is still here," said Pilar.

When the driver pulled away, Rebecca looked after the car and wished she had obeyed Rinaldo's orders.

"My goodness, what brings you two here this evening?"

Yamilet met them on the front porch, dressed in tattered clothes and her hair unkempt.

"Who did this to you?" She reached for her daughter's face and examined the raw bruises.

Bembe who must have heard the commotion from his room came running down the stairs in his underwear, waving a pistol in the air. When he noticed Pilar and Rebecca, he tried to hide his weapon, then his bare chest, with his arms. Yamilet motioned for him to go back up the stairs. As she tended to her daughter, Rebecca decided to wait until morning before heading to her mother's cabin. She slept in a room by herself, using the time to process the major event that had just happened in her life. When she was alone it dawned on her that Rinaldo would get the wrong impression if he returned and found her gone. She smiled, imagining his pain over her absence. By her calculation, that would make things even.

The next morning when Rebecca prepared for the long walk down the dirt road, Pilar left with her. As they passed the old barn, she told Rebecca the story of how she and Zuellie snuck out of the house late one night to dance with the laborers. Pilar breathed heavily as she struggled to keep up with Rebecca's determined pace.

"I'm thinking your Mama can help me, she's always had something special about her…do you have the same gifts?"

Rebecca kept her focus on the path ahead. When Pilar repeated the question she hesitated before answering.

"I don't believe in anything beyond what we can see or touch," said Rebecca.

Pilar scratched her head as Rebecca quickened her steps. As they drew closer to the cabin, a colorful array of polymita shells began to jingle in the tree branches from where they were hung.

"A surprise visit from my daughter, and my dear friend!"

Zuellie appeared in the doorway.

"Who told you we were here?" asked Rebecca.

"My shells, of course, but your vibration is slightly off—something happened."

Zuellie looked her daughter over as she handed them each a cup to drink from.

"Oh Ma, you know I don't believe in that stuff."

After their embrace, she stepped aside for Pilar.

"Your vibration is off too, and now I see why."

She turned Pilar's face to look over the bruising, as she sucked her teeth.

"I should've killed him when I had the chance."

"No! Please don't resort to violence on my account."

When Zuellie's back was turned, Rebecca whispered that she shouldn't take to heart everything her mother said.

After they finished their drink, Zuellie pulled her drum to the middle of the floor and began to beat a rhythm. Slow and almost woeful at first, then she picked up the tempo. It seemed as though when the rhythm began to enlighten their mood, the beating slowed to a low almost undetectable tap. Somehow Pilar fell asleep. Zuellie continued playing until her eyes glazed over.

"*Manman*, what's wrong? You're scaring me!"

Zuellie's hands stopped.

After several moments of silence, she began to chant in her native language, her voice horse and scarcely audible. She crawled over to her daughter and placed a hand on her belly.

"This one is next in line to wield *La Clairière*," she said.

"No! *Manman*, there are no more cane cutters in this family. From now on we're educated people—we live in big houses and have servants, with a car in the driveway."

33

February 1934

REBECCA CAREFULLY CONSIDERED her options during the long journey home. She knew it was going to be awkward having to explain Pilar's decision. With any luck, she would make it to her bedroom undetected before the arduous conversation ensued. By the time Rebecca reached the front gate, her hopes vanished seeing Obi standing near the front door. Her steps slowed as she decreased her determined steps on the pavement. When she looked again, Obi waved in her direction. Rebecca took a deep breath before returning the gesture as her steps quickened. There was no luggage for him to retrieve, and if there had been, his shaking hands would've made it difficult to carry out the simple task.

As soon as she entered through the door, Rebecca noticed a shadow standing in the hallway. Ijemma folded her hands as she blocked the entry to Rinaldo's bedroom. As they glared at one another, Obi approached and removed the small bag from her hand.

"Two left, and only one returns?" said Ijemma, as she moved to stand before Rebecca's room door.

"Pilar decided not to return."

Ijemma's body began to rock, as her foot aggressively tapped the decorative tile. When Obi passed between them, grinning proudly as he carried her handbag, Rebecca followed him into her room.

"With her mother?" Ijemma sucked her teeth.

"No, she chose to stay at the cabin."

Rebecca held onto the doorknob as Obi left the room.

"And why would she choose to live like a savage, when there's such a fine house there?"

When Obi turned to face her, Rebecca realized he had expected an answer as well. She shrugged, hoping they would be satisfied, but neither of them would budge.

"She believes it's safer for her there, and for the baby."

Ijemma placed her hands on her cheeks, and then covered her mouth. Obi left the room after hearing the news.

"Well, I guess that settles it then…and with Señor on the run, maybe it's best we all head back," said Ijemma.

"The decision is yours to make, but I won't be going back there to live," said Rebecca.

When they were both gone, she shut the door, closed her eyes, and took two deep long breaths. There was no time to rest, especially since her plans were to take over managing the house in Rinaldo's absence. For starters, she needed to find employment, and there was her own matter to consider.

Rebecca used her time wisely, setting out immediately to find work with whoever would employ an uppity mulatta. Her reputation as a talented singer and pianist paid off. Two weeks later, she accepted a position at the Peyrellade Conservatory as a music teacher. As the weeks passed, her personal matter grew more noticeable. There were no discussions, but Ijemma's attitude changed toward her as she prepared meals with extra protein and vitamins on the side. Nor did anyone question when she paid the staff and kept the household functioning like a well-managed factory. And by the time

Rinaldo resurfaced, six months later, he was welcomed into his home by an industrious and frugal woman.

His return was on a Saturday morning. Had it been any other day the change may have gone unnoticed for several days. It was what Rebecca called her scheduling time, used for planning meals and assigning chores for the upcoming week. When he entered the kitchen, Obi stood at attention, but the women gave as much notice to him as they would've given a paperboy or milkman. After the list was completed, Ijemma took Obi by the arm and left the kitchen. Rinaldo waited until they were gone to approach Rebecca.

"What's happened here?"

"You were probably expecting to find the house had been abandoned."

Rebecca rose from the chair with one hand over her round belly.

"No, no that's not what I meant—how are things?"

He followed her into the front room.

"I'm glad you're back, my feet are swollen, and I'm not sure how much longer I can continue working this way."

She removed the hand from her stomach to close his gaping mouth.

"I'm sure there were pregnant women wherever you eloped to."

She laughed when his mouth flew open again.

"You're having a baby?"

Rinaldo removed the glasses from his eyes to clean them. Rebecca moved closer. With one hand still holding her belly, she used the other to gently stroke the side of his face.

"Who—where is the father?"

When she gave no answer, Rinaldo began rubbing his eyes until they were swollen and red. He pulled her toward the sofa, and as they sat, he made sure to put some distance between them. Rebecca sighed as the cushion eased the strain on her backside. Had he not been shell-shocked by the news,

Rinaldo would have noticed when Ijemma returned with a tray of fruit and placed them on the end table nearest Rebecca. He stroked his beard as he gazed at the decorative wallpaper, a new feature added while he had been in exile.

"If only I could give you and the baby a proper surname, or make this right somehow," he said.

"It's enough we're together now. We'll continue on as we always have."

Rinaldo moved across the seat, narrowing the distance between them. No matter how many ways he imagined the outcome nothing seemed right, not in a world that frowned upon inter-racial marriages. He reasoned with her words, realizing what mattered most was that they stayed together.

• • •

December 1934

Three months later (two days shy of New Year's Eve) Rebecca gave birth to twins. The boy was given the name Leonardo, and the girl was named Consuelo Lynnette. The boy came out first and seemed to be sick from the moment he took air into his lungs. Consuelo Lynnette was born second, kicking and screaming, but healthy. The boy was darker complexioned, like Rebecca, but long-limbed and frail like Rinaldo. The girl had her father's red hair and pale skin, but she had her mother's temperament, which was first evidenced by the way the carriage rocked back and forth as she clenched her tiny fists and wailed.

By the time the proud Grandmama arrived from Baracoa, it was the day after their birth. Rebecca was asleep when Zuellie entered. Sensing a change in the room (along with the smell of eucalyptus and sage), she awoke to greet her *manman* who was gallantly dressed in all white, from the turban on her head, down to the sandals on her feet.

"What did you name the baby?"

"I can't believe you came—and you're wearing shoes!"

As Rebecca wiped at the tears forming in the corners of her eyes, Zuellie placed a cup in her daughter's hand and then instructed that she drink.

"This is for strength, and it'll enrich your milk."

"There are two—a girl and a boy. The boy was born first, but he's such a tiny little thing. The girl is chubby and round, and she has your large eyes."

"A boy? I didn't see the boy in my vision. How could it have slipped by me?"

Zuellie sat on the edge of the bed and took a sip from the cup intended for her daughter's nourishment.

"Well, she's the one next in line. The girl will be given *La Clairière*…she'll hear the call of the drums—drink up!" Zuellie placed the cup at Rebecca's lips.

The contents were coagulated and thick. Rebecca drank the familiar substance as she had done many times as a child. As she continued to work the bitter and lumpy herbs down her throat, Zuellie began to give advice on how to build baby Leonardo's immune system. As she listened, it dawned on her that the instructions not only revolved around traditional remedies (like bone broth and herb-infused teas) but religious superstitions as well. Rebecca knew she would never be the kind of mother who could identify the names of roots and plants or their many benefits, but she was willing to give Religion a try—for the children's sake.

"So, it's settled then, the girl should be named properly as a Dupont," said Zuellie.

Rebecca offered her cheek as her mother leaned to kiss her goodbye. By the time she made it to the exit, a nurse returned with two bundles wrapped snuggly in her arms. Zuellie's countenance softened as she admired both the boy and the girl, and her eyes stung from the tears she refused to shed, but when she looked into the large eyes of Consuelo

Lynnette, Zuellie was deeply moved. She placed a finger in the boy's mouth and he began to suckle. Consuelo Lynette wriggled from her Grandmama's touch on her delicate skin. When she reached to remove the babies from the nurse's arms, Rebecca gave her approval.

"Will you stay at the house with us—just for a little while? I could use your help, especially with the boy."

"No-no, I'm sorry but I just can't. If me and their Father are around each other the hex will find us…has he ever mentioned anything about how we arrived in Cuba?"

Zuellie held her breath as she waited for an answer. Rebecca opened her mouth but closed it when she heard Rinaldo outside the room door. His voice was louder than either of them had ever heard before. Zuellie and Rebecca listened as he insisted the twins be given his surname. There was some discussion of the paternity, to which he emphatically vouched for the integrity of the mother. Not happy with the conversation, Rinaldo dismissed the staff and entered the room.

"To hell with the world, we're getting married!" He announced defiantly, as he held the door to keep steady.

Rebecca could smell the alcohol on his breath from across the room. Zuellie tried to leave before he noticed her, but as she slipped through the door, Rinaldo reached for her hand. She confirmed his gesture with a firm handshake, never looking up to meet his eyes, and then she was gone. He seemed to sober up for a moment as he questioned if he should pursue her. When Rebecca called to him, he frowned at the missed opportunity to ask for forgiveness.

Their encounter was brief, but it was enough to scare Zuellie into fleeing Havana immediately. When she found her seat on the passenger train, she swore in her native language. Raising her fists toward the general direction of Haiti, Zuellie let her flurry rage for everyone to hear. Onlookers believed her to be a mad woman, but upon further inspection, most of them could tell by her garments that she was, in fact, a bush healer. Zuellie ignored their curious glances as she recited every incantation and prayer she thought would cancel out and ward off Pieter's voodoo curse.

Back at the hospital, Rebecca chose to ignore the exchange between her mother and Rinaldo. She reminded him of their plan to remain as they were. Marriage was an unnecessary formality in her opinion, all that mattered was for them to stay together and raise their children under one roof.

"Do you think your mother is upset about us?"

"No, but she asked if you've ever mentioned Haiti."

"I just wonder if she hates me, or blames me for the way her life turned out."

He put his head down as he wiped the sweat from his forehead with a handkerchief.

"But why would she hate you? You gave her work as the other laborers, to give me a better life."

The answer seemed to give him peace. Rinaldo kissed her cheek before doing the same to each of the newborns.

•　•　•

When Rinaldo took Rebecca and their children home on New Year's day, they committed to each other as if they were husband and wife. Rinaldo was 41 years old, and Rebecca was a tender but very mature age of 20. Cuba and the world at large had their own affairs to sort out; beginning with the revolt that ended with Ramon Grau as acting President of Cuba. The great depression was still a factor, with threats of more wars, race, and discrimination. There was a rather vile situation in Germany with a gentleman named Hitler and his Nazi party. With hatred spewing across the globe, who had time to regard a highly intelligent black woman raising two mulatto children with her presumed Spanish employer. It was nothing new after all, except such arrangements would usually have the woman and her children living in separate and less suitable quarters.

At the end of President Grau's term (100 days to be exact), Cuba's new government continued to elect and replace President's at will, and within the turmoil, Rinaldo somehow avoided having his property confiscated by transferring deeds to Rebecca and the children. Former associates who had not survived the fall of the previous regime were stunned by his ability to maintain his status, leading Rinaldo to believe they were secretly plotting against him. When he was home he drank himself into a stupor, and when he was gone, he stayed away for months at a time.

After nursing her children until they learned to walk (and with the help of Ijemma), Rebecca was able to return to the University as a student where she completed a degree in liberal arts. Thereafter, she took a position as a Professor of Arts and Culture. During her tenure, a co-worker at the University extended an invitation for her to visit the Iglesia Evangelica Pentecostal, and to everyone's surprise, she began attending regular Church services. When Rinaldo was home (and happened to be sober) he accompanied her to Church.

34

1938 – 1939

WHEN LEONARDO AND Consuelo Lynnette turned four, Rebecca became pregnant again. Another boy was born, and they named him Nicolas Machado. This one was healthy and fair-skinned. While Rebecca cared for the newborn, Rinaldo took odd jobs part-time, managing a hotel and a nightclub, in addition to a full-time position as a banker. He often spoke of a desire to move someplace where a marriage between them would be accepted. Whenever the subject was discussed, Rebecca would respond in the same manner, "it's enough that we're together."

Rinaldo continued to drink, although less due to the increase in his workload, which puzzled Rebecca, especially as the newly legalized communist party could be seen as a threat to his financial liberties. By the start of World War II, Rebecca gave birth to another girl they named Carmen Machado. Rebecca had her hands full with the two younger children, and Leonardo, who she kept nearby due to his sickly nature. The many distractions left her little time to curb Consuelo Lynnette's growing boredom, who would then resort to pinching her siblings or stealing food from their tiny hands just to laugh as they cried. Rebecca tried to refrain from punishing the girl, but each day became more of a challenge to keep her in line. By the time Ijemma offered to take her along for a train ride to Baracoa, Rebecca gave no argument.

While they were gone, Rebecca found more time to rest and nurture the other children. However, after three days, she began to miss Consuelo Lynette's antics which she realized broke up the monotony and offered some comedic relief throughout the day. When she heard Ijemma at the front door, Rebecca couldn't wait to tell her daughter how much she was missed, but there was no Consuelo.

"Have you lost your mind! Why would you leave her?"

Rebecca cornered the older woman at the door.

"They both said to leave her—your Mama and Pilar, and she was playing so nicely with the other children, I'd never seen her so well behaved before."

Ijemma wrung her hands as she whimpered her excuse. Blinded by her anger, Rebecca yelled to a sleeping Rinaldo and told him that she was going to get their child if he cared. She packed her sleeping children into the backseat of the car and began the long drive to her mother's cabin. With Ijemma along for the help, they reached Baracoa by early evening. It was still light out, so the children were awake but hungry. Pulling as close as she could to the dirt trail, Rebecca unloaded her tribe (Leonardo, Nicholas, and Carmen), then marched them down to their Grandmama's cabin. Consuelo was first to notice as they approached. She ran to her siblings, smiling with dirt smudges around her face and hands. After hearing the commotion, Zuellie stepped onto the porch.

"Here are your other grandchildren, if you care to meet them," said Rebecca.

She touched the top of each child's head, like when one played a game of duck-duck-goose. Zuellie went to Leonardo first, opening his mouth to check the flesh of his cheeks and then the swell of his belly. Satisfied with his condition, she examined young Nicolas next, and then the baby in Rebecca's arms.

"I don't see any of me in them—none of these will ever hear the call of the drums."

"Enough of your silly superstitions, every one of them was born by me, that means your blood runs in them too—and you!" She pointed to Pilar whose mouth dropped when the attention turned on her.

"I expected more from you."

"Leave her out of this. I need more time to teach my granddaughter our ways—she's like me you know."

Rebecca ignored her mother as she moved to face Pilar.

"What happened to you? You were the one who took me from this very place when I was a child."

"But me and my girl will be here too, we'll make sure she's well cared for and safe," said Pilar.

Rebecca flat out refused to leave Consuelo (whom they insisted on calling Lynn). However, before leaving, she agreed to allow more visits as it was obvious the girl's wild tendencies were better exercised in the countryside.

35

1950

CONSUELO LYNNETTE BECAME known by her family and friends as Lynn. At 15 years old, she was wild by nature, preferring to climb a tree rather than sit underneath one in a pretty dress. Her expository vocabulary overwhelmed classmates, and she found their conversations to be tedious and insufferable. Thankfully, at Pilar's urging, a phone line was installed in the cabin, which served as a meaningful outlet in-between weekend visits with her Grandmother. During their phone calls, Zuellie would remind her of the charge to carry on the family legacy. Lynn would check to see if her parents were listening before confirming that their secret was still safe. After the reassurance, Zuellie suggested that Lynn occupy her time with something useful, like finding unique specimens from the backyard to bring on her next trip.

Everyone agreed that Lynn blossomed in the countryside. Having the freedom to roam and explore the land kept Lynn out of trouble, which equaled peace for her siblings. Like her Grandma, she believed the earth revealed its mysteries underneath her bare toes, so the pull toward the secret culture of the healer was born naturally. Lynn became everything Zuellie had missed out on with Rebecca.

During her visits, it became customary for Lynn to assist with setting the dedication table as part of a ritual or ceremony. Her grandmother taught her in stages, which was painfully slower than Lynn preferred. Timing and patience were everything, she heard these words more times than she cared to count. Zuellie wanted to make sure none of it was forced upon her. If her premonition were correct, Lynn would hear the call of the drums for herself. Nine years had already gone by, and she still heard nothing outside the rituals in her Grandmother's backyard. Pilar had failed to hear her own calling as well (which was no surprise) but she seemed contented by fulfilling her role of maintaining the offerings of meat, fruit, flowers, and candles.

On her last visit, Lynn had an experience that changed everything, which is why she now had the secret family relic in her possession. During the last celebration, she fell to the floor after dancing so hard she could barely stand. Later that evening, when all the guests had gone, she told her Grandmother of the episode, explaining how it felt as though the beating of the drums seemed to jump into her bones and consume her entire body.

"The ancestors are ready to speak, but if your Mama finds out, she won't allow you to come back," said Zuellie.

"You mustn't mention a word of this to anyone," said Pilar, who stopped sweeping the floor to join the conversation. "I didn't understand it before, so I made the mistake of taking your mama away, for which I have suffered for...this is your way, I know that now."

Lynn and her grandmother were sitting together on the sofa and there was a rare breeze blowing through the open window, which helped to clear the musty odor from patrons who had crammed into the small room the hour before. Pilar moved from the table and knelt before them.

"Your Guardian will help you in bad times like it helped me get rid of—"

"What she means to say is that an Orisha has chosen you, and it's my duty to guide you through the process."

Zuellie swatted Pilar away with a piece of garment that would later be used to cover the offering table. With Pilar gone, she walked Lynn into her bedroom and closed the door.

"The time has come for you to have this."

Lynn's large eyeballs watched intently as her Grandmother bent to pull a long object from behind a chair. Zuellie removed the burlap sack as she handed it over and placed the blade in Lynn's hands.

"This belonged to my papa, and his papa before him…and now it's yours."

"A Machete? But I'm not a bracero."

"This is not just any Machete, what you're holding happens to be *La Clairière*, a family relic. Take it home and keep it somewhere out of sight, but you should make sure to carry it with you on special occasions."

Lynn did as she was instructed. Back in Havana, she kept *La Clairière* in a safe place, although she couldn't quite understand the reason why. Not much longer after bringing the relic home, it became clear that Lynn had heard the call of the ancestor's drums. At first, it was nothing more than a subtle thumping, as she lightly tapped along to her parent's music. Then one night, while in her room studying, the drums were so loud she yelled for her parents to please turn off the music. When they refused to listen, she left her room to complain, only to find them both resting quietly in bed. Later in the night, the sound returned, this time it lured her out of bed as she began to sway and dance. After the first night, it happened several times a week, always after midnight when the house was dark and her family slept. On one occasion, Ijemma caught her swaying in the hallway. After wagging a wrinkled finger in her direction, she reminded Lynn of what could happen if her parents caught her behaving that way.

Threats no longer had any effect on Lynn. She was past caring, as the proverbial door opened and pulled her through. Unbeknownst to her parents, she had been taught her grandmother's native language and knew almost everything there was to know about remedies to heal and even to kill, if necessary. Lynn knew how to host a sacred ceremony, and now she had heard the call of the drums. The only thing left to do was to assume her position as she waited out the time of adolescence (which was the hardest part). When you're young the days seem to drag. Sitting in a classroom learning about mathematics, historical figures, dates or geography was no fun for Lynn. Recess provided little relief, as she navigated around peers who long gave up attempts at friendship. She was either perceived as black trying to pass for white, or white trying to act black. Thankfully, life had been kind enough to gift her with two friends, one black and another white.

The tone of acceptance was much the same in Baracoa. The children in the countryside were just as cruel as the ones in the city. However, due to their much-appreciated services of Zuellie, youngsters were more careful with their slurs as parents warned them to be mindful of how they treated the Healer's granddaughter. Lynn grew tired of feeling like an outsider everywhere. One evening, she approached her mother in the study, who sat with a book in hand as the younger siblings listened to a story before bedtime.

"How have you managed to get away with all of this? No one seems to harass you for having mulatto children—why?"

Rebecca waited until the little ones were gone, then she had her older daughter sit next to her.

"I never gave anyone a chance to reject me. Besides, we're all the same inside, that's all that matters."

"*Mwen diferan!*" Lynn answered in Creole.

Soon as the words were spoken she cupped both hands over her mouth.

"So, *Manman* has been teaching you her language, eh?" Rebecca stood with her hands on her hips.

They both stopped talking when the room door opened and Rinaldo entered. He paced the floor as he mumbled to himself. Rebecca had grown used to seeing him this way since the cold war brought tension with the United States, placing his financial interests in jeopardy once again.

"I'll always be nothing more than an outsider here—and now I'm told there's a mark on my head," he murmured.

Rebecca tried to hush him, but sensing he would not be easily consoled, she asked her daughter to give them privacy. As Lynn walked slowly to her room, she listened to the paranoid ramblings of her Father and realized he had been just as miserable living in Havana. Tonight he had been drinking (as he did on most nights), evidenced by the slur of his words, and the strong odor of alcohol on his breath. If she could ever catch him sober, he would be the one to petition for her release.

Trips to Baracoa were less during the school season, and at her age, throwing a temper tantrum was unacceptable. As Lynn prepared for bed, she considered making minor adjustments to her personality which could help to temporarily improve her situation. Lying awake most of the night, she imagined ways to be friendlier to her siblings and even her peers at school. She thought hard, as she tried to envision herself happy or interested in normal things the others her age found interesting. By morning, she had slept a total of two hours, at best, and the only conclusion she could reason with was to leave.

At the breakfast table, she noticed her Father was clean-shaven and dressed in his suit, which meant he would be leaving for work at the bank soon. Her mother's expression matched her own, the lines across her forehead revealing weariness and lack of sleep. Her twin sat to her right, slurping the remainder of his cereal from a bowl. Nicolas and Carmen bickered over their favorite seat, next to Leonardo. No one was prepared when Lynn asked for their full attention.

"There's a change coming soon," she said.

She waited for the younger siblings to stop fussing before continuing. Rinaldo adjusted his tie and smiled at his daughter. Rebecca blinked away tears as she faced him.

"You told her? But we agreed—"

"Yes, some changes are coming for our family. How would you feel if we left Cuba?" said Rinaldo.

The children stared at their father, faces frozen with shock. They were used to him being somewhat unpredictable with his drinking, but this was different.

"Your brother's not able to go this time, on account of his upcoming treatments, but how would you like to accompany me on a business trip?"

Rinaldo turned to Lynn, as Leonardo put his head down. Lynn knew her brother well enough to know he was not upset, only pretending so she wouldn't catch on to their scheme. Their father would have asked him along on the trip first, and knowing him, he had whined until Lynn was the second choice. Not to mention, she knew Leonardo was not sick, just a scrawny fellow who had been a picky eater from birth. Also, he was popular at school and excelled in academics, no offer would have been tempting enough to lure him away from his friends or his books.

"OK, I'll go, but only to keep an eye on you. Besides, nobody likes me around here either," said Lynn.

Her twin perked up when she agreed to go, and so did her mother, knowing Lynn would deliver on her promise, and return with a full report of her father's business trip.

36

January 1951

TWO WEEKS AFTER her 16th birthday, Lynn and Rinaldo left their home with three suitcases between them: one of them contained the hidden family relic within a burlap sack. As they approached the large passenger ship, Lynn held onto her father's hand. Living around the water was one thing (she loved the fishy smell of the ocean, or splashing in the waves on the beach), but boarding a vessel and sailing out into the deep unknown was unsettling and intimidating. Rinaldo smiled at his daughter when the time came for them to board. As she steadied her legs, she squeezed his hand tighter.

Ever since waking up that morning, she had an overwhelming sense of something evil lurking that made her knees tremble from terror. Lynn believed had she been a few years younger, her parents would've shown more sympathy for her uncontrollable nerves, but not at sixteen, especially since she was almost as tall as her father. When the line began to move faster than she preferred, Lynn reminded herself that she was about to embark on the opportunity of a lifetime.

"Something's different about you today," said Rinaldo.

Lynn took a deep breath, as she anticipated the conversation where she hoped to bare her deepest secrets.

"You're so much calmer, and I can see your relief at leaving your problems behind…I feel the same."

"Dad, are you always this clueless? I'm a nervous wreck, and you should've brought Leonardo too!"

Rinaldo's eye's widened, as he realized her hands were shaking. He kicked the ground and wished he could think of how Rebecca would respond in this situation.

"I've never told you this before, but you're a lot like me. We focus so much attention on what's down the road that we can't even see what's right before our eyes."

Rinaldo paused to stroke a hand through his thinning grey hair.

"Perhaps this trip will be the change we both need."

Most of his words seemed to fly over her head, but at least her knees had stopped knocking. Once they were on the ship, she turned to face the city and blew a kiss with her hand. Rebecca would be working at the University this afternoon, and her siblings would be heading home from school soon. When Rinaldo imitated her gesture they took a moment to wave goodbye as if their family was waiting down by the dock. When the smile left her father's face, Lynn turned to see what caused the shift in his behavior. There wasn't a familiar face in the crowd, that she could recognize. After wiping his brow with a handkerchief, he reached for her hand. She could see the tightness of his jaw, and his stiff back as they walked.

"What happened, who did you see?"

"It's nothing—we should get you settled before dinner."

It wasn't until they found their stateroom, and the door closed behind them, that Rinaldo released his grip. Lynn massaged her hand, as he wiped more sweat from his forehead.

"It's nothing really, just a few business matters needing to be sorted out."

A flask materialized from his jacket. As he drank, Lynn moved around the cabin as she checked the room's accommodations. There were two beds, a small closet, and an even smaller area for the tiny commode. As she considered using the bathroom, there was a knock at their room door.

"I was just about to come looking for you," said Rinaldo.

Lynn noticed the slight trimmer in his voice. She stood behind the bathroom door to peep through the crack. Four unsmiling men entered the room with two women following behind them. One of the women draped herself on the arm of the man standing closest to her father. The other three gentlemen observed the room and the suitcases on the floor.

"As I explained earlier, I'm going to America on a short business trip. My wife and three other children are at home."

The man standing near her suitcase frowned behind her father's back. He was much younger than the others, probably in his early twenties. She noted the way his eyelashes curled, and there was a dimple in the center of his chin. He was the pretty boy who probably had to frown to prove he was as tough as the others. He pointed a finger at her father's head and pretended to pull a trigger. Rinaldo who must have sensed something evil, turned around and told the youngster to leave.

"We just stopped by to wish you all a safe journey," said the man with the woman on his arm.

He pointed at his crew and they followed him out of the room. It wasn't until her father closed and locked the door that Lynn emerged from her hiding place. Rinaldo took another sip of his drink.

"Dad, who were they?"

"It was a mistake not to have flown to Miami...I thought the ship would've kept us under the radar."

He shook the flask as he swallowed the last drop.

"This is what I've been feeling since morning, it's those people— who were they?"

Lynn touched her father's arm to get his attention.

"Th-they work for some powerful people who have invested a large sum of money with me."

His shoulder's tightened, as he paced the floor, and Lynn found herself doing the same thing.

"They haven't decided if they can trust me yet."

"But, have you given them any reason to doubt you?"

"No, no, it's nothing like that. Some people need more time to check things out for themselves, I'll prove to them their money is safe with me—"

"Maybe if you quit drinking…I know it would make Mama happy too."

"Don't worry, they won't bother us again…for now, let's see what this ship has to offer for dinner."

Lynn kept an observant eye on her father as they ate the unremarkable meal in the crowded dining hall. He continued to drink, and as the alcohol saturated his throat, the one nervous hand on his glass eventually stopped twitching. When the room cleared, the hardened lines across his face smoothed and rested. In the brief moment of seeing her father relax, Lynn's stomach settled, giving her some hope the earlier threat had passed.

"Let's catch the sunset," he said, as he escorted her onto the promenade.

The cool breeze was a relief after sitting in the crowded hall. Lynn shivered as the wind rustled her frizzy hair. It had been two intense hours at sea. Not to mention, the feeling of terror that had attached to the pit of her stomach like an anchored buoy since morning. Now there was the motion sickness, which she refused to mention to her father. They stood side by side, but miles apart as the day's events washed over them like the waves of the wide blue ocean. Lynn recalled the conversation with her grandmother when she phoned to say goodbye.

"I fear I'll never see you again, my sweet girl, you must do something for me?" she said.

Ignoring the concerns of her superstitious grandmother, she promised to visit upon her return.

"You must take *La Clairière* with you, for protection and to keep us bonded," said Zuellie.

From out in the middle of the ocean, she could hear her grandmother's voice perfectly, much clearer than her father's heavy sighs beside her. With each passing kilometer, the sound of her grandmother's drum began to beat louder. As she listened, the rhythm grew stronger. Lynn closed her eyes until the image of Zuellie standing in her white robe and turban materialized.

Her grandmother sat with the palm of her hands on the drum. Droplets of sweat formed along her hairline as her unsmiling face drew her granddaughter into a deep trance. Lynn began to rock with the ship. She gripped the railing for balance but kept tumbling forward. The sound of the drums caught her fall and lifted her above the water until she hung like a cloud in the sky. When she looked around, Zuellie held out a hand to pull her up.

"There's no turning back now, my sweet girl—but at least you have the relic to keep you safe."

"Gran, I'll be back before you can even miss me."

"You must watch for the one—"

Lynn could hardly make out her grandmother's words over the beating drums.

"The one who points the finger."

They were the last words she heard before the vision ended. Lynn's back was on the floor when she awakened, and her father was leaning over her. Rinaldo dabbed at her face with his handkerchief.

"Oh, thank God you're okay!"

He removed the cloth from her face to wipe his mouth.

"You fainted and almost fell overboard—come on, let's get you in bed to rest."

As they made their way back to the stateroom, Lynn clung to her father's arm, oblivious to the concerned stares from other passengers. By the time she reached her temporary sleeping quarters, it was 8:30 pm. If she took a hard nap, by the time she awoke the journey would be over. When her father's back was turned, Lynn pulled the burlap sack out of her luggage and placed it underneath her pillow. Her fingers clamped around the blade as she fell asleep.

Sometime later, she was awakened by her father's voice as he spoke with someone outside their room. The conversation was muffled but she could tell the words were fueled with anger. When they were finished speaking, he entered the room and punched the closing door behind him.

"Are you ok? Was that the angry men again?"

When Lynn attempted to sit up, the awful feeling returned in her stomach and anchored her to the bed.

"It's been straightened out now…once we arrive in Miami, I'll withdraw the money from my account to keep them happy, and we'll never have to see them again."

When Lynn checked the time on her watch, it was 9:15 p.m. They weren't due to arrive in Florida until a little past midnight. She bit her bottom lip as she decided against sharing her vision and the warning from her grandmother.

"You're going to love Florida," said Rinaldo.

He filled his glass with a drink as he pretended to be calm about the unsettling situation.

"We'll spend a day, or so, there before heading to Louisiana, that's where my business is, and the surprise…I hear there's a live band playing in the showroom, should we go check it out?"

"No, I still don't feel well, and the constant rocking is turning my stomach upside down."

"Then you should rest, I'm going up for some fresh air."

Lynn watched as her father put on his glasses and patted his pocket for his hipflask. She knew it was better to stick together, but his nerves wouldn't allow him to stay put, and her stomach kept doing somersaults. She laid back down and listened with her eyes shut as her father's hurried footsteps left the room. An hour passed and she was still lying on her back staring at the ceiling. Somehow while in her thoughts, *La clairière* seemed to magically appear in her hands.

Lynn turned the bedside light on for a better look at the rusted blade, which was many years past its usefulness. There were grooves imprinted into the steel, possibly from being dropped, which caused imperfections that resembled facial characteristics. If you looked hard enough, in the right lighting, it seemed as if eyes and lips were staring back at the wielder. Some of the mouths gaped open with words never spoken. Of course, the facial impressions were imagined but as she held onto the handle, she could feel the heartbeat of every unnamed face staring back at her.

A knock at the door caused Lynn to drop *La Clairière*. Thinking it might be the gang of thugs from earlier, she quickly retrieved the blade. As she waited for another knock, the hallway outside the room went silent. The night grew darker and quieter. When she checked the time on her watch, it was 10:30 p.m.

PART III:
America

37

THE BOAT RIDE from Cuba to America was a manifestation of Lynn's worst nightmares. It was like a bad dream you wanted to end but it never does, growing more ominous and terrifying each second. The crisp new document in Lynn's hands read, Terra-Lynn Machado. She held the paper up to the car window and repeated the words slowly. Realizing it was her broken English that was to blame for the misunderstanding, she crumpled the paper before shoving it into her pocket.

"Terror!"

That was what she had said to the first kind face that approached her, along with a few other words in Spanish. The name change made about as much sense as her now riding in the back seat of a 1949 station wagon, without her father. The same men who entered their stateroom yesterday sat in the first two rows and their two female counterparts were on either side of her. The issue was not that Lynn could not remember what happened last night. She had not been drugged, nor had she lost track of time from a blow to the head. It was more like she wished to forget it all—same as you would a bad dream. She pinched herself again, this time leaving a nasty bruise that needed massaging and a little spit to stop the blood.

Lynn was very much awake now, as she had been since the knock at the stateroom door last night at 10:30 p.m. As she sat in the car that held her captive, the full events of the evening hours flooded her mind. After the knock at the door, she rushed to pick the family relic up from the floor and put it away. Then she remembered waiting, for at least another thirty minutes, for her father to return. Growing more worried by the second, Lynn had left their room to search for him. Her father was not at the bar or the dining hall, nor anywhere on the decks. After circling and backtracking her steps, the anchored dread in the pit of her stomach returned, causing her more grief.

"Excuse me, have you seen a Spanish man about this tall and wearing glasses?"

Lynn held a hand over her head to emphasize his stature. No one had seen her father. She searched the area where the band had left their equipment out after ending their session. Then she went to the smoking lounge, even though her father was not a smoker. Afterward, Lynn doubled back around the promenade and searched over each face and shadow before heading back to her stateroom. When she returned, the room was dark, and in the same condition as when she had left. It had to be around 11:15 or so when a knock interrupted her thoughts. And without hesitation she opened the door, hoping to find her father leaning against it for support after drinking his problems away. The four angry men from earlier entered as if they had a right to be there, and the two women trailed in behind them.

"*Hola*, allow me to introduce myself…my name is Patrick, you can call me Pat—these are my associates, Ángel, Zachary, and Jerrold." He pointed out each one as he spoke.

"I thought you were my—you'll have to leave now," said Lynn.

But the one who called himself Pat, along with Ángel, took a seat in the two foldable chairs that served as an eating nook. Lynn held her breath as the two women made themselves comfortable on the bed her father should have been sleeping on. The two younger men remained standing by the door. The youngest, with smooth skin and a hairless face, answered to the name of Zachary. The other named Jerrold fiddled with something in his coat pocket. He was startled when an older couple passed by in the hallway. Zachary glared at him until he became more on edge.

"WHAT MAN? I didn't sign up for this," he mumbled.

As they bickered, Lynn went to the door and was about to leave when Zachary caught her arm. He wasn't rough, but it was clear by the way he blocked her path that she wasn't going anywhere. When he walked her to the bed, Lynn remembered *La Clairière* tucked inside her luggage.

"My papa said you'd get your money in Florida, so please leave us alone now!"

"Shut your mouth," said the nervous man by the door.

"Be cool, it's not her fault," said one of the women.

When Lynn looked at her, the woman shrugged.

"Hey kid, things got out of hand tonight, and messed-up things happen in life sometimes—you know?" she said.

That's when Pat explained that her father ran off after an altercation with one of his men. There was no real damage to either man, but their pride and principle were on the line. When Lynn looked at the nervous gentleman standing at the door, she noticed his bruised lip. It served him right, they had been a nuisance from the moment Lynn and her father boarded the ship.

After waiting for an hour, Pat and his girlfriend, Joleen, remained in the room as the others left to search for Rinaldo. Deciding against using the old family blade, Lynn went into the bathroom and began reciting secret incantations for protection her grandmother had taught her. By the time she finished the chant to her guardian spirit, there was a knock at the door. She stepped out of the bathroom, not expecting to see her father by this point, just as Pat's crew returned. Zachary entered first, and she noticed the way his eyes sparkled at the sight of her. Lynn couldn't help to think, that if the situation had been different it would have been nice to get to know him better. She resisted an urge to brush her hair or to smile in his direction. Zachary jabbed his finger in the air, signaling that Pat should follow him into the hallway.

Joleen kept an eye on Lynn while they were gone, as Lynn sized her up to see if she could take her down. When Pat returned, he seemed shaken like he had seen the ghost of the *loa Agau* (her guardian spirit). Her grandmother had once told her that the *loa Agau* was an angry Haitian spirit who entered its host with tremors and violence, and that's who she had just summoned. As the rest of the gang filled the room, each bore expressions from fear to worry. The other female, they called Raquel, pulled Lynn over to the bed as the men stepped back into the hallway.

"Listen, I don't have much time, but gather your things and anything of value to take with you. Don't let anyone see you, but hurry up," she said.

"Did they find my father, is he okay?"

Lynn braced herself for the bad news.

"What I know is he is a wanted man, he probably intended to pay, but they ran out of patience."

That was all Lynn needed to hear. She gathered her father's wallet and tucked it into the sack with her grandmother's relic and kept it nearby. When the right moment presented itself, she planned to escape. There were two men posted outside the door, and two standing inside, so she decided it was best to wait for a safer opportunity. The last three hours of that boat ride passed in slow motion.

When the time approached to leave the ship, she watched as Pat put her father's hat on, then begin searching around the room and under the bed.

"Where is it, where's his identification?" he said.

Raquel trembled beside Lynn, who remained calm. While his back was turned, she slid her father's documentation on the bed but kept the wallet. When he rose from the floor and found the papers, he frowned at the two girls. After returning his glare, Lynn stuck out her tongue.

"I demand to see my father!"

"Shush girl, you don't want to push him," said Raquel.

But Lynn stood in her face, long legs like her father's and a sturdy hand like her Grandma Zuellie. She could wield a machete like any bracero, and after chanting for the last two hours, she felt the strength of the angry *loa* and was ready to fight. She clutched her fists for the first blow.

"You can't punch a bullet," said Raquel.

She touched Lynn's arm, then pointed to Pat's hand resting on the bulge of his pocket.

"But this is a crime! Do you think no one will be looking and expecting my father when we exit the ship?"

Pat grinned as he waved her father's papers in his hand. When she went to open her luggage, Lynn heard her grandmother's voice.

"Hold off, the time for revenge will come later."

Trusting the voice as her beloved grandmother, she decided to wait. That night was the first time Lynn had felt pure rage. Also, it was her first time seeing human bloodshed. Chicken or pig's blood was a regular occurrence at her grandmother's rituals, but never a man's blood. Just as they were about to leave the room, Zachary and Jerrold closed the door behind Ángel, who then walked over to Patrick and plunged a knife deep into his gut. And if it weren't enough, he removed the sharp knife and jabbed it several more times into Pat's collapsing body.

Joleen fell to the floor, her painful cries caught somewhere in the back of her throat. Raquel placed a hand over Lynn's mouth just before she could scream. She was going to bite Raquel's hand, but Ángel's sinister grin caught Lynn off guard. The roles had changed, and he was now the gang leader. Lynn watched as he commanded the others to take Pat to a room two doors down. That's when the spirit of *Agau* slid from the dying corpse, with a sound of dark sputtering as it entered her body. Lynn bowed at the waist, almost too weak to withstand the possession, and then she heard the polymita shells outside her grandmother's cabin begin to jingle.

"Hold your peace, the time for revenge will come," she heard her grandmother's voice repeat.

That's how Lynn ended up now riding in the station wagon. When Ángel said it was time to move, she moved. When he said she could speak, she spoke. Besides the one moment of weakness where she believed the man at the border could help, she had been compliant as she awaited the command from her grandmother's voice to take her revenge.

"They terror me—" she had begun to say to the border patrolmen, as he grew annoyed at her broken English.

"What is that? Speak up—who is Consuelo Lynnette?

"Terror—"

"Terra is your name?" He rolled his eyes.

"Her name is Lynn," said Ángel as he snatched the paperwork from her hand.

"Alrighty then, Terra-Lynn, welcome to America sweetheart." He handed the new papers to Lynn as Ángel handed him some money.

Lynn had been silent ever since being given the new name. So had Joleen, who must've been secretly planning her escape or retaliation. Occasionally, Raquel would try to bait Lynn into a conversation.

"We should speak English here as much as possible," said Raquel. "Otherwise we'll be at their mercy, and that won't be good for either of us."

Lynn watched as Raquel's lips moved but she couldn't process the words. Small talk had to be saved for later (much-much later), after the time for her own revenge. The luggage with the family relic never left her side, even now as it rested under her feet; and her eyes never left the sight of Ángel, except to stare at the paper which she now held up to the sunlight.

"Terra-Lynn Machado," she read the name once more.

38

THE DRIVE TOOK twelve hours in total. The car stopped twice, once for a bathroom break in a town called Alabama, and once somewhere in Mississippi. Lynn was surprised at how well she managed to control her rage, even while vividly imagining ways to sever each of their heads with *La Clairière*. The car headed toward a two-lane road and passed through an oak forest. After a while, the trees parted, giving a view of fields of cotton. At one juncture, the station wagon passed through a small town where a group of people gathered on a sidewalk as they waited to enter a building. The giggling young girls were dressed in poodle skirts and hair-ties, and the cool-mannered boys wore cuffed jeans and leather jackets. Lynn's gaze rested on a sign that said something about coloreds.

"Blacks aren't allowed to mingle with whites here, it's called segregation," said Jerrold, as Joleen translated his words to Spanish for Lynn's sake.

"It's dangerous for negroes in America, and especially in the south, that's why we're bypassing the bigger cities and sticking to the back roads."

As she listened, Lynn touched the kinky edges around her hairline. She had long reddish-brown hair that hung mid-back, but her roots were too thick to deny her genetics. She would have the same problem here as in Cuba; too light for her grandmother's people, but not light enough to be white. If she straightened her hair the way her momma taught her, she had a chance of passing, not that she wanted to, but if it were a matter of saving her hide she had to at least try.

After Jerrold announced that they were in Louisiana, he pulled to the side of the road.

"We're stopping to use the bathroom," said Raquel.

"Here! But we're in the middle of nowhere—couldn't we wait until the next town?" said Lynn, as she watched the men disappear behind the huge oak trees. She did consider the location as a perfect place to enact revenge, but what if Ángel had the same intentions?

"No, thank you…I'll wait here."

Raquel rolled her eyes and then hurried to follow the others. Within moments they all returned, and the journey resumed. A few hours later, just as the temperature changed and the sun dropped, Jerrold announced that they were in a place called, Cecilia, Louisiana. When the car stopped outside a gated property, Zachary and Jerrold whistled and began talking excitedly to each other. Ángel grinned at the sight of the home, which to Lynn was an eerie replica of *La Casa Grande* in Baracoa. Following behind Raquel and Joleen, she exited the van and faced the two-story, Victorian home.

This was the place her father disappeared to when he was away on business. There were wide steps leading up to a long porch, with tall pillars that held up the upper veranda. Lynn moved toward the house, observing the immaculate hedges and full magnolia trees marking the landscape. As she placed a foot on the first step, her eyes rested on the vibrant garden framing the raised platform; inside the planter was her mother's favorite plant, the Cuban orchid. Snapping one of the flowers, Lynn stopped to smell the bloom before placing it behind her ear.

Ángel removed a keyring from her father's coat pocket and opened the door. When the gang followed him inside, Lynn watched the back of his neck, imagining the tomato-red blood at the place *La Clairière* would rip into his flesh. She waited for a moment at the screen door and listened for her grandmother's signal. All she needed was one rat-a-tat on the drum, and she would know it was time to make her move. The wind was silent and the air was brisk and biting, but quiet. The only sound for miles was the steps from Ángel, and from the rest of the gang, who were now inside the house her father had built to surprise his family.

Still clutching her suitcase in one hand, Lynn shut the door behind her as she admired the layout. Beyond the foyer, decorative metal sconces lined the walls of the hallway, and a rather ornate chandelier hung from the high ceiling. Just like in *La Casa Grande*, there was a sitting room to the left of the hallway, and an office to the right. Further down the hall were the dining room and kitchen, but there were bedrooms downstairs, which was different from the house in Baracoa. Also, besides the back exit at the far end of the hallway, there was another exit down a side hall, that led to the most beautiful garden gazebo she had ever seen.

After her brief inspection, Lynn went to find the other women, who she found resting on a claw-foot sofa in the sitting room. Joleen's face was buried into the rolled arms as Raquel begged her to say something.

"I want you to know that we were never a part of any of this," said Joleen. "We are victims, just like you."

Raquel's eyes searched Lynn's face as they waited for her response. Maybe it was the unfortunate comparison, but Lynn found herself irritated with their presence. Exhausted and grieving, she sat her suitcase behind the door, pausing momentarily when the handful of polymita shells she took from her grandmother's yard clinked against the blade. Regardless of what the foreign documents said, she was the granddaughter of the Haitian *Mambo*. And with that revelation in mind, Lynn marched over to the sofa, pulled the hair on Joleen's nape, and smacked her across the face. When she yelped, Raquel gasped but quickly covered her mouth.

"I don't want to hear any more of your sobbing, where is my father?"

Lynn yanked the woman's hair into her fist. When she could no longer stand their whimpers, she loosened her grip.

"W-we should stick together—you know these men are real gangsters," said Raquel as she moved to console Joleen who was trying her best to hold in her cry.

Stopping first to retrieve her suitcase, Lynn left the women to stew in their fears. In the hallway, she waited several seconds to see if the men would come running, but no one stirred. The front door stood between Lynn and freedom, as she realized there was no one to stop her now. But this was her father's house, he should be here and not a gang of hoodlums. She belonged here. Her heavy eyelids and aching back reminded her of the need for rest after the long journey. Maybe by the time she awoke her father would arrive, putting an end to the horrible nightmare.

Lynn climbed the wide stairs feeling a little relief as the ball of nerves in her stomach relaxed. At the top of the stairs, there were windows at both ends of the hallway. The front view overlooked the driveway and entrance gate. The rear window looked down on the backyard that loomed with sagging trees above a swampy and enchanting bayou that trailed the outskirts of the property. Taking note of the moon's reflection off the surface of the water, she inhaled the beauty of nature all around.

Lynn chose the master bedroom at the top of the stairs. Inside the room was a fireplace on one wall, complete with a sturdy screen and tools. After admiring the iron fire-poker, Lynn removed *La Clairière* from her suitcase and wedged it at the back of the empty firebox. She ignored the temptation to lie down on the bed, choosing to sit on the floor with her back against the wall. As she faced the bedroom door, Lynn's stomach began to settle. She reminded herself that there was still a good chance that her father was alive, instead of floating between the Gulf of Mexico and the Atlantic Ocean as she imagined. Upon his arrival, she determined he would find her safe and strong, not fragile and broken like Raquel and Joleen. Her parents would be grateful for her intuitive survival skills, and her grandmother would expect nothing less. Pulling herself from the floor, she switched on the baroque lamp beside the pencil-post bed and retrieved a clean outfit from her suitcase. With the rest of the contents, she marked her territory by arranging the multi-colored polymita shells in a pattern around the bed.

There was a bathroom across the hall, so she decided on a quick bath. It wasn't until she entered the bathtub that Lynn began to hear the first rat-tat-tat-rat-tat of her grandmother's drums. With a racing heart, she quickly entered her room and began to get dressed as she thought of her next move. She was about to retrieve *La Clairière* when Joleen and Raquel's giggles filled the air. Standing at the doorway she followed the direction of their laughs to the back window where the sound of beating drums grew louder. If she closed her eyes, she could envision her grandmother's white robe and tribal markings across her cheeks. The cool evening sparkled from a show of brilliant stars in the night sky. One of the stars made a jarring move across the sky before it fell somewhere beyond the bayou. Lynn's bare feet smacked against the floor as she hurried down the stairs.

"This is my father's house!" she whispered.

Lynn ran through the house with a determination aimed at stopping the hoodlums from their celebration. At the back entrance, she observed Ángel's smug demeanor. He was pointing one of his scathed fingers at Jerrold and Zachary as he held Raquel by the waist. As they laughed together, she imagined how easy it would be to catch them off guard with *La Clairière.*

Whoosh!

In mere seconds, she could chop off that pretender of a fingertip he so enjoyed pointing at the others.

Thwack!

Just the way her grandma Zuellie had shown her, clean and swift leaving no trace of blood on the blade. As she prepared to exit the house, Lynn noticed a telephone on a console table. She reached for the receiver and dialed her home number. When the call was connected, she whispered.

"I haven't seen mi papa since we were on the ship…there are some bad men here who say they're not leaving until he pays them."

"Have they threatened you? Stay put, I'll call the police and also your papa's associate there—are you safe?"

Rebecca tried to remain calm for her daughter's sake, but Lynn could tell she was shaken.

"Yes, I'm safe, all they want is their money."

Lynn peeked to see what Ángel was doing before she rested her back against the wall. After telling her mother about the house in Cecilia, she promised not to play the heroine. She would wait for the authorities to arrive, she promised again. Lynn placed the phone back on the hook, just before Ángel entered through the back door. Wreaking of body odor and alcohol, he approached and blew her a kiss.

"I like you, you're tough and beautiful—just the way I prefer my girls."

He licked his cracked lips as he propped a hand on the wall above her head. Lynn stepped away, but not before uttering some words in her grandmother's creole language.

"You'll be lucky if *La Clairière* doesn't clear your shoulders this night!" The words shot from her tongue like a serpent's bite.

There was something in her eyes that caused Ángel to sober up and began to carefully back away. His eyes never left her glare, until he reached the front door and opened it. Once he felt there was safe enough distance between them, he lifted his pointer finger and pretended to pull a trigger.

"This is my father's house, I belong here, not you!"

When she opened the back door a gust of wind blew her hair high above her head. Lynn held her chin up, as her toes sank into the ground and connected her to the foreign land. Joleen and Raquel approached cautiously, and they too saw that there was something wild and dangerous swimming beneath the surface of her pupils.

39

DROPLETS OF SWEAT formed on Zachary's forehead as he beat the drum. Transfixed by his own demons, his vacant eyes looked beyond a dancing Lynn, who now swayed before the crackling firepit. With her hips bucked, she raised her hands and reached for the stars above. The time had come to summon the spirit of rage to exact her revenge. When it seemed the earth stopped spinning, she welcomed her host.

A bloody vision of violence snatched the air from Lynn's lungs. Down on her knees, she panted and clawed for relief. As she squirmed around on the ground, an outstretched hand broke through the trance. She heard a gentle voice begin to say, *"My way is easy."* As Lynn contemplated whether to receive the kind offer, the sound of Zachary's drumming resumed. Rising on her feet, she spun with the world; fast and faster until the stars from the sky were flung into the roaring of the firepit. The next thing she knew, it felt as though Lynn had been thrown into the pit with the fire and the blazing stars. Breathing in the embers, she watched as the extended hand slowly withdrew and faded. Ultimately the decision came down to her grandmother's ways versus her mother's beliefs—vengeance or forgiveness.

The raging spirit offered her a milder version of violence, but still, a sacrifice would be required. As she made her decision, the drummer went silent and the stars returned to their place in the sky. Eventually, Lynn found herself alone with the dew of morning against her face and wet grass sticking to her legs and arms. When she rose from the ground there was no mistaking the task, although she wished the terms could be negotiated. Chicken bones and blood were not satisfactory for her new spirit host, and the demands were clear; the sacrifice required access to a lifetime servant. Lynn stood in the middle of the yard and surveyed the land. As she admired the dangling Spanish Moss spawning across the bayou, an eerie chill crept up her spine.

"Be patient, you'll have your sacrifice soon enough."

A beautiful, yet sinister grin erased her fatigue as the chill subsided. With each sluggish step, a ghostly force strengthened her countenance as she accepted her fate. When Lynn entered her home, Ángel watched from where he sat in the study. Her muddy feet clumped on the floor as she entered the kitchen. When she moved out of sight, Ángel locked himself inside the office. Lynn sucked her teeth, just as Grandma Zuellie would do when a patron claimed they couldn't pay for her services. Afterward, her gran would say, "pesos, chicken or blood—we all have to eat!" They would almost magically produce the payment from their pocket.

To her delight, a warm stack of pancakes sat on the counter. Quickly snatching up the plate and a cup of freshly-squeezed orange juice, she reminded anyone within earshot that this was her house and her food. She left the kitchen with her nose held high in the air. At the stairs, she skipped the steps two by two. Without stopping to rinse the sticky earth particles from her skin, she gobbled the food down just before sleep pulled on her eyelids. It was a heavy sleep, the kind that made you forget about your troubles and reality. Lynn slept for most of the day and when the sun fell below the tree line, she rose from her bed in search of food. This time Joleen and Raquel were in the kitchen.

"Look who decided to give us a hand," said Raquel, as she turned the ladle inside a steamy pot.

"I give the orders from now on." Said Lynn.

She frowned at the two women who were now staring at her with their mouths wide open.

"Please, don't let him hear you talking like that." Raquel dotted the air with the large spoon in her hand.

Joleen avoided eye contact with her, which was smart. Lynn had to act fast before the police arrived. There was still an offering to be made to her spirit guide, and as of yet, the men avoided her. The two women could leave now or end up a casualty. When Joleen finally looked her way, she handed Lynn the fish knife she had been using.

"Please don't encourage her," said Raquel, her eyes pleading with each of them.

Joleen grabbed a smaller knife and continued filleting fish. For a second, Lynn considered that she had not been the only one who made a deal with the dark side.

"My blade is much bigger than this, but I could always use a backup." Lynn smiled at Joleen.

"What's going on in here?" said Ángel.

When he entered, Joleen and Raquel quickly returned to their cooking. As he glared at her, Lynn hissed like a cornered cat until he froze and began to back away. When he cleared the doorway, she batted her eyelids before turning in the direction of the backyard. She found the drum propped against a cypress tree. Sitting down on the same stool Zachary used the night before, Lynn began a slow melodic beat as her toes burrowed into the earth. When her feet rested in a warm spot, she began to groan as a vision of perished souls of former slaves cried out. Playing soft and calm, she listened to their labor pains, heartaches, and tears. After paying homage to their passing, she switched to a louder more intense beat.

Jerrold and Zachary watched her from the upper veranda; Raquel and Joleen viewed from the kitchen window. With her focus on the men above, she ignored the women. One of them had to offer himself freely, but the only one who had shown her any interest was Ángel. Zachary was her preference, he was closer in age and good-looking, and Jerrold was second best. After narrowing down her selection, Lynn returned to the house.

"Where have all the hombres gone?"

Joleen and Raquel tried to act as if they had not been watching her the whole time.

"They went to check on the hotel," said Raquel.

Realizing she had said too much, she looked to Joleen to bail her out.

"What business would they have at a hotel?"

"Maybe I owe you the truth since it's—" She placed a hand over her mouth when a figure entered the kitchen.

Lynn's evil eye greeted his wicked grin. She was no match for him in strength, but he could not gauge her emotions and that is what he feared the most. She reminded him of a girlfriend he once had who could seduce a man while slitting his throat (she had done so on many occasions at his request). Lynn had the same dance of beauty and rage lurking beneath the surface; that's what kept drawing him closer.

"Calm down pretty thing! No one wants to harm you, we all want the same thing."

As Raquel cowered in a corner, Joleen offered him a plate of food which Ángel gladly accepted. When he suggested they join him in the dining room, they each looked at Lynn. She thought to tell them to enjoy their last meal, but instead, she shook her head. After they were gone, she went to the telephone and dialed home.

Rebecca informed her daughter that an investigation was underway, and at some point, police officers would have answers about her father's disappearance. Lynn's shoulders relaxed as she listened to her mother's voice.

"You'll love it here; the house is beautiful, and the women dress in fine clothing."

Lynn listened as her mother breathed on the other end.

"Ma, can you hear me?"

"Yes, I hear you…let's discuss that after we find your father." Rebecca sighed on the other end of the receiver.

After their phone call, Lynn dialed her Grandmother's number; relieved that the stubborn woman had installed a telephone line to keep in touch with her grandchildren. She exhaled her tears when Zuellie answered.

"Don't cry, you were chosen from birth to cross the Ocean," said Zuellie. "It's your time now, so be strong!"

"There's a big house and land here for us, but the men want some money—they say my father owes them; and there's a sacrifice I must offer, but I don't know if I can."

"Don't be silly, you've watched me all your life, and you have help, the guardian spirit, and the other thing I gave you."

When the call ended, Lynn's stomach was in knots. With a heavy heart at missing her family, and deciding to move forward, she returned to her room and locked the door. For the next two nights, she continued her vigil in the evening, dancing until the stars fell into the fire-pit and the dew woke her in the morning. On the third day, she called home again. Lynn's twin brother gave her the awful news. Their father's body had been found, and it would not be long before Ángel and his gang would be arrested for the murder of Rinaldo, and another mystery man, who she knew had to be the one they got rid of before leaving the ship.

That night as Ángel and the others were in the backyard drinking, Lynn watched him from the upper window. After filling himself with liquor, he staggered to the house. It was time to make her move. Lynn crept down the stairs intending to meet him in the study. When he kept going, she slid from behind the door and followed him in the shadows of the candlelit hallway. Ángel went up the stairs and entered one of the empty bedrooms. By the time she reached the room, Ángel had fallen across the bed, his legs dangling off the side. Lynn approached carefully. As she ran a hand up his thigh, his body stiffened and then relaxed when she touched the pants zipper.

"I-I'm sorry," he said.

Lynn placed a finger over his lips.

"Do you willingly make this offer?"

When he said yes, she laughed at how easy he had complied. Lynn removed his pants as his head rested on the pillow. Climbing on top, she began to rock as he hardened. Within about ten minutes, the exchange of blood and semen had been made. Afterward, Ángel rolled onto his side and fell asleep. She waited for the change in his breathing as he began to snore. Timing the moment, Lynn hurried to her room and retrieved *La Clairière* from inside the wall. She stood over Ángel with her head raised high above her head. When the glow from the candlelight sprang from the wall and danced on the ceiling, she lowered her arm.

Thump! The blade slammed into the mattress.

Ángel wailed as he leaped from the bed. Lynn laughed as she watched his naked body hop around the room. The hand she had hit dripped blood across the floor as he cursed and wailed. Between his drunkenness and the dancing candlelight, Ángel was confused about which way to run, so he continued to run in circles. When Zachary and Jerrold came to his aid, Lynn slipped away to her room and waited for whoever was brave enough to challenge *La Clairière*.

40

PATCHES OF MUD and fallen leaves clung to the sides of Lynn's face and hair. When a strong gust of wind rustled the leaves, the Spanish moss shivered on the tree limbs. For a second, she imagined being at her grandmother's cabin with the hanging shells and glass bottles in the front yard. When her leg knocked over Zachary's drum, she recoiled from the ground and scurried behind a tree. It was early dawn now, and thankfully, there was no sight or sound from Ángel and his gang. It was foolish of her to have fallen asleep, especially knowing Zachary and Jerrold had come out several times in the night searching for her. They never bothered checking under the short pier by the water's edge, or the bed of leaves she buried herself under. After the noise settled and the lights went out, she crawled from the soggy hide-out and tucked herself between the drum and the cypress tree; leaving Ángel's severed fingers buried in the mud. Now with the daylight, the unwanted houseguests would awake, and remember what she had done.

Stooping low to the ground, Lynn began to crawl down the bank; this time she planned to hide below the surface of the murky water, and if there were any wild animals or mammals around, they would have to move over. As she approached the water a large Egret snapped its bill several times until she stopped moving. While scanning the ground for something to throw, the back door opened. Lynn froze—and so did the person at the door. It was too late to hide.

"Consuelo, is that you?"

She turned around slowly, and to her relief, a uniformed officer stepped off the back porch. Lynn nodded as pieces of mud and leaves fell from her face. As she swiped the dirt from her clothes, she noticed the dried blood mixed in with the mud beneath her fingernails.

"Your mother sent us to fetch you. We searched the entire house earlier but gosh darn-it no one bothered to look back here." He shook his head, before spitting on the ground.

Lynn marked the place where his spittle landed just in case she needed to retrieve the specimen later.

"Did you catch Ángel—and the others? Good, I'll let my mama know they're gone…thank you." Lynn side-stepped the officer as she headed toward the house.

"Hold on there, you'll need to come down and give us a statement…" he paused when she wrinkled her nose. "About what happened on the ship, and the last time you saw your father?"

"Oh, that—couldn't we just go over everything here?" She brushed the strands of hair from her face.

The dallying officer looked down at her bare feet, and then at her muddy dress. When she remembered her fingernails, Lynn hid her hands behind her back.

"Well, that's not usually how we do things over here, but seeing as though you've had such a terrible welcoming committee, I'll make an exception," he said, and then winked.

The officer and his partner took Lynn's report on the front porch until the clear morning sky turned charcoal grey. A third officer stepped from the doorway after making a final inspection of the house and remarked about the approaching storm. When she asked about her father's body the elusive officers bid her goodbye.

"What about the car?" she asked.

The first officer stood near the station wagon, the other two entered their cruiser and started the engine.

"The bigger question is what to do with you," he huffed. "With what's going on between the U.S. and the Soviet Union it's amazing you made it this far, more likely you should—"

"But I'm staying here," said Lynn, anticipating his response.

"—better for you to get on back to where you came from, otherwise the Welfare Department will come for ya."

"My father brought me here to help with the family business, I have to stay."

"And how old are you again?"

She answered with her eyes, as her hips whipped back and forth like a feline's swirly tail. Lynn batted her eyelashes as the lawn shrunk between them. The officer cleared his throat and adjusted his collar as she came closer.

"If anyone comes around bothering you, make sure to give me a call."

Lynn watched as he fumbled with the door handle and got inside his car. After putting a safe distance between them, he wiped his forehead with a shaky hand as he started the car engine.

"Goodbye officer Bowles, I'll be in touch," said Lynn.

The car wheels spun and rolled out the driveway. After they were gone, she latched the gate and shut herself inside the house. The door to the study was opened so she entered there first. The officer's search turned up valuable information about the house and the hotel; both owned by her mother and father, which meant she had been gifted with a new life, complete with a source of income. Scouring through the closed drawers she found a lump of U.S. dollars and a stack of Cuban pesos.

"Why didn't you just pay them back?" she whispered.

She took the money and placed it inside the wall next to *La Clairière*. After securing the home and its contents, Lynn went to the telephone and dialed home.

"Yes, I'm fine, everyone's gone now," said Lynn.

"I'll book your flight soon as I'm able, money's tight now with your papa gone."

"Don't worry about it…did you know about dad's business here—the hotel?"

"Yes, we'll have to sell it, along with the house."

"I can manage things here, and send money home every month to help out?"

Lynn held her breath as she waited for a response. Rebecca went silent. It seemed even the wind stood still to consider the proposition. Lynn knew she was asking her mother to sacrifice a child, but she also knew her mother was a smart woman, who liked nice things. With the loss of her husband's income and his protection as a white man, their future was in grave jeopardy.

"If you knew someone there you can trust to help, like a guardian—maybe your father's business associate can help us," said Rebecca after a long dreadful silence.

Lynn touched her pocket where she had placed officer Bowles' card. After telling her mother she knew just the person, they ended the phone call. As she mulled over a plan, she decided it would be best to get rid of Ángel's fingers. Before she made it out of the backdoor, there was a knock at the front door. Lynn watched the shadow behind the glass pane, a small figure bounced up and down, then rapped on the door once again.

"Hi, I'm selling magazines to earn money for a school trip, could you help me out?" A shiny-faced girl about Lynn's age stuck her face in the door.

"My English is not good," said Lynn.

"Oh, what language do you speak?" The girl pushed her glasses up on her nose as she adjusted the stack of magazines in her hands.

"Spanish, and a little Haitian-Creole."

Lynn took the magazines from the girl's arms.

"Perfecto, mi nombre es Diane," she extended a hand. "My Papa is Black and my mama is from the Dominican Republic."

"Nice to meet you, would you mind helping me with a few things? I could pay for these," said Lynn.

After finding a resting place for the stack of magazines, the two unusual teens became friends with a handshake. They made a to-do list, in the most haphazardly way young people do; first, change all the door locks, and then go shopping for food and personal items. Later in the week, Lynn would remember to add English lessons and learn to drive to her list. Each day Diane would come straight from school and after her homework was complete, they cleaned the house before she oriented Lynn to the fine American cuisine of hamburgers, and frankfurters.

During their talks, Lynn discussed her regret over not being close to her siblings. Diane shared how she had the burden of being the oldest of seven children. When she brought up the topic of her Protestant faith, Lynn's breathing quieted. Overlooking her avoidant silence, Diane took her friend's hand and bent her head.

"What are you doing?"

Diane held her hand firmly and refused to let go.

"We should be praying for you, you're all alone in this big house and if someone finds out child welfare will come for you," said Diane.

She cocked her head to the side when Lynn snatched her hand away.

"Thanks, but I've already taken care of that."

Lynn squirmed in her seat as her friend tried to read her body language.

"Good—we should pray, just this one time together."

Lynn offered her hand slowly, her pulse quickened at the warmth of her friend's touch. After a few short words about the Lord Jesus, Diane said "Amen." Lynn quickly excused herself. Standing in the bathroom she dabbed at a tear in the corner of her eye.

"It had to be done, the deal was already made," she whispered to her somber reflection in the mirror.

When the tears dried on her face, she met Diane on the front porch. Lavender and purple hues chased away an orange sky, which Diane said was a signal to school-age children to return home for supper and family time.

"What do you plan to do here by yourself?" said Diane.

Lynn shrugged as she diverted her gaze to a salamander scurrying across the wood railing.

"Continue living and dealing with whatever comes next...my mama needs me to stay here and work so I can send money home to help out now that my papa is gone."

Diane touched her arm as she promised to return the next day. As she left, a crumpled napkin used to wipe her mouth fell to the ground. When she was gone, Lynn retrieved the stained tissue, and after wrapping the sample tightly in cellophane, she tucked it securely in the back of the refrigerator icebox.

41

Summer, 1951

LIKE THE REST of America, Louisiana was segregated by color and fear. Zachary and Jerrold had already schooled Lynn on the trauma and terror of the black-American experience, so she cringed when a bus ride was suggested, "just for fun." At Diane's giggling persistence, Lynn's frizzy auburn curls were pressed straight using a hot comb. And with a heavy dose of face powder, her mother's genes were subdued as the new Lynn was made-up to pass as white. Being a shade too dark to pass herself, Diane relished their secret with a devious grin as she skipped to the back of the bus.

At their stop, Lynn exited through the front and approached her friend who waited on the sidewalk.

"I can't do it," said Lynn.

The words weren't fully out of her mouth before her persuasive companion stormed off.

"There's no difference really, except the people in America are more honest about how they feel," said Lynn, as she ran to keep up.

"I'm only asking for one favor," said Diane, stopping momentarily to check the traffic on a side road.

When the street cleared, she kept her eyes on the ground like she had been taught to do in public.

"I know, and I'm sorry, but I—please wait!"

"One favor, that's all I'm asking for."

Diane held up one finger.

"I need that skirt, and they won't sell it to me—but you can pass," Diane whined, as she kicked the ground.

"You win, I'll do it this once, but please don't ever ask me to do this again." Lynn exhaled dramatically.

Diane's smile returned as she reached inside her handbag and retrieved her makeup bag. After reapplying the face powder on Lynn's cheeks and nose she reapplied the lipstick.

"It's like I said before, we play our roles," said Diane. "I'm like Dorothy Dandridge, sassy and troubled," she stuck out her chest. "And you are the sophisticated bombshell, you know, like Ann Sheridan in that movie, The Unfaithful— you're beautiful like she is, and with all this luscious red hair."

"But I would prefer to play the role of someone like Fredericka Washington or Josephine Baker, they wouldn't sell out their race for a poodle skirt."

Diane hid around the corner as Lynn entered the all-white boutique. After circling the floor, she pulled the skirt from the rack. When her handbag slipped from her shoulder, Lynn checked her surroundings. Two clerks helped a sobbing girl and her whining mother at the back of the store, and another clerk rang sales near the front door. Lynn removed a silk scarf from the stand, and after making her purchase the smiling clerk said, "come again soon!"

Withholding an urge to announce how they had just been tricked into selling to a colored girl, Lynn sucked her teeth at the confused clerk before retrieving her purchase. The second sales clerk approached, along with the mother and daughter. The girl who had gotten her way smiled; Lynn returned the gesture—to the girl only.

"I owe you big time for this," said Diane, when she saw Lynn come around the corner. She squeezed her friend's neck, but her expectant grin fell when she opened the bag.

"What is this?" She held the silk material in the air.

Lynn removed her purse while Diane's head was down, and retrieved the hidden skirt.

"What did you do?" Diane's mouth hung open.

"Why would I give money to someone who won't serve me properly—let's go, I know how you can repay the favor."

Diane was still explaining the difference between manipulating the system, versus stealing, when they exited the bus together from the rear. Lynn stopped in front of a modest two-story hotel, the fresh paint and windows barely smudged or weathered. Diane pointed to the neon sign underneath the Bayou Inn marquee which displayed the words, No Vacancy.

"Do you need a job?" said Lynn, as they approached the entrance. "I could use the help, and you do owe me a favor."

A woman held the door open for them as the two girls entered the lobby. Diane waited nervously as Lynn eyeballed the two women behind the counter. Joleen choked on her saliva when she noticed Lynn, as Raquel backed away and tried making a run for the front door. Diane blocked her path just before she could reach the door handle.

"W-we had nowhere else to go," said Joleen, with her hands raised in surrender.

"So you decided to take over my father's business?"

"I told her we shouldn't be here—If you let me go you'll never see my face again," said Raquel, cowering three feet away from her escape.

Diane shrugged when Lynn looked in her direction.

"You can stay, but you work for me now…and you," she pointed to Raquel. "You'll have to toughen up if you're going to stick around. You're not a hostage, but you don't ever want to cross me."

A thorough search of the building proved the hotel had zero occupants, besides Joleen and Raquel. Not only were there vacancies, but twenty elaborately decorated rooms were cleaned and waiting for guests. Lynn pulled Diane into the manager's office to go over the books.

"What have they been doing? The rooms are all empty."

"And look here…the rooms have names on them, and they've already paid according to this ledger."

It took them another hour to circle through the building, front door to the back entrance, floor to ceiling. Ten rooms per floor, five on each side of the hall. An additional room behind the manager's office, but no trace of other humans in sight. When they were convinced the guests were ghosts, Lynn moved to the front entrance and switched the neon sign to vacancy.

"Actually, there aren't any available rooms this evening, it's already Friday," said Raquel. "It's hard to explain, but—well, they do pay."

"I don't like this, it feels wrong," said Diane, reaching for her bag with the stolen skirt as she prepared to leave.

No sooner had the words left her mouth, than a car light shone through the window, then another, as the lot filled.

"Oh no, you can't leave me now. Remember the favor you owe me?" Lynn's mouth was still open as a swarm of people flooded the entrance.

They were the classiest black folks Lynn had ever seen in her life. The elegant women's hair had been pressed and rolled neatly into buoyant curls. As their expensive perfume thickened the air, the jewels draped around their necks and fingers sparkled under the lighting. The men wore fine suits and wing-tipped shoes. They each brandished plump leather wallets and sturdy pocket watches; all of them smiling and laughing as they waited for the good time to begin.

"Welcome to the Bayou Inn hotel, I'm the new owner, Terra-Lynn," she introduced herself to each patron.

Raquel and Joleen checked in the guests, falling easily into position with their new employer. Diane spoke with the female guests who had lingered outside to have a smoke. With careful prodding, she learned the Bayou Inn had a reputation as the place to go where you could "forget about your troubles," said the women with a side wink. The rooms were paid for in advance and the festivities never began until each room had been booked. None of the women dared repeat what exactly happened in the rooms, the only concern was if the new management would allow the business to continue under their secret terms. The guests would begin arriving on Thursday evening and stay until Sunday night. Most of the rooms were cleared by then, except for a few stragglers on each floor; those customers were charged a weekly rate.

After Lynn (who now called herself Terra-Lynn) learned that Joleen and Raquel sterilized and cleaned the rooms during the week, she suggested they should sleep in the manager's quarters, but they insisted on paying for their own room. With the new arrangement, they were both officially hired as live-in staff.

◦　　◦　　◦

By the time Terra-Lynn returned home the following Wednesday, she crashed on the sofa and did not move until the phone rang sometime after sunset.

"It's just me," said Diane, "I don't know about you but I'm dog tired, I overslept this morning and missed school. You should hire extra help for the weekends—and why aren't you using your real name?"

"Because it's my official American name, and it suits me better for now. Do you know anyone looking for work?"

"I'll ask around, but we need to find someone by Friday, my legs couldn't take another weekend working like that."

Terra-Lynn massaged her aching lower back. Not only was every muscle in her body throbbing from being on her feet for days, but she was nauseous and needed a decent meal. After the phone call, she went to the kitchen and stared at the groceries she and Diane had purchased and stocked the week prior. She had never learned to cook, her mother reminded her of the fact when she made the case for her return. Thankfully, she could boil rice and fry an egg, which she reasoned should keep her from starvation.

Months had gone by without any interference from the welfare office or any other government official; which she could only guess was the doing of Officer Bowles. He had come looking for her a few weeks ago. She stood stiffly behind the embroidered drapes, watching as he slid a note in the mail slot and retreated. She wanted to thank him for his kindness, but if he saw her now it would draw more concern. At night, Terra-Lynn would stand before a starry window and rub her growing belly. Speaking gently, she reminded herself of the spirit guardians terms to be given a lifetime servant. It would not be right to offer an innocent soul for her own, no matter what the benefit. She and the unborn child would bear the load together and would make themselves available whenever her spirit host required servitude.

In the early morning hours, Terra-Lynn heard the light tappings of her grandmother's drum. Before her eyes could open, her twitching feet craved the floor. She danced from her bed and throughout the house until her legs were flimsy like old rubber bands. Afterward, she ate her stale breakfast of white bread and fried eggs as she listened to the downpour of rain outside her window. When the sun pushed back the clouds, she would call for a ride to work, each day promising to learn to drive the station wagon still parked in the driveway. There was always a reason to put off the driving lessons, the same as learning to cook. One thing she never put off was calling home once a week, even if she failed to mention her condition.

"What's this name they call you now," said Zuellie.

"Terra-Lynn…it has a nice ring, don't you think?"

She had purposefully made fewer calls to her grandmother on account of her seeing eye and keen discernment.

"I always knew you were going to leave, and are you calling on your spirit guides for help as I taught you?"

"Yes, I know what to do," said Terra-Lynn, as she sighed and thought about Diane's insistence on praying to Jesus.

"I was hoping you would consider coming back home, at least for a visit before things get worse. Cuba is changing and there are talks of a revolution."

"That's why my papa wanted us to leave. It's lovely here, and there's enough room for us all."

"Even with the baby coming?" said Zuellie.

In the silence, Terra-Lynn imagined her grandmother's poppy eye's as they admired her enlarged belly.

"I gotta go, someone's at the door, I'll call again soon."

After peeping through the drapes, she opened the door.

"I bought food, do you like crawfish?" said Diane.

"I'm not sure, never had them."

Terra-Lynn frowned as she held a hand over her mouth.

"I should've asked before buying them, does the smell make you sick?" Diane withdrew the pan.

"No, it's not the food…it's the baby."

"Can you repeat that, what did you say about a baby?"

Diane followed Terra-Lynn into the kitchen as she went to get a drink of water from the faucet.

"I'm sure you've noticed, and in case you're wondering, the baby belongs to the man arrested for my father's murder."

Terra-Lynn smiled as Diane touched her stomach.

"You were raped? Are you giving it up for adoption?"

42

ON THE MORNING Terra-Lynn's baby lowered into the birthing position, she had just rolled over at the sound of her grandmother's drum. After her laboring contractions began, the imaginary cadence silenced in homage to the new life. The plan had seemed so simple up until that moment, but now with waves of agony rolling through her body, Terra-Lynn curled into a ball and prayed for help. When the contractions slowed enough for her to stand, she limped to the stairs and moved slowly down each step. There was a single knock at the door, that quickly became louder and more impatient.

"Help me!" She hollered between quick breaths.

"Lynn, is that you—are you okay?" said Diane, her voice muffled behind the stained glass.

Terra-Lynn used what seemed like her last ounce of strength to open the door. Diane could tell by her heavy breathing that the baby was ready to be born. Moving quickly, she sat her expecting friend on the sofa, then ran through the house to retrieve Terra-Lynn's shoes and purse. By the time she returned, Terra-Lynn was panting on the floor.

"I'm not going to make it." She clutched her stomach.

"You'll make it, but please stop pushing!"

Diane was focused on searching for the keys to the station wagon when she heard the loud grunt. The next moments seemed to happen in slow motion. She watched in shock as Terra-Lynn's bent knees locked in position and her body shook. With another push came water and blood. Another grunt and there was the baby covered in a pasty-brown substance and dangling from a pulsating cord.

"Call for an ambulance!" said Terra-Lynn, as she held the baby in her quivering arms.

When Diane snapped out of her shock, she went to the door which had been left open during the ordeal. From the porch she noticed a slow-moving vehicle, so she ran and hailed the driver to stop. The middle-aged couple was polite and wasted no time helping Terra-Lynn and the newborn into the backseat. Still holding the keys in her hand, a shaken Diane stood near the driveway watching as the car pulled away. She had never driven a car before, so when Diane and the monster of a vehicle jerked to a halt outside the St. Martin hospital in Breaux Bridge, she attributed her safe arrival to the rapid-fire prayers she had hurled to heaven while swerving down the road. By the time she located the appropriate room, Terra-Lynn was lying in a hospital bed. Her eyes opened when Diane entered the room.

"You named your baby Josephine Fredericka Lynn?" said Diane, after the Doctor left them alone.

"Yes, I named her after Josephine Baker and Fredericka Washington," said Lynn, through her cracked lips.

Diane raised the cup of water to her friend's mouth so she could drink. After a few sips, Terra-Lynn lowered her head and closed her eyes.

"But why so many names, couldn't you leave off Lynn?"

"We'll call her Josephine for short, but Lynn has to be a part of her name."

"Oh, that's right, the curse." Diane refrained from rolling her eyes. "Josephine Fredericka-Lynn it will be," she said as she squeezed her friend's hand.

The baby was quiet-natured and easy to console, which made her mother smile. Terra-Lynn had committed both their souls to a life of solitude together (never marrying or knowing love outside of each other), to fulfill her sacrificial obligation. Under no circumstances would she tell Diane or anyone else of her vow, but Terra-Lynn did thank the gods for her small companion; including her grandmother's *Bondye* from Haiti, and the *Orisha's* she'd served in Cuba, even her mother and Diane's Oneness God they called Jesus.

"At least she'll never have to struggle with her identity, as it's already been decided for her. And if anyone ever tries to come between us they'll have to deal with *La Clairière*."

"Who—who's that?"

Diane looked away from the swaddled baby in her arms.

"It's different here in America, and don't you think it's better to wait and see the child's temperament? Besides, she'll choose her path, outside the perimeters of racism and segregation, of course…are you considering going home?"

"Racism exists everywhere, America is just more open about how they feel. Besides, the social worker said my baby is a U.S. citizen so this is officially my home now."

"Social worker?" Diane's mouth widened. "What did they want, did you tell him anything?"

"She was nice, she's going to stop by the house after I'm discharged and check in on me and the baby."

Diane gently rocked the delightful newborn as she considered the situation. If they could give the appearance that Terra-Lynn and the baby were not alone, maybe child welfare would call off their dog aka the social worker.

"We'll have to hire a live-in nanny for the baby…and someone to clean and cook during the day, that way when the social worker comes—"

"I don't think it'll be necessary."

Terra-Lynn watched as her friend's concerned gaze grew more frantic by the second.

"Hand me the baby, she'll be all shook up like a milkshake by the time you're through with her." Terra-Lynn reached for the newborn.

"I'm sorry, but the truth of the matter is, you're a minor living alone with a new baby. I'm worried you'll draw the wrong attention."

In three months Terra-Lynn would turn 17, but for now, she was 16 years old, fresh off the boat as a foreigner without supervision or guidance. The hotel was doing well and bringing in a consistent cash flow. If she followed her friend's advice, the decision would mean sending less money home to her mother, but if Diane was correct, this would be a temporary situation and all would return to normal within a short time. Diane left the hospital after promising to have two trust-worthy individuals ready for work by the time she and the baby were discharged.

The woman Diane chose as a nanny was named Eugenia, who was an afro-wearing granny in her mid-sixties. She had been known for her fish fries, and other cajun plates sold off the back stoop of her home, so there was no need to hire a cook. Still, Diane wanted another person in the house, and running out of options at such short notice, Raquel was pulled from the hotel to act as housekeeper between the hours of 10 and 3 pm.

By the time the welfare office got around to sending an agent out the following week, Eugenia had made herself comfortable with the baby, and in the kitchen. The social worker, who was more impressed with the plantation-style home, gawked at the heavy wood-carved furnishings as Terra-Lynn gave her a tour of the rooms. Eugenia met them at the bottom of the stairs with a steamy wrapped plate, to which the amazed and speechless woman accepted. When she was gone, Raquel tossed the broom aside and fell on a side chair.

"Can I go get some sleep now?"

Between the hotel and Terra-Lynn's home, she had been working almost around the clock. With the threat past, Raquel was no longer needed around the house. Eugenia was given a door key and told her new working schedule would be 8:00 am to 4:30 pm, Monday through Friday. Diane took over managing the Bayou Inn with another person she said was a cousin. With the particulars settled, Terra-Lynn shut the rest of the world out, refusing to leave her home or property for any reason outside of an emergency. The whole first year of her daughter's life was spent in seclusion.

About 9 a.m. every morning, Eugenia would serve them breakfast in a room opposite Terra-Lynn's bedroom, which had been converted into a communal space for the mother and child. In the afternoon, she walked in the backyard along the Bayou's edge with her baby, until the water curved and trailed off through the Cypress trees. On the way back, she would stop at the spot where Ángels' severed fingers were buried, and thank her spirit guide for protection before returning to the house. When the weather permitted, she would sit on the shaded porch until the baby fell asleep.

Most days when the child slept, Terra-Lynn relished the alternating phone calls from her mother and grandmother. Each of their conversations brought more distressing news about the growing unrest in Cuba and a revolt that kept gaining momentum. Terra-Lynn warned her mother if she kept hesitating to join her in America, the window of a safe escape out of their country would soon close. For reasons unknown, the phone calls became sparingly and few.

"Well, it looks like it really is going to be just you and me kid," said Terra-Lynn to the sleeping child.

43

December 1955

TERRA-LYNN AND HER daughter spent four cozy years protected behind the walls of their expansive lair. Besides her mother, the only people little Josephine encountered were Eugenia and Diane. Eugenia shopped for their groceries and other household needs, and Diane's visits brought needed social interaction. Her conversations alternated between business updates and leisure, occasionally she would provide hilarious reenactments of the hotel's flamboyant guests. If not for the mail carrier who stopped at the mailbox each day at noon, or the groundskeeper who came twice a month, Josephine would've never seen a real male figure outside of the television set (which her mother tried desperately to shield her from).

Terra-Lynn was just as unimpressed with America's political climate as she had been with Cuba. It was not long after the Montgomery bus boycott ended in Alabama and each day brought more reports of violence, anger, and rage; beatings that led to lynchings and hangings were the worse. The "bad juju" (as Diane called it) seemed to be spreading everywhere and had finally caught up to Terra-Lynn. A match was lit, then a flame devoured the front end of the Bayou Inn, shattering the lobby window and charring the neon sign. The insurance policy would cover costs to replace furnishings and interior damages, but a remaining balance of $20,000 for the roof and structural damage was left.

Diane sulked on Terra-Lynn's sofa as Josephine was instructed to wait upstairs. After the child was out of earshot Diane suggested they solicit hotel guests for help.

"It's all my fault, I never checked the trash bins in the lobby before leaving."

Diane cupped her hands over her face.

"But what about the others, was there no one managing the front desk?"

"Everyone was asleep in their rooms until we reopened for lunch—you know how exhausting the weekends can be."

Diane sunk her head until the skeletal frame of her spine replaced her neck. Terra-Lynn turned her back to check for a small crouching shadow at the top of the stairs. When she heard the familiar sounds from Josephine's toy chest, she returned to her apologetic friend.

"I should have paid closer attention; before I left a woman was standing near the entrance wearing a scarf and large glasses."

As Terra-Lynn listened to her friend's whining, her mind continued to calculate the repairs. From what Diane shared of the hotel's guests, the men were nothing less than over-dressed gamblers and pimps; going to them for help would be opening the door for eventual mutiny. The decision was clear, and Terra-Lynn knew what had to be done. After she was able to usher her sorrowful friend out the door, Terra-Lynn sought her spirit host for answers. Believing to have received clear instructions, she placed the call.

• • •

The insurance adjuster met her on the front porch of her home the next afternoon. At first glance, he was a business-minded gentleman with a straightforward approach. There was a genuine concern expressed for the financial burden as he reminded her to be thankful that no one was hurt. Terra-Lynn was cautious with her words as she spoke with a floral Latin accent reserved for special occasions. If she could pull off her plans, the man behind the suit would expose his true nature by nightfall. After checking for silence from the sleeping child upstairs, she invited him inside.

"Could I offer you something to drink, coffee or tea?"

As he entered the home, Terra-Lynn cringed from the blustery weather nipping at her bare feet. Eugenia stuck her head out of the kitchen to scrutinize the agent, after the greeting, she returned to the simmering meatball stew. Terra-Lynn sat him in the front room, then left momentarily to retrieve his glass of water. She wasted no time with small talk. The repairs had to be covered in full—all of them. Casting a tempestuous smile in his direction, Terra-Lynn leaned close enough for him to catch the scent of her alluring body cream. He took less than a second to consider her options as he explained the impossibility of the request.

"Would you mind taking another look? There must be some kind of loophole in the fine print, there always is."

Her bare feet brushed against his pant leg as she took a seat and crossed her leg.

"No, I've had plenty of time to review the policy," he said, before moving to put distance between them on the sofa.

"Hmm, suppose you come back later, say about 10ish? We could read through the fine print together?"

The agent cleared his throat. As he reached for the glass some of the water splashed onto his lapel.

"Sure, I'll come back later and we'll review it together."

Terra-Lynn lifted on her toes and thanked him with a light kiss on the cheek. His pen and paper fell to the floor with a thump, where they were left in his rush to leave.

To pass the time until his return, she tired little Josephine out by running around the yard and then a long phone call to her granny in Cuba. After a warm bath, Josephine was ready for bed. When the time drew near, Terra-Lynn considered her plan as she chewed on her fingernails. The insurance adjuster arrived shortly after 10 pm with a bottle of wine in his hand. To thwart any plans of a quick escape, Terra-Lynn led him to a dimly lit room upstairs. After closing the door behind them, she sat him in a chair and poured a glass of wine.

"I was thinking—" he said.

Terra-Lynn held the glass to his mouth and gestured for him to sip. Each time he tried to speak, she offered him another drink, which he accepted thanks to his nerves. When his speech began to slur, she moved him to the bed. First, his polished shoes were untied and placed aside, then the freshly washed shirt and trousers were unbuttoned and removed. When she tied one of his wrists to the bedpost, he giggled from the wine and reached for her. Terra-Lynn kissed him once on the mouth before offering him another drink. They laughed together as she held the bottle for him to finish the last drop. When he passed out, she sat in a chair and waited. As she suspected, twenty minutes later he awoke in full panic.

"What's happening here, untie my hands!"

Terra-Lynn had positioned herself snugly alongside him just before he came to. When he tried to free himself, she wrapped her youthful legs around his body.

"Unh-unh, you must promise not to renege."

When he yelled for help, she left the room and returned wielding *La Clairière* high above her head. The blade sliced the air several times until he froze in fear.

"Please, my wife doesn't deserve this!"

She almost felt sorry for him when he whimpered, but there was no turning back now, she had needs and he had access to her solution.

"Does your wife know you like young colored girls?"

Terra-Lynn held up his identification and a photo of his wife and two small children. She watched as his will to fight surrendered under the reality of her plan. He would sign off on all the Bayou Inn's repairs, after which she would return his driver's license and photos to his place of business.

44

Summer, 1956

AFTER THE FIRE at the Bayou Inn, Diane left Louisiana to attend Shaw University in Raleigh, North Carolina. When she returned for summer break, her first stop was to locate her friend and little Josephine. Standing outside the restored hotel, she admired the new flashing marquee. Diane smiled at the elaborate new furnishings as she peered through the front window. She pushed on the door, but it was locked. As she turned to leave, two young girls who looked to be about fifteen and sixteen entered with a key.

"Excuse me, do you work here?" said Diane.

Both girls nodded. When she asked for the owner, they gave the time Terra-Lynn was expected. After thanking them, she hopped in a waiting car and sighed her relief as she neared the gate of the home in Cecilia. She entered and knocked on the front door.

"It's me, aren't you going to let me in?"

Terra-Lynn flung the door open to welcome her friend with a teary embrace. After the greeting, Diane reached for little Josephine who shirked away with a frown.

"Don't you remember me—auntie Diane?"

When Josephine hid behind her mother's hip, Terra-Lynn reached for the girl and led them into the front room.

"You stopped responding to my letters, is something wrong? I went to the hotel first—I like the renovations but your workers are a bit young, don't you think?"

"I don't see why it's a problem now, you remember how old we both were when I took over the place."

As Diane contemplated the argument, Eugenia appeared and announced that supper was ready. As platters of blackened fish with rice and beans were placed before them, Diane elected to put off her concerns for the moment. After finishing the meal, they retreated to the front porch so Josephine could have some playtime in the yard, but she remained at her mother's side. Diane began her conversation with the movement led by Dr. Martin Luther King, Jr., and other activists across the south.

"The world is changing for us, black children can now attend schools with whites. There's more work to be done, but at least our children have access to better education."

Diane stared at the interaction between mother and daughter as Terra-Lynn's attention remained on Josephine.

"And just in time for this little beauty to enter school. She's 5 years old now, right?"

Josephine pressed a butterfly kiss on her mother's forearm, and Terra-Lynn returned the gesture with a kiss on her forehead.

"Is my little one ready to leave her Mama all alone?"

"Nope, I'm here with you always," said Josephine.

To Diane, it appeared as if they had rehearsed the answer over a hundred times.

"She has a private tutor, that along with learning the family business should give her plenty enough education. I'm teaching her everything while she's young."

When it was time to leave, Diane waved goodbye to the two of them standing on the porch. Terra-Lynn and Josephine waved back.

"Next time you're in town I wouldn't mind another visit. And I promise to write back from now on."

Diane smiled as she closed the gate behind her.

*   *   *

May 1961

A Cuban revolution delayed plans for Rebecca's travels to America. Even if she were able to cross the ocean, the situation was not much better on the other side as the Ku Klux Klan had been seemingly trying to burn down everything tainted with negro blood in the deep south. Then a group of civil rights activists left Washington, DC by bus with the idea of testing the climate of the segregated south. When Terra-Lynn learned that the "freedom riders" journey ended in violence she decided it was best to keep *La Clairière* close at hand. Of course, Terra-Lynn and her daughter were safe, but the name she had embraced served as a daily reminder of the constant terror hiding in the shadows of every joyful moment.

For the most part, Terra-Lynn no longer lived in fear of Ángel's return, but she was ready if he ever thought about it. Life had proven thus far to be a constant stream of evil, so she pressed into the darkness, only stepping out of the shadows for the one ray of light she found in a now 10-year-old Josephine. It was during this time that the Bayou Inn's reputation grew as a flow of black entertainers traveled the music circuit throughout the south. Terra-Lynn had no choice but to keep Josephine away from the hotel until she could gain control over the new crowd.

Joleen and Raquel (who had remained loyal throughout the years) promised they had a handle on things, but Terra-

Lynn's gut intuition told her otherwise. Late one Saturday evening, she took the keys to the station wagon and sat behind the driver's seat. Ignoring the fact that she had never learned to drive, Terra-Lynn handled the situation as she did everything else in her 27 years of life—she acted on instinct. Thirty minutes later, Terra-Lynn arrived at the hotel and parked in the back of the building. Full of adrenaline from the wobbly car ride, she pulled the silk scarf over her head (the very one she had stolen from the boutique many years ago) and slid through the back entrance. When she was sure no one had noticed her, Terra-Lynn ducked into the manager's office and stood behind the door as she listened.

A group of young attractive girls waited behind the desk as Joleen took payment from a patron. After the transaction was complete, one of the girls was selected to accompany the guest. When she had seen enough, Terra-Lynn readjusted her headscarf and left out the back entrance. The following night she returned in the same manner, and again the next weekend. After gathering enough facts, Terra-Lynn was ready to make her move. Dressing in a flamingo pink evening gown, she placed a string of pearls around her neck and let her wild red hair fall down her back. Stopping to kiss her sleeping daughter first, she made her way down the stairs. At the door, she caught sight of her toes underneath her dress and had to run back upstairs to grab a pair of heels. When she entered the station wagon, she tossed *La Clairière* onto the passenger seat.

A pipe-smoking crowd of handsome men gawked at Terra-Lynn when she entered the front door of the Bayou Inn hotel. Mesmerized by her flowing hair and gown, none of them paid attention to the machete in her hand. Raquel noticed, and so had Joleen who left one guest's hands open as he waited for change. She passed through the group of young girls and looked them over carefully before instructing Joleen to send them one at a time into her office.

What she quickly learned, was that each of the girls had a tragic story. Whether abandoned at an early age, abused by a family member, or just about any other horrible situation had happened to them. After hearing each girl out, Terra-Lynn introduced herself as the owner of the Bayou Inn and their new employer. The last girl she met was the only one to challenge the new arrangement.

"I ain't scared of you and that silly thing you carry around—I work for no one but myself," she said, as she leaned forward to mirror Terra-Lynn's cold stare.

It happened so fast and was over before the girl could defend herself. In one motion Terra-Lynn had reached underneath her desk to produce *La Clairière* and brought it down swift as if she had cut a melon in half. The sassy girl froze at the sight of the crooked blade. With a swoosh of air, three fingers vanished. Terra-Lynn felt a release of her hidden rage as the girl sprung from her seat.

"MY FINGER, MY FINGER!"

The girl hopped around the room as she squeezed the bloody hand. When Joleen appeared in the doorway, Terra-Lynn instructed the girl to be driven to the emergency room.

"I can't—I have a warrant out for my arrest," said the girl, as she whimpered in Joleen's arms.

"I know a doctor who can treat her, he's one of our regulars," said Raquel, who had joined them.

After they were gone, Terra-Lynn surveyed the room behind the manager's office. With a touch here and there, another bed for Josephine, it could be cozy enough for them to sleep there as she managed the Bayou Inn.

45

1963

SOME OF THE guests were seasoned cons who could charm the pocket-watch off of a politician and sell it back to him for double the price. Mostly they were decorated and finely tailored blacks who earned their money from secret ventures. Terra-Lynn greeted her guests with a smile from behind the counter. Opting for a more mature look, she wore her hair pressed straight to accentuate the diamonds around her neck, and her body zipped tight into the flowing pink gown that concealed her bare feet. At her side was 12-year-old Josephine, who had been schooled on the likes of their patrons, and was known to openly scrutinized the girls.

During the transition from living alone with her mother to working and staying permanently at the hotel, Josephine had decided that words were exasperating, so she rarely spoke to others. When the need to speak was unavoidable, she could be toothy and sharp-tongued, especially to new arrivals who had heard the owner was known to employ young runaways.

"Turn around and go back home," were her usual remarks, as she pointed a commanding finger at the door.

Terra-Lynn liked when her daughter sassed the men, but she cringed when the girls were chased away. If a worker complained about "house rules," Josephine pointed to the exit sign, always with a cheeky side glance in her mother's direction. Later in their sleeping quarters, Terra-Lynn would remind her of their charge to care for the girls.

"Think of us as their guardians, we were sent here by the ancestors to care for them," said Terra-Lynn, as she turned her back to avoid seeing the rolling of eyes.

"I don't know what the ancestors told you, but what we're running is called a broth—"

"Hush, girl!"

Terra-Lynn shot a stern look at her daughter.

"Don't let the guests hear you saying things like that."

Josephine would say no more. The next day she ignored the girls, speaking only when unavoidable or until someone else's stray child made the mistake of seeking their help. To her disapproval, the female runaways kept coming, drawing in more elite men along with a few gangsters and musicians. The girls who were honest about their situation and openly discussed ways to get out of the business were the ones Josephine favored. These she greeted with a welcoming smile and would offer a fresh cup of coffee for comfort.

On one stormy evening, Raquel and Joleen were making cleaning rounds in between check-outs as Terra-Lynn checked in guests at the front counter. To make herself useful, Josephine handed out towels to drenched guests in the lobby. In one corner sat a girl with her face buried in a book. When Josephine nudged her, she reached for the towel without looking away from the page. As Josephine leaned to see what she was reading, a gust of damp air disrupted the warmth of the lobby. A boisterous young lady marched up to the desk and asked for a room.

"HEY!" said Josephine, before her mother could greet the guest.

"Go back to where you came from." She pointed to the settling door.

"It's okay, my sweet girl—mama can handle this one."

Terra-Lynn gritted through a fake smile. The guests stopped what they were doing as mother and daughter stared at each other. When Josephine stormed off and disappeared down a hallway, they returned to their conversations. The disruptive new girl reached over the counter to admire the diamonds around Terra-Lynn's neck. When she noticed the look on Terra-Lynn's face, she withdrew her hand and laughed nervously at the group of ogling men dressed in fine suits. When one bold man stepped forward and nodded, Terra-Lynn passed the girl a room key.

Several minutes later, Josephine returned with a rolling cart and began collecting the dampened towels.

"You sent her off, right?"

She watched her mother's smile fade as she turned away. Josephine left the cart and followed her into the office.

"Mama, I know things about them that you don't. They think I can't hear 'cause I don't talk much—but I hear it all."

"And you don't think I know things too? I'm running the show here, not them, or you."

Josephine watched as her mother slid the family relic from its hiding place and reached for a bottle of lemon oil. When Terra-Lynn pulled *La Clairière* from its new sheath and began rubbing the steel, Josephine stepped closer. There was nothing magical or special about the blade at all. In fact, her mother's coveted family relic was nothing more than some old backward tool.

"You wanna hold it? Go on, it'll be yours next." Terra-Lynn flashed a proud grin.

"No thank you—I should go check on things out front," said Josephine as she observed the way her mother began to whisper to the blade.

Later as she worked, Josephine contemplated her mother's mental state while preoccupying herself with receipts and ledger balances. After the files were updated, she eavesdropped on the remaining guests until the lobby cleared. Raquel dropped off room keys to the empty rooms before clocking out from her shift. Josephine nodded as she snatched tags from the wall to update the new vacancies. While her head was down, she heard the scampering of feet as the front door shook from the gusty wind. Seeing no one in the lobby, she left to check on her mother. As her hand reached for the doorknob, an angry man began swearing in the lobby. By the time she reached the front desk, Terra-Lynn met her there.

The irate man clutched his belt buckle, as the other hand beat down on the counter. As his face contorted to match the anger spilling from his lips, Terra-Lynn slid *La Clairière* from her back and stepped forward.

"M*en mwen se yon rezoud pwoblem!*" She said, the words rolling off her tongue like a seductive potion.

Josephine held her breath when she heard her mother's native language—and so did the man, who took a few steps back. Terra-Lynn lowered *La Clairiere* when he told them how the girl he was with (the same one Josephine warned her mother about), robbed him while he was asleep. Stealing from customers was a major violation. She had even spiked his drink (violation two), unaware of his status in the community as a local official (violation three). As he departed, Josephine saw the badge sticking out of his pocket. She frowned at her mother before leaving her alone at the desk.

Terra-Lynn picked up the telephone and asked to speak with someone. An hour later, the thieving girl returned and was escorted to the manager's office. Josephine slid in before the door closed behind them, crossing her arms over her chest when her mother asked her to leave. Mother and daughter stared each other down refusing to budge. When the girl reached inside her pocket their focus shifted.

"There's your cut, now can I go?" Several crumpled bills landed on the desk.

The bottom of Terra-Lynn's gown swept the floor as she crossed the room and began mumbling in her native language again. Josephine readied herself to save the girl's life.

"I know what I did was wrong, but I had good reasons, he put his hands on me—see?" As she pointed to her bruised cheek, she looked to Josephine for sympathy. When Terra-Lynn reached for the radio and turned the volume up as loud as it could go, Josephine lost her nerve and left the room.

"THE WHIRLWINDS OF REVOLT WILL CONTINUE TO SHAKE THE FOUNDATIONS OF OUR NATION…"

Josephine paused as the voice of the civil rights leader, Dr. Martin Luther King thundered through the speaker.

"BUT THERE IS SOMETHING THAT I MUST SAY TO MY PEOPLE…" He said.

Terra-Lynn faced the speaker as she listened.

"…WE MUST NOT BE GUILTY OF WRONGFUL DEEDS…"

Terra-Lynn's eyes shut as she allowed his words to douse her inner rage with refreshing water she hadn't known existed.

"WE MUST RISE TO THE MAJESTIC HEIGHTS OF MEETING PHYSICAL FORCE WITH SOUL FORCE…"

As he finished orating his dream, her hand withdrew from the blade underneath the desk. The powerful speech lasted for seventeen minutes, and when he finished speaking, the applause from the crowd who were present at the March on Washington protest was earth-shaking.

"This man almost persuades me to believe in humanity again," said Terra-Lynn.

Josephine exhaled when her mother's shoulders relaxed. The girl sat trembling in her seat unsure if her life had been spared or still in danger.

"Get out!" said Josephine. "And don't ever come back here again, you hear me?"

As the girl shuffled from her seat and hurried out of the office, Josephine shook her head. If she ever met the man on the radio, she would have to tell him how his speech had not only given hope to the nation but also saved a foolish girl's life and kept her mother out of jail—at least for one more day.

"I'm thinking about hiring a few bodyguards for us," said Terra-Lynn.

Josephine cut her eyes and sucked her teeth.

"No time for us to bicker about who's right or wrong. It doesn't look good to have me doing the dirty work, and it's getting to be too much keeping up with you and these other fast-tail girls around here." Terra-Lynn reached for the phone on her desk and began dialing.

"I don't want you ending up like these girls. You should be focusing on your education and going off to college someday, like Diane."

Josephine smiled as she imagined school and making friends with normal girls her age. Then she thought about her mother managing the hotel with a twitching hand holding an old rickety blade, ready to chop the ligaments off of anyone who crossed her up. On the surface, Terra-Lynn seemed fearless and terrifying at times, but she was also incredulously naïve and hyper-spiritual. If she left, who would keep an eye on her mother when she walked in her sleep or danced to silent drums all night long until she fell out from exhaustion?

There was also the awareness of the flickering darkness that lurked beneath her mother's eyes, just a glimmer of evil, but enough for Josephine to recognize it—and she had a bizarre obsession with fingers. Terra-Lynn hated when anyone pointed, which is why Josephine pointed whenever she was mad at her mother.

46

February 1964

SIX MONTHS AFTER she vowed to hire bodyguards, the positions were still unfilled. The process took longer than Terra-Lynn anticipated and much longer than Josephine cared to be bothered with. Most of the applicants had been more interested in pleasure than business, which became obvious once the interview ended and they lingered in the lobby to meet one of the girls. There was one applicant who showed promise of employability. An even-tempered man dressed in a tweed jacket and matching cap marched up to the front desk and introduced himself as Mr. Stackhouse. When Josephine escorted him to her mother's office, Terra-Lynn rose from her desk to greet him.

"You can call me Vernon," he said, as his thick mustache gave way to sturdy white teeth.

Vernon told them how he had lost his employment while traveling with a band after the singer was jailed for reasons he'd rather not disclose to a lady. He interviewed on a Monday and returned on Thursday for a trial run with the girls. After his orientation, Terra-Lynn left him with Josephine as she went to speak with a notable guest. When her mother was gone, Josephine couldn't resist smiling back at the man with pretty teeth.

"So, how do you like working in the hotel business?"

"It's not too bad, except for when—"

Josephine paused to acknowledge a young girl who had just entered the lobby. She blew a large bubble with her gum as she waited to be greeted.

"I need somewhere to sleep tonight, my mom's second cousin is in town and she needs my bed," said the girl as she sized up Mr. Stackhouse.

"The same excuse every week, as if we both don't know you'll be back next Thursday, Friday, and Saturday night."

Josephine turned to grab a room key.

"Here you go, same room as usual."

The key crossed the air between them and popped her in the nose, knocking the chewing gum out of her mouth. Mr. Stackhouse coughed into his cuffed hand to keep from laughing. After the disgraced girl left the counter, Mr. Stackhouse returned his attention to Josephine.

"Wouldn't you rather be in school?"

"I have a private instructor, and I'm passing all of my grades if it's any of your concern."

"But wouldn't you prefer to be in a school, doing whatever it is kids your age do?"

"What kind of things would that be?"

Josephine leaned on the counter, close enough to smell the musk of his cologne and cause her heart to skip. Mr. Stackhouse took a step back before he answered.

"Well, first off, they have best friends and they're probably at the cinema on weekends or listening to the jukebox while doing the mashed potato or the twist—do you know what that is?"

"Un-unh, seem like those kids are just as worthless as little Ms. Chewing Gum who came in here looking for a room." Josephine frowned.

Mr. Stackhouse shook his head and smiled. As she returned to her work, he took a seat and held a newspaper to his face. Every so often he would look over to monitor her interactions with guests. As the early muggy evening turned into a sticky hot night, Josephine removed her steamy glasses and pulled her hair into a bun. She had just sassed another worker when her mother appeared and summoned Vernon Stackhouse. Before leaving, he watched as Josephine tossed a room key at another girl's face. When he bypassed, she stuck her tongue out at him.

Terra-Lynn and Vernon were smiling at each other as she shuffled papers on her desk to find a writing pen. Neither of them noticed when Josephine entered the room. Her mother was saying something about the girl's work, and thanking him for taking on the job. That's when he pulled out his badge and identified himself as an undercover agent. Josephine watched her mother's hand as it moved underneath her desk. She froze when her eyes met her daughters, as did Mr. Stackhouse, who had just handed Terra-Lynn the court papers to shut down the Bayou Inn; effective immediately.

•   •   •

After the undercover agent gave orders to shut down the Bayou Inn, Josephine helped her mother empty the rooms of its guests. Terra-Lynn was the last person to leave the building, she paused to frown at a group of lingering men in the parking lot. Josephine watched from the sidewalk, her smile widened as two black officers stepped around her mother and crisscrossed the doors with a heavy chain lock. As they prepared to leave, Terra-Lynn motioned for Josephine to wait as she approached Mr. Stackhouse. While her back was turned, several squad cars pulled into the parking lot. Josephine's mouth gaped open as three high-chested white officers exited and began to survey the scene.

When Terra-Lynn overheard them ask for the owner, she waved for Josephine who quickly followed her to the station wagon parked in the back lot. As they drove away, Josephine watched the rearview mirror. It was not until the car pulled into the driveway of their home and Terra-Lynn closed the gate behind them that she was able to exhale. Once inside, her mother stood against the door holding her chest.

"I knew that girl was bad news," said Josephine.

Her lips poked out as she fell across the sofa.

"Now what do we do? You think they'll come here?"

"No-no, it wasn't the girl, there was a storm that night."

Terra-Lynn shook her finger in the air.

"This is the doing of a greater force and it's because I never repaid the debt I owe."

Terra-Lynn mumbled some inaudible words as she moved from the door. Josephine's brow squinted.

"Mama, sometimes you don't make any sense at all."

"These papers say I have a court date."

The documents swirled to the floor as Terra-Lynn kicked the wall with her bare feet.

"At least we still have our house, no one will bother us here, will they?"

Terra-Lynn observed the dust-free surroundings kept cleaned by Eugenia in their absence. Josephine expected to see a smile on her mother's face but instead, she was met with the flickering darkness beneath her mother's brown eyes.

"Keep the curtain drawn and the lights off, don't answer the door for anyone, you hear me?"

Josephine nodded as her mother left the room and went upstairs to place *La Clairière* back in the wall. After making herself a sandwich, Josephine went to her room and locked herself inside. Behind the door, she continued smiling until her puffy cheeks throbbed from the excitement. When she awoke the next morning, her face had stiffened from the grin that had remained throughout the night.

When Eugenia arrived for work she was surprised to find a smiling Josephine in the kitchen.

"It's so good to see you home, but you know I don't like anyone messing around with my pots and pans!"

After their embrace, Eugenia slid a frying pan from underneath the counter before moving to the refrigerator.

"I heard about what happened over to the hotel yesterday, how's your Ma handling the news?"

"I'm not sure, she's been locked in her room ever since."

Josephine placed her head down on the table.

"Well, I'm sure glad to have you back home. Maybe now your Ma will enroll you in school so you can meet some decent folks your own age."

*   *   *

During their first week home, Josephine spent her days helping around the house and in the kitchen. After Eugenia left for the day, Terra-Lynn would emerge from her room and drag herself to the backyard where she remained until the glow of morning. Depending on her mother's mood, in the evening they would sit together on the deck and count the first stars as they appeared in the night sky. When her mother's eyelids lowered and began to wrestle with her inner demons, Josephine faked a yawn before kissing her goodnight. Terra-Lynn reminded her to keep the lights off as she retreated inside.

As Josephine entered through the back door, she was startled by the candlelight halo that danced along the walls and illuminated the idols that had been placed on a corner table in the front room. In the morning, Eugenia would place a sheet over the table, but until then Josephine looked away and tried to ignore the eerie presence that touched the nape of her neck as she passed. After she had made it safely to the stairs, the phone rang on the hallway console. Staring at the idol-erected table, Josephine waited for any signs of movement besides the dancing flame. When she was sure none of them had come alive, she ran to answer the phone.

"I hate to call so late, but do you think your Ma will come to the phone?" said Raquel.

Josephine sucked her teeth as she put the caller on hold.

"The phones for you," she yelled out the backdoor.

After her mother took the phone, she crouched on the steps to eavesdrop on the conversation.

"I can't right now, and you know my Josie won't go for that—they'll have to lay low until this madness blows over."

When Terra-Lynn's shadow moved toward the stairs, Josephine pressed her body flat against the wall.

"Meet me at the back entrance, and make sure nobody sees you," said Terra-Lynn in a whisper.

The phone clicked on the hook as Josephine tiptoed up the stairs. After closing her door, she listened to her mother's movements as she dressed in the room down the hall. When footsteps approached her door, Josephine stubbed her toe on the bed frame while running to get in the bed. She had to bite her lip to keep from crying.

"I know you're up," said Terra-Lynn.

She entered the room and sat on the bed. When Josephine pretended to be asleep, she placed a hand on her daughter's head to remove the blanket.

"It may seem as if I'm choosing them over you, but I owe a debt, and if it's not paid…I'll be back before morning."

Josephine knew her mother wouldn't return before she awoke, because Josephine never went to sleep that night. She had seen *La Clairière* swinging from her mother's side when she left, which could only lead to more trouble. After she was alone, Josephine blew out all the candles and covered her mother's alter with a sheet. Then she checked the locks on all the doors, even the side entrance which was never used, and waited in the family room upstairs to watch for approaching headlights in the driveway.

By morning, a swollen gray sky covered the home as thunder cracked somewhere above the clouds. When the front gate opened, Josephine watched the old station wagon as it came to a halt in the driveway. After her mother slid from behind the wheel, she ran to her room, this time mindful of the bed frame, and covered herself with the blanket. Terra-Lynn's steps were quiet and delicate as she entered the house and went straight to the bathroom. The sound of running water disrupted the silence, and as she entered the bathtub, Terra-Lynn's angry chant seeped through the closed doors and reached Josephine's ears. When she finished bathing, Terra-Lynn went to her room and shut the door. The mattress squished as her mother fell into the bed.

Heavy rain and winds surrounded the home as Terra-Lynn slept through the morning. Josephine watched the ticking clock until Eugenia arrived sometime around 11 am when the storm slowed. After giving Josephine a soggy greeting, she looked to the corner table and rolled her eyes.

"Those things should be in a more discrete setting."

"Yeah, like the basement or attic, any place where that thing can't stare at me," said Josephine as she pointed to one image representing the goddess Yemaya.

After their conversation, Josephine went to check on her mother. Terra-Lynn's back was turned away from the door and her face was covered with the bedspread. As Josephine entered the room, her foot kicked one of the polymita shells placed around the floor for protection. When she bent to look for the misplaced shell, her eye caught sight of several drops of blood that trailed to a plate near the empty fireplace. Several dry bones were placed neatly on the blood-stained plate. Josephine watched for the rise and fall of her mother's body before backing out of the room.

The trash in the kitchen was empty, and so was the larger bin to the left of the backdoor. Finding no trace of a dead animal or anything else inside their home, Josephine searched by the deck and then around the muddy swamp. As the stormy wind picked up, she heard a clinking sound above her head. Colorful objects had been strung through the limbs of the tree where her mother liked to sit with her drum. When she reached to touch one of the pretty shells, the sky cracked open as dark clouds poured down more rain. By the time Josephine reached the back porch, Eugenia handed her a dry towel and ordered for her muddy shoes to be removed. Josephine shivered from the cold rain.

"Have you looked in my Mama's room?"

"I don't know what I see half the time, but it sure ain't wise to leave all that stuff lying around, especially while an investigation is going on."

Eugenia sucked her teeth before returning to the stove. As the smell of jambalaya and cornbread filled the air, Terra-Lynn emerged from her room. When Eugenia blessed the food before serving them, Josephine and Terra-Lynn imitated her bowed head and folded hands.

"I'll have to leave before the storm gets worse, but I want you two to keep your head up, it'll all blow over soon enough," said Eugenia.

As she was preparing to leave, someone knocked at the front door. Eugenia left the kitchen and returned in seconds with a hand over her mouth.

"There's an officer and a social worker here," she whispered. "What should we do?"

47

April 1964

EUGENIA CREATED A diversion at the front door as Terra-Lynn led her daughter upstairs. Josephine poked out her lips and frowned when her mother nudged her toward the attic. As the social worker said goodbye to Eugenia who hurried to leave, Terra-Lynn pushed Josephine into her bedroom instead. As the door closed, she went downstairs. When she was sure her mother had gone, Josephine tiptoed from her room and down the stairs. From the window in the study, she was able to spy on the visitors standing on the front porch. An overweight officer stood with his hands on his hips as his stomach threatened the buttons on his shirt. He shrugged at his associate, a middle-aged black woman wearing a business suit. They exchanged a few words before she stepped forward and rattled the screen door with her fist.

After the second knock, Terra-Lynn stepped from around the corner. It wasn't until the door was opened that she noticed Josephine sitting on the sofa. Her eyes glitched as she looked from the stranger to her daughter. After making eye contact with Terra-Lynn, the officer returned to his car.

"Aren't you coming in with me?"

"I'll wait out here, good day to you ma'am," he said, tipping his cap at Terra-Lynn.

Officer Boyles had aged and gained a considerable amount of weight, but his concern for the young displaced Cubana had not changed throughout the years. She acknowledged him with a head nod, then opened the door for the social worker who introduced herself as Mrs. Adeline.

"I've read over your file and let me first start by saying how sorry I am for your troubles."

Mrs. Adelinehe extended a rather masculine hand, which Terra-Lynn rejected as she gestured for the woman to enter.

"Perhaps we should speak in private," said Mrs. Adeline.

Both women turned their attention to Josephine who was now sitting crossed-leg and defiant in her seat.

"I told you to stay in your room," said Terra-Lynn through a fake smile.

When her mother nodded toward the stairs, Josephine poked out her lips. As she left the room, she turned to observe the woman's demeanor and when their attention was diverted she ducked into the study to hide.

"The department's only concern is your daughter's education. If she were enrolled in school, like all the other children her age, I'm sure that would make—"

She stopped talking when Terra-Lynn went to the corner table and removed the sheet. Mrs. Adeline gasped when one of the candles fell against a clay pot and disrupted a pile of colorful polymita shells.

"Oh my—what's that one called?"

She pointed to the image that resembled a robust black woman with a protruding belly.

"She's the one that gave me my Josie, and the other girls I've been sent here to watch over."

Josephine cringed in the other room as she thought about making a run for the backdoor. When she peered into the hallway, she watched as Mrs. Adeline's strong hand rapidly moved across a notepad as she took notes.

"For heaven's sake, Ms. Machado—"

"Machete!" said Terra-Lynn, her back still turned.

"Excuse me? Your birth name is Consuelo Lynnette Machado, correct?"

Josephine could see her mother's mouth moving as she whispered a prayer to the goddess. Josephine looked around the room before moving to hide underneath the wooden desk. In the other room, Mrs. Adeline put her pad and pen away as she prepared to leave.

"Will you at least consider putting the idols out of sight until the investigation is closed?"

"Today you're a lucky one," said Terra-Lynn, as she stepped away from the table and took the social worker gently by the elbow. "You weren't chosen because the offering must be a man."

At the front door, the two women searched for the appropriate parting words.

"Perhaps I could come back another time, here's my card should you—"

When the door shut abruptly, Josephine jumped causing her head to hit the desk. By the time she made it to the door, Terra-Lynn was marching down the hallway.

"What's wrong, are you hearing the drums again?"

"You have to learn quick, I can't put you in school until you learn how to call on the ancestors."

Josephine sighed as she watched the two cars drive off.

• • •

October 1964

Josephine watched as her tutor left the porch and hiked across the lawn to her car. After starting the engine, she waved goodbye.

"We call him Twitch, on account of his Tic's disease, but don't let that worry you none, he's a bright kid and real easy to get along with—besides he's family."

Josephine wiped a tear from the corner of her eye. How could she not be worried, the woman who'd tutored her since the age of 5 was backing out the driveway with a packed car bound for Chicago, and her mother had possibly become a vampire. The only way to know when Terra-Lynn had returned was by the mud prints tracked from the front door to the back, sometimes there would be blood streaks on the banister and the knob of her bedroom door.

Josephine went to her room to prepare for the meeting with Twitch. It wasn't until she was standing before the mirror deciding on an appropriate outfit that she remembered her mother's cardinal rule.

"Ma, are you awake?"

The door creaked as Josephine watched the rise and fall of her mother's body. She approached slowly and seeing the thin pool of saliva in the corners of her mother's partially opened mouth, she turned to leave the room. A few seconds later, Josephine returned with a washbowl and rag.

"We're having company today," said Josephine.

She placed the damp rag on her mother's face and neck. The stubborn dirt clung to her skin, forming oily patches in the crevices of her bent neck. That's when Josephine noticed the strand of beads in place of her diamond necklace.

"He's not really a man, per se, but if you insist on the rule of no men in the house, I'll have to take my school lessons on the hot porch."

Josephine watched for her mother's reaction as she wiped smudges from her forehead. Terra-Lynn reached over and touched her daughter's wet hands. She managed half of a smile before turning her back and within seconds she began to snore. Only God knew what she had been up to in the late hours of the night. Making sure the girls from the hotel were safe was one thing, but the dirty fingernails and feet were telltale signs of her mother's superstitious activities.

After dumping the soiled water down the drain, Josephine took a moment to freshen up before her tutor arrived. She blushed at her reflection in the mirror as a nervous smile spread across her face. Passing an unstable hand over two thick pony-tails, she continued practicing different greetings. When she felt somewhat confident, Josephine picked up her schoolbooks. The doorbell rang while she was in the kitchen preparing drinks and snacks. Before opening the front door, Josephine checked herself in the hall mirror. A lanky young man with a reluctant grin pushed his glasses onto the bridge of his nose before introducing himself, prompting Josephine to do the same.

"Hi, I'm Twitch, my cousin sent me over—let me get that for you."

Josephine blushed when his extended hand took the tray. As he moved, she observed the ripple of his arm muscles and the way his long back curved as he placed the tray on the patio table. From her quick observation, there was nothing twitchy about her new tutor besides the flex of his biceps.

"I was expecting someone else."

"Sorry about that, childhood nicknames are hard to shake around here. You can call me Raymond if you prefer?"

He waited for Josephine's response who had remained gaping near the screen door.

"And how old are you?" She managed to ask.

"I will graduate high school next year, I'm a member of the national honor society and top of my class. I know my cousin has been with you for a long time but she's leaving you in good hands."

Josephine nodded. Feeling relaxed from their introductions she stepped onto the porch and sat down on one of the patio chairs.

"It'll be like you're getting a younger version of her, except I'm a guy and she's a woman. Oh, and I wear glasses, but so do you."

Josephine pretended to look away when he tapped a fist to his mouth to keep from babbling. The two of them sat quietly for several minutes, allowing the tweeting birds and croaking toads to memorialize the moment of their first encounter. Josephine sighed when she realized the absence of stomach flutters that had been present during her talk with Mr. Stackhouse.

"I have tutored others before, and I've even helped two students with entrance exams, one's at Howard University and the other's at Tuskegee, where I plan to apply—I'll pass on the sugar, it makes me hyper."

Josephine handed him a glass of tea but held back the sugar cookies. After finishing his drink, Twitch seemed to breathe easier as his speech calmed. He removed the pencil from behind his ear as he bent to write in a notebook.

"Math is my favorite subject."

While his head was down, she checked to see if there was a ring around his shirt collar or stains on his converse shoes, both were clean.

"See here, a negative and a negative makes a positive."

"What a relief," said Josephine.

"Excuse me?" He blinked twice.

"I meant, that's what I got too."

The front door swung open as a bug-eyed and shaken Terra-Lynn emerged from the house.

"WHO ARE YOU? Josie, get in the house!"

Josephine's glasses fell to the ground, as Terra-Lynn pulled her by the arm and shoved her inside. On the other side of the closed door, she listened to Twitch's trembling voice as he explained himself. When his voice cracked and he began to plead for mercy, Josephine opened the door. To her astonishment, Terra-Lynn marched him into the house as she held a knife out.

"I'll slice him down like a cane stalk if he tries to run!"

Twitch whimpered when his back encountered the wall. While his hands were in the air, she reached for the telephone and began dialing the number he wrote down on a piece of paper. After the caller confirmed his story, the knife lowered from his throat.

"Why would you send someone here without my permission—especially a man?" She yelled into the receiver before slamming it back down.

"If my Josie is okay with you, then we'll try you out but come back tomorrow."

Twitch fixed the glasses on his face and thanked her from the doorway. Josephine watched his shadow as he hurried down the walkway and out the front gate.

"Why would you open the door for a stranger? You know what I've told you about opening the door, especially for a man!" Terra-Lynn's shoulders relaxed as she put the knife back on the rack in the kitchen.

"What does it matter, you'll chase him away like you do every other man...now who's gonna tutor me?"

"Because men are too unpredictable, you see what that fine Mr. Stackhouse did to us...I'm wasting time on damage control instead of taking care of you and the girls."

When her mother's back was turned, Josephine took the torn paper with Twitch's phone number from the table and slid it into her pocket.

48

May 1965

THE STORMY SEASON began with howling winds and what Josephine referred to as the heaviest tears from heaven she'd ever seen. The rain fell the hardest during the day, causing the swamp water in the bayou to rise and claim new territory in the yard. At night, the cypress and oak trees cracked under the pressure and made the ghastliest noise as they surrendered to the force of nature; and as the sky poured out its fury, Terra-Lynn's hunger for retribution came alive. In the evenings, after they ate dinner together, Josephine took a warm bath before bed, as Terra-Lynn prepared to leave. Dressed in one of her most provocative gowns, her beautiful yet bizarre mother embraced the darkness with the battered family relic at her side. When Josephine heard the front door close she ran to the window to watch as lightning from the sky illuminated her mother's figure. From her viewpoint, it appeared as if Terra-Lynn floated across the lawn before entering the car.

In the morning, Josephine awoke on the sofa where she had fallen asleep waiting for her mother's return. Moving quickly to the window, she was surprised to find the station wagon parked in the same position as if it had never left.

Josephine scratched her head and marveled at how her mother was able to reenter the house without a sound. Each night was the same routine; she left around 10 p.m. to sneak the girls into the back entrance of the hotel, and upon her return, she slept until noon every day. After waking, she took long baths in the afternoon, then spent time down by the bayou with her drum and the empty bottles swinging in trees above her head. When Eugenia left, they ate together, and the night repeated itself.

Josephine accepted things for what they were, and she was elated to be free from the business at the Bayou Inn. Then came the eeriest twelve days that sent several edgy men to the emergency room with missing fingertips. The story first broke on the evening news, the same night Josephine had invited her tutor over for a rather late session. It was a Tuesday evening, and a little more than an hour ago Twitch had been waiting in the hedges near the driveway (just as his young pupil had instructed the day before). Had it been on a Monday, Wednesday, or Friday afternoon, he would have an excuse for the visit, but on a Tuesday night was gambling with his life. Josephine was persuasive with a blushing smile, even now with him sitting beside her - much closer than he would have dared if Terra-Lynn were home.

The grainy television picture glitched as the storm continued to ravage surrounding tree-tops and other stationary objects. He relaxed into the seat with one arm on the headrest as he read from a list of college choices.

"Have you talked to your mother yet?"

"No, she's so obsessed with the hotel, we barely see each other…besides, I'm still short on credits, it'll take years before I'm eligible to graduate."

Josephine shrugged.

"Yes, but with your grades and brains you could get into any college that'll take coloreds—shoot, even some of those uppity Universities would be foolish not to accept you."

As the howling wind increased, Josephine found she had inched close enough where his pant leg brushed lightly against her own. When he suggested they light the fireplace, she agreed. After the fire was going, he noticed the book she had placed between them on the sofa.

"Just so everything looks proper, I wouldn't want to send my mother in an uproar—you do remember how she carried on with you that first time?"

Twitch nodded as he took another peek out the front window. If there were headlights, the plan was for him to run out the back door and hop the fence.

"You seem tense, I'll get us something to drink."

When Josephine returned with two cups and a bottle, his neck was still turned toward the window.

"I don't think that's a good idea," he said.

But Josephine had already opened the bottle and began to fill their cups. The drink helped them to forget about the raging storm and the threat of Terra-Lynn. Before long they were deep in a conversation about President Lyndon B. Johnson's speech detailing his plan to end racial injustice.

"Yeah, but there's still more strides to be made, racism seeps into the fiber of our nation like a stain on a mattress, after a good sponging you can't see it on the surface, but it's still there," said Twitch.

"Why so pessimistic? Change starts small, but eventually it gains momentum and we mustn't overlook the many accomplishments of Dr. King and the civil rights movement."

"Turn on the news, you tell me how far we've come. A black man and a white woman are still prohibited from cohabitating. God help them if they think to marry."

At his insistence, Josephine turned the television volume up. A hospital spokesperson gave an update on the bizarre case of the first man with missing fingertips. The details were rather vague, as the confused victim gave a loose description of a shadowy assailant. When the reporter switched to the weather forecast, Josephine thought of her mother's secret nighttime activities. Terra-Lynn had become so distant, almost avoiding her on purpose, as if she needed to shield her daughter from the darkness that freely emerged.

"And on that note, I should take my leave," said Twitch.

Their goodbye was an awkward hug before she bid him farewell, but not before they each checked the driveway for approaching headlights. After he had gone, Josephine went upstairs and entered her mother's room. Searching in the darkness, she reached inside the chimney flute for what she knew would be missing.

The next morning she awoke to find her mother soaking in a steamy hot bath. When Terra-Lynn noticed her daughter standing in the doorway, she mumbled something about washing away the past.

"It's about time we put the investigation behind us and get on with our lives," said Terra-Lynn.

"I would love for things to be normal again, the way it was before the hotel changed us."

Terra-Lynn closed her eyes and sunk further under the water, but not before Josephine noticed the flicker of anger in her mother's demeanor at the mention of the hotel. When the phone rang downstairs, Josephine left to answer the call.

"Eugenia can't make it over today, I'll make us breakfast," she said, from the bottom of the stairs.

After an hour, Josephine returned with a tray of food and placed it at her mother's night table. She found her mother still soaking in a tepid cloudy bath.

"Keep it warm in the oven for me, please," she said, before reaching to refill the tub with hot water.

Two hours later, Terra-Lynn's old friend Diane knocked at the front door. After Josephine gave the message that her mother was unable to come down, she handed her two pamphlets on the Azusa Street Revival and left. As Josephine began to read, she was immediately drawn to the story of

William J. Seymour and decided to write a report on the Pentecostalism movement. When she went back upstairs, Terra-Lynn drained the tub and entered her room.

"Diane left these, it's about her new religion."

Terra-Lynn stood in the doorway and smiled at her daughter, who had spread the pamphlets and papers on the desk as she wrote in the family room.

"You remind me of my mama and twin brother, they're both smart…I was cursed with my Pa's good looks and my granny Zuellie's rage."

Terra-Lynn turned her back when their eyes met. The floor creaked as she moved across the hallway and tiptoed down the stairs. Josephine listened as the back door opened and after several moments, the familiar sound of her mother's drum began a guttural rhythm that made the charms in the cypress tree clank together. She moved to the window at the end of the hallway and watched. Terra-Lynn's eyes were closed and she had the most peaceful expression on her face. She continued to beat on the drums until the palm of her hands ached and turned red. Josephine watched as her mother left the drum and began dancing - around and around - in circles. When the phone rang, Josephine held the wall for balance as she ran down the stairs to answer the call.

"GRANNY'S ON THE PHONE!"

Terra-Lynn stopped spinning at the sound of her voice and stared into the bayou.

"I need to fix this mess first, the *mambo* will understand."

"Maybe you should come inside and lie down for a little bit? You haven't been getting much rest lately."

Terra-Lynn turned around to face her daughter.

"I can't, not until this is settled, then we can move forward. It's almost over though."

Terra-Lynn approached her daughter and stroked her face, then kissed the smudge left behind on Josephine's cheek. Josephine followed behind her mother as she went inside and hung up the receiver without saying goodbye. Afterward, she lay across the living room sofa, and within seconds, fell into a deep sleep. Josephine moved quietly when Twitch arrived at 3 o'clock for her school lesson. She stopped him from taking a seat on the patio chair and whispered how they should meet later that night. When he protested, Josephine pointed to her sleeping mother. Twitch's shoulders were hunched forward as he shook his head no.

"She said not to wake her, so you'll have to come later, please? I'm a hostage here, I have no one else besides you."

As he left through the gate with his head down, she prayed he would be brave enough to return as promised. Hours later, like clockwork, Terra-Lynn awoke when it was time for dinner. By 9 p.m., she removed the hair rollers from her head, stepped into her gown, and spritzed her favorite fragrance behind each ear. Twenty minutes after the station wagon left the driveway, there was a knock on the front door. Soaked from the rain, Twitch shivered in the doorway as he explained his worry about her being left alone on a dark stormy night. After removing his wet jacket and shoes, they sat by the fireplace sipping tea and nibbling on grilled cheese sandwiches.

Their time together was innocent as he told tales of the townspeople she would never meet. Josephine shared several of her own stories of the runaway girls who worked at the Bayou Inn.

"Have you heard there was another man with missing fingers?" said Twitch, just as he prepared to leave.

Josephine nodded.

"I'm more worried about the situation in Cuba. If things don't improve, I may never meet my grandmother."

Her diversion was intentional as she calculated the days of the missing family relic and the strange occurrences of dismembered men.

49

JOSEPHINE MAY NOT have ever caught her mother returning in the night but quickly learned to clock her movements in other ways. After Terra-Lynn awoke at noon, she would always soak her secrets in a tub of hot water until the unforgiving pipes ran cold. For the third day in a row, Josephine slipped into her mother's room and stuck her hand inside the crack in the firebox. Feeling nothing more than heaps of ash and air, she stretched her hand deeper into the hole, but there was still no sign of *La Clairière*. Chewing on her bottom lip, she made a quick check underneath her mother's bed and closet. *La clairière* had gone missing.

Josephine tiptoed into the hallway and back to her room. Standing before her bedroom window, she watched the falling rain and the swirling winds as it played ring-around-the-Rosie with the tousled leaves and debris. She looked to the place where the receding water had reached during the peak of the storm and wondered if the family relic had been buried there in the mud. Before she could make a move for the stairs, her mother opened the bathroom door.

"There's my sweet girl, could you make us breakfast?" Terra-Lynn forced a weak smile.

"We both know you won't eat, besides Eugenia's here."

"Oh, in that case, I'll be down in a little bit."

"And then you'll go straight outside to play with your silly drum—if you don't have time now then maybe we can talk tonight when I go with you to the Bayou Inn."

"Alright, give me a moment to get dressed first."

Terra-Lynn sucked her teeth as she adjusted her towel. Josephine stepped aside and then followed her mother into the bedroom.

"I've decided it's time I went to public school and even apply to college after that."

As Terra-Lynn reached for her clothes, her eyes scanned the floor and then rested near the wall where *La Clairière* should have been.

"It's time I met some friends and did what normal girls my age do, and with you running around town half-crazy who knows what'll happen to me if they take you away."

"What about our business? No one can keep the girls in line better than you, we were born for this."

Josephine searched for the right words as her mother sat down and began brushing the frizz from her tangled hair. When she turned to leave, Terra-Lynn called after her.

"I know you don't understand what I'm doing now, but in time you will—Please, just trust me."

Josephine nodded. She stood still when her mother approached and reached for her. In the few moments of their embrace, she was reminded of the years spent alone - just the two of them – and how happy they had been then. It would be nice to have that mother again. Maybe Terra-Lynn was right, if the threat to their livelihood was resolved they could at least get back to business as usual; and *La Clairière* could return to its rightful place, hidden out of sight where it could do no harm.

•　•　•

The fourth day of the storm brought the strongest winds that shook the roof and rumbled the ground that held tree roots in place. That day, Terra-Lynn skipped her usual bath and slept all the way till evening. And just when Josephine thought she would have to cancel her late tutoring session with Twitch, the sound of running water filled the tub. When Terra-Lynn left the bathroom, Josephine was waiting.

"You're going out in this weather?"

Terra-Lynn followed the direction of her finger as her daughter pointed to the window.

"The girls need a warm place to stay, and we almost got caught last night, so I can't have you there yet."

"Okay, suit yourself," said Josephine as she left the hallway and went into her bedroom.

"You can't go with me, not tonight!"

Terra-Lynn rushed into her room, where she dressed much quicker than she preferred, leaving several hair rollers in her hair as she fled from the house. From the upstairs window, Josephine watched as the old station wagon pulled out the gate, and when the headlights were out of sight she ran to the telephone.

"You can come over now...don't tell me you're afraid of a little wind...ok, let's agree it's more like a hurricane, but are you still coming?"

An hour later, Twitch stood on the porch as he explained the fallen trees and the flooded roads he had to drive around to get to her house. When Josephine opened the screen door he shook his head. She shivered from the damp winds as he stood on the porch and continued the dramatic tale of his drive. When a flash of lightning caused them to jump, he reached for the door and followed her inside.

"Maybe a little of your mother's private stock will help?"

Josephine rolled her eyes as she left to get the drink. When she returned, his knobby fingers reached for the glass.

"Do you understand how dangerous it is for me to be here at night?" He said, as his trembling hands held the glass.

"If we get caught I'll say I called you because I was scared, does that make you feel better?"

Twitch held the drink to his lips but stopped when he looked at his hands.

"What's wrong with you?" she said.

He chuckled nervously.

"What if she chops off my fingers or something worse, like those other men showing up at the emergency room."

"What are you saying? Do you think my mother is responsible—"

"No, no, it's just a stupid rumor—nothing really, but some folks around town are spreading stories about that billhook machete your mother carries."

"Billhook what?"

"It's bound to draw attention, the tip curves like this..."

Twitch stood with his arm bent at an awkward angle.

"Hard to find a blade like that around here."

After his demonstration, he moved to the front door.

"I should get going, the roads are so bad your mother is bound to return soon."

Josephine followed him onto the porch, and when he went for the stairs she continued with him down the walkway. At the front gate, he pointed in the direction of a large oak tree where the nose of his car was barely noticeable in the shadows.

"You should get back inside before you catch a cold."

Josephine followed his eyes as they rested on her flimsy shirt. When his back turned to unlatch the gate, she lifted on her toes and planted the gentlest kiss on his jawbone. Before he could react, she ran to the house. Closing the door behind her, Josephine braced herself against the wall and waited for her heart to stop racing. When her breathing returned to normal, she looked out the front door and was surprised to see Twitch still standing near the gate. With a hand touching his cheek, he mouthed the words, "see you tomorrow," as he disappeared through the gate and into the stormy night.

•   •   •

On the fifth day of the storm, Josephine pulled out a notebook and began writing as much information as she could about the case of the men with missing fingers. She recorded the names, and physical descriptions, along with the exact words and the similarities of their stories. The men were always vague with their account, and none of them would say where they thought the missing fingers were. At the bottom of her page, she wrote,

La Clairière has gone missing.

To better keep watch on her mother's coming-and-going, Josephine tried staying awake through the night by drinking multiple cups of coffee. By 3 a.m., she was so annoyed with running to the bathroom that she abandoned the mission and crawled into bed. No sooner did she close her eyes, she heard the front door gently open and shut as her mother stepped lightly across the floor. Standing against the wall, Josephine positioned herself behind the door and watched as her mother's figure moved to the end of the hall. Terra-Lynn opened the attic door, and after several minutes of moving around in the dark, she returned to her room.

•   •   •

On the next morning, a shaken and contradictory gentleman was the first to give a significant clue in the mystery of fingerless victims across the parish. Josephine held her breath as the reporter described what was believed to be "some kind of long knife." Pressed for more information, he went on to say that the attacker, who was "thin in stature but sex undetermined," approached in an unlit parking lot, swinging wildly, and narrowly missed dismembering his arm.

Later in the afternoon, Josephine noticed the lop-sided silhouette of her mother as they passed each other from the far end of the hallway. There was a disturbing flicker in her eyes, that almost mocked the dance of fire in a bottomless pit. It was easy to avoid her mother when she was outside or sleeping, but sitting at the kitchen table for lunch, Josephine fought an urge to stare into her eyes. Ignoring the fear from the lurking evil that seemed as if it could reach out and snatch her soul, Josephine forced a smile.

"In case you're wondering about my limp," said Terra-Lynn, as she hobbled to the table. "That nosey police officer came snooping around the hotel again, I took a tumble trying to get down out of sight." She grimaced when her weight shifted into the chair.

The warmth of her mother's voice encouraged Josephine to lift her head. Her shoulders relaxed when she saw the softness of her mother's smile. Terra-Lynn was a beautiful woman in her early thirties, with plenty enough time to find a husband and live a normal life - despite her growing madness. After lunch, Josephine recorded her thoughts and observations in her notebook, ending with...

She's walking with a limp and the evil eyes are back, and scarier than ever.

•   •   •

On the 7th day of the storm, Terra-Lynn awoke earlier than usual with grandiose ideas of remodeling their already larger-than-necessary home. To Josephine's surprise, Eugenia added her desire to have a separate kitchen for cooking, as the two of them searched through the yellow pages and checked off suitable contractors. Skipping her long bath, her mother sat at the table for breakfast and laughed as if the past five month's crisis was long behind them.

That afternoon the rain slowed enough for the water to recede in the backyard, allowing for Terra-Lynn's preferred afternoon stroll down by the pier. Josephine thought to refuse her mother's request to join her on a walk, but not wanting to add to the growing distance between them, she agreed. As they turned onto the bank and followed along the edge of the bayou, the open sky revealed a dramatic cloud formation that billowed like a mystical temple.

"You see that one over there," Terra-Lynn pointed up. "It's a sign that my offering has been accepted."

"Or maybe it's from the storm."

"Yes, the goddess of the storm made it possible."

"What exactly are you saying?" said Josephine, as she frowned and pulled her arm from their interlocked embrace.

Terra-Lynn gestured that they should keep walking, but her daughter's tight jaw and tense shoulders told her otherwise. When her mother refused to answer, she turned and ran as fast as she could - away from the storm, away from the danger of her mother's mysterious words - back to the house where she could write in her notebook from the safety of her room. Eugenia tried to stop her at the stairs, but Josephine blew past her. Skipping the steps by twos, she continued running until she reached her bedroom. The walls of the aging home rattled when the door slammed behind her. With trembling hands, she began to write,

A goddess in the clouds who accepts offerings! Is there no end to this madness?

After making the inscription her breathing returned to normal and her eyes grew tired. Downstairs she could hear Eugenia's scolding voice rise through the ceiling as she scolded Terra-Lynn.

"If you don't stop this foolishness, and stop it quickly, you'll lose everything, including your baby girl!"

Josephine fell asleep with the book clutched at her chest. Later when the smell of savory meat drew her from sleep, she unlocked her bedroom door and followed her stomach to the kitchen. Terra-Lynn was at the stove stirring with a ladle.

"This is just about ready, and cornbreads warm and buttered fresh out the oven."

"Why isn't Eugenia cooking, or did you run her off too?"

Josephine made sure to stand out of reach to avoid her mother's backhand.

"It's just you and me tonight kid, like old times. After we eat, let's do something fun - whatever you want - how does that sound?"

Her face tensed into a smile, as she thought about Twitch. When her mother excused herself to use the restroom, she raced for the telephone and dialed.

"There's a change in plans, don't come tonight."

50

DAY EIGHT BEGAN with blue skies and a lingering chill that entered through the window shutters and slipped beneath Josephine's bedspread. After rubbing her arms and legs like matchsticks for heat, her cramped fingers reached for the pencil and notebook.

She left this morning, sometime around 4 a.m.

After Josephine made the brief inscription, she scampered from bed and ran down the hall. At the bottom of the stairs, movement in the study caused her to stumble into the wall as she checked for the intruder.

"WOO-HOO! The Bayou Inn is back in business."

Terra-Lynn stood to her feet, kicking both legs in and out as she imitated the mashed-potato dance craze.

"There are a few changes we'll discuss later, but we are officially open for business—isn't that wonderful news?"

Josephine lifted on her tippy-toes to avoid the cold floor, as she entered the room. When her neck careened to read the document on the desk, Terra-Lynn flipped them face down.

"This is who we are, a high-class establishment where runaway girls can work and seek shelter—"

"It's called a brothel," said Josephine, as she frowned.

Terra-Lynn threw her hands in the air.

"Whatever you call it to make yourself feel better is fine with me…we aren't like ordinary people, never have been. Tsk! By the time I was 15 like you are now, I was studying roots and rituals with my grandma in the bush."

As she spoke, Josephine searched the darkness of her mother's eyes for the dancing fire. Seeing nothing more than the hard lines of fatigue with the faint subtleness of aging around her jawbone and cheeks, she inched closer.

"You said I was smart like your mama and your brother, I should be in school and preparing for college applications."

She folded her arms when Terra-Lynn moved to slip the papers inside a desk drawer.

"Yes, and you will, when the time is right. Look, someone very important told me that the chains will be removed tomorrow, and all the charges are being dropped— can you believe it?"

When Terra-Lynn leaned to kiss her on the cheek, Josephine took two steps backward. Her mother reached to stop her from running, but her young legs carried her almost as fast as her racing mind. Within a few seconds, the walls in her bedroom rattled as the door slammed behind her. Josephine's hands were trembling as she wrote.

The papers on her desk were signed by the victim who reported seeing a wild swinging blade.

*   *   *

The next day greeted them with heavy black clouds and a roaring angry rain. To Josephine, it seemed as though her mother's fanatic superstitions had finally manifested directly above their house, opening a portal to the ancestors and every other spirit host. The cracking of tree roots being ripped from the ground caused Josephine to fall on her knees and beg the Lord Jesus (whom she secretly believed in) for mercy. By midday, the dark clouds lifted like a dirty carpet being shaken out, leaving behind shades of gray and blue in the sky that resembled a handcrafted Persian rug.

Josephine checked the phone line for service before dialing the number to the hospital. The chatty clerk who answered the phone freely offered details of how the fingerless victims were high-ranking men, including two district attorneys and a judge, and were all attacked while soliciting prostitutes. After swearing Josephine to secrecy, the line clicked. It was hard to make out the light tapping over the rain that began falling on the roof, but as she moved toward the stairs there was no mistaking the familiar sound of her mother's drum. Terra-Lynn's bedroom door was open and the bed was empty. Assuming her mother would be sitting beneath her favorite tree, Josephine moved down the hall and looked out the window. The rising swamp water had returned to reclaim the back half of the yard and the spot her mother would usually sit. Figuring the sound was nothing more than her imagination, she turned away from the window, and just as she passed the attic door, the light tapping commenced.

The storm grows more violent. Prostitutes continue to lure men to La Clairière. She now plays her drum in the attic.

• • •

On the 10th day of the storm, Terra-Lynn left the house to help the girls prepare the hotel for its reopening. Josephine was not invited, nor did she ask to join the cleaning committee. When her mother was gone, she picked up the phone and dialed Twitch's phone number. After provoking him with a debate on Louisiana's slow movement toward ending segregation, he agreed to come right over. Due to the lingering storm clouds, the evening was darker than she preferred but not enough of a deterrent to change her mind.

Josephine tugged on her rain boots and snatched an umbrella from the stand near the door. After pulling the hood over her head, she zipped up her coat and stepped outside. Twitch arrived 30 minutes later.

"Do you mind driving me to the hotel?" said Josephine.

Without hesitation, Twitch pulled away from the curb. During the drive, he seemed jumpier than times before, and more talkative if that were possible. He rambled nonstop about details from the morning newspaper, then on to gossip around town, and finally what was troubling him the most.

"My cousin is back, and she says your mother wants her to take over the tutoring. So, I was wondering if we could keep in touch just until I leave for college?"

"No, she won't—I'll tell her I prefer to keep you."

They were silent until the car pulled beneath a lamppost in the hotel parking lot and Twitch turned off the engine.

"I leave for college at the end of summer, remember?"

He grabbed the keys from the ignition before opening the car door to pursue Josephine.

"You wouldn't dare leave me now?"

She studied his face in the nightlight. When he refused to answer she grabbed his hand and led him through the backdoor which was no longer locked. She listened for a moment to the voices coming from the front lobby, and when it seemed clear, she pulled him through the management sleeping quarters. Bypassing Terra-Lynn's closed office door, they scurried down the unlit hallway. As if there was a need to caution the barely breathing young man, Josephine pressed a finger to her mouth as she dragged him up the back stairs. As they hurried, she noticed the cleaned rooms still waiting for guests. At the far end of the second floor, she opened a room door and clicked the lock behind them.

"I'm as good as dead if she catches me here," said Twitch, more nervous than ever.

"And I'll die if you leave me in this town alone."

Her lips quivered from the damp air.

"What's here for me if I stay, would we be allowed to keep seeing each other?" He almost begged.

Sitting close to each other on the bed, they began to remove the wet layers of clothing. When his shoulders began to shake more than usual, Josephine reached over and kissed him on the cheek, and then the lips, until his body relaxed.

•   •   •

On the tenth day of the storm, Josephine smiled from the sweetest of secrets. Unbothered by yet another fingerless male victim, she fixed herself breakfast and hid out in her room as the clouds rumbled and the rain pattered against the window. When Terra-Lynn awoke in the afternoon and stuck her head in her daughter's room, she found her still in bed.

"I'm okay, it's just warmer in here," said Josephine, over the music playing on her radio. "Without Eugenia here in the mornings to start a fire, the house gets so cold."

"I'll get that started for you…hey, would you like to come over to the hotel with me tonight?"

Josephine shook her head, as she reached for her notepad. When her mother refused to leave the doorway she set her pencil down and pretended to pay attention.

"You sure you're fine?" said Terra-Lynn.

"Yes, just cold and a little busy with writing."

"Okay, I'll go light that fire," said Terra-Lynn as she moved from the door.

When she was gone, Josephine picked up her pencil.

The fingers and the men, and the reopening, is not a coincidence. She blames it on the ancestors and sacrifices but it's all been for revenge. Now we all have secrets; Momma, Me, and La Clairiere.

•   •   •

Another stormy day. No victims to report and the hotel is almost ready for guests. We took another drive this evening. He held my hand so tight I almost thought the bones in my fingers would snap. He is sweet, but he sure can be awfully nervous and jumpy at times. Except when he's lying down.

●　　●　　●

On the 12th day of the storm, Terra-Lynn and Josephine both slept until noon. Earlier that morning, sometime around 4 a.m., Josephine had scarcely made it home when the headlights from the station wagon illuminated the front porch, right after she had slipped through the front door. By the time she reached her bedroom, Terra-Lynn was unlocking the front door and tip-toeing across the same floor her daughter had moments before. Now they were both awake as if the secrecies of morning never existed, each preparing for another evening of moving shadows, prohibited activities, and concealed sacrifices all over again.

When her mother descended the staircase - dressed in her signature flowing gown and hair pressed down her back - Josephine pointed to the television set. The bizarre case of the fingerless men had stalled at twelve victims. All of the men, except for one, claimed to have injured their finger in a freak accident with a chain link while cutting wood, meat or gutting fish. Terra-Lynn shrugged as she checked her reflection in the wall mirror.

"Oh well, that's the end of that freak show."

"Unless more men come forward with information, they have nothing to catch the person responsible for all this."

The reporter mentioned how the victim's appeared to be in a state of shock. Each of them reported feeling fine after being treated for their injury and now wished to put the whole ordeal behind them, especially as there were no new victims.

"They owe me one more," Terra-Lynn whispered beneath her breath, "but twelve seems to be good enough, at least the storm eased up."

"What was that you just said?"

"I said, you should finish up your assignments today because I'll need you back at work tomorrow."

Before leaving, she kissed her daughter on the forehead. When she was gone, Josephine dashed up the stairs and entered her mother's room. Her hand felt around the dark hole in the wall until her fingers found the long blade resting in its place as if it had never moved. Josephine went into her bedroom and began to write.

For the first time in months, the Bayou Inn will receive guests after twelve days of La Clairière went missing, twelve violent days of storm and rage, and twelve fingerless victims.

• • •

JULY 1965

The cautious girl stood before Josephine with her eyes toward the floor, as she twiddled her thumbs. She had no doubt been warned about the owner's smart-lipped daughter, who was prone to throw things across the counter if she disliked the way a girl spoke, dressed, or smelled; but for some reason, Josephine liked this one. She came in wearing glasses and a school uniform with her hair pulled into two pigtails. When asked about her story, she said it was the lingering eyes of her mother's new husband that ran her off. Josephine turned to check the room register, and out of her peripheral, she caught the girl slipping a pen from the counter into her pocket.

"Here's the key to your room, enjoy your stay."

Josephine placed the key gently on the counter.

"Aren't you Josephine, the owner's daughter?"

She took a step back after asking the question.

"Mm-hmm, here's a care package on the house."

Josephine handed the girl two bundles, neatly wrapped in a box, and tied with a silk tie. Inside were seven items; toothpaste, toothbrush, sanitary napkins, animal crackers, a Jet magazine, a writing pad, and a pencil. When the girl took the key and package, Josephine reached across the counter and grabbed her arm.

"This room isn't for business—you hear me? If it's work you want, then I'll have to switch you to another room."

"No ma'am, I mean yes ma'am, I only need a few nights to rest and figure things out."

"I mean it, I catch you in there with anyone and I'll boot you out while your heads still spinning."

Josephine released her grip as she snapped her fingers. After swearing on her life there would be no funny business, hanky-panky, or any other good times of any sort in the room, the girl hurried off. Any other room would be fine, but the mousy school girl would be occupying the room she and Twitch used on nights when Terra-Lynn slinked out the back door to her own clandestine affairs - which Josephine overlooked, so long as there were no new victims.

Josephine stared out the window as she sat on a stool, watching nothing in particular. Her mind flowered with the most cherished moments in the room with Twitch until a faint rattling drew her to the present. Before she knew it, the lobby filled with scantily clad ladies, hand-picked by men dressed in suits and wide-brimmed hats. As a peculiar sound closed in behind, Josephine turned to face a long clinking necklace strung with shells that resembled bone fragments around her mother's neck.

"It's a gift from my spirit guide, do you like it?"

Terra-Lynn clutched the pouch dangling at the end.

"Why does it look like bones?"

Josephine frowned.

"I told you it's a gift, don't you like it?"

The necklace clanked as she moved from around the counter to greet her waiting patrons. Josephine watched her mother work the room until the noisy pouch fell silent beneath the pitch of their laughter and shouting. After the revengeful days of *La Clairière*, things were different between them. There were so many secrets now, which only served to divide them more as the small chasm stretched into a gorge complete with stone walls, deep valleys, and rocky mountains. All while working and living together Thursday through Monday and three days off at home. Their only time apart was on the nights when Terra-Lynn disappeared, and on those nights so did Josephine.

51

October 1965

ON THE DAY Josephine received the best news of her life, Terra-Lynn announced they would be taking a three-week vacation from work.

"Why are we taking off just to sit around home?"

Josephine pouted when they pulled into the driveway.

"A vacation is when you actually go somewhere, like Florida, Jamaica, or even Cuba."

After hopping out of the car, Josephine slammed the door. By the time she reached the porch.

"What if I brought Cuba to us?" said Terra-Lynn, yelling from the car window.

Josephine turned, leaving her key dangling in the door.

"What are you talking about?"

"Your grandmother is coming and so are my twin and other siblings."

"And what about Zuellie, she coming too?"

Josephine lept from the porch and ran back to the station wagon. Lynn shook her head.

"That stubborn old woman will never leave that island, she believes a zombie curse will catch her if she does."

Terra-Lynn sucked her teeth.

"That's too bad, I really wanted to meet her, but if she's scared then how much of a witch doctor can she be?"

"Never mind that," said Terra-Lynn as she shooed her away from the car door. "Help me with the bags, we don't have much time to get the house ready."

The house was spotless, thanks to Eugenia's three times a week cleaning. What she really meant was Josephine would have to help her pull the altar and idols from the front room and out of sight. Josephine nodded toward the back door.

"What about the junk hanging from the branches?"

"They're called charms…" Terra-Lynn moved to the back door as she wrung her hands. "She'll understand, it's not like she hasn't seen them before."

As Terra-Lynn rationalized her decision to leave the trinkets hanging from the tree, she went around to the side of the house and pulled out a step ladder. By sunset, every swinging bottle and shell, along with the idols, had been neatly tucked away in the attic.

•   •   •

Early the next morning, an unusually chatty Terra-Lynn drove them to meet her family at the Lafayette airport. Josephine watched as her mother checked the mirror seven times during the 25-minute drive. Twice she removed the bone necklace from around her neck, only to place it back on again. When they pulled into a parking space she shoved the necklace back into her purse.

"The last time I saw my mother I was a little older than you are now," said Terra-Lynn as she removed the key from the ignition. "And I was never close to my siblings, so I'm not sure why they agreed to come."

During the walk through the parking lot, Josephine listened to her mother's concerns. Her stomach tied into knots with each step closer to the terminal. It was not hard to recognize her grandmother amongst the passengers standing at baggage claim. She had heard many stories about Rebecca, but her mother never mentioned how much Josephine resembled her grandmother. Same slanted eyes underneath eyeglasses with a serious and stern expression, and a long torso that made them both appear taller than they actually were.

Rebecca began to weep at the sight of the daughter she lost over sixteen years ago on that fateful boat ride. Terra-Lynn melted into her mother's arms as her siblings embraced the sister they affectionately called, Consuelo. When Josephine managed to wiggle her way out of the huddle, she stood back and took a deep breath. As she looked at her grandmother, two uncles, an aunt, and finally her mother, she recorded them all to her memory. From her uncle's high-water bell bottoms, her aunt's curly afro and micro-skirt, to their varying degrees of tans and browns. Her grandmother was the richest shade of brown sugar and the darkest, her aunt the color of raw cane, and the two uncles were light-bright and could pass for white, just like Terra-Lynn.

Her mother's twin, Leonardo, held his sister at arm's length as he looked her over from head to toe. When their hands locked together, it seemed as if a pause button froze the two in a moment, transporting them back in time to their dual conception, combined gestation, and shared birth. Their other two siblings joined hands, as Rebecca re-closed the circle. Then they began to talk and cry and laugh, all at once.

Leonardo broke free from the group and stood beside Josephine. After drying his face with the back of his hand, he pulled her into his arms, her feet lifted off the ground when he spun her around.

"Hello, I am your tio!"

He swung her until they were both dizzy. When the others came near he placed her back on her feet. Josephine giggled as they each began poking and touching her at once. This was the family she had dreamed of for so long (much longer than she could remember), and she prayed they could stay like this forever.

After piling into the Station wagon, Terra-Lynn was much calmer than when they arrived, overlooking the mirror and ignoring her smeared make-up. During the drive, they took turns discussing their careers and accomplishments. The two brothers, one an Educator like his mother and the other a Businessman like their father had been. Their sister and the youngest, Carmen, was a singer and performer, just as Rebecca once was as a young girl. When it was Terra-Lynn's turn, Josephine noticed how her cheeks flushed.

"Business is good, but Josie is the scholar in our household, she gets that from you all," she said, nodding at Rebecca and Leonardo,

"Don't mind your mother, she's my smartest, but would you believe she's the only one who hasn't completed her education?" said Rebecca.

"Mama, it's not her fault, it was those greedy *barbudos*—even here they tried to take everything Papa had worked so hard for," said Nicolas, the other brother.

"We should change the subject, *por favor*, the past is the past," Rebecca sighed. "You've done a wonderful job taking care of yourself and this little beauty, I can't get over how much she looks like me."

Josephine smiled at her grandmother, who had turned around in the front seat for a better look.

"When are you going to give me a grandchild, as your sister has?" She said, turning to Leonardo.

"He already has, he just doesn't know it," said Nicolas.

He ducked when his brother swiped at his head. Carmen yelped when his hand knocked her in the chest.

"Quit it you two, unless you want us to look like bait meat for every hoodlum in America!" said Carmen.

"They've been like this ever since you and papa left."

Rebecca rolled her eyes as she turned to face forward. When Terra-Lynn pulled into the driveway and parked beneath the carport, Leonardo and Nicolas straightened up to view the property. Carmen was the one who whistled as they exited the car.

"If I had known you were living this fancy, I would've hopped a ride to America a long time ago," she said.

"And who'd you say was managing everything, how're the numbers at the hotel?" said Nicholas.

"Papa kept very detailed records, I just duplicated what he had already done."

"See, I told you she was my smartest," said Rebecca as she whispered to Josephine.

At the door, Eugenia took their coats and handed them a warm cup from a nearby tray. Afterward, Terra-Lynn led them down the hallway that wrapped behind the stairwell to the right where the two guest rooms were located. Then she pried Josephine from her grandmother's arms and instructed them to freshen for lunch.

"How come you never told me that I looked like her?" said Josephine, when they were alone in the front room.

"I did, in my own way," she smiled.

By the time Josephine made it back to her room, her stomach was in knots as she sat and began to write.

My Grandmother Rebecca is everything I imagined she would be. Poised, elegant, and a true matriarch, who would never ever be caught in a brothel like the Bayou Inn. My two uncles, Leonardo and Nicolas, on the other hand, are smart, silly, and just as I pictured brothers to be like. They would fall in love at the Bayou Inn. Aunt Carmen is only twelve years older than I am. I fear what a place like that could do to someone like her.

When she finished making her entry, Josephine sprang from her bed and ran down the hall. She swung her mother's bedroom door open without knocking first.

"You can't take them to the Bayou Inn!"

"Shhh, keep your voice down."

Terra-Lynn pulled her daughter in and shut the door.

"My mama and siblings are dignified educated folks, they wouldn't understand that kind of work."

"And what about us—what about me? I'm more like them than you are."

Josephine's blood boiled under her skin. She knew the words would sting, even before her mother's mouth gaped open and her eyes watered over. Terra-Lynn moved from the door and returned to her clothes rack, the hangers slapped against the other as she flipped from one dress to another. Josephine thought about apologizing but her lips pressed tight for fear of speaking what she truly felt, about her mother, and the prison she called a life.

"I know how intelligent you are, and I should have put you in school a long time ago…I was just too scared to let you go," said Terra-Lynn.

Josephine imagined what it would be like to finally leave the house and the Bayou Inn to attend school. She longed for friends to go dancing with, and laughter floating over root-beer drinks while watching a movie at the cinema - all the things Twitch had told her about during their times together. She couldn't wait to tell him that they would be able to meet at the park with the other teenagers and hold hands as they walked through town. She smiled when her mother approached, not hearing the words she spoke until much, much later.

As the family all met at the dining table, the room exploded with clanging plates, and a chatter Josephine had never witnessed in their home. She watched as her two uncles hugged their sister and the way Carmen compared their similar traits. Terra-Lynn threw her head back and hollered when they began sharing forgotten stories from their childhood. Josephine tried to follow the story, but when they began speaking in Spanish it was easier to watch the melting ice cubes in her glass. Watching them together gave her mixed emotions. These were her mother's people, no matter how much Josephine thought she took after them more than Terra-Lynn. Just as a twinge of jealousy clouded her mind, Rebecca stood to remove the empty plates. When the table was cleared, she asked if her granddaughter could show her the garden. Terra-Lynn's face glitched for a moment as she watched the two of them leave the room. When Leonardo asked if Terra-Lynn was okay, Josephine could hear the pause in her mother's response.

They started the tour on the east wing of the house where the long-forgotten gazebo sat covered over in vines.

"My mother used to bring me out here every day for lunch when I was little, that was before she became obsessed with work."

Josephine stopped when she spied two small wooden blocks on the ground left nearly ten years ago.

"Do you mind if I keep them?" said Rebecca.

When Josephine nodded, she placed them in her pocket for safekeeping.

"We sleep at the hotel during the week because she can't pull herself away from it."

Josephine realized confiding in her grandmother was much too easy, which was probably the reason for her mother's concern. Rebecca listened instead of giving advice and respected the silence when Josephine bit her lip after saying more than she should.

"She gets that from her father," said Rebecca, as she pulled at the twigs wrapping around the railing.

"I feel like I have to keep an eye on her all the time, and her paranoia and superstitions are bound to land her in trouble, and I'll never get to college at this rate."

"And that would be my mother's doing, which I never wanted her to learn; but I'd rather her here and not there, doing only God knows what down in the bush with her grandmother."

Rebecca shivered and quickly changed the subject.

"Tell me about your friends?"

Josephine blushed before she could turn away.

"Who is he? Come on, your secrets safe with me."

Rebecca kept silent as Josephine told her about the only friend she had, a former tutor turned boyfriend, whom she called Twitch (on account of his Tourette syndrome). As they sat alone with the sound of birds chirping in the trees, Josephine divulged information she would have otherwise told a sister or a close friend.

"We're in love, but mama's so strict we can't go out as a normal boyfriend and girlfriend would. I can't even go to school or anywhere else except by her side."

Josephine pouted.

"She's afraid to lose another person," said Rebecca.

She put her head down, remembering the day her heart broke when she lost Rinaldo, and how difficult it was to pull herself back together and finally leave Cuba to face the land that changed her life.

"If only you all could stay here with us, I know she would get better," said Josephine.

"Let's see how the month goes first, you just might change your opinion after six weeks with your uncles."

• • •

After two weeks had gone by, Josephine felt like they were no longer just her mother's people, but a family she could call her own. In the mornings she ate breakfast alongside her loud and animated uncles. In the afternoons, she and her grandmother went on walks where they wandered beyond the front gate and waved to neighbors she had never met before. On a shopping spree with her aunt Carmen, she bought trendy teenage fashion; polka dots and bold stripes, shapeless shift dresses, shoulder strap bags, hair ties, Mary Janes and slingback shoes. She replaced her notebook with a real diary, and a second journal to record her grandmother's favorite recipes and the lyrics to the songs her uncles sang by the fireplace in the evenings.

One afternoon, she and Carmen swapped outfits and went downtown where Josephine watched a movie at the theatre for the first time in her life. She couldn't wait to tell Twitch about all the new things she had done, but he had stopped calling after her uncle Leonardo answered his last phone call and demanded to know what he wanted with his niece. When she and Carmen returned home, she dialed his number while everyone was distracted. To her surprise, her grandmother took the phone and invited him over for lunch the next day.

When he arrived, Josephine and her grandmother met him outside the gate. Twitch stood at attention, his pants pressed stiff and shoes polished to an impeccable shine as if he were a recruit at basic training. Rebecca asked him to accompany them on their afternoon walk, where she listened mostly to their plans to go off to college and start a life together. At the end of the dirt road, just before it turned back toward the bayou, Twitch said his goodbyes. Her grandmother was silent as Josephine continued to express her longing for a different way of life. At some point, they stumbled upon a canoe sitting on the bank and decided to take it for a ride. Rebecca watched the ripples cross the surface as she considered her next words.

"In my day it was nothing for a girl your age to get married, but nowadays there's so much more to hope for, especially here in America."

Josephine covered her face with her hands.

"Grandma, we love each other but it's not like we're thinking of running off and getting married."

Rebecca raised her eyebrows.

"Oh, well what else are you supposed to do with a blazing love like the two of you have?"

Josephine's cheeks burned as she tried to better explain her situation. She reminded her grandmother of their previous conversation in the gazebo. What it was like being an only child, and never having attended traditional schooling, not having friends, and how she felt imprisoned in the house. College with Twitch was her only hope.

"I know what it's like to be an only child living with an unconventional parent. Maybe it'll help if I spoke with her about how it was for me growing up alone with my mama."

Josephine clutched her grandmother's hand.

"Would you do that, please? It would mean so much."

After traveling as far as they felt comfortable rowing, they returned the canoe and went back home. Terra-Lynn was on the porch singing with her brothers as Carmen sat by the telephone on a long-distance call to her sweetheart in Cuba. That night they ate a simple meal of red beans and rice with fried chicken. Rebecca waited until her sons had left the kitchen and returned to their singing, then she asked the question that shocked both Terra-Lynn and Josephine.

"So, what do you think about Josie coming back to Cuba for a while with me?"

Rebecca folded her hands and waited, as Terra-Lynn thumped her mug on the tabletop.

"She can learn about her roots here with me."

"I'm not talking about any roots, the girl needs to be properly educated, and she should be attending church regularly—do you know she identifies as a Christian?"

Terra-Lynn snickered.

"Why would I send her over there for that? If anything, she'd go to meet her great granny Zuellie so she can be properly connected with her spirit guide, I've tried everything but she's not getting it here."

Rebecca rolled her eyes.

"When I was alone in the bush with Zuellie I never heard any drums from the ancestors either," said Rebecca.

Terra-Lynn cut her eyes at her daughter.

"You never said anything to me about wanting to live in Cuba, or going to Church."

"That's not what I said—I mean, it would be nice if we could both go for a visit," said Josephine as she squirmed in her seat. She put her head down, ashamed to face her mother and grandmother's disappointment.

Each day after dinner, Rebecca would ask the question again, and Terra-Lynn would ruffle her feathers like a bird being poked in a cage. Finally, on the last night of their visit, her grandmother asked a different question.

"Well, if you refuse to let her go back with us, at least send her to school so she can make friends her own age."

"Fine, all she had to do was ask. I'll enroll her in school tomorrow," said Terra-Lynn as she pushed away from the table and marched upstairs.

When Josephine heard her mother's bedroom door shut, Rebecca reached across the table and gave her granddaughter a high-five.

"There's more than one way to cross a busy intersection," she said. "My daughter's bright, but there's so much going on inside her brain you just have to learn to outthink her."

Ignoring the heaviness inside her chest, Josephine returned the smile. Tomorrow her grandmother would be leaving, carrying all her granddaughter's secrets with her on the plane ride home. Josephine knew it had been a joke, but each night she fantasized about packing a bag and leaving with them to Cuba. She imagined what it would be like to watch her aunt perform live at a Cabaret, or even herself as she sang some of the songs her uncles had taught her.

"When you're gone, she'll go back to doing what she always does with her charms and that other stuff. She might even bring that weird machete back out," said Josephine.

"You mean she has that old thing?"

Josephine nodded.

"It doesn't mean anything, it's just something my mama held onto to keep her connected to the family she left in Haiti," said Rebecca.

When it was time for bed, Josephine gave her old notebook to her grandmother and made her promise not to read it until she was back home in Cuba.

52

December 1965

JOSEPHINE HATED TO see her family leave, but she knew when they had arrived six weeks ago that the trip would end with goodbye. When her mother asked Carmen to come again soon - to help keep an eye on Josephine and the house – she agreed, as did her uncles. There were no empty promises from Rebecca, she would be waiting in Havana until Terra-Lynn and her granddaughter were ready to return to their true home. Then they were gone and the world shrunk back down to regular size. The Bayou Inn had to be managed, her mother's paranoia needed to be monitored, and the girls at the hotel had to be kept in line - and then there was Twitch. Had it not been for their secret love, Josephine would have stopped at nothing to be on that flight to Cuba.

During her morning shift, Josephine waited at the front desk with a ready-made script for each of the girls. The message was intended to be gentle, but there was always an unsettling sting to her delivery. If she had to be honest, Josephine knew her words were sharp enough to cut through skin and leave a gaping wound. She started off kind.

"Is this all you want for your life, to be someone's picked over trash and—"

Like clockwork, the boney necklace around Terra-Lynn's neck would clink from behind the office door. Josephine took a deep breath before she continued. Her eyes pleaded as she released the key clutched in her hand and sat it on the countertop.

"Why not give your life to Christ? He can give you a better future, just try it."

Josephine knew she was pushing the limits with her mother, which is more than likely the reason Terra-Lynn announced that the time had come for her to start school. The only surprise was Josephine's lackluster response to what she previously imagined would be the best day of her life. For Josephine, attending school meant showing up to an unfamiliar place to meet strangers, like the ones she'd seen at the movie theatre with aunt Carmen, and proving she knew just as much (if not more) than the average student her age. Josephine shrugged.

"I've decided not to go."

The boney necklace rattled as Terra-Lynn stood and walked around the desk.

"After the grief you and your Grandmama gave me, now you say you ain't going to school—oh, you're going alright."

Terra-Lynn's slender fingers cupped the dangling pouch to keep it from swaying. Josephine's gaze fell on the tiny pieces of the necklace as her mother moved closer.

"I made it this far without school, what's the use now?"

Her mother's eyes narrowed as she studied her daughter closely. Josephine held her composure, refusing to break a sweat as she spoke. She would work her shift until 4, then go home in the evenings to give them space as she figured out what she wanted to do next. Terra-Lynn seemed happy with the arrangement. She sashayed off with one of the girls, humming a tune to her favorite song.

At 4 p.m. when Josephine's shift ended, she stuck her head in the office and saw that her mother was in a meeting. When Terra-Lynn said she'd be free in about 30 minutes, Josephine said she had a ride, and blew her mother a kiss before closing the door. At the end of the block, she entered a waiting car and gave him a peck on the cheek.

"Drive anywhere, as fast as you can," she said.

Josephine never worried about her mother when she and Twitch were together. She certainly was not thinking of her mother when they went to dances or to watch a movie. There was a moment when meeting Twitch's friends, and finding out how much she had in common with other teens who were annoyed by their parents, that she thought of sharing the experience with her mother. Then she'd return to work the next morning, only to find Terra-Lynn speaking bizarre things, as she waved *La Clairière* at hooligans while her bone-necklaced rattled back and forth. For Josephine, the Bayou Inn represented chaos, the outside world with Twitch and his friends became her sweet escape.

On the morning of Christmas Eve, Josephine arrived with a duffel bag for her stayover that night. The hotel was at its peak for the Christmas holiday, when guests were in their all-time festive moods. Drinks were served until the lounge closed at 7 p.m., and those who were not ready to sober up stumbled two doors down to a liquor store that stayed open until midnight. Terra-Lynn was not much for drinking, but she was known to finish a glass (or two) every so often. With Josephine gone in the evenings, it seemed she was enjoying every bit of her free time in the company of a special friend, as the scent of his cologne lingered throughout the manager's sleeping quarters.

"I see you brought a change of clothes, does that mean we get to spend Christmas together like a real family?"

Terra-Lynn rolled over and patted the corner of the mattress for her daughter to sit.

"Do I have a choice? You haven't been home in weeks."

"It's been real busy around h—"

"I know, I know how things are at this time of year. I'll stay over tonight if it's okay with whomever you've been keeping company with."

Josephine tossed her bag on the floor.

"Come and lay with me like you used to."

Terra-Lynn adjusted herself to make room as Josephine came near the bed. She pinched her nostrils and frowned from the smell of cologne. When Terra-Lynn reached for her arm, Josephine relaxed, realizing it was the first time they had touched since her grandmother's visit.

"What's this?" said Terra-Lynn, as she began to gently poke at Josephine's belly.

For a moment the room fell silent, the only sound coming from the ticking grandfather clock against the wall as Terra-Lynn calculated the last two months. After several seconds lapsed, Josephine removed her mother's hand as she sat forward.

"I guess Grandma's rice and beans put a few extra pounds on me."

Terra-Lynn's mouth puckered as if she had eaten spoiled roux or bad fish. Josephine did not move when Terra-Lynn's hand reached and touched her stomach again.

"No, it's my fault, I never should've left you alone…now this Parrish owes me another sacrifice."

Josephine clutched her stomach.

"Mama, it scares me when you talk like that, please don't worry about me."

Terra-Lynn sprang from the bed, her lean body bent over to pick up her dress from a nearby chair.

"I should've killed him the day he stepped foot on my porch!" she said, slipping her hands inside the nightstand to retrieve the bone necklace.

"Mama, please don't hurt him. I love him, and we're planning to leave and go to college together."

"You silly girl, this is a baby, not your grandmama's beans and rice!"

Terra-Lynn paced back and forth.

"Tell you what, have him meet us at the house tonight and we'll decide how to handle this like civil adults, okay?"

Josephine searched her mother's eyes to see if the darkness had returned. At that moment, what she saw was a mother's concern for her daughter, so she picked up the telephone and dialed his number. When he answered, Josephine was shocked at how quickly she told a lie, saying her mother wanted to have a Christmas Eve dinner with family and friends and she was allowed to invite one friend. After the phone call, Terra-Lynn took her daughter in her arms and consoled her.

"We've dealt with worse situations than this, we'll get through this together, as a family."

• • •

When they arrived home, Terra-Lynn began cooking to cover her daughter's story. By the time Twitch arrived later in the evening, he was so nervous he forgot to question the absence of the other guests. Dressed for the occasion, his suit and polished shoes bore droplets of water from the fresh bouquet in his hand. After Josephine took the flowers, he wiped the hair grease from his forehead with one arm.

"I'll take those," said Terra-Lynn, as she snatched the bouquet and clicked the door lock behind him. "Come in, take a seat."

Twitch adjusted his bowtie before he sat down. Josephine remained standing, even after her mother was seated.

"If this country hasn't taught me nothing else, it's taught me how to properly dispose of problems," said Terra-Lynn.

Josephine bit her lip as she positioned herself between her mother and Twitch.

"And that's what I like most about you, ma'am, you and your daughter are true survivors no matter what anyone has to say about you," said Twitch as he swallowed the lump in his throat.

"And what about you, are you a survivor?"

Terra-Lynn fingered her necklace as she waited for his response. When he noticed the streak of madness dancing around her pupils, Twitch looked from Josephine to her mother. Josephine began to cry, which caused him to look across the room to the locked door.

"I know we—I mean I-I was wrong. My mother taught me better, she raised me in a good Christian home, and I know to do right by all people…"

"So, you expect to do right by your child?"

"Oh, yes ma'am, when that day comes and I'm married, I'll be the best father and husband a woman could want."

Josephine put her head down when her mother's dark glare turned toward her.

"And what about the one you got coming?"

When Terra-Lynn pointed to Josephine, Twitch noticed her stomach just as his face began to jerk.

"What's wrong with you boy?"

Terra-Lynn jumped to her feet.

"He can't help it, he has Tourette's syndrome," said Josephine, as she tried to calm him with a soothing tone. "It's my fault, I should've told you sooner."

When his breathing settled, Twitch used a trembling hand to pull a handkerchief from his pocket and began to wipe the sweat from his face.

"No need for dramatics, I know people around here like to talk about me and my machete, but you're safe for now, I just need to know your plans for my Josie and the baby?"

"If it's okay with you, ma'am, I'd like to ask for her hand in marriage?"

Josephine slid across the seat and put her hand in his. Twitch kissed her briefly on the lips, then placed a hand on her belly. She smiled as he explained how he would get a job to take care of them, and hopefully by the time the baby was born they'd find a small apartment for rent. As he spoke, Josephine forgot about her mother's anger. This was her chance at true happiness. Twitch was going to save her from the bizarre world she had been born into, and their baby would never set foot in the Bayou Inn, or know anything about charms and alters or drums. Josephine knew at any moment the darkness in her mother could flare up and lash out, but for now, she was calm or in shock. Terra-Lynn's body was stiff as a log, except for her fingers stroking the pouch on her necklace.

"Don't be a stranger, you hear me? You're like family now," said Terra-Lynn as she left the room.

When she was gone, Josephine led Twitch to the door, just in case her mother had plans of returning with *La Clairière*.

53

May 1966

A TINY GLIMMER of hope began to bud inside - and outside - of Josephine's body. With every wave of morning sickness throughout her first trimester, and then the slightest barely noticeable stomach flurries around the fifth month, she became more aware of the possibilities that life could offer. Getting married and having a child would be her way of escape - not fleeing to Cuba or fighting with the girls at the Bayou Inn. Josephine rubbed her stomach and smiled at the growing bump.

"If you get me through these next few months, I promise to raise this child as a good Christian," she said with her eyes closed in prayer.

Josephine rested her hand over the general area where she believed the baby was and waited for movement.

"And it won't be just listening on the radio, but a real church building where we can hear the choir singing and see the preacher's face."

She waited a few seconds, scarcely breathing so as not to miss the quick flutters.

"When me and your daddy are old enough to get married we'll all go together as a family should."

She imagined Twitch sitting on the opposite side of their child, dressed in a clean suit and a new pair of shiny shoes. They would clap and sing together as they thanked Jesus for helping them make it out of her mother's house and the Bayou Inn. Josephine would have to wait three years until she turned 18 and she counted every second of every day. There was still another trimester of pregnancy ahead, and then the birth, nursing, and weening of the child. Not long after that waiting period would come her 18th birthday, a wedding, and finally freedom.

When she heard footsteps in the hallway, Josephine's hand jerked away from her stomach. To ensure she was eating properly, Eugenia was now coming every morning. Twitch arrived in the afternoons and stayed until bedtime, but he never slept over for fear of another unpleasant face-off with Terra-Lynn. Today was a Saturday morning, which meant her mother was home for the weekend and the tension between them would be as unsteady as a tightrope walker balancing 20 feet high. Josephine wiped the sweat from her forehead before stepping from her bedroom.

"Have the girls been behaving?"

Her hands rested in front of her stomach to shield the baby bump.

"What do you think? I'm left to manage things on my own now." Terra-Lynn zeroed in on her daughter's growing stomach. "Thankfully, I still have *La Clairière* around to handle the larger problems."

Josephine took a step back when her mother approached and reached for her stomach.

"Don't worry, I would never hurt you or my grandchild—but I can't say the same for the boy who has decided to act like a man with what belongs to me."

The first signs of gray strands had begun to curl at her mother's hairline. At thirty-three, she was more beautiful and vivacious as Josephine had remembered from her youth when it was the two of them alone romping around the estate. That was before the sacrificial altar, the strange offerings, and before the darkness changed her mother's soul. Terra-Lynn rubbed her daughter's stomach until the tension lifted. When she pulled back, Josephine held onto her hand and nodded toward the window.

"I decided to raise my baby—your grandchild, the same way you were raised with grandma Rebecca, to go to school and to be taught Christian values - outside that front gate."

Terra-Lynn threw her head back and chuckled loud enough to cause a low ringing sound to bounce off the window glass. As the flicker of evil replaced the warmth in her mother's eyes, Josephine removed her hand to shield her stomach.

"You hate him enough to kill him, I can tell. You would do that to me and your unborn grandchild?"

Terra-Lynn stood before the window and gazed out over the property. Her lips were moving but the words were inaudible. Josephine looked beyond her mother to the treeline with storm clouds forming just above them. There was danger and something tragic ahead, not because of the clouds or anything nature could predict, but a weeping that came from somewhere deep within her gut. She held her stomach tighter.

"Please explain this to me, if your own father had to pay the consequences, what makes that boy any better?" said Terra-Lynn with a clenched fist waving in the air. "He marched right through those gates and slithered in like a crocodile stalking a small animal on the muddy banks."

"But it was nothing like that, you're twisting things around to make it sound bad. He was all I had when you kept disappearing during that big storm."

"What's wrong with a little revenge? I was the one out there fighting for our livelihood and your birthright—without that hotel we have nothing. You should be thanking me that it's just a finger and not his life."

This time it was Terra-Lynn who walked away. Josephine jumped when the door to the study slammed. She thought about ways to spare Twitch from her mother's rage, but nothing short of tipping off the authorities would save him. In the end, she figured marriage to a man with a missing finger or two couldn't be so bad.

"It's just a finger, not his life," she repeated the words to herself while standing in her bedroom.

•　　•　　•

That night, Terra-Lynn tossed and turned as the low thumping sound grew to a pulsating beat. One eyelid flew open as it searched the darkness of her bedroom. She was at home in her bed, and here is where the beating drums would not allow her to sleep, not until she obeyed the call to dance. With both eyes now open, she listened as the beating of her grandma Zuellie's drums crossed over the oceans and hovered over her bed. The rhythm intensified until she was on her feet. As she danced, her shadow lept onto the wall and played hide-and-seek with the moonlight. Throughout the years, Terra-Lynn had learned to dance in silence to keep from waking Josie, but now the clanky necklace made a noise with each movement. She danced until her ankles throbbed and knees wobbled. When the drums stopped, Terra-Lynn faced her still shadow and accepted what had to be done.

It was past midnight. The full moon cast light along the road as she drove her car to Breaux Bridge and parked underneath a huge oak tree on a side road. When she left the car, Terra-Lynn's silhouette danced onto the asphalt as the moon stretched to illuminate the mocking shadow. She began moving faster, the sound of her breath now much louder than the rattling of her necklace. After finding the protestant church at the center of town, she stopped for a moment to rub out the pain from the stones that pricked the bottom of her bare feet.

"Just two more streets to go," she whispered to her shadow, which sprung back into action upon hearing the command.

Terra-Lynn stopped outside a small home with a Nova parked in the driveway. She tried opening the front and back doors and then jiggled the windows but the house was locked on every side, and so was his car. When headlights approached and moved down the road, she moved to hide in the bushes. In a few hours, the good boy and his family would be getting ready for church, if she waited, she could make her move first thing in the morning. Terra-Lynn lost track of the hour, but somewhere around the time when dawn chased away her dancing shadow, the front door opened. Twitch was dressed in all-white, a pair of white gloves stuffed into his pants pocket. Terra-Lynn slid out of the bushes and checked over her shoulders before she pursued him. He didn't notice her until she was close enough to reach out and touch him.

"Ms. Machado, you startled me—what are you doing here, is Josephine alright?"

"I came as quick as I could, Josie's waiting for you at the hotel, she refuses to go to the hospital without you."

When Terra-Lynn hopped in the passenger seat, he may have wanted to ask how she knew where he lived, but he never did. Twitch gripped the steering wheel and turned corners without stopping for red lights. Once they arrived at the hotel, Terra-Lynn had him wait in the front lobby while she stopped briefly in her office. When she returned, he followed her upstairs to an empty room.

"I don't understand, why is she here and not at home?"

He turned around just as Terra-Lynn locked the door behind them.

Thwish! *La clairière* sliced through the air.

She had been aiming for his neck but missed when he raised his hand to block the blow. They watched as four of his fingertips flew across the room and thumped against the wall, leaving a stream of blood dripping from his hand.

"I'm giving you until sunset, if I ever see your face again, I won't miss your head."

Terra-Lynn unlocked the door and watched as the blur of his frame fled the room.

$$54$$

June 1966

THE HEAVY RAINS returned, and with it came the howling winds. Josephine waited at home for Twitch, calling three and four times a day with hopes he'd answer the phone at least once. She expected him to be nervous, but not enough to stay gone this long, especially with the baby due in a couple months. As she reached for her journal, she listened to the footsteps that came to a halt outside her locked bedroom door. It was Sunday, which meant her mother would still be home for the weekend.

"You okay in there? I cooked breakfast, why don't you come down and get a plate?"

Josephine reached for the radio and turned the volume up before she began to write.

If I can help it, I will never speak to her again. She's a wicked evil woman and has already taken far too much from me. I won't let her anywhere near our baby!

Josephine waited until the rattling around her mother's neck left the door and descended the stairs. She couldn't bear to see or hear that sound coming from the pouch as the bones of her mother's victims fell on top of one another—and maybe a piece of Twitch had recently been added to the collection. But with the sky growing darker and her stomach starting to growl, Josephine knew she would soon need to leave the room and face her mother. A major storm had developed in the Gulf of Mexico and would make landfall by evening, and who knew how long the residual winds and rains would hang around. She could brave out a day or two locked in her room with the blankets over her head, but from the shape of the clouds, she knew it'd be more like a week. Josephine found Terra-Lynn bent over a stack of papers in her office.

"So, are you going to tell me where he's at so I can identify the dead body?"

Josephine placed a hand over her large belly. Terra-Lynn sighed as she peered over the rim of her reading glasses and watched her daughter waddle into the room.

"You know that's not my style. Besides, a stern warning gets the message across every time, and I've found the endless favors to be most helpful."

A playful smile covered Terra-Lynn's face.

"But I can't do this alone, so can you make him come back now, please?"

Josephine cringed when the sound of thunder cracked somewhere in the not-so-far distance.

"How am I to do that? I don't even know where your scary little boyfriend ran off to. Looks like you'll have to come with me to the Bayou Inn until the storm passes."

When a series of rolling thunder barreled across the sky, Josephine moved closer to the desk. She whimpered when her mother stroked the back of her hand.

"My Josie, you were always afraid of the storm. Come on, let's get you a bag packed…he'll turn up sooner or later."

"What if he comes back and I'm not here?" she whined.

"You're being silly, who doesn't know to find us over at the hotel?"

Josephine nodded.

•   •   •

August 1966

The day began with greyish-black clouds that chased away all hopes for sunshine. Josephine closed the curtains after checking in both directions and propped herself onto the pillow. There was a time when she knew Twitch would be standing out there waiting for her signal. Yesterday, his mother answered the phone and promised to have him call soon as she heard from him. But Josephine knew it was a lie, she could tell from the detestable way his mother hung up the phone, just as Josephine was thanking her for her kindness. She rubbed her belly pretending it would slow down the process. The time was drawing near, she could tell from the increased abdominal pressure over the past week. When she rolled onto her side the baby turned in her stomach. A sharp pinch, then a cramp spread across her hips. Josephine took several deep breaths and grunted.

"Hold off my little angel, at least until the storm passes."

After the sensation passed, she massaged her stomach as she washed her face and put on a work vest. First, she checked the manager's office and then proceeded down the hall.

"Good morning, I hope you don't think I'm going to let you work in your condition?" Said Terra-Lynn, as she placed her coffee cup on the counter and bent to kiss her daughter's stomach.

"But I'm bored, and I can't stand waiting any longer."

"And I'm sure you heard all the thunder this morning."

Josephine blushed at first, but when the front window darkened from the passing clouds she put her head down.

"You can keep an eye on things while I run over to the Piggly Wiggly."

Terra-Lynn reached for her umbrella and coat. Besides a girl reading a newspaper against the wall, the lobby was empty. No sooner had her mother left, a heavy downfall covered the ground. The sound of rain beat against the portico as some of it puddled into the downspout. Then the thunder, which was always the worse of it in Josephine's opinion. She cupped both hands over her ears.

"Hey, maybe you should take a load off," said the girl.

Josephine tried to sit on the stool but the abdominal pressure made it impossible to move.

"Oh, no, something's happening!" She grunted.

The girl tossed the paper on the floor and ran to her side.

"Don't move, let me get help—no, sit here first."

She escorted Josephine to an upholstered chair. "Breathe slowly, and whatever you do, don't push!"

The girl ran out the front entrance and within seconds she was back with help.

"He's going to take you to the hospital, but don't worry he's a friend of mine."

Josephine watched their lips move as she blew tiny puffs of air to calm her nerves. On the way to the hospital, the car bypassed the street where Twitch lived. When she looked to see his Nova still not parked in the driveway, she cried out over the thunder and the rain.

"Don't worry, we're almost there," said the girl. "I'll let your mother know you're here after we get you checked in."

Josephine cried until they reached the emergency room entrance, the whole time she was being checked in, and even more when her birthing pangs began.

"Don't push yet, you have a few more centimeters to go," said the nurse.

Josephine refused to wait any longer, she bore down with a loud grunt that caused her whole body to tremble. The nurse began to yell, and then a Doctor hunched over between her legs. When he resurfaced, a tiny human bounced in his hands.

"You have a healthy baby girl," he said.

The nurse took the baby for a moment and then placed the child on Josephine's breast. The newborn was light-skinned like Twitch and had a healthy set of lungs like Josephine. She kissed the wailing baby.

"We'll call you Rebakah, to remind me of the promise I made my grandmother."

The baby stopped crying long enough for Josephine to hear the rattling necklace approach outside the door. Terra-Lynn entered the room and rushed to her side.

"I knew it was a bad idea to leave you alone—oh, just look at this precious gift!"

"Were you able to find Twitch? It's a girl, we were hoping for a boy."

Josephine began to sob.

"It'll be alright, I'm sure he'll turn up soon."

Terra-Lynn kissed her daughter and grandchild on the top of their forehead.

"Need I remind you about my grandmother's curse? The only way to protect this child is if she's named appropriately."

"I already named her Rebakah," said Josephine, as she passed the baby to her mother's opened arms.

"Well, she'll be named Rebakah-Lynn then, to be on the safe side."

Terra-Lynn moved the pouch from against her chest to keep from snagging it on the baby's blanket. She mouthed a silent request to the spirit guides to pay homage.

"It's been a long time since I held such a tiny being. I'll have Eugenia fix your room for you and the baby, and we'll hire a nanny to help out when I'm not there."

The baby squirmed and started to whimper at the sound of Terra-Lynn's voice. When she let out a shrill, Josephine reached for her baby but Terra-Lynn moved away.

"You'll have to get used to this voice, precious one. We're going to be in each other's life for a long long time."

She rocked the baby until she became inconsolable. Josephine reached out again.

"That's enough, give her back to me now."

When Terra-Lynn leaned forward to place the baby on Josephine's chest, little Rebakah-Lynn's tiny hand snagged the pouch around her grandmother's neck. Josephine and Terra-Lynn watched as the necklace snapped in half and fell like broken glass at her feet. Terra-Lynn chuckled nervously as she bent to retrieve the pieces.

"I'm so sorry, can it be fixed?" said Josephine.

Her mother had backed away from the bed and waited near the door. She watched as the now silent baby nursed at her mother's breast. Josephine knew her mother would take this as some kind of sign or bad omen.

"Did you hear what I said, can you fix it?"

Terra-Lynn nodded, her eyes never leaving the newborn. Did her daughter say the curse can be fixed? Or did she say it was a hex? She left the room without saying goodbye. With each step, her toes searched for answers from the ground. When she found her way outside onto the rain-soaked roadway, Zuellie's drum began to beat against the storm. As she listened to the danceless rhythm, Terra-Lynn became aware that she had just encountered a problem *La Clairière* would never be able to fix.

ABOUT THE AUTHOR

Laura Caldwell Gaisie lives in San Luis Obispo, CA with her husband and children. She spends most of her time with close family and friends and enjoys Church, reading, writing, hiking, and painting. Laura is also a book writing coach and has published her Writer's Workbook, 12-month planner, and notebook, along with other books through her independent publishing company, Purple Pearls Publishing. Laura is co-founder and Executive Director of a nonprofit organization, Authors Inside (a writing program and publishing service for incarcerated authors). For more information visit:

Website: www.lauragaisie.com
Facebook: LauraGasie
Instagram: author_lauragaisie

THANKS FOR READING!

Reviews are extremely important for Authors. Please consider adding your review on Amazon and/or Goodreads! Don't forget to share your review on social media.

Thank you for your support!

Acknowledgments

I would like to thank my husband, who always encourages me to keep writing. My children for being so understanding, and my mother for being my biggest cheerleader.

I was unable to travel for research as planned due to the pandemic, thankfully, there are a few people who helped bring Haiti and Cuba alive for me. Thank you, Marie Sainvaliste, (Youtuber vlogger: Life In Haiti) for your eye-opening work in Haiti. Thank you, Yasnai Osorio, for sharing your experiences growing up in Guantanamo, Cuba. Thank you, Leonard Carpenter, for the long talks as you discussed your travels throughout Cuba, your many photos, and your expansive knowledge of Cuban History.

Especially want to honor my faithful readers, namely Diana, who continued to reach out regarding my forthcoming book release. And most of all, I want to thank my Lord God Almighty for the gift of writing. Jesus Christ is Lord!